REDEMPTION

THE SOPHISTICATES SERIES

• Book Three •

CHRISTINE MANZARI

This book is a work of fiction. Any references to historical

events, real people, or real places are used ficticiously.

Other names, characters, places, and events are products of

the author's imagination, and any resemblance to actual events

or places or persons, living or dead, is entirely coincidental.

To my brother, Johnnie —

For always sharing my love of books

and everything geeky.

LIST OF CHARACTERS
Code Name, Skills, and Twins (aka Others)

Cleo — Code Name: Malaysian Fire Ant
Skills: Explosions and fire
Twin/Other Counterpart: Persephone (Alive)

Ozzy — Code Name: Archerfish
Skills: Perfect aim and tracking
Twin/Other Counterpart: Euripides/Euri (Alive)

Rune (Leader of surviving Others)— Code Name: Pistol Shrimp
Skills: Snaps hands shut to create a blast of air that can stun or kill
Twin/Deviant Dozen Counterpart: Sebastian (Dead)

SECONDARY CHARACTERS IN ALPHABETICAL ORDER:
Arabella — Code Name: Indonesian Mimic Octopus
Skills: Transforms looks with just a thought, exceptionally strong, body stretches, theoretically can regenerate body parts
Twin/Other Counterpart: Ambrosia (Dead)

Cassie — Code Name: Horror Frog
Skills: Long claws that extend from her knuckles at will
Twin/Other Counterpart: Sphynx (Dead)

Dexter — Code Name: Spitting Cobra
Skills: Saliva can burn through almost anything
Twin/Other Counterpart: Egan (Dead)

Eva — Code Name: Tiger Moth

Skills: Ultrasonic Noises, scrambles sonar and radio waves, can replicate voices

Twin/Other Counterpart: Echo (Dead)

Marty — Code Name: Spitfire Caterpillar

Skills: Ejects hairs from his arm that turn into blades

Twin/Other Counterpart: Pirro (Dead)

Quinnie — Code Name: Electric Eel

Skills: Electric shocks, creates magnetic forcefields

Twin/Other Counterpart: Elysia (Alive)

Sadie — Code Name: Ring Tailed Cat

Skills: Agility and acrobatics

Twin/Other Counterpart: Daphne (Dead)

Sterling — Code Name: Hummingbird

Skills: Super speed, theoretically can fly

Twin/Other Counterpart: Aison (Dead)

Theo — Code Name: Bull Shark

Skills: Electroreception, seeing in the dark, navigating. Skilled with video equipment.

Twin/Other Counterpart: Pollux/Lux (Dead)

Wesley — Code Name: Bald Eagle

Skills: Keen eyesight. Can see through anything but osmium.

Twin/Other Counterpart: Argus (Dead)

RUNE

SCARS

The road was desolate and little more than a rugged dirt trail carved through the dark forest. Persephone scratched at her arms as she surveyed the woods around us. Her 8-ball hadn't survived the fight with Cleo. Without the distraction to keep her hands busy, her agitation was visible in long, red, vicious gouges on her skin. I reached over and pulled her shirtsleeve down for her, drawing her attention to me and away from the habitual motion. Even after all these years, the network of scars on her arms disturbed me. One day, the cuts and gashes she made wouldn't be enough. She'd need something deeper. Longer. More permanent. Something to stop the voices that whispered lies to her. My stomach clenched with the realization that I wasn't exactly sure how I felt about that.

We were all a little crazy, but Persephone had gotten a bigger slice of the pie than the rest of us. The Program never intended for us to exist. Our genetic material was supposed to be discarded like waste, but Delia defied orders and gave us life. We might be unexpected by-products of the Deviant Dozen experiment, but we were alive. And I intended for us to stay that way, no matter how crazy we might be.

"Why did we come back here?" Persephone leaned against the car we borrowed—or rather stole. Her nails dug into the skin on her inner arm, scraping along the ratty fabric.

"We're here because we need answers." I knocked her hand away and she turned to scowl at me.

"Actually, what we need is to be as far from here as we can get." Elysia stared down the long driveway that we traveled less than two days ago. We left death and destruction in our wake then. I had no idea what waited for us this time or why I thought it was a good idea to return.

"No one said you had to come. You're free to leave any time you want." I pushed away from the car and turned to glare at her.

Elysia snapped her mouth into a tight line and looked away. I knew she wouldn't leave. None of them would. Without each other, we had nothing but borrowed faces and unnatural skills that might eventually get us killed. The idea that we could just go our own ways and enjoy the illusion of our freedom was nothing but a handful of wishes and dreams. Freedom wasn't an option for us. Not after what we'd done in Vegas. And Andrews Air Force Base. And the Academy. Not after what happened down at the Inner Harbor with the Deviant Dozen. The memory of that night still made me sick.

We lost eight of our brothers and sisters, and it was my fault.

We also lost Delia—and that was my fault, too.

Most of all, we lost our purpose and this was the only place I could think to go. This was where answers, and our chance at mercy, were located. Just a few months ago we were anonymous and non-existent in the eyes of the Program. Now we were targets and eventually the Dozen would come after us. If we ran, we'd be hunted. We wouldn't win. I knew that much.

The only solution I had was to come here. We might be enemies of the Program, but we still had special skills we could offer them. I was hoping their greed for power would be just the thing to save our lives, miserable as they were. I was choosing to offer myself up to the Program's mercy, and Persephone, Elysia, and Euri followed me. Out of loyalty? Doubtful. Most likely because they were feeling as lost as I was.

"Come on," I said, starting down the long driveway.

We abandoned our borrowed vehicle by the main road so we could walk to the entrance. We'd be less threatening without the vehicle. As we got closer to our destination, I could see that no attempt had been made to repair the front gate. It still hung, broken and battered, from its massive hinges, and debris still littered the ground nearby. It didn't look like anything had been cleaned up since we came through two nights ago.

"That's odd." Euri looked around at the wreckage.

After the time spent at the Academy under the guard of Ozzy and the Hounds, it felt a little odd being in a leadership position. I had to remind myself I wasn't a prisoner anymore and that Euri wasn't Ozzy, even if they did look exactly alike.

"Yeah, this is an accident waiting to happen." Elysia kicked a blackened hunk of metal further into the grass to the side of the road.

"No, I mean it's odd that no one has come outside to apprehend us yet." Euri's hand twitched as if reaching for the weapon that he no longer had.

He was right. Usually there were a few Hounds guarding the gate, but as we entered the grounds, we could see that there was no one around at all. We continued up the driveway to find that the door to the Academy wasn't just broken, it was missing all together. I entered the main hall first, the echoes of my footsteps fading into the darkness as I came to a stop in the middle of the room. No sound, no movement, no Hounds, no Mandates.

Where was everyone?

"Come on," I said, motioning for the others to follow me toward the back of the building. When we reached the balcony that over-looked the training field, I was surprised to find the area vacant, the doors of the weapons cabinets hanging open to reveal empty shelves.

We searched the dorms, classrooms, infirmary, and even the prison cells.

St. Ignatius Academy was abandoned.

OZZY

∞ 2 ∞

MANHATTAN MOAT

"How do you know this isn't a trap?" Dexter asked.

"I don't." We were hidden across the street from the old Exchange Place station, one of the terminals for the subway system that was once used to get from Jersey City to Manhattan. If our information from Sterling was correct, the building in front of us would have only one guard. "There are only a handful of ways in and out of Manhattan. The few vehicle tunnels and bridges that are open are heavily guarded. This is our best chance of getting Sterling out of Headquarters."

Marty shook his head. "The entire subway system into Manhattan is barricaded, though, isn't it? I heard that all the tunnels from surrounding areas were blocked." Marty stood next to me and crossed his arms as we kept watch over the building across the street.

"They were. Sterling said there are massive, metal barricades at the entrance to each tunnel," Arabella answered as she paced in the shadows behind us. "These stations are monitored, but mostly overlooked. It would take something big, like an explosion, to get into the tunnels. And even if you managed to break through the gates, you'd still have to trek three miles in an old, unused tunnel death trap. They'd never expect us to try to get in this way."

"So if it's a death trap, why are we using it?" Eva pulled her coat tighter around her shoulders, her body shivering in the cold night air.

Arabella stopped pacing and I turned to watch her stomp across the pavement toward us. She was glaring at Eva. "Sterling's tattoo is disabled, but he's in hiding and it's only a matter of time until someone finds him. And when they do, they'll kill him." She grabbed Eva's shoulder and spun her around. Arabella's hair fanned out around her head in a sudden burst of bright red as if her anger and fear couldn't be contained. "If you were stuck in there, we'd come for you, so don't you even think about backing out." Arabella jabbed her finger into Eva's shoulder.

Eva cringed and took a step back. "I wasn't...I won't..."

"Every minute he spends in there is another minute he could be discovered." She bit the inside of her lip.

I reached out for her shoulder. "Arabella, it's going to be fine."

She shrugged my hand off. "Don't. You're the one who let him stay. This is all your fault."

My hands went up in defense as she stepped toward me, worry and rage making her shake. "We'll get him out," I promised. "As soon as Theo is done, we'll be on our way. It won't be much longer." I looked back toward the building across the street. The Hound guarding this station was more formality than security, but we still needed to be careful. The Program was no doubt looking for us and one guard could place the call that would have every Mandate and Hound in the area surrounding us in minutes—which was just one of the reasons why I wanted to get this over and done with as quickly as Arabella did.

The other reason was stowed away in a stolen van in an abandoned garage.

We'd been on the run since Younglove called to warn us that the Program wanted us terminated. We managed to successfully get out of Baltimore without being apprehended, but Cleo was still recovering from her ordeal at the Inner Harbor. I left her in the van with Quinnie, Cassie, and Wes to protect her. I didn't like splitting up, but we didn't have a choice. Cleo could barely walk let alone be part of a rescue mission. And as Arabella said, we needed to get Sterling before the Program found him. Splitting up was our only option.

"I don't like this," Dexter said. We stared into the darkness, waiting for the signal from Theo, who was disabling the security camera. Before I had a chance to answer, a light flashed three times in quick succession. Theo was done.

"Let's go." I motioned for the others to follow me and we hurried across the dark street, joining Theo in the shadows of the building we'd been watching.

"I didn't even need to bother with the cameras. He's asleep anyway." Theo jerked his head toward the window where we could see the Hound leaning forward in a chair, his head propped on the desk next to the monitors he was supposed to be watching. "Clearly he doesn't get much action around here."

"That's because we're the only ones stupid enough to want to get *in* to Headquarters." Eva shook her head. "I can't believe we're going back. Once was enough for me." She shivered like she was shaking off bad memories.

"Don't worry, you're not going into the city with us," I reminded her. "How is your shoulder by the way?" The stab wound she got from Pirro during the battle at the Inner Harbor had been treated by a Program doctor before we ran, but everything happened so quickly that I hadn't really had time to check in on her.

"It's fine. The wound wasn't deep and Sadie helped me clean and bandage it earlier. I can't move my arm well, but the pain killers seem to be working."

"Good. Take it easy, okay?" She nodded and I turned to Theo. "We want to make sure that we don't leave any evidence."

"Once we're inside, I'll make sure the footage is useless so that the Program won't have proof it was us." He shrugged. "It'll be like we were never here."

"Good. Dexter, want to do the honors?" I pointed to the door with the unsophisticated lock that stood between us and the sleeping Hound.

One dose of Dexter's corrosive saliva, and the lock was gone in a melted mess of steaming metal. Marty pushed the door open and I was grateful, yet surprised, that there wasn't an alarm. Arabella's arms stretched across the room and had the Hound restrained against his chair before he even woke up. I reached his side in a few long strides.

It was almost scary how easy it was.

"What's going on?" The stunned Hound struggled against Arabella's grip as I disarmed him. His handgun became part of the small arsenal we managed to retrieve from the Academy SUV before we escaped Baltimore. Arabella held the guard down as Marty and Dexter stripped him of his uniform and tied him up. They dragged him off to another part of the station where he couldn't be seen from any of the windows. From the things I could hear the Hound shouting, it hadn't taken him long to realize who we were. The Program probably had our pictures sent to every Sophisticate in the country after we disabled our tracking tattoos and disappeared off their radar.

The entire takeover took less than a minute. The Program was right to fear us.

"I can't believe you're making me stay here," Arabella hissed as she pulled the Hound's uniform over top of her clothing. "And I can't believe I agreed to it. I should be the first one through the tunnel to save Sterling." Her voice wobbled and then she cleared her throat, pulling her shoulders back, a look of determination on her face as she fastened the buttons on the shirt. "I owe him a piece of my mind for shooting me with that freaking dart."

We both knew the dart wasn't the reason she wanted to go. She probably *would* give him more than a piece of her mind for shooting her with a dart and taking her place as prisoner to Dr. Steel, but Arabella wanted to go because she loved Sterling. She'd never admit that to anyone, though. Especially to herself.

"We don't have a choice." I watched Theo's fingers fly across the Hound's keyboard as he removed any evidence of our arrival. "Eva has to stay here to do the hourly radio check-ins because she's the only one who can mimic the Hound's voice. But we need you here to *be* the Hound."

"Why?" Arabella's eyebrows pulled together and she frowned. "No one is going to come here. If he felt comfortable enough to take a nap while on duty, it's only because he knew he wouldn't get caught."

"That may be true, but we can't take the risk. Besides, we don't know how long it will take us to get to Sterling and back again. I hope we can do it before this Hound's shift is over, but we have to be prepared if that doesn't happen. What good would it be to rescue Sterling if someone discovered how we got into Headquarters? We need you and Eva here to make sure we can get back out. Otherwise, we're as good as dead."

She rolled her eyes.

"We need you here." I didn't have time to argue with her. She'd been right before. Every minute that wasn't spent going for Sterling was another minute he was at risk.

Arabella crossed her arms and glared at me. She didn't say anything as she stalked over to the desk, allowing her features to morph into those of the Hound who had been sitting in the chair only a few minutes earlier. She handed me her phone and I placed the call that would put us in contact with Sterling.

"Arabella?" Sterling answered.

"No, it's me. Ozzy. We've taken control of the Exchange station. We're heading down to the platform now." I turned on my headset and shoved the phone in my pocket so I could keep in touch with Sterling and still have use of both of my hands.

"Good," Sterling responded. "Once you're in the tunnel, it will take you at most an hour to get here, less if you run. It's only three miles and pretty much a straight shot. At least that's what it looks like from the map I found."

"Just a friendly, morning run through a tunnel, right?" I took a deep breath thinking that the Program's daily training regimen had at least prepared us for a quick rescue mission. I motioned for the rest of my team to follow me as I descended the stairs that would lead us to the platform for the old subway trains. I got a look at the barricade as I reached the top of the steps. "Damn. The gate looks like something that belongs on an old castle. I hope Dexter can get through it," I said.

Sterling laughed. "Welcome to the Manhattan Moat."

"The Manhattan Moat?" I laughed. "Well at least you haven't lost your sense of humor while in captivity."

"No, that's what everyone calls it around here. The Hound who helped me escape the main building told me all about it. A couple decades ago, Hurricane Lilith flooded most of the subway and Path tunnels."

"Don't tell me we have to swim. I forgot my speedo." We would already be in miles of tunnel underneath water, it would make the rescue a hundred times harder if we had to swim or wade, too.

"No, they're not flooded anymore. There's only a little water down there."

"I thought you said it was a straight shot. Why do they call it a moat if it doesn't go around the city?" I descended the stairs until I reached the platform, my eyes transfixed on the thick metal gate and the darkness beyond.

Sterling's huff of breath was an audible shrug. "I have no idea. I guess because it's barricaded to keep people out."

I pushed my hand back through my hair as I stood on the platform staring at the formidable gate in front of me. The Manhattan Moat. Trekking three miles through a tunnel under water was the last thing I wanted to do, but I didn't have much choice. We had to rescue Sterling and this was the easiest way in.

"Huh," Marty grunted, looking at the gate. "Sterling forgot to tell us to bring a battering ram."

I turned to look at Theo. "Guess we're going to have to use your hard head, buddy. At least it's good for something."

He flipped me the finger and I grinned.

I jumped down off the platform and walked toward the barricade. "Come on. Let's go storm the castle."

CLEO

❧ 3 ❧

ASHY TRUTHS

The van was chilly. Almost everyone had gone on the rescue mission for Sterling, and only four of us were left behind to wait in the cold, abandoned parking garage. Even Quinnie's heated glare wasn't enough to warm up the dark space. We didn't dare start the engine for heat because we couldn't risk being discovered. It was bad enough my injuries caused us to split up into two groups, I wasn't going to put us at additional risk by complaining about my frozen fingers. At least I was in the van. Cassie and Wes were outside freezing their asses off. The fact that I was cold, despite my deviation, was just proof that I wasn't even close to fully healed yet.

I'd gotten so used to sticking up for myself that needing someone else to take care of me was a hard pill to swallow. I hated being dead weight. When Ozzy insisted that Cassie, Wes, and Quinnie stay with me, I argued. I didn't need bodyguards, especially not three of them. I wasn't a hundred percent, but I wasn't completely helpless either. I could still feel my powers simmering deep inside, even if

13

they were weak. I wasn't confident I was strong enough to use them, but I wasn't going to admit that.

Quinnie argued too. She hated being kept out of the action, but I think mostly she just hated me. Neither of us were keen on the idea of being trapped together in a dark, frigid van.

Ozzy put his idea to a vote, and Quinnie and I were outnumbered. It was ridiculous he would waste three people just to sit with me in an empty garage. I thought Arabella at least would be on my side and support my argument to let me go along on the rescue mission, but she didn't care who did what as long as someone was going after Sterling. Since she could make that happen more quickly by siding with Ozzy, that's what she did.

I sighed, hoping that my friends were okay, and that everything was going to plan so far.

Wes and Cassie were outside patrolling the area while it was Quinnie's turn to be stuck in the van with me. She was twirling her fingers together in boredom, making a cat's cradle out of strings of electricity. Everything in my body still ached. My arms were heavy, my head was throbbing, and I was exhausted. Nearly dying can do that to you, apparently.

I managed to sit up, resting my back against the wall of the van. I took a few deep breaths to recover from the effort that small movement took and then pulled the osmium box toward me. Ozzy suggested we spend some time going through it to see if there was anything useful inside. Professor Younglove insisted that the box contained information on people who could help us, but I didn't think such a thing was even possible at this point. We couldn't hide from the Program forever. They were the most powerful organization in the country—more powerful, even, than the government.

They controlled the businesses, the military, and every secret agency that existed. Who could possibly help us against that?

Opening the lid to the box, I pulled out the glossy black binder on top that was labeled "Dozen Donors." This binder should have all the dirty details about our parents, the people who created us and handed us over to the Program. A thrill shot through me as I realized I might finally get the answers I'd been looking for about my parents. Months ago, I hacked the Program's secure files and found out that the names of my donors were Sarah and Michael. When I snuck into the Restricted Section of the library looking for information, I dug up an article about a Sarah and Michael Cross who had received IVF treatment to have a child who was unknowingly genetically altered by the Program and eventually taken into custody. The article never mentioned the name of the child, but I desperately wanted to believe it was me and that one day I'd be reunited with parents who were eager for my return. I hadn't been able to find out any of my other personal details in my searches.

Who knew that all this time the information I wanted was in a simple black binder that Professor Lawless had hidden in a strange metal box?

Quinnie ignored me as I flipped open the cover. I was surprised to find that the first page didn't have a picture of Ozzy like I expected. He was the leader of the Dozen and the first to exhibit, it made sense that his information should be first. Instead there was a picture of Quinnie. I was about to turn to the next page in search of my own answers when an unexpected name caught my eye. I went back and read the information slowly before finally tearing my eyes away to look up at the distracted girl in front of me.

"Your last name is Baker." The shock of realizing the identity of

Quinnie's important sponsor was like a punch to the gut. No wonder she never had to do work detail.

Her head jerked up as she met my accusing gaze, the strings of electricity blinking out to leave us in thick darkness. "My last name is Dracone." Her disembodied voice cut through the shadows, harsh and deadly. "Just like yours."

"Russell Baker is your *father?*" I pressed. "The man in charge of the Program. The one who created the Deviant Dozen. He's your father?"

Quinnie didn't say anything. She didn't move.

"Have you known all along?"

She grunted in annoyance before answering. "He didn't exactly keep it a secret from me. He was proud of his DNA." She paused and I tried to imagine the look on her face. Was she disgusted? Embarrassed? Angry? "I've always known who my donor was." She tried to sound superior, but failed miserably. I knew what Quinnie sounded like when she was acting arrogant. Her reply was a poor imitation of that arrogance.

"You mean father?"

"He's not my father." The words snapped through the darkness as she forced them through her teeth.

Technically, he was her father, but it would do me no good to push it. "Did you ever tell anyone? Does Ozzy know?"

Her laugh was bitter. "Are you kidding? Ozzy doesn't even know who *his* donor is and he should have easily figured that out years ago. I did."

"Who's his donor?"

Her words were low and menacing as they snaked their way through the dark. "Don't you think he deserves to know before you do?"

She was right. I wanted to be the first to find out about my donors. "Don't you think the others should know about Baker?"

"If I did, I would've said something a long time ago. It's no one's business. It's definitely not your business. Give me my page and swear you won't tell anyone about it." Her voice was threatening, but she had nothing to threaten me with. She could attack me, but I didn't believe she would. Even if I was injured, she couldn't be sure I wasn't strong enough to use my deviation. Fighting would only draw more attention to us.

I clenched the paper in my hand. "Why do you care if people know?"

"Are you serious? Would you want everyone to know that you share DNA with the asshole who created the Program?" Quinnie's disgust filled the darkness like a physical being. My silence was enough of an answer for her. "I didn't think so, princess. Not only would I be a target for every Hound, Deviant, Mandate, and Vanguard in the Program, every person on this planet who isn't a Sophisticate would hate me, too."

Quinby Baker. The entitled daughter of the Program's highest officer. Princess of the privileged. Or at least, that's what people would think.

She wasn't stupid. Even though the Program had been a necessary evil after *Wormwood*, people still hated it. It was easy to hate your savior when your savior eventually turned out to be your oppressor. And if Quinnie was the daughter of the Program's most powerful leader, she would be just as hated as he was. The truth would put a huge target on her back.

"But you don't seem to care if people like you or not," I pointed out. "I mean, you act like a bitch most of the time." I could almost feel her glaring at me. "Actually, all of the time," I corrected myself. "Sorry, but it's true."

"Are you going to give me the page or not?" Quinnie's voice was cold, but it was laced with something else. Fear.

"Are you really going to keep this from everyone else?" How could she? How could I?

"I have this long. The question is, are you?" All haughtiness was gone. She was pleading and I had to make a choice.

I was quiet for a moment, weighing my options. After what happened with Rune, I vowed that I wouldn't keep dangerous secrets from Ozzy anymore. But was this secret dangerous? Russell Baker had given the order to have us terminated. All of us. Quinnie was just as much a target as the rest of us. If I really thought that she would betray us to Baker, I wouldn't even consider what she was asking of me. But deep down, I believed she wouldn't. She chose to disable her tattoo and come with us. It was obvious she wanted nothing to do with him.

The page I held in my hand was a momentous truth that could destroy Quinnie's reputation with the Dozen. No matter how much I disliked her, or how many reasons she'd given me for vengeance, could I really reveal her dirty secret? The most important thing right now was for the Dozen to stick together, not suspect one another. If I shared her secret, not only would everyone begin to doubt her, but it could be the beginning of a complete collapse of trust in the group. I couldn't risk that. We needed each other too much.

"I'll keep your secret on one condition. You have to tell Ozzy. If you don't, I will."

She took a deep breath and released it in defeat. "Fine. But not until we rescue Sterling and we get somewhere safe. I don't want him worrying about this on top of everything else."

"Agreed."

"And we're not telling anyone else," she demanded.

"That's between you and Ozzy." I gripped the edge of the page and pulled, tearing it from the binder. "Here." I held the paper out toward where I thought Quinnie was sitting. I'd give it to her and let her make the decision about what to do with it. In fact, I was going to give each person their own information without looking at it. I wanted to be the first person to see my personal details, it was only fair to give everyone that opportunity.

Sparks of electricity flickered to life between Quinnie's fingers and she leaned over the paper I held out to confirm that I was giving her the page she wanted.

"Burn it," she ordered.

"You burn it." I snapped at her and shoved the paper into her stomach.

"If you burn it, then you're destroying the evidence. You're keeping my secret for me. Prove to me I can trust you."

A harsh laugh tumbled out of me and I shook my head in disbelief. Quinnie hadn't earned my allegiance or trust. She didn't deserve it, and I really didn't want to give it. Keeping her secret went against everything that I felt she deserved. I didn't *want* to keep her secret, I was only doing it because I thought it was best for the group. I looked up to tell her where she could shove her demand for trust. I was surprised to see that for once, Quinnie's face was stripped of its confidence and superiority, her eyes clouded with vulnerability.

"Please," she pleaded.

Damn it all to hell. That one word pushed aside all the animosity I felt toward her and I didn't want it to. It was easier to hate the girl who'd caused me so much trouble and pain. Looking into her eyes, I could see how broken and damaged she really was. Her attitude and actions were part of the armor she wore to protect herself against the truths she kept hidden, and what people would think of her if they knew who she really was.

For a moment I forgot we were enemies. I forgot that the Program wanted us dead. I forgot that I was worried about using my deviation inside the van. My power surged beneath my skin, crawling through my veins like liquid flame. When I released the breath I was holding, I felt the heat seep through my fingertips, raging against the fragile paper in a silent, obliterating promise. Seconds later, the space between us was nothing but streams of artificial light and a pile of ashy truths.

Rune

❧ 4 ❧

A Chance

We walked the empty halls of the Academy, wary and alert.

"Why do you think they left?" Euri asked.

"I have no idea." I hadn't been able to come up with a single explanation as to why the entire Academy was deserted. It was unnerving.

"Whatever the reason, if it scared them enough that they abandoned this place, then maybe we should leave, too." Elysia had been jittery ever since we left Baltimore, which was odd because she was always hostile and eager to do Delia's bidding. There hadn't been a hint of her usual confidence since our showdown with the Deviants. The death of our brothers and sisters was a catastrophic loss, and that loss left us all scarred in different ways. Elysia's scars were just more visible.

I thought about my scars. Now, those were scars that went deep. Too deep for anyone to see. I knew the choices I made that night were irreversible—like the decision to kill Delia Younglove.

She created me. She raised me. She turned me into a tool for her revenge. Her death was something I'd thought about many times during my childhood. I wished for it during the beatings she gave me to encourage my deviation to manifest. I yearned for it every time she yelled at me to protect myself. I craved it whenever I had to watch her torture one of the others. I should feel ashamed that the thing I wanted most in the world was the death of the woman who gave me a chance at life. Should it matter that life was dark and tortured? Did my lack of shame over her death prove that I was as corrupt and wicked as the Program assumed I'd be?

I wanted to believe the Program was wrong, that even though they considered me to be a mistake in their perfect science, I was still human enough to feel guilt. I didn't feel guilty that I wanted Delia dead—only that my actions resulted in deaths I hadn't wanted. When I knocked Cleo aside with a blast of air, her fireball ricocheted and hit the glass building that shattered and crushed my family. Ambrosia, Daphne, Aison, Egan, Lux, and Argus were buried underneath all of that glass, their lives cut short unnecessarily. Pirro's death was also on my hands. He fell on his own blade when I tried to throw him out of the way to protect Cleo.

I was too impulsive. I never considered the consequences. If I hadn't killed Delia, if I hadn't tried to protect Cleo, the others would probably still be alive. I would have to live with that for the rest of my life. I just kept telling myself that despite my inferior genetics, I could still choose how I reacted to situations. I wanted to believe that small shred of guilt that found its way into my chest meant that there was something human inside me worth saving.

Persephone, on the other hand, seemed to be unaffected by the events of the other night, aside from the loss of her 8-ball that is. I wondered if she was truly callous enough to not care, or if she buried her guilt even more deeply than me. I was inclined to think she didn't care.

"Maybe they left because they're scared of us," Persephone said in response to Elysia's suggestion that we leave. "Maybe they knew we'd be coming." She flicked her hand toward a door in the hallway that was closed, causing a ball of fire to smash through the wood in an eruption of searing heat and fiery splinters.

There was nothing on the other side of the door, but she would have insisted that she was just being diligent in making sure the room beyond was empty. Scolding her would do no good. In fact, that's probably what she wanted—a fight. Now that she knew we weren't in any danger, she was bored and fearless again. Pain and discord was always her way of dealing with things. I think I almost preferred an agitated and worried Persephone. At least then she was too distracted to be destructive to anything but herself.

"I doubt they'd be scared of us." My voice echoed down the empty stone hallway. "There are only four of us left, and they know that. They might hide behind their precious Deviants, but they wouldn't run from us. Whatever it is that caused them to leave is far worse than the threat we pose." I continued to walk through the empty halls, the others following me. I had no clue what we should do next. I kept expecting an answer to come to me, but I was all out of ideas.

"We have no place to go and no money. Do you think we should just sleep here for the night?" Euri suggested. "There's plenty of empty space." He laughed but it was full of nerves and uncertainty.

"We might as well." My breath rushed out of my chest. We were no better off now than we had been yesterday. "We can decide what to do tomorrow."

"A night in the enemy's stronghold," Persephone purred. "It'll be like spending the night in a haunted house."

Elysia slowed down and wrung her hands. "Maybe this isn't such a good idea—"

"Stop being a coward, Elysia, it's not a good look for you." Persephone sneered. "Come on, I know where the faculty suites are. If we're going to spend the night here, we might as well be comfortable." She turned to go down one of the hallways, leading us into a section of the Academy I'd never been. Since I spent most of my captivity following Ozzy, Quinnie, and Cleo around, I had no idea where the staff slept. Persephone, however, knew the Academy like the back of her hand. Before she was discovered sneaking around and causing trouble, she had the opportunity to snoop around every nook and cranny of the Academy looking for the information Delia wanted.

But even with all of her sneaking around, Persephone never did find what Delia sent us for. Delia's destructive invasion two nights ago hadn't been successful either. She never uncovered what she wanted—information on all of the donors of the Deviant Dozen. Delia believed that if there was anyone who was willing to join her and get revenge on the Program, it would be the parents who hadn't willingly given their children to the Sophisticate Program to be genetically modified. Delia knew, only too well, that those parents existed. She just didn't know what happened to them after they were forced by the courts to give their children over to the Program. She believed there was an underground group of anti-Program rebels, and that we'd find them by finding the donors of the Deviants. She wanted to lead the rebels against the Program. She was convinced that revenge would fix everything.

I was convinced Delia was insane.

I was also convinced we were better off now that she was gone, even though it was strange to feel both relieved and guilty in that conviction.

"I'm hungry. Let's stop in the kitchens and get something to eat first." Persephone made an abrupt turn and led us down a different hallway. No one argued since none of us could remember the last time we ate a proper meal.

***

Half an hour later, Persephone led us back toward the faculty suites. Before we reached the first set of doors, she stopped suddenly, staring at a piece of paper that was placed in the middle of the floor. It was folded and the word "Rune" was written on the front.

"Looks like someone knows you're here," Persephone sang. Instead of being afraid, she gazed leisurely around us, daring the writer of the letter to appear.

Euri immediately took a defensive stance, using one of the knives he liberated from the kitchen as a weapon. I bent over to pick up the note.

"What does it say?" Elysia asked, her voice breaking with worry.

Persephone whirled around and glared at her. "Stop being terrified of everything! You can control electricity," she spat, jabbing her finger into Elysia's shoulder. "He has perfect aim," she said, gesturing toward Euri, "and Rune can kill people with the snap of his fingers. We are like gods among men. Don't you dare act like a coward!" Heat swirled outward from Persephone, her hair lifting with the warm air that spun angrily around her.

"We're not gods." Elysia's voice was quiet. "We're accidents. We're unwanted. We're survivors. But we're not gods. Gods don't die and I can tell you with certainty that we are going to die. Probably very soon."

"Coward," Persephone hissed again.

"Cut it out." I used my hand to snap a blast of air in Persephone's direction. The small burst of air pushed into her, nudging her back and away from Elysia. "We have bigger problems than bravery right now. Listen to this," I said, reading the note to them.

I'm not sure you deserve my mercy, but I'm giving it to you because if I don't, it would be as if I slit your throats myself. The Program has given the order to terminate the Deviant Dozen experiment. The Deviants have been sentenced to death and are currently on the run from the Program. This means that you, too, will be terminated if you are captured. The Dozen knows they are being hunted and the Program has no idea where they are or what they intend. To avoid retaliation from the Dozen, St. Ignatius Academy evacuated to Headquarters. Your arrival here has not gone unnoticed, and Hounds are on their way to eliminate you. I am in a difficult position. You have done terrible things, but terrible things have been done to you, too. I can't stand by and watch you be slaughtered. In a way, you are victims in this as much as you are the threat. Rune, I know you didn't help Delia kill the

26

Hounds, even though you could have. I believe you can be redeemed. I would suggest that you not be here when the Hounds arrive. And now that Delia is dead, I would suggest you think about what you will do with the rest of your lives. You can change the course of your future.

I finished reading the note and flipped it over, looking for a name or signature. There was nothing. "I guess we're not going to sleep any time soon. Let's get out of here."

"Where are we going to go?" Elysia asked.

"There's only one other option we have right now. If I can remember the phone number, we might have a chance." I spun on my heel, heading away from the faculty suites and toward the main entrance.

"A chance at what?" Euri asked.

"A chance at not dying. Here." I handed the letter to Persephone. "Burn it."

Ozzy

ONCE BITTEN

Thick metal grates covered the entrance to the tunnel on either side of the platform. Beyond the rusty barrier, the tunnel was pitch black, all of the overhead lights burnt out. Peering through one of the openings, I shined the light from my headlamp into the shadows. As Sterling mentioned, there was a dark river of water along the floor, but it was shallow, no more than shin height. The curved walls on the side of the tunnel were dingy and missing many of the decorative tiles that had once given it a tidy appearance. The tiles that were still there were cracked and broken in places, and the beam from my headlamp was choked off by the thick darkness about twenty feet in.

I turned to face my team—Dexter, Marty, Sadie, and Theo. "Ready?" I asked Dexter. He nodded and I motioned for him to start dismantling the medieval looking barricade in front of us. He stepped forward and worked quietly, the only sound of his efforts being the hiss of the water as melted bits of metal fell down from the grate and splashed into the murky sludge below. We watched in silence as the hole he created in the grate got larger.

"We're almost ready to enter," I told Sterling through the headset I was wearing. "Dexter's about halfway done. It won't be much longer before we get to you and then you'll be a free man."

He laughed. "Free or not, I have a feeling some vicious form of punishment awaits me at the hands of Arabella."

I grunted in agreement. "I wouldn't be surprised if the stun gun was involved."

"I don't think she'd want to knock me out. She'll want to see me suffer," he joked.

"Definitely. Hope you're wearing a cup."

"Thanks for the warning. So...how has she been?" Sterling asked quietly.

I took a deep breath. "You know. You've been in touch with her over the phone."

"I only know what she tells me."

I paused for a moment, debating the value of telling him the truth. Arabella despised pity and worked hard to be unbreakable. But that wasn't the real Arabella. The real Arabella was as vulnerable as a kitten, albeit a kitten with a serious hissing and biting problem.

"At first, she was pissed at both of us. Things got pretty ugly between us for a while. But after the initial rage wore off, it's been mostly fear. If this doesn't work, she'll probably try tearing down the front gate herself."

Sterling released a frustrated sigh. "I didn't want to do it, I didn't want to stay behind. She knows that, right?"

"She knows."

"I had to do it. I couldn't let Dr. Steel experiment on her." His voice broke and he cleared his throat. "Better me than her. I'm not much of a threat, but she is."

"You did what you had to do. You made the ultimate sacrifice."

He was quiet for a moment. "Don't you feel the same way about Cleo? Wouldn't you do anything you had to do to keep her safe, even if that meant sacrificing yourself or someone else?"

"You know the answer to that," I said, refusing to admit the truth. There wasn't much I *wouldn't* sacrifice for Cleo's safety. This situation was proof of that. I left three people behind to guard her, making our rescue mission more vulnerable than it should be. If I had been thinking with my brain and not my heart, I would have left her in the van by herself, maybe with one guard at most. But her safety was more important to me than anything else.

"I couldn't expect anyone else to make that sacrifice for Arabella. I couldn't risk that they might change their mind," he said.

"I understand." For the first time since we met, Sterling and I were in complete agreement.

Sterling was quiet and I let the conversation die away as I watched Dexter work. A huge chunk of the massive gate fell away from the sides of the tunnel, clattering against the cement below, and splashing us with stagnant and filthy water. As more pieces fell onto the floor and crashed against one another, the echoes that filled the tunnel were deafening.

"This isn't very stealthy of us. I hope no one can hear this," Marty pointed out.

"All done." Dexter pushed one last piece of metal to the ground and stepped aside for me to lead the way.

"Put on your headlamps." I adjusted mine and made sure the

phone was secure in the pocket of my jacket. "We've got a long trek ahead of us."

There was a fair amount of rustling in backpacks before five headlamps flickered on, bathing the old, filthy walls with tight beams of light. We were huddled together, staring into a darkness so intense and endless, it was hard to believe there was an opening anywhere at the other end.

"The faster we get started, the faster we get back." I stepped through the jagged hole in the metal barrier as I entered the tunnel. The cold, motionless air seemed to swallow me whole, the thin beam of light barely cutting through the oppressive darkness in front of me. The rest of the Deviants followed, their awkward steps through the water filling the tunnel with white noise as the dank liquid lapped around our ankles and up against the sides of the walls in heavy ripples.

"Are you guys on your way now?" Sterling's voice was impatient.

"Just started." I stepped carefully, unable to see what was under the water. "I don't think we'll be running, though. We can hardly see ten feet in front of us and we can't see the tracks at all since they're under water."

"That's okay." I could hear Sterling shifting over the line and I wondered where he'd managed to hide himself. "Even walking you should get here in less than an hour. I don't think anyone will find me, but I'm ready to get out of here."

We continued to trudge through the tunnel, the only sounds being the splashing of five pairs of feet and our labored breaths as we carefully navigated the submerged tracks.

"Wait. Did you hear that?" My arm flew out to the side to halt everyone. With the heightened tracking abilities of my deviation, my hearing was more sensitive than everyone else's. I looked around for the source of the noise. Looking behind us, I could still see the opening of the tunnel that led to the platform. We hadn't gone very far.

"I couldn't hear anything but water splashing." Sadie leaned around me to look out into the darkness.

I peered down the tunnel, allowing my headlamp to search out the strange sound I heard. We stood still and I could just barely hear a scraping noise, although I wasn't sure what was causing it.

"Can you see anything, Theo?" I asked.

"Not yet."

"Look at the water." Sadie pointed at our feet.

I looked down to see that the water was slapping against our legs in smooth ripples like tiny waves crashing on a non-existent beach. We weren't moving, but it was as if something else was in the water with us.

"Look out!" Theo yelled.

I glanced up in time to see the flickering glow of two orbs in the darkness right before something massive came hurtling toward us.

"Go back," I yelled, spinning around while pushing the Deviants toward the opening. As I reached for my gun, something hit me in the back, knocking me into the water. The impact caused my headlamp to fly off my head and out of reach. The light was still shining, however, and what I saw when I spun around caused my blood to freeze. The thing in front of me was like something out of a science fiction movie. A nightmare.

"What is that?" Marty yelled out.

A creature the size and shape of a large jungle cat was poised in front of me, its eyes pinning me in place. Slowly stalking forward, it growled in warning. I'd heard the old urban legends about the New York sewers being infested with alligators and huge rats, but we weren't in a sewer. And this wasn't an alligator. It looked like a tiger, but was covered in bony plates that protected it like armor. I'd never seen anything like the creature in front of me. What was worse, I could see the intelligence in its eyes as it inspected me before casting a quick glance over the rest of my team. Its tail flicked possessively behind it, the sound of the plates along its body clicking against one another as it moved.

The beast stopped and crouched low as if preparing to pounce. When its tail flicked sharply and the plates snapped against each other in a creepy cadence, the tunnel was suddenly filled with more pairs of glowing eyes. I couldn't see what the eyes belonged to and they appeared to float in midair. I put my arms out to the side as if to keep the others safe as I backed away from the creature in front of me. I hadn't taken more than two steps when the flicking tail clicked out another series of sounds and the walls seemed to come alive as the outlines of four more bodies came into focus. Creatures, just like the one in front of me, were clinging to the walls, their perfect camouflage fading as their tails twitched in response to the noise the first one was making.

"Oh my god." Sadie's voice shook with disbelief. "It's like they were invisible. Were they there the whole time? What are those things?"

I reached for my gun, pulling it out of the holster. "Clearly we weren't the only weapons in the Program's arsenal," I answered. My anger was sharp and bitter.

The creatures crawled forward, clinging to the curves of the walls and knocking more tiles loose.

"Pull back," I ordered, lifting my gun to aim at the closest threat. I backed up toward the entrance, never taking my eyes off the creatures. The splash of my team's retreating steps echoed around us as we hurried toward the opening in the barricade. The noise we were creating agitated the closest beast, causing its tail to snap angrily back and forth. It scanned the scrambling bodies of my friends, eyes narrowing as its spine curved upward like a pissed off house cat. Its lips pulled back from its muzzle revealing a jagged row of teeth that gleamed in the scattered beams of the headlamps.

When I clicked the safety off the gun, the small sound pulled the creature's attention back to me. Faster than I was expecting, it lunged, attacking in a blur of wet fur, slimy scales, and sharp teeth. As it jumped, the animal curled in on itself until it was an armored ball, launching through the air. Instinct took over before my brain could, and I fired a shot. My bullet bounced off the bony plates, ricocheting wide. I jumped to the side to avoid being crushed under the weight of the beast, and it crashed into the water beside me, unfurling as it rolled onto its feet again.

"What's going on?" Sterling yelled through the earpiece. I realized it wasn't the first time he'd asked the question, but I had no time to answer.

I was about to shoot again when I was struck from behind. The force lifted me out of the water, slamming me into the tunnel wall. My head cracked against the unforgiving concrete before I slid down into the muck in a confused daze. I looked up to see that one of the other creatures had come up behind me and knocked me off my feet with its tail.

The creatures dropped one by one from the walls to the ground, each of them fixing a predatory gaze on me. Their movements pushed the water around me in heavy waves. I reached for my headlamp as it floated by, but it disappeared under the deluge of the dirty river on the tunnel floor. I couldn't see much of anything except that the beast that lunged at me was now blocking my exit. Standing up, I regained my footing, and took aim again. I fired just as the animal pounced, a massive shadow that I shot at until my gun was empty. From the sounds of the bullets pinging off, I knew I'd hit it, but not fatally. The bullets couldn't pierce the armor.

The animal came at me like a wrecking ball. I dodge, but one of the plates from its back slashed across my arm. I hissed in pain and reached for my bicep where the jacket and shirt were sliced clean through. Sticky warmth welled along the cut, soaking the edges of my torn shirt. More gunshots rang out from the other side of the grate as the creature turned to face me again. The beams of light from the headlamps whirled across its scales like it was a Hollywood movie premier. Unafraid, it curved its body so the bullets being shot at it rattled harmlessly against its back. The four other animals crept toward the opening in the grate, stalking my team. The animals kept their heads down, the armor protecting them.

"Be careful," Sadie shouted, "or you'll hit Ozzy."

My gun was empty and I realized my backpack with my ammo had been ripped off me when I was attacked the first time. I reached for the daggers in my boots, carefully watching how the beast turned its scaly side toward me to defend itself as it approached.

"Don't worry about this one," I yelled, gesturing to the first creature. "Try to keep the others away from the opening. As long as they're on this side, we have a chance of keeping them contained." I was still dizzy from hitting my head and the moving lights didn't help my vertigo, so I blinked hard to clear my sight. Just as I took a step forward to attack, the creature curled around itself into a ball and disappeared, its armored scales camouflaging it against the surrounding darkness. My heart lurched in my chest and I resisted the urge to look wildly around for it.

Focus. I needed to force myself to calm down and focus. I was a tracker. I didn't need to see it to know where it was. I could hear it, sense it. I could almost taste it if I concentrated hard enough. I could trust my deviation. I could trust my tracking abilities.

I went completely still, my body on high alert. I heard the creature move and what had been nothing but shadows, suddenly was clear to me. I could hear the scraping of the plates rubbing together. I could feel the air stir with its movements. I could see the ripples in the water. I could smell the rancid stench of its breath. I couldn't see the creature with my eyes, but I could see it with my deviation.

And it was leaping at me.

I took aim and let my dagger fly into what looked like empty air. When the blade found its mark, the beast screamed in pain and crashed to the side. It skidded along the ground, armor screeching against concrete in protest. Water sloshed around its body as it became visible again. In the meager light, I could see that the dagger was embedded in the throat of the beast, exactly where I was aiming. The limbs and tail thrashed a few seconds before finally going still.

An unearthly howl filled the tunnel as the other armored cats realized one of their own was down. They turned toward me, the rest of my team forgotten.

"Shit," I muttered. I had one dagger and four creatures ready to rip me to shreds. "Aim for the throat or underbelly," I called to the others.

As if hearing my warning, the creatures faded one by one, cloaking themselves in darkness. I held my dagger in front of me, barely breathing. I saw the water splash to my right and just had time to jerk to the side as one of the creatures flew past me, clipping my arm. Pain shot through my elbow as it was bent backward and it was all I could do to drag my body out of the way before the creature could come at me again.

Sterling's voice was deafening through the earpiece as he demanded to know what was going on. My gun was empty, I had one dagger left, my left arm was hanging limply at my side, and my vision was nothing but shadows and dark blurs.

"Watch the water," I told the others. "You might not be able to see them, but they can't hide their movements."

"Hurry, Ozzy," Theo called. "If you can get behind the barrier, we can pick them off one by one."

"What the hell is going on?" Sterling yelled into my ear. "Talk to me Ozzy!"

"Monsters," I managed to say as I edged away from where I could sense the animals. "The moat has monsters."

When ripples appeared in the water, gunshots rang out again from beyond the barrier. The sound of ripping flesh was followed by another loud howl. One of the beasts flickered back into view, its head thrown back in pain. That was all it took for one of Marty's blades to come flying through the air, slashing the soft underbelly of the cat clean through. It stumbled forward and then fell face first into the water, twitching.

Three left.

Marty was suddenly around the barrier, splashing his way to my side. "I've got the weapons, you just have to tell me where they are." He pressed his gun into my hand as blades the length of swords materialized along his inner arms.

From my peripheral, I watched as Dexter stood in the opening of the barricade, spitting when ripples appeared close by. Threatened, the invisible creature started to lunge for him. Before it could attack, it jerked to a stop, its camouflage fading away when Dexter's corrosive saliva burned through the plates on its back and reached tender skin. Uncurling its head from its protective posture, the creature attempted to figure out where the pain was coming from. That small movement was all I needed to put a bullet between its eyes.

Two left.

I was still scanning the darkness when one of the beasts came out of nowhere, tackling Marty to the ground. He struggled to keep his head above water as the weight of the monster pinned him down. I threw myself against the invisible boulder and felt the armor cutting into me as I knocked it off balance. As the weight of the monster lifted off Marty, he spun onto his back and thrust his blades deep into the chest of the animal, twisting them before pulling them free. My momentum carried the animal's dead weight to the ground and I landed on top of it, nearly shredding myself against its sharp armor in the process.

One left. The entire battle happened in a matter of a few minutes and there was just one left.

Marty struggled to stand up, the back of his jacket torn with gashes where the beast's claws had sunk in. "Thanks, Oz."

I nodded, regaining my footing and searching for the last creature. Out of the corner of my eye, I saw Arabella running down the steps to the platform. She was still wearing the guard's uniform, but her features were her own.

"What's going on?" She looked around wildly, noting the carcasses scattered about the water. "What are those things?"

"Stay back, Arabella," I answered. "There's another one here somewhere." I scanned the darkness.

"Look out!" she screamed, leaping over the edge of the platform and down into the shallow water. She pointed into the darkness as if she could see something in the endless shadows. She grabbed the gun from her own holster as she came through the ragged hole. Arabella jumped, her arm reaching upward in an unnatural stretch as she caught the edge of a beam in the ceiling. Her arm instantly shrunk back to its normal size, causing her to rocket through the air. She swung over the area where she'd pointed, screaming and shooting. As the creature unwound from its protective position and dove for Arabella, it became visible again.

The creature was so fast that I heard Arabella scream before I had a chance to take my first shot. The beast's head launched upward and clamped down onto her arm as she dangled above it. I squeezed the trigger repeatedly as Arabella dropped from the ceiling. My bullets shredded their way into the side of the creature's head as one of Marty's blades impaled it dead center in the chest. There was a moment of complete stillness and then in slow motion, the battered beast crumpled down into the water with a deafening crash, its body falling into a pile of twisted flesh, fur, and scales.

The beast was dead, but it was too late. Arabella had already fallen into the dank water next to the animal and she was clutching what was left of her arm. Her screams were the worst sounds I'd ever heard in my life—like they were piercing my soul. I had a feeling that when they stopped, the absence of those screams would forever change me.

"Is that Arabella?" Sterling yelled into the earpiece. "What happened? Is everyone okay? Ozzy! Talk to me!"

I stumbled to Arabella's side. Her eyes were clenched shut, her head tilted back as she continued to scream. The creature had bitten her below the elbow so that her hand and the bottom part of her arm were completely missing. The skin just below her elbow was torn and bloody. It looked like a Halloween prop. She thrashed around in agony, clutching the remaining half of her arm to her body. I shrugged my jacket off and then peeled my t-shirt away from my body. She was losing a lot of blood.

"Oh my god," Sadie screeched. "That thing bit her arm off!"

"Whose arm? Arabella's arm?" Sterling howled into my ear. "Ozzy, is Arabella hurt?" I was the only one who could hear Sterling, but he could hear everything that was going on around me.

"Yes." That one word tore something deep inside. "She was trying to distract it." I forced myself to remember all the first aid I'd learned over the years as I twisted the t-shirt into something I could use as a tourniquet. "She's hurt badly. We have to get her help. If we don't, she's not going to make it. I'm sorry Sterling. We'll have to come back for you later."

"I'm coming," Sterling said, his voice laced with panic. "I'm coming. Tell her I'm coming." I heard the click of the phone call ending, but I couldn't worry about Sterling right now. Not when Arabella was bleeding to death.

I pulled her arm away from her chest, my elbow screaming in protest with every movement I made. I attempted to wrap the shirt around her arm, but Arabella's hips bucked up frantically as she struggled against the agony I was causing her.

"Hold her down," I told Marty. "We can't help her if she keeps thrashing around like this. Dexter, you'll have to do the tourniquet. I hurt my arm and I won't be able to get it on tightly enough." Dexter and Marty hurried over to do what I asked. Arabella let out another heart-wrenching scream as Dexter tied the shirt tightly around the area right above the stump of her arm where I indicated. Her body bowed out of the water, trying to escape.

"We need something clean," I said, motioning with my good hand. "A jacket or something to wrap around it, too. To protect it." Sadie shrugged out of her jacket and handed it to Dexter and he did as I asked, protecting the bloody remains of her arm with the fabric.

Another scream tore out of Arabella and I felt the echoes of her pain like whip marks. This was my plan. My fault. I was responsible for keeping the Dozen safe and I failed Arabella. As her scream finally ended and the sounds of her agony faded into the darkness around us, her eyes rolled back in her head and her body collapsed. My hand flew to her neck and I was relieved when my fingers found her pulse. It was there, beating wildly. She took in a deep breath and then she continued to breathe heavily, her chest contracting wildly in harsh, ragged pulls.

Everyone was waiting for me to tell them what to do. I was the leader and the decision was mine, no matter how much I wished it wasn't. "We have to get out of here," I managed. "We have to get back to the van and get her some help. We'll come back for Sterling later, but if we don't get Arabella to a hospital, she'll die."

"I've got her," Theo said, bending down to pick up Arabella, hugging her small unconscious form to his body. Dexter rushed forward to help Theo get her up and out of the tunnel. Eva must have come down with Arabella because she was standing on the platform watching us, the look of horror in her eyes telling me what I already knew—Arabella was in really bad shape.

Just as we were about to make our way up the steps, there was a deafening explosion like the sonic boom a jet makes as it breaks the sound barrier. That noise was the only warning we had before the windows of the building shattered inward, throwing shards of glass all the way down the steps and across the platform where we stood. My arms flew over my head for protection.

When the glass finally settled and I dropped my arms, the first thing I saw was Sterling standing at the top of the steps—a broken-hearted, avenging angel. His hair was wild and on end, his eyes wide and mad as they quickly searched the space and found Arabella huddled in Theo's arms.

Sterling jumped down the steps so quickly I never saw him move. One moment he was at the top, the next he was in front of Theo, gently taking Arabella into his arms.

"How did you get here?" Eva asked him.

"Where's the van?" Sterling demanded instead of answering her.

I couldn't even consider how Sterling was here, because Arabella needed help. "This way." I took the lead, moving as quickly as my battered body would allow.

We ran up the steps to find that the main floor of the station looked like a war zone; every pane of glass reduced to jagged shards that were scattered over every surface like discarded diamonds. Even the lights were broken. Carefully, we navigated outside and then down the dark streets. If we had been in a residential area, there would have been plenty of witnesses, but we were lucky that it was the middle of the night and no one was around. The noise of Sterling's arrival, however, had been so loud, people surely would be investigating the source. Emergency response teams and curious onlookers would be coming around soon.

As we ran through the deserted streets, Sadie grabbed my arm. "Do you think there are more of those creatures?"

I cast a glance back over my shoulder to where the ruins of the station were. "I don't know," I answered honestly. "Maybe."

"But there are innocent people here. If one of those things gets out..."

I swallowed down the guilt. "I know, but we can't risk worrying about that. We have to worry about Arabella first. If there are more...the Program will just have to take care of the problem. They created them. They must have a way to control them."

Sadie's laugh lacked all humor. "Yes, because they have so much control over us, too."

I clenched my jaw. We didn't have a choice. Arabella came first. She had to. Thankfully, our luck held and we didn't cross paths with a single soul on our way to the parking garage.

"Wow, that was quick," Cassie said as we approached the van. "Did you guys hear that noise a few—" She finally noticed Arabella in Sterling's arms. "Wait, what happened to her?"

"Just open the van," Sterling demanded.

"Hurry," I instructed. "We need to get out of here now." Cassie gave the group a quick scan, noting Arabella's blood all over us, the glass shards clinging to our hair, and the wet and filthy clothing that spoke volumes of what we'd been through. Without another word, she swung open the door to reveal a surprised Cleo and Quinnie who were huddled over a black binder. They jumped back from each other quickly, Cleo brushing away the dirt between them as they moved toward the back of the van to let us in. My gaze swept over Cleo and despite our situation, relief settled over me that she was safe. If she was safe, everything would be okay. It had to be. She gave me a small smile in return.

"I need you to drive," I told Wes. "I want to be back here to monitor Arabella."

He nodded and rounded the side of the van to get into the driver's seat. Theo got in the passenger side and the rest of us piled into the back. I sat next to Cleo, my fingers immediately finding hers. My heart was slamming in my chest and I knew that every second wasted was one that was stealing a bit of Arabella's life.

"Where to?" Wes asked as he started the vehicle and then pulled out of the space.

"South," I responded from my spot next to Cleo. "Just go south. We'll go to the nearest hospital."

"Hospital?" Cleo asked.

I turned to look at the worried faces in the van. They knew if we showed up to a hospital, it wouldn't be long before the Program found us. "Arabella will die if she doesn't get medical help. We'll figure the rest out once we get her there."

We jostled around in the back of the van as Wesley sped down the empty streets. Everyone was staring at Arabella who was laying in Sterling's lap, Sadie's jacket still wrapped around her arm.

"What happened?" Cleo asked.

"There were...creatures in the tunnel," Sadie answered. "Monsters. One of them bit off Arabella's arm."

Cleo's body jerked in surprise and her hands covered her mouth. "What?"

"A monster?" Quinnie asked. "Is that code for something that actually exists?"

"Those things...it looked like a tiger mated with a dragon or something," Sadie said defensively. "They were like big cats with scaly armor."

"Like a big armadillo?" Cassie's eyebrows were scrunched over her eyes as she looked between those of us who had been in the tunnel.

"No. Armadillos aren't scary. These things were like freaking mutant tigers wearing battle armor." Sadie wrapped one of her braids around her finger as she shivered. "They could camouflage themselves. Sort of like Arabella." She glanced down at our friend who was curled up in Sterling's lap. "We couldn't even see them half the time."

"We need light," Sterling ordered, ignoring the conversation about the creatures. "And something to make a tourniquet."

"We already put one on her." Marty nodded his head toward the bundle of fabric around Arabella's arm.

Sterling glared at him. "No offense, but I'm still going to check it." This was not a side of Sterling any of us were used to seeing.

The lights in the ceiling flickered on as supplies were quickly handed to Sterling. Arabella's chest rose and fell in harsh movements as she continued to breathe rapidly. Sterling gently unwrapped the jacket from around Arabella's arm and then paused as he peeled back the last piece of fabric covering her skin.

Those of us who were in the tunnel stared in disbelief. We saw the creature bite her arm off, which was why what we were looking at made absolutely no sense. Arabella was in Sterling's lap, and all I could see was her arm—perfect and complete—right down to every single one of her five unblemished fingers.

How was that possible? Her arm was still covered in blood, but it was whole. Not even a scratch or bite mark.

It had...grown back?

"I thought you said something bit her arm off." Quinnie scoffed. "It looks like it's all there to me."

"It *was* bitten off," Sadie said. "I saw it."

Theo laughed. "She grew her arm back. I can't fucking believe it. Younglove said the Indonesian Mimic Octopus could regenerate, but who would have believed Arabella could actually grow back a body part?"

Sterling's fingers trailed a leisurely path from Arabella's elbow down to her wrist and back again. When he looked up, there was a relieved smile on his lips. "If anyone could do it, it would be her."

"Ugh," Quinnie said. "Pull over, I'm allergic to lovesick idiots."

The van sped down the streets, but inside we were all frozen into quiet astonishment.

Finally, Eva turned to Sterling. "Now that we know Arabella isn't dying, are you going to tell us how you got out of Headquarters?"

"You guys didn't go get him?" Cassie asked.

"No. We entered the tunnel, we were attacked by the mutant tigers, Arabella's arm was bitten off, then all the windows in the building exploded, and next thing we knew, Sterling was standing there like he materialized out of thin air," Sadie explained.

All eyes were on Sterling, but his gaze was fixed on Arabella as his fingers slid over the flawless skin of her arm.

"Spill it, bird boy. What happened?" Quinnie was feigning boredom, but she was just as curious as the rest of us.

A smile spread over his mouth. "Apparently, Younglove was right. I can fly," Sterling said matter-of-factly.

"You can fly?" Sadie crossed her arms over her chest.

Sterling shrugged. "I guess that's what you could call it." He met Sadie's eyes briefly before glancing back at Arabella. "Younglove suggested it was possible, but I never believed her. I never tried it. I guess I just needed to be properly motivated."

I couldn't even comprehend how he got over the wall that surrounded Headquarters and travelled three miles over open water to reach us in just a matter of minutes. And it didn't look like he was going to give us any details either. Nobody said anything else, but I knew I wasn't the only one looking at Sterling with newfound respect.

Sterling could fly and Arabella could regenerate body parts. What other secrets did we not know about ourselves?

I grinned. "Skip the hospital, Wesley. New plan."

The van was silent as Wesley navigated to the freeway and we all stared at the unconscious girl in Sterling's lap. I could've sworn I heard sirens in the distance, but for just a moment, I wasn't worried. After what we'd been through in the last few days, and especially the last hour, it was amazing that we were all still alive. We had stared death down over and over again, and yet, we survived.

The Program was right to fear us.

CLEO

❧ 6 ❧

HELPFUL HAYSEEDS

We drove for hours and were safely away from the disaster we left at the Exchange Place station. At first, everyone was too stunned to speak once they heard the details of what happened, but after Arabella gained consciousness and shrugged off her miraculous healing as if it were nothing more than putting on a new pair of pants, the argument for where we should go next began.

Dexter wanted to drive out to Los Angeles. The University he had trained at was located there and he wanted to get as far from Headquarters as possible. Sadie wanted to go to Penn State. She had a boyfriend who was in the Vanguard program there. Marty wanted to go to Dallas and Wesley wanted to go to Chicago. Most everyone thought that we should go to the university where they trained, each insisting they might know someone who could help us.

"They're going to be watching the universities," Ozzy argued. "That's where they'll expect us to go."

"No place is safe," Sadie countered. "At least if we go where we know people, they might be able to help, or at least give us a place to hide until we can figure out what to do."

Ozzy cleared his throat and stared out the window. "We need to get a new vehicle," he finally said. "This van could be linked to what happened at the Exchange Place Station. We don't know if anyone saw us or if we were caught on any surveillance cameras in the area." He ran his hand back through his hair and I knew the stress he felt over the responsibility for all of us was wearing on him. Every injury, every mistake, every failure—he took them all personally. He had the weight of eleven other lives on his shoulders and I wished I could do something to share the burden.

"Go to the Philadelphia International Airport," Ozzy finally told Wesley.

"Are you planning to hijack a plane?" Sterling asked. "Because I've always wanted to fly on a plane."

"Says the boy who actually flew without one." Cassie smirked.

Sterling smirked back. For once, he was feeling pretty good about his Hummingbird skills. Running fast was cool, but flying...there wasn't a single person in the van who wouldn't want to be able to do that.

"We're not flying anywhere." Ozzy leaned against the side of the van, trying to get comfortable before pulling me in close to him. "We need to get a new vehicle. If we go to long term parking at the airport, we can borrow something that won't be noticed missing for a while. It might buy us some time."

"We also need to eat," Marty pointed out. We'd been living off of protein bars and water since we left the hotel. We didn't have much money and had been too busy running for our lives to get real food.

"I know. First things first. We need a new van." Ozzy pointed to the sign for the Philadelphia International Airport, and Wesley took the exit.

***

It only took one loop through the airport parking lot and fifteen minutes for Theo to disable nearby cameras and then hotwire two SUVs for us. We couldn't find a van big enough, and Ozzy reasoned that two SUVs were probably better anyway. At least it was more comfortable now that we all had our own seats and weren't sliding around on the floor of a cargo van. I felt a moment of guilt for the people who owned the cars we were taking, but when it came to our safety, there wasn't much we wouldn't do to survive. Stealing two vehicles was a much smaller price to pay than an all-out battle with Mandate soldiers and Hounds. I told myself we were doing everyone a favor and keeping innocent people from being caught in Sophisticate crossfire.

Wesley was driving the vehicle that Marty, Dexter, Sadie, and Eva had gotten into, so I climbed into the third row of the SUV that Arabella and Sterling were already sitting in. It looked like even after everything we'd been through, the Deviants continued to gravitate toward their usual cliques. That's why I was surprised when Quinnie slid into the seat next to me.

Arabella was still a little weak from her ordeal, but not too weak to turn around and give Quinnie a dirty look. "You're riding with us?"

Quinnie didn't bother to look up as she pushed herself into the corner of the seat and hooked her ankle under her knee to get comfortable. "I didn't know there were assigned seats."

"Didn't anyone tell you? I put your place card in the trunk of that Honda." Arabella pointed to the beat up car next to us.

Quinnie flipped Arabella the middle finger before pulling her phone out of her pocket and giving it her attention. When Arabella realized she wasn't going to get the argument she wanted, she turned back around to lean her head on Sterling's shoulder. Since we were all accounted for, I was wondering who Quinnie was planning to call. Her father?

"You're not planning to turn us in are you?" When she looked up and met my eyes, she was frowning. I nodded toward the phone.

Quinnie blinked slowly, that small motion saying more than an entire monologue. "Yeah," she finally said. "Because I'm so eager to be *terminated*." She rolled her eyes and returned her attention to her phone.

"They can still track it," I pointed out.

She took a deep breath and then pushed it out in annoyance without looking at me. "How stupid do you think I am?"

Arabella turned around in her seat. "Do you want the full blown explanation, or can I sum it up with a few important bullet points? Because I have plenty."

Quinnie set the phone down and laced her fingers together before pushing her hands in front of her body, cracking her knuckles. Sparks of electricity danced along her fingertips. She glared at Arabella and for a good thirty seconds they were locked in a stare so full of disgust and dislike I could almost taste the bitterness. "Too bad that monster didn't bite your face off instead," Quinnie told Arabella. "It would have been an improvement."

Arabella's elbow was resting on the seat behind her and she squeezed her hand into a fist, ready for a fight—verbal or physical, it probably didn't matter. Before she could make a move, Sterling stretched his arm along the back of the seat, pulling on her shoulder until she curled into him and had to look away. "Hag witch," I heard Arabella mutter.

Quinnie's eyes narrowed as she stared at the back of Arabella's head, but her mouth quirked up into a satisfied smile. I had a flash of panic, wondering why I'd agreed not to share her secret, and worried just how much trouble I was getting myself and everyone else into. Could Quinnie really be trusted? And when was she planning to tell Ozzy?

If she tried to make a call or send a message, I'd toss the phone out the window and take care of her myself.

As if she could feel the weight of my gaze, she finally looked at me. "This wasn't an official Program phone. They don't know I have it and it's not being tracked. So you can just go ahead and get your panties all untwisted."

When she pulled some earbuds out of her pocket and plugged them into the phone I felt the worry ebb a bit. She was just listening to music. Although I wondered if she was just going to tune out and listen to music, why was it so important for her to ride with us?

I continued to watch Quinnie because I knew she had a very specific reason to choose our vehicle instead of the one where all of her friends were riding. She hated me more than anyone else; she would never choose to sit next to me unless it was important. When she finally looked up from the screen on her phone to meet my gaze, I lifted my eyebrows in question. Her eyes darted to the box in my lap and it all made sense. She wanted to know what else was in the osmium box, and she was also making sure I was keeping my word to keep her secret to myself. There was no need for that.

I meant what I told her earlier. I had no plans to divulge the information on her page, but I could understand why she was sticking close to make sure. If our roles were reversed, I wouldn't trust her either.

The front doors of the car opened and I looked up as Theo got into the driver's seat. Cassie entered through the side door and frowned as she realized Quinnie was next to me. Instead of squeezing into the spot between us, she took the empty seat next to Arabella. I had a quick, desperate hope that Ozzy would climb in back with me and force Quinnie to sit elsewhere, but no luck. With a quick glance to take a headcount, he slid into the passenger seat up front next to Theo. He said something to Theo I couldn't hear, the car started moving, and then we were on the move again.

Ozzy turned in his seat, his eyes meeting mine, his fierce expression softening. His gaze was full of promises and I didn't have to hear him voice them aloud to know what he was thinking—when this was over, it would be us. Freedom. Together. I knew this because every time he'd gotten near me since the altercation with the Others in Baltimore, his body was always reaching out for me as if to make sure I was real. Safe. His fingers would wrap around mine in a silent reassurance that no matter what we faced, we'd face it together. We'd survive.

Would surviving always mean a life on the run from the Program?

To distract myself from that depressing thought, I opened the osmium box which I'd been holding since the rescue party had returned to the van with a nearly dead Arabella. Quinnie elbowed me and when I looked up from the box, her eyebrows arched up in question. Were we really going to continue communicating in questioning eyebrows and meaningful looks? This was getting ridiculous.

"Lawless and Younglove both said that we'd find information in here that could help us. We can't drive around stealing cars forever, we have to find some place to go," I explained.

Quinnie nodded her head toward the box as if granting me permission, and I started rifling through the information looking for anything that might be useful. She kept a careful watch over everything I touched. Underneath a stack of large, white envelopes, I found what looked like an address book. I flipped open the front cover and a thrill shot through me as I read the note on the front: *Dozen Contacts*. This had to be what Lawless was talking about.

"I think I found something that might help," I said. Ozzy turned around and I held up the address book before passing it toward him.

He gave me a smile, the first one I'd seen since we left Baltimore. In his gaze, I could see all the things he couldn't say in the moment. He was relieved that we were all still alive, but he wished, as much as I did, that he wasn't so far apart from me. His smile turned apologetic and then he gave his attention to the address book.

After a few minutes, Ozzy started giving Theo directions.

He turned around in his seat to look at us. "We'll be there in about an hour."

"Where are we going?" Arabella asked, yawning.

"A farm in Eastern Maryland. Daniel and Gina Knight were the first entry in this book. I hope that means they can help us."

Daniel and Gina Knight. I wondered who they were and how they were involved with the Program. I closed the box and set it on the floor under my feet. I had an hour to try to resist the desire to look through it. Inside were the answers to the past of the entire Dozen and it was only fair that we discover those answers together.

I hoped Lawless was right and that this address would take us to someone who could help us. Without money and someplace safe to go, it wouldn't take the Program long to find us.

***

My head jerked to the side, banging against the window. Sitting up, I rubbed the heels of my palms across my eyes to clear the sleep from them. Our SUV was on a long dirt driveway, jostling violently with every pot hole we drove over. To either side of the driveway, white pristine fences enclosed pastures that were still boasting some green grass, but were mostly browning with the coming of winter. Trees lined the driveway, guarding the entrance like soldiers standing at attention. Leaves littered the base of the trees, their bare branches reaching into the lightening, pre-dawn sky.

"Where are we?" I groaned.

"Some horse farm out in the boonies." Quinnie was wide awake and grumpy. "I think your little black book was faulty. Don't see how these hayseeds can help us."

Outside the window, the sky was still a deep purple, but dawn was inching over the trees on the horizon. Off in the distance, a large stone home was visible. To the right of it, there was a long tan building that had a red roof, numerous dormer windows, and first floor windows and doors with large "X"s across them. I assumed that it was a stable.

For once, I had to agree with Quinnie. I couldn't see how these people could help us, unless we chose to face down the Program on the backs of horses. I giggled at the thought and Quinnie glared at me.

"I was just imagining..." I started to explain and then shook my head.

"What?" Quinnie snapped, annoyed that I left the sentence hanging.

"Nothing."

She rolled her eyes and returned her attention to the window.

We pulled up to the stone home, which had a large covered porch extending along the front of the house and wrapping around the side. All along the porch, I could see the remains of what was probably a gorgeous garden during the spring and summer, but was now a mass of brown bushes and overgrown weeds. Several metal poles with glass butterflies on top were scattered throughout the garden, brightening the otherwise colorless area. A man stood on the porch. His hand rested on the rifle leaning against his side as he watched our cars approach and come to a stop. Theo turned off the engine, and Ozzy got out of the SUV, leaving his door open as he approached the man cautiously.

"Who are you?" the man asked. He had dark hair that was graying at his temples, but he seemed familiar, and totally out of place on a farm. He was distinguished and looked like he should have been wearing an expensive business suit, not jeans and a plaid, button-down shirt.

"Ozzy. Osbourne Dracone. Professor Lawless gave us your information. We're hoping you might be able to help us."

"Professor Lawless sent you?" The wary look in the man's eyes brightened into hope as his eyes scanned the two dark vehicles in his driveway. "Who else is with you?"

Ozzy stood with his hands raised even though the man hadn't

pointed the gun at him. "Just the rest of the Dozen. I assume you're familiar with who we are."

"All of the Dozen?"

Ozzy nodded.

"Does the Program know you're here?" The man shifted, lifting the gun slightly.

Ozzy shook his head. "The Program is trying to kill us. We disabled our tracking tattoos a few days ago. We've been on the run ever since."

The man's mouth tightened into a thin line. "Drive your cars around back and park them in the garage," he said, pointing to the side of the house. "Then come inside. We'll talk." He threw another hopeful glance at the SUVs and then went inside the house.

As Theo pulled around back, two doors on the detached garage lifted and we parked inside. When we exited the garage, I could see the man standing on his back porch. He pressed the button of a remote in his hand and the doors rolled down again to hide our stolen SUVs. Or prevent our escape. Only time would prove which of those scenarios was true. I wanted to trust Lawless and hope that he could, and would, help us. But in all honesty, the only people we could really trust at this point were each other. Who knew how far the Program's reach was?

I looked around at our group and realized just how bad we looked. We were dirty, many of us in torn and bloody clothing, and we were exhausted. Sleep and food had been scarce in the last few days, but terror and danger had been plentiful. Those truths were easily visible on each and every one of our faces. We stood awkwardly in the yard waiting for the man to tell us what to do.

"Come inside. You look like you could use something to eat and a little rest."

"Thank you," Ozzy said gratefully.

"We can discuss everything after that, but I'll just reassure you now that you're safe. You can trust me." He leaned on the railing of the porch, as he took the time to look at each of us.

I exchanged looks with Cassie, Arabella, and Sterling who were standing nearby. The only people we ever really trusted were each other and sometimes even that was difficult. In our world, supernatural powers and evil twins could really put a strain on relationships. I understood why my friends hadn't trusted me when Persephone was wreaking havoc at St. Ignatius and casting the blame to me, but it didn't change the fact that in the life of a Sophisticate, trust was hard to come by. The problem was: we didn't really have a choice. We could turn away from this man and his farm and stay on the run, or we could hope that Lawless was on our side and pointed us in the right direction.

Just then, the back door was flung open and a middle aged woman with tousled dark hair rushed out onto the porch. She had a robe pulled tightly around her body, one arm clutching it against her waist, the other hand gathering it against her throat to keep out the chill. By the state of her dress, it appeared that our arrival woke her up, but her eyes were alert and searching as she scanned our group. Her breath came out in heavy clouds in the cold morning air. Her bright blue gaze skimmed easily over me before settling on Arabella and halting.

"Arabella." The woman said her name like it was a prayer. Her hands released the fabric of her robe and as she ran down the steps toward us, I could see a necklace resting on the neckline of the nightgown that was beneath her robe. It was a turquoise butterfly wrapped in gold, a symbol I had seen before.

I held my breath as the woman came to a stop in front of Arabella, seemingly oblivious to the torn and bloody clothes she was wearing. The woman was staring at Arabella as if every wish she'd ever hoped for had been granted all at once.

Arabella took a careful step forward, her eyes flicking to the necklace at the woman's throat and then back to the strangely familiar face above it. Arabella's head tilted to the side as she said, "Mom?"

The woman folded Arabella into a hug and I was surprised to see my usually aloof friend accept it willingly. I felt a moment of jealousy, but it was replaced by the hope and wish that a similar fate awaited me in my future. If we could find Arabella's parents, we could find mine, too. I felt a smile creep across my mouth, but when I looked away, my gaze found Quinnie and the hope for myself turned into pity for her. With a father like Russell Baker, Quinnie had no hope of something like this in the future. Her father wanted to put a knife in her back, not hug her.

Quinnie must have felt me looking at her because her head lifted up to meet my gaze and when she saw the pity in my eyes, she set her face in a mask of indifference before walking toward the porch. She stopped in front of the man who was fondly watching the woman hugging Arabella. "You said something about feeding us?"

RUNE

✑ 1 ✑

TRUTHS & LIES

After quickly raiding the Academy kitchen and grabbing as much food as we could carry, we started making the long trek out to the road where we left our vehicle. I didn't know how much time we had before the Program showed up, but it would be a shame to die of starvation before they had their chance to kill us. I figured since the Academy evacuated to Headquarters in Manhattan, it would be a while before anyone would arrive. We could spare the few minutes to grab some food.

"They have a huge garage out back with tons of vehicles, we should take one of those," Persephone suggested as she stumbled under the weight of the food sack she was carrying. "It's much closer than walking all the way out to the end of this freaking driveway."

"Who knows what kind of tracking systems those things have on them? If we take one of their cars, we might as well put a huge neon sign with a flashing arrow above our heads that says 'shoot here.' We can't risk it." I tried to take the bag from her but she pushed me away and gripped it in a way that suggested she would use it as a weapon if I dared insult her by trying to help again.

Persephone huffed. "Our car is a piece of shit."

I couldn't argue with her on that point. When we left Baltimore, we'd taken care to steal an old car without all the bells and whistles on it so that it would be less likely to be traced, but that also meant it was little more than a death trap on wheels. Luckily, I had a new plan and place for us to go and we didn't have far to travel. The death trap should be able to at least get us as far as our next destination.

I still hadn't told Persephone, Euri, and Elysia where we were going because I didn't think they'd agree to follow me. There was a small part of me that wanted to let them know, let them go their own way so I wouldn't be responsible for them anymore. I had a much better chance at surviving without them, of getting mercy if they weren't with me. But at the same time, I felt like it was my duty to at least try to keep us safe. I wouldn't make any of them stay if they decided to leave, but I'd give them the option for us to stick together. It was the least I could do.

The car was just as we left it—hub caps missing, blue paint chipping off, front fender dangling precariously, and rust taking hold on the dent in the front panel of the driver's side. The pink pine tree air freshener hanging from the mirror was probably the newest thing on the car. We were tossing the sacks of food into the back seat when I heard the sound of dead leaves being crushed beneath boots.

"Don't move," a voice ordered.

Against my better judgment, I did as I was told and stood still even though every cell in my body screamed for me to run. I looked over the hood of the car and scanned the woods to find Mandates hiding behind trees, their guns pointing directly at us. There were at least a dozen that I could see and probably even more that were hidden. They were all our age—young and just as scared as we were.

"Don't attack," I murmured under my breath, just loud enough that Persephone, Elysia, and Euri could hear.

"Why not? They're going to kill us," Persephone hissed.

"They haven't yet."

"Exactly why we shouldn't give them the chance," she countered.

"Ozzy." It was one of the guys in the front.

I shared a quick look with Euri and gave him a small nod that I hoped he understood. These kids thought we were Deviants. Well, at least the other three were. As far as these cadets were concerned, they were holding their friends hostage and had no idea who we actually were.

"Yeah?" Euri answered, moving forward as if he recognized the guy who had spoken. "What's up?"

"The Program gave us the order to terminate you." The guy said the words as if they were a question, as if he couldn't believe the order had actually been given and was hoping we'd tell him it was all a joke.

Euri turned to look at the rest of us with a raised eyebrow that asked what he didn't dare say out loud. *Do we attack now?* There was a part of me that remembered all that Delia had ingrained in us—attack first and stay alive. As hard as it was, I fought the compulsion that told me to strike first. I could be better than Delia planned for us to be. I wanted to be.

I answered Euri with another shake of my head. *Not yet.*

"Terminate us?" Euri looked around at the Mandates and chuckled like it was a joke. "That's a surprise to me." He leaned against the car, giving off an air of easy confidence that looked every bit like Ozzy.

"What did you do?" the guy asked. "Why does the Program want you dead?" The guy nervously ran his hand back through his hair. It looked like he wished he was anywhere but in the middle of the road with a gun pointed at his friends. Just last week these kids were taking classes and training with the Deviant Dozen. To them, we looked like their classmates, not threats.

The Program should have sent seasoned Mandates to apprehend us instead of a bunch of cadets whose uniforms still had creases in them. They easily had us outnumbered, but it was clear they didn't want to kill us. And that was a good thing because I didn't want to die.

"I don't know, but there must be some mistake," Euri said, feigning surprise.

"Maybe it has something to do with him," the guy suggested, gesturing to me with his gun.

Interesting. The Program hadn't told these Mandates anything. They had no idea who I was or the danger I posed. The Program merely gave the order to terminate the Dozen and they assumed the order would be followed no matter how many Mandates they might lose in the process. The question was, how far would these kids go to follow orders? The fact that we were still alive proved that they didn't want to do as they were told, and probably didn't fully trust the Program. That could work to our advantage.

"We were on a mission for the Program," I said, looking to Euri, encouraging him to say something to gain the support of the Mandates.

Euri shrugged. "We have important intelligence about the recent attacks and we were supposed to return here to give a briefing. But when we got here, everyone was gone."

The guy's posture relaxed and I noticed his grip on the gun wasn't nearly as severe as it was initially. "The Academy was evacuated because it was attacked," the Mandate explained.

"We were wondering what happened. Who attacked?" I asked.

He turned to look at me and his dark eyebrows furrowed over his eyes. "I don't know. It's classified. All they told us was that we were supposed to terminate you." The gun was still pointing in our direction and his finger twitched around the trigger as if it was fighting an internal battle: follow orders, or spare a friend? The guy, and his finger, couldn't decide.

I realized that we were going to have to make the decision for him. We would do whatever we had to survive, but at the same time, I didn't want to kill these cadets. They were victims in this as much as we were.

"We didn't do anything wrong," I said, slowly raising my hands in surrender. "This is all a mistake and once we get a chance to talk to the officials, they'll be glad you spared us." I didn't know what the Mandates knew about the Dozen, but I was confident they were observant enough to notice how important Ozzy and Quinnie were around the Academy. That had to mean something to them.

"Maybe." He was lost in thought for a moment, the gun still pointed in our direction. "But we did have orders, so we'll at least have to take you into custody and bring you to the officials ourselves." His statement sounded more like a question, and when he lowered his gun a little to look around at the rest of the group for support, that's when I made my move.

I snapped my hands shut as I spun around, pushing blasts of air out at the cadets around us, knocking them to the ground before they realized what happened. I heard surprised grunts and cries as branches and leaves were thrown about by my thunderclaps of air, making it hard for the cadets to see as they scrambled to get to their feet again.

"Burn the trees," I told Persephone. "Just the ones on the edge. Don't kill anyone."

"You're no fun." She muttered something about me being a pansy ass, but I noticed she took care to fling fireballs with careful precision at the base of the trees around us, the piles of leaves immediately igniting and throwing tongues of flames up the trunks. She didn't hit a single cadet and her meticulous accuracy gave them a chance to retreat safely.

A few gunshots rang out, but since the cadets couldn't see, the bullets missed us. I could hear them hitting trees, the ground, and even parts of our car.

"Don't shoot," the guy shouted to his fellow Mandates. "You could hit one of us!"

I continued to use my deviation to blast leaves and dirt into the air so we couldn't be seen. "Get in the car," I told everyone. "Hurry, before they decide to start shooting again." My hands created mini tornadoes of leaves and air that fed Persephone's fire and drove the cadets further into the trees. Behind me, the car started.

"Go!" I yelled, jumping into the back seat and yanking the door shut behind me.

The car revved and then spun in a tight circle, heading for the opposite direction. All I could hear were gunshots, screams, and the sound of bullets making contact with different parts of the car. We'd be lucky if they didn't shoot out all four tires.

"Hurry!" Elysia screamed from the front seat.

The car was swerving so erratically that I was having trouble getting into a sitting position. I finally managed to get into the seat and was about to roll down the window to stir up the dirt and leaves when the glass shattered. Instinctively, I threw my arm up over my face, blocking most of the shards.

"Shit!" Persephone screamed next to me. She was gripping her elbow to pull her arm close to her body. There were cuts across her face and arm and blood was starting to trickle down her face. "Those assholes shot out our window! I should have killed them." Before I could stop her, she flung her good arm across my body. A fireball rolled off her fingertips and howled through the broken window, exploding magnificently against the nearest tree.

Our car sped past, and I saw a few bodies fall to the ground, flames racing up the clothing they wore. I didn't know if they were hurt...or dead...or soon to be dead. My stomach clenched in disgust. I hated a lot of the things that Delia had forced us to do to each other and to innocent people in the name of revenge, but right now, I hated myself for how badly the situation got out of hand.

As our car fishtailed around the corner at the end of the long driveway and headed away from the Academy, I glanced back at the carnage we left behind us—bodies, flames, pain. Nothing had changed for us. So much damage in so little time. It seemed even with Delia gone, we still managed to destroy everything around us.

OZZY

❦ 8 ❦

No Choice

The kitchen was large, but not nearly large enough for all the revelations that were sure to come. Mr. Knight pulled in chairs from another room to place around the wooden farm table and along the walls. All of the Deviants collapsed into them, the first promise of safety in days taking its toll. Mrs. Knight was cooking breakfast, but it was slow going since she couldn't seem to pay attention to anything other than Arabella, who offered to help her.

God help us all if Arabella was cooking. We'd be lucky if we didn't end up with food poisoning. Although honestly, I was hungry enough to risk it and not think twice.

Cleo sat in the chair next to me, her hand tucked into mine, her head on my shoulder. From the even rhythm of her breathing, I was pretty sure she was asleep. Most of the Dozen were in various forms of exhaustion. They hadn't been on as many missions as me and their bodies just weren't used to the stress and lack of sleep we'd faced in the last few days.

"So you say there are others like you? They look like you and have the same abilities?" Mr. Knight asked. I had just finished telling him about the events of the last few days that led to the Program's order to have us terminated.

"There were Others like all of us except for Cassie," I corrected him, pointing to Cleo's best friend who was sitting next to Theo. "There are only four Others left, but we have no idea where they are now."

"But you said they helped you even though you were sent to apprehend them?" Mr. Knight poured juice into glasses and passed them out as he spoke.

"Rune helped us—well, he helped Cleo," I said, looking down at the sleeping form nestled into my side.

"Well, that's a good thing. Maybe that means you have an ally in him."

"I don't know. I think Rune felt he owed Cleo a debt and that the debt was repaid when he saved her life." I took the glass that Mr. Knight held out to me.

"But if the Program is hunting them as well, you have a common enemy."

My spine stiffened at the word 'enemy.' Now that we were here, I couldn't envision what the future held for us with an enemy like the Program. "Are you certain we're safe here?" I asked. "No chance the Program would come looking here?"

Mr. Knight stopped and looked at me with a stern expression. "Geoffrey Lawless wouldn't have given you our name if we couldn't help protect you."

"How do you know, though? Doesn't the Program keep tabs on the parents of Sophisticates? Especially those of the Dozen?" Sterling asked.

"They do until they think you're dead." The smile that crept across Mr. Knight's face was very much like the devious smile that Arabella often wore.

"How did you convince the Program that you're dead?" Having lived my life constantly tracked and monitored, I couldn't imagine such a possibility.

Mr. Knight laughed. "We weren't chosen as parents for the Dozen for nothing you know. To get the best you have to start with the best."

"Daniel," Mrs. Knight admonished from her spot near the stove. "Don't be so arrogant."

Daniel turned to look at his wife, his gaze turning soft at seeing Arabella standing with her at the counter. "I'm not saying anything that's untrue." He turned back to me and Sterling. "All of the parents of the Dozen were chosen for their mental and physical superiority to be donors for the most elite Sophisticates. The only problem was that we didn't know we'd been chosen. Like many of the other parents, we needed IVF treatments to make our dreams of parenthood come true. We had no idea what the scientists did without our permission."

His jaw tightened in anger before he continued speaking. "They genetically altered our child without our knowledge. And once they did that, we lost rights to our baby. No exceptions. You can't imagine the terror of having your child taken away and to be completely helpless to do anything about it. Of course, we tried to fight it legally, but science was on the Program's side and we lost custody. Gina was devastated," he said, casting a tortured look to his wife. "We both were. But we decided if the Program wouldn't give our child back, we'd bide our time until we could make our move. Faking our deaths was the easy part. The difficult part has been making the connections we needed to ensure that when we did finally try to rescue our daughter, the attempt would be successful. And now, here she is, delivered to us by the Program's ignorance and fear."

"You faked your death?" To fool the Program...I couldn't imagine.

"I was in the CIA for many years." He crossed his arms and his expression was stony. "You learn a few tricks of the trade."

"You said something about connections. Who are your connections? What were you planning?" I asked.

"Honey, can we put a halt on all the mastermind plans for a bit?" Gina set down a bowl of scrambled eggs and a plate of bacon. Arabella followed with a stack of plates. Seeing Arabella helping cook and setting the table was really throwing me off. She was the last person I ever expected to act domestically. The concept was as strange as the idea of putting a wolf in an apron.

I must have had a strange look on my face because when she saw me staring, Arabella rolled her eyes at me. "What are you looking at? You were less surprised when I grew my arm back."

"You grew an arm back?" Daniel asked, his calm expression fading into fear. He turned to glare at me. "What does that mean?"

"I didn't make it that far in the story," I said. After we entered the kitchen, I'd managed to tell him about Andrews Air Force Base when we found Rune and took him back to the Academy. I filled him in on the mission to apprehend Janus Malleville which resulted in Malleville's suicide and Sterling being kept at Headquarters by Dr. Steel. I even told him about the unsuccessful trip to Conowingo Dam and the battle at the Inner Harbor, but I still hadn't told him about the rescue mission for Sterling and how Arabella had been injured. How was I supposed to tell a father that his daughter's arm was bitten off by a monster because she was trying to protect me? He continued to stare at me expectantly.

I sighed. "In our attempt to rescue Sterling, we accidentally discovered that Arabella can regenerate. We don't know the extent of her ability, but she grew back part of her arm."

"Really?" Daniel smiled as he looked at his daughter. I expected him to be horrified, but he was actually impressed. Leave it to Arabella's father to be fascinated by the ability to grow back severed body parts. It explained a lot about her. "How long did it take? Was it painful to grow back? Does the new arm work just as well?" He took a step toward her and lifted her arm, inspecting it like it was something he might want to purchase.

"Really, Daniel. Let it go for now," Gina interrupted. "These kids are starving and tired. Let them eat and get some rest. Your questions will still be here in a couple of hours." Despite her words, she cast a curious look over her husband's shoulder.

"You're right," he said, dropping Arabella's arm and patting her on the shoulder as he looked around the room. "Dig in kids, and then I'll show you were you can get some sleep. Thankfully, we don't have any grooms in residence right now. There is plenty of lodging above the stable. We can talk later."

"I did have one question."

Daniel turned back to face me.

I cleared my throat. "When we went to rescue Sterling from Headquarters, we went through Exchange Place Station."

A dish fell to the ground and shattered. Gina turned, ignoring the broken pieces at her feet, and fixed a terrified gaze on me. "You tried to go through the Manhattan Moat?" Her eyes flicked over toward Arabella and she reached out, pulling her into an embrace. "You're lucky you only lost part of an arm!"

"You know about the Manhattan Moat?" I asked. Daniel nodded. "So you know about the creatures in there?"

Daniel ran his hand over the edge of the counter, lost in thought. He was quiet for a long time. When he finally looked up, his eyes were full of burning hatred. "Those creatures were another of the Program's experiments. If humans could be weapons, why not animals? Right?" He clenched his jaw. "Luckily, most of those experiments failed. The few that survived were sent as an extra precaution to guard the tunnels that led into the city."

I huffed. "Yeah, well the Others were supposed to be failed experiments and look how they turned out. The Program's failures are more dangerous than their successes."

Daniel's mouth thinned into a tight line. "There's some truth to that. Delia was a failed experiment too. I'd say it's about time the Program was dismantled before they create anything else." Daniel's fingers curled into a fist and he bumped his hand lightly on the counter twice as if he were warding off the past. "But first we eat."

I really wanted to know more about Mr. Knight's connections, how he knew Professor Lawless, how he knew about the Moat, and how he faked his death and avoided the Program's notice. But right now, I wanted nothing more than to eat a nice hot meal, even if Arabella did help make it.

***

After breakfast, Daniel led us out through the yard toward the stable to where the lodging rooms were. The sun was fully seated in the sky, turning the frost covered grass into a sea of shiny blades.

He unlocked a door that entered through the side of the stable and then led us to a stairwell. On the second floor, a hallway stretched across the length of the building with half a dozen doors leading off of it. He handed me keys to the rooms.

"Sorry there are only six rooms. Hopefully you don't mind bunking up with each other. I'll leave it to you to organize room arrangements. When you're all rested, we can talk more."

"Thanks. For everything." I held my hand out and he shook it.

"No. Thank you. You brought Arabella back to us. She is *our* everything." Daniel smiled as he turned toward the steps and left.

"Do you think Arabella is going to be okay?" Cleo asked. Gina had asked her daughter to stay in the main house and Sterling insisted on staying with her. I had a feeling he wasn't going to be letting her out of his sight any time soon.

"She'll be fine." I slid my arm around Cleo's waist and pulled her close. "We're all going to be fine."

Cleo nodded, biting her lip, and I wondered what she was thinking and whether she believed me. I wasn't confident that *I* believed me.

I unlocked the first door and peered inside. The room was sparse, but neat and clean. There were two twin beds, a couch, dresser, and television. "How do you want to split up?" I asked, turning to the group.

"Cleo and I will take this one," Cassie said, stepping forward and pulling her friend out of my grip.

By the look on Cleo's face, I knew she was feeling the same way I was. After everything we'd been through in the last few days, I just wanted to be with her. I wanted to have her in my arms and know she was safe. And we still needed to discuss what happened with

Rune and the Others both at the Academy and at the Inner Harbor. If we were going to have a relationship, which I was determined to, we had to know that we could trust each other. We'd both kept secrets and the time for that had to end.

"Now isn't the time." Cassie's glare could have rivaled Arabella's in intensity. "We all need to get rest—you most of all, Ozzy. I don't think you've slept at all in the last few days. You're no use to us as a zombie."

I released a breath and rubbed my hand over my head as I grinned at Cleo. "Make sure you get some rest, too. I plan on keeping you very busy once you wake up." I reached out and ran my thumb across her lips.

"Bloody hell," Quinnie whined. "I swear to God I'm gagging on the hormones. Get laid already and stop with the mushy shit. It's giving me hives." She stormed down the hallway taking the last room on the left and slamming the door behind her

"Come on," Cassie said, pushing her best friend into the room. Before Cassie could shut the door, Cleo darted back through the opening, closed her hand in my jacket, and pulled me forward until her lips pressed against mine. Her mouth was warm and soft and I had to fight the urge to drag her into the room behind me and ignore common sense. My body might need rest, but it wanted Cleo.

Cleo pulled back from the kiss just enough so she could look into my eyes, but our lips were still touching. "Dream of me?" she whispered against my mouth.

As if I had a choice.

CLEO

~ 9 ~

CROSS IT OFF THE LIST

I'd been lying next to Cassie staring at the ceiling for hours. She fell asleep right away, but I couldn't turn my brain off. Maybe it was because I'd had more opportunity to sleep than everyone else. Or maybe it was knowing that the answers to the truth about my parents were finally within my reach—a short walk out to the garage and into the back seat of the SUV where the osmium box was hidden. Or maybe it was knowing that Ozzy was just down the hall and that there was no one to tell us we couldn't be together. The Program no longer micromanaged every second of our lives and we were finally free from the Academy's prying eyes. Our freedom had come at a great cost, but I couldn't deny that there were some definite benefits, too. I just hadn't had the opportunity to enjoy those benefits yet since we'd spent the majority of our time avoiding death. Would there ever be a time when we would be truly free to pursue our own happiness and desires? Was the life we were given genetically charmed in some ways, only to be cursed in the ways that mattered the most?

I tried to force myself to sleep, but it was no use. It was the middle of the day and my mind and body refused to rest. The bedroom curtains had been pulled closed, but they were no match for the sunlight that crept around the edges of the drapes and bathed our room in morning light. After another ten minutes of counting the squares in the checkered pattern of our quilt and listening to the sounds of geese flying overhead, I convinced myself that I had to go to the bathroom—anything to escape the boredom of wakefulness. I slipped out of bed, careful not to wake Cassie. I didn't need to worry, though. She didn't even so much as flinch when I got up.

I put on the unfamiliar jacket that had mysteriously become mine over the last few days and then grabbed our room key off the dresser. Opening the door just wide enough to squeeze through, I snuck out into the quiet hallway...and bumped into someone.

"Jesus!" I whisper-yelled. It was Arabella's mother, Gina. "Oh, Mrs. Knight. I'm so sorry." I couldn't control the warmth of the blush that spread up from my neck and across my cheeks. Cursing wasn't exactly the way I wanted to greet my friend's long-lost mother for the very first time.

"Call me 'Gina.' And it's okay." She reached out and patted my shoulder. "I'd be surprised if you weren't a little skittish after all you've been through."

"I was just on my way to the bathroom." I stammered a bit because I was actually nervous she might realize I'd been thinking about sneaking into Ozzy's room. He and Quinnie were the only ones with their own rooms.

"Down there, hon." Gina pointed toward the end of the hall. "It's a communal bathroom, but it has three separate shower stalls.

Hopefully you all can make that work."

"Absolutely. Thanks for everything you've done for us."

Gina waved her hand. "It's nothing, really. We're just glad you're all here and safe." She tucked her lips between her teeth and when she looked away, I could see tears in her eyes. After a few seconds, she cleared her throat. "We'll be having dinner later up at the house after you've all had time to rest and clean up. But if you're already awake, you might need these." Gina pointed to some bags that were placed at our door. I noticed that there were bags at each of the doors. "I ran into town and picked up some toiletries and clothes for you all. Arabella told me that you didn't have anything with you and I noticed that the things you were wearing were in rough shape after the events of the last couple of days." She cleared her throat again. "I don't know if I got your size right—"

"I'm sure it will be perfect," I said. I felt the urge to hug her. As Sophisticates, we'd never been treated with this kind of empathy. Sure, we were provided for—fed and clothed well—because we were valuable to the Program, but I couldn't remember the last time that an adult had been kind to me because they actually cared about me. My heart was overwhelmed with gratitude. There was also a lingering sense of jealousy knowing that this sweet, kind woman was Arabella's mother. She was exactly what I would have wished for in a mother for myself, and I kind of hated myself for being envious of my friend for having such good luck.

Gina reached out hesitantly and then finally rested her hand on my arm. "If you need anything, just let me know, okay?"

"Thank you." I grinned.

"No, thank *you*. You helped bring my daughter back to me and we're so grateful to have you all here with us." Gina's smile was sad, but genuine. "She's already told me so much about everyone."

"She has?"

Gina nodded and looked down at her hands. "She went with me into town to help choose some clothes. With her ability to change her appearance, we didn't have to worry about her being recognized, and I really needed her help. I'm not really up to speed with what young people wear these days." She shrugged. "I don't get off the farm much."

"Arabella picked out our clothes?" I laughed. "This should be pretty interesting."

"She was a little disappointed with the selections," Gina admitted, looking up at me again. "One of the things about living in a small town is that you don't have many options for interesting clothing choices." Gina winked. "But I think you'll be fine, there's nothing too crazy in there." And with that, she waved and headed down the stairs.

Cautiously, I peeked into the bag. Jeans, long sleeve henleys, hoodies, underclothes, and two pairs of converses in mine and Cassie's sizes. Thank God for small towns to thwart Arabella's fashion sense. Desperate to get out of the disgusting clothes I'd been wearing since my unexpected almost-drowning at the Inner Harbor, I snatched the bag and made my way to the bathroom.

After that, I was going to get some answers out of the osmium box.

***

Despite the fact that it was the middle of November, the day was sunny and warm. The ground was covered in dry, brittle leaves in many places and as I made my way to the garage, I detoured my path to shuffle through the random piles. There was something tempting about the brightly colored leaves that begged me to kick them around a bit—an act of defiance, an act of freedom, an act that made me think of childhood memories I never had the chance to make with parents or friends or siblings.

The side door to the garage was open and I was relieved to find that the SUV hadn't been locked either. The osmium box was shoved under the seat where I hid it. With the confusion of the night before, I'd forgotten all about it. I opened the black folder and found my page without giving in to the urge to look at Ozzy's or anyone else's. I tore out my sheet and then shuffled through the box until I found the envelope with my name on it that I'd noticed earlier. Satisfied with my findings, I closed the box and placed it back under the seat for safe keeping.

Wanting privacy, I found a porch swing hanging from a huge oak tree and I curled up on the wooden seat, sunlight drenching me as it filtered through the bare branches above. My hands trembled as I held up the sheet I tore out of the black binder. Most of the information was familiar to me: my name, the schools I attended, my deviation, and my talents with computer hacking and languages. But my eyes immediately found the line about my parents. There were names. And a hometown.

Michael and Sarah Cross of Bel Air, Maryland.

I hugged the paper to my chest, my eyes squeezing a few tears from their corners as I closed my eyes in gratitude. My parents were the ones in the article I read in the Restricted Section all those weeks ago. I had parents and they had wanted me. They fought for me. It was everything that I'd hoped for when I began my search.

And I had a last name. Cross. Clementine Cross.

I spent my entire life at Program facilities in Maryland, and all this time they had been so close. Did they still think about me? Were they still hoping I'd come home one day like Gina and Daniel had hoped for Arabella? Did Gina and Daniel talk to my parents? Maybe they were friends.

Excitement bubbled through my chest at the thought of that possibility.

My mind was made up. I had to see them. Bel Air wasn't far away and I was sure that if I asked, Ozzy or Cassie or even Arabella would go with me to visit them. Bel Air was close to where the Academy was, so it was a risk to go, but I had to try. I couldn't have this information and do nothing. I just needed an address...

Remembering the envelope with my name on it, I tore it open, happiness spreading across my lips in a manic smile. I pulled out the stack of papers ecstatic to see that there was an address on the first page. I wanted to jump into the SUV and leave immediately to find it, to finally see the faces I'd dreamt about all these years. I continued to read, wanting to know everything about them. What did they do for a living? What did they look like? Did I have siblings? Were my grandparents still alive?

As I continued to read, however, I could feel my smile melting away with every word. When I flipped the page, the next sheet shattered my hope into a million pieces, leaving me feeling as bare as the branches of the tree I sat beneath.

My breath stuttered out of my throat. I clutched my chest, the pain making it hard to breathe.

There would be no trip to Bel Air, Maryland.

I would not get to meet Michael and Sarah Cross.

I would never know what it felt like to be hugged by my mother or my father.

Michael and Sarah Cross were dead. And they had been for 16 years.

CLEO

❧ 10 ❧

RED

It was odd that I couldn't cry. Tears of happiness were so easy just a few moments ago, but I couldn't even muster the strength to cry. There was an emptiness in my chest and I knew what it was that was missing: hope. At first, I convinced myself that the copies of the death certificates were nothing more than a brilliant ruse by my parents to stay off the Program's radar, much like what Daniel and Gina must have done. But then I turned the page and saw the pictures and the accompanying newspaper articles.

The story was all there in black and white. When my parents were denied custody and visitation rights for me, they took matters into their own hands. They found out who the nurses were that worked for the Program, and they made friends with one who was sympathetic to their plight. Six months after my birth, the nurse smuggled me out of the Program's nursery and into the arms of my parents. For nearly a year, they were on the run and we were a family. Until the day that the Program finally found their missing property—the day my parents surrendered their lives to try and keep me.

The newspapers called what my parents had done kidnapping, but that wasn't technically true. The Program kidnapped me; my parents had merely been trying to right a wrong. They were smart, resourceful people, which was why they'd been selected for the Program in the first place. The only problem was, they never agreed to the selection. In the end, it didn't matter that the Program modified my DNA without their consent. Once it was done, I was no longer Clementine Cross, cherished daughter of Michael and Sarah. I was Clementine Dracone, property of the Program. A weapon.

The paperwork in my files was thorough. Apparently, after my unexpected removal from the Program nursery, the Sophisticate tattoo was born. The Program designed the tattoos so that they could keep track of their valuables, so they'd never have to worry about a Sophisticate ever disappearing again.

My fingers curled around the sheet I'd torn out of the black binder, deforming the words as they folded in on one another. The heat of my anger and the disappointment of my lost hope licked under my skin as my fist crushed the details of my past into a tight ball. I held my breath to keep my anger contained where it couldn't hurt anyone.

No. I wouldn't cry. I couldn't cry. There were no tears to shed because I was filled with so much rage that I was surprised I hadn't gone up in flames myself. I counted slowly, pushing and pulling my breaths into even measures, wishing I could deny the truth about how loving me had cost my parents their lives. And even after their sacrifice and efforts, I had nothing to remember them by—no family heirlooms, no memories, not even any photos of us as a happy family.

The only photos in the envelope were images of the day the Program finally caught up to us. My mother was spread out across the floor of what appeared to be a cozy living room. Her arm was bent in an awkward position as if she never had a chance to try and break her fall. Sarah Cross' dark hair was strewn across her face, some of it falling into her mouth which looked as if it had been silenced mid-plea. Her eyes were brown like mine, but they were blank, forever gazing into a future she would never see. She was wearing a red coat and the white shirt underneath was marred with a blood stain that spread across her chest and down her side. Next to her, Michael Cross was lying on the floor like discarded laundry, his hand still clutching a suitcase. His shirt was covered in so many blood stains that I couldn't tell what the original color had been.

There was so much red in that picture.

I ran my finger along my mother's jacket, as if I could still feel the soft fur that lined the collar, and recognition flickered to life. I didn't remember this day or how the events unfolded, but somewhere deep in my soul, I remembered the red jacket. I remembered gentle fingers stroking my hair, vanilla perfume scented kisses on my forehead, soft fur tickling my nose when I snuggled in for hugs.

I didn't remember my parents. I didn't remember the time we had together. All I had were snippets and strange recollections that were fleeting and unformed. I felt cheated. To be given the promise that those eleven months existed, but to be unable to remember them with any amount of clarity was cruel. Maybe it would have been better to think they'd never wanted me, because knowing that they died trying to keep our family together was...soul shattering.

And still...the tears wouldn't come.

No tears, but plenty of rage.

I folded the pictures and articles so I wouldn't have to look at them anymore, and then stuffed them back into the envelope.

My hope for my parents might be dead, but I had a new hope.

To destroy the Program as effectively as they destroyed my family.

***

"How long have you been out here?" It was the middle of the day already, but Quinnie's breaths were visible in soft clouds that puffed out of her mouth. By the way she shivered slightly in her new jacket, it was clearly cold outside, but I hadn't noticed since my emotions were on a slow boil. Being my own personal heater was one of the benefits of my deviation when it was fueled by my anger.

"I see you found the clean clothes," I said to her. It was none of her damn business what I did or how long I'd been out in the cold.

"Yeah, this is the perfect disguise. Now we *all* look like a bunch of hayseed hillbillies. The Program will never recognize us." She looked down at her generic, no-name jeans and plain sneakers. Quinnie was used to spending her leisure time at the Academy decked out in name brand clothes and flashy accessories. Without her usual fashion sense, she looked normal and completely non-threatening. It was a nice change.

"It's not that bad." I pulled my feet up onto the seat of the swing and wrapped my arms around my knees. "Especially since Arabella helped pick out the clothes. You know how much she loves the color black and anything with skulls on it. We could have ended up looking like Satan's minions."

Quinnie tilted her head and smiled. A real smile. Not the arrogant or mocking sneer I was used to seeing. "Did you just make a joke for me?"

I shrugged. "Maybe."

"Careful. People might get the wrong idea if we start acting friendly." She didn't smile this time, but she didn't say it with malice either. I stared at Quinnie for a moment, surprised to see a touch of insecurity in her expression.

"Yeah. We wouldn't want that," I agreed. "We have reputations to uphold."

"They expect drama. We have to give the people what they want." Quinnie stared off across the sun-soaked farm, her hands shoved into the pockets of her jacket. "You didn't tell anyone about Russell Baker being my donor." The way she said it was almost a question, like she couldn't quite believe it was true.

"I promised you I wouldn't."

"I know. But if things had been reversed, I probably would have broken my promise." Her eyes met mine. She seemed disappointed in herself to admit that was the truth.

"You still have to tell Ozzy," I reminded her.

"I will. I just...I will," she said, more determined.

I don't know why I felt compelled to let her off the hook. Quinnie had never done anything to deserve my sympathy or support, but maybe that's why she needed it. She had always gotten her way at the Academy because of her "sponsor" and by the fear she was able to instill in others. But now that I was taking the time to really understand her, I was beginning to see that her behavior was really a defense mechanism. For Quinnie, it was easier to demand people's respect and allegiance than to earn it.

"You want a second chance?" I asked.

Her eyes cut to me, hopeful and wary at the same time. "What do you mean?"

I held out my envelope to her. "Read this."

"What is it?"

"My envelope from the osmium box. These are my secrets. I wanted to know who my parents were."

Quinnie stepped forward slowly and then settled on the swing next to me. She took the envelope out of my hand and opened it. I remained quiet as she read the papers. When she was done, she huffed and put them back in the envelope, slapping it in my lap. "Is that your way of proving that you're better than me? That your donors were good and mine weren't? That you were loved and wanted by your parents and I was just a means to an end?" She crossed her arms and shifted her body so that she was facing away from me. Cruelty was slipping back into her words, infusing her entire being with the cold withdrawn attitude I was used to.

"No. I wanted you to know my biggest secret."

"And what is that?" she snapped. "That your mother had shitty taste in furniture?" Her voice cracked, almost like she was ready to cry, as if it hurt her to insult me. I didn't allow her vicious jab to bother me. I knew she was saying it out of jealousy and a fierce desire to not be weak.

"No. My secret is that it's my fault that the Sophisticate tattoo was created."

She huffed and rolled her eyes. "First of all, it was your donors' fault, not yours. Second of all, who gives a shit? It's not even nearly the same thing as my secret. Your donors were the cause for a tattoo, but my donor was the cause of the Deviant Dozen. I'm pretty sure everyone would hate me if they knew whose DNA I shared, but I really don't think people would give a rat's ass about the tattoo."

"I care." I slapped my hand against my chest. "That tattoo is basically keeping every Sophisticate a prisoner of the Program. It was created because of me."

"But it's not even a big deal. Who cares?"

"Probably every Sophisticate who has ever tried to run away and was caught because of their tracking tattoo. Sterling was whipped for running away. Cassie was, too. Who knows how many other Sophisticates have suffered the same fate because of me and the actions my parents took?" I stared at her profile, willing her to open up again.

Quinnie's expression softened and she turned to look at me. She wanted to be convinced that we were the same, that we shared some horrible secret. "It's still not the same thing."

I shrugged. "Maybe not exactly, but it's something I don't want to be common knowledge."

"Then why tell me?" Her voice was quiet. Hopeful.

"Because I'm trusting you to keep my secret. I'm giving us a chance at redemption."

OZZY

11

FREEDOM & VENGEANCE

I couldn't believe what I was seeing. Maybe I was still asleep and trapped in some sort of Bizarro universe, because it looked as if Quinnie and Cleo were sitting on a swing together. Talking. There were no fireballs or bolts of electricity. And was Quinnie...smiling? Strange. I didn't even know she was capable of it.

From my window, I watched them for a few minutes, expecting a fight to break out at any moment. I wanted Quinnie to go away so I could go down and talk to Cleo myself, but it seemed that whatever they were talking about was important, so instead of interrupting, I watched. As if aware of my attention, Cleo looked up, finding my gaze immediately. Her lips turned up in something that was just short of a smile before she laid a hand on Quinnie's arm, in a surprisingly gentle way, and said a few words before standing up. After Quinnie answered her, Cleo made her way back to the stable, and me, keeping her gaze firmly rooted to mine until she finally had to break it and enter the building. I watched Quinnie as she continued to sit on the swing, staring off in the distance. When I heard steps outside my door, I turned around to lean against the sill of the window to wait for Cleo.

A few moments later, the handle turned and she slipped inside, quietly closing the door behind her. She leaned up against the wall, her hands tucked behind her, watching me from across the room, looking uncertain.

"Hi." Her voice was calm and quiet, but the look in her eyes was stormy, and it was hard to pin down exactly what emotion I was seeing in them. Passion? Insecurity? Anger? Fear?

"Did you sleep well?"

Cleo pushed off the wall and walked towards me. "I wasn't tired."

"Is that so?" She continued to walk toward me, confidence bleeding into her with every step. What a difference a few months had made. "What were you and Quinnie talking about?"

"Redemption." Cleo stopped in front of me, leaving hardly any space between our bodies. Her gaze was fixed on mine—intense and searching.

"Not that I'm complaining, but why did you come up to see me?" I smiled the cocky smile that I knew she liked, hoping it was the same reason I'd been watching her out the window. Now that we were safe, I couldn't think about anything but her. For once, the responsibility of looking out for the Deviant Dozen was a worry tucked deep down inside. We were together, we were away from the Program, and for now, we were safe. All that was on my mind now was Cleo. I needed to know that there was a future that included us. I needed to have her in my arms. And I needed her to need me.

"I want to get lost in you," Cleo said. "I want to forget everything else until you fill every space in my mind." She reached up, her fingers wrapping behind my neck to pull me down until our lips barely touched. "I just want you," she whispered against my mouth. I pulled her into me, pressing a kiss firmly against her mouth. She parted her lips, the kiss becoming insistent, as if we were taking deep breaths of fresh air after being locked away for too long. After everything we'd been through in the last few days, we both knew what this kiss meant—that we were survivors. We were still alive, and it was the only thing that mattered.

I walked back, pulling Cleo with me, until I could sit down on the edge of the bed. Unwilling to allow her mouth to leave mine, she lowered down on my lap, her knees resting on the bed on either side of my legs.

"Make it go away," she said, her lips moving against mine, her words barely understandable due to the way she nearly choked on them. She slowly opened her eyes and the storm I'd seen earlier in them had been replaced with an emotion I could only describe as broken. "The pain. Make it go away," she begged.

"You're hurt?" Maybe I hadn't seen what I thought I had. Maybe she and Quinnie got into an argument after all.

Cleo wrapped her fingers around my hand and pulled it up to her chest, pressing my palm to the spot where her heart was. Her breath shuddered out of her mouth, the look on her face wounded.

I pulled the edge of her shirt down to see the skin that was under my hand. I expected the worst, but it was perfect and unblemished. "I don't understand. How are you hurt?"

Her head fell to my shoulder and she wrapped her arms around me, pulling me close. "I feel empty and it hurts," she confessed.

I rubbed Cleo's back, offering comfort even though I didn't know for what. She wasn't making any sense, but her pain seemed genuine. After everything that had happened at the Inner Harbor, I could understand. Her lips found my neck, feeding on my skin with urgency while her fingertips dug into my back. It was almost as if she thought if she could just pull me close enough, she'd be able make us one living thing. That I could somehow shove the pain away by taking its place.

"Tell me what happened, Cleo."

Her lips moved up my neck, reaching my jaw and kissing along it until her mouth was pressed against the dip just above my chin. "I couldn't sleep." The warmth of her mouth met mine and I matched her kisses, letting her take whatever she needed. "And then I read my file," she murmured. "The one that was in the osmium box."

My hands settled on her cheeks and I gently pushed her back so that we could look at each other. "We all have terrible secrets, Cleo. What's written on those papers has nothing to do with the real you. Those files don't tell you who you really are. They're nothing but random facts—observations and theories of scientists who see us as opportunities, not people. Whatever it was you saw means nothing. Okay?"

She blinked and tears filled her eyes. "My parents are dead. Because of me." She pressed her hands to her chest in a way that made it look as if she was holding herself together. Her eyes closed and her lips trembled in an effort to speak. "That means everything."

I noticed that she said "parents" and not "donors." I knew that Cleo wanted to find out more about the people who had given her life, she'd mentioned it that morning at the King and Queen's seat. I just didn't realize how much hope she pinned on a future with them. I never would have expected her to feel the loss so deeply. Sure, I was curious about my donors, but I was so young when my deviation exhibited that I never really had the opportunity to yearn for something like parents. I never entertained the idea of being part of a family.

But I *had* considered a future with Cleo, and just imagining the possibility of that future being ripped away made me understand a little more what she was going through. When she'd been pulled from the Inner Harbor lifeless and close to death, I thought my soul would die with her.

I laid back and twisted to the side, laying Cleo next to me. I pulled her in close, wrapping my arms around her as if my embrace could keep out anything that wanted to harm her body or heart. Her face was tucked into my chest and I could feel her tremble every once in a while even though she never cried. After a few minutes, exhaustion overtook her and she fell asleep.

***

A few hours later, there was a knock on the door and Cassie called out, "Cleo, are you in there?"

Cleo stirred, but I answered for her, squeezing my arms around her to keep her against my chest. "She's here."

"Okay. Well Arabella just came by to let us know that dinner will be ready in about fifteen. Gina and Daniel want to talk to all of us afterward." Cassie said through the door.

"We'll be there."

Cassie left and Cleo tilted her head up to look at me. "I'm sorry. About earlier."

She was still tightly wrapped in my embrace and I lifted my arm to run my hand down her head, using my fingers to gently unravel the tangles in her hair. "No apology needed. You know I'll always be here for you."

"I came up because I wanted to be with you. I was looking for a little harmless kissing. But as soon as I saw you—" Her hand came up to the side of my face, fingers trailing down my jaw and along my neck to my shoulder. "As soon as I saw you, something cracked inside. It was like I didn't have to hold myself together anymore."

"Because you knew I would do it for you." I held her gaze, noticing that the storm in her eyes had calmed.

She nodded. "It was almost a relief to give up control. To share the pain."

I rubbed her back. "How do you feel now?"

Cleo was quiet for a moment, her eyes following the movement of her fingers as they traced the collar of my shirt. "Heartbroken that they're gone." Her eyes met mine. "And vengeful. I want to make the Program pay for taking everything from me."

"They didn't take everything," I reminded her. "You have Cassie and Arabella."

"Yeah."

"And me."

Her mouth finally curved up in a smile. "Yes, you."

"And Quinnie..." I suggested. "I saw you two getting all chummy down there. Best friends forever?"

Cleo's finger swept along the inside of my collar before she pulled the top of my t-shirt down and leaned in so she could kiss along my collarbone. "Let's go back to the part where I have you."

"No argument here." My skin warmed under her touch.

"There's no one to tell us what to do anymore. We don't have to hide or sneak around." Cleo hooked her leg over my waist, bringing our bodies as close as possible before she tipped her chin up, offering me her lips. They were opened slightly and when our mouths met, everything else blurred into non-existence. I could only feel the places where our bodies touched, only taste the sweetness of her kisses, only hear the pounding of my blood as it thundered through my veins and pushed my heart to race.

Cleo's scent of roasting creamsicle flared in a heady mixture and I closed my eyes and dipped my nose to the base of her throat where it was strongest. We were a tangle of emotions and limbs and tongues and heat—the chance to be with one another an unfamiliar freedom that was so strong I wasn't sure either of us would ever be able to stop.

Cleo's hands pressed along my chest, heat flaming against my muscles. She kissed me again, her breath searing me inside and out. Having her safe—kissing her again—it was so right I could almost ignore the pain of her fevered touch. When her hands gripped my bare arms, the brief touch of her fingers branded my skin and I flinched. Cleo tore her lips from mine and stared in horror at the red welts her fingers left on me. My shirt was scorched with her fingerprints and yet I still leaned in for more, trying to capture her mouth and kiss it again, reckless and needy.

"Again," she whispered, staring at her hands as if she didn't recognize them. "Why does this keep happening?"

I reached for her as she scrambled to get out of the bed to avoid touching me. "Cleo..."

"We should go." Cleo readjusted her clothing, looking everywhere but at my face. "They're expecting us."

Her gaze lingered on my arms where the red marks from her fingers still remained. The marks stung, like a sunburn, but I pretended not to notice. I grabbed a long sleeved shirt and slipped it on so she couldn't look at them anymore. She began to head for the door and I grabbed her elbow, turning her so she could look at me.

"Don't worry. We're going to fix this, okay? It's just a minor setback of your deviation. We all had them when we exhibited."

She nodded, but I could tell she didn't believe me. I knew she was wondering the same thing as me: Why was there always something standing between us? Hadn't we earned a free pass after everything we'd been through?

***

I'd been on a lot of missions in the last two years and I'd seen command centers in a ton of different countries, but none of them had ever looked like the one we were in now. Daniel and Gina's living room had been turned into our unofficial War Room, as Arabella insisted on calling it. The Deviant Dozen—instruments of death and destruction—sipping hot chocolate out of fancy tea cups while sitting on flowered sofas and plaid kitchen chairs. It was as if someone had taken a high security prison and dropped it into a retirement home. Lace doilies on the arms of the chairs, a tea set on the coffee table, and a basket of knitting on the floor next to a rocking chair. The Knights' living room was definitely not the place for twelve of the deadliest Sophisticates ever created.

It still didn't seem real that Gina, a quiet farmer's wife, was Arabella's mother. They couldn't be more different. Where Arabella was dark and antagonistic, Gina was light and nurturing. But the obvious difference between them didn't seem to bother Arabella in the least. She was seated on the couch next to her mother, stealing looks at her as if the sun rose and set in the older woman's hands.

"So," Daniel said, capturing our attention. "Now that everyone is rested and fed, we should probably talk about plans. For the immediate future at least."

"What are our options?" I leaned forward so that my elbows were resting on my knees. "I'd imagine it's too much to hope we all have families waiting for us to return home. Besides, I'm not sure splitting up is the best idea. We'd just be easy pickings for the Program."

Daniel was standing in front of the fireplace. He took off his glasses and cleaned them on his shirt, taking time to consider his answer. "First, let me make it abundantly clear, that you are all welcome to stay here as long as you like. However, that being said, if you choose to go, you put the rest of us at risk. Since the Program is looking for all of you, every decision from this moment forward must be made with the knowledge that the safety of every person in this room lies in the hands of everyone else. I won't make anyone stay, but I do insist that we make safety our top priority."

He put his glasses back on and turned to me. "And no, not everyone will have families waiting for them to return. There are some people, like Gina and me, who never agreed to have their children genetically altered. But sadly, there were some who did. And even those who are like us and would love to have you back, don't have that luxury. We faked our deaths. As far as the Program is concerned, we don't exist. The other donors are monitored closely. You wouldn't be able to get close to them without the Program knowing."

There was a brief moment when I wondered which category I fell into, but then I noticed how Cleo tensed beside me. I grabbed her hand, intertwining our fingers, and pulled it into my lap.

"Do you know all of our donors?" Sterling asked.

Daniel shook his head. "Not all of them. I met some and was able to keep in contact with a few of them through Geoffrey Lawless, but we don't speak one-on-one. It's just not safe."

"Professor Lawless?" I asked.

"Of course. He and Twyla Younglove worked together to watch over you. It was always their hope to be able to help you escape the Program's custody, once you knew how to protect yourselves. She was determined that you all should master your deviations because that would be the best way for you to survive."

I always knew that Professor Younglove cared about the Dozen in a way that the Program didn't. I just never realized that she was hoping to find a way out for us. "Why didn't she ever tell me?"

Daniel shrugged. "What good would it have done? It would have just made you reckless if you knew your freedom was at stake. She figured the best way to protect you was to make you strong. That way if the opportunity ever arose to set you free, you could protect yourselves."

All that time I told Cleo and the others not to use their deviations to keep them safe from the Program, and Younglove was encouraging the exact opposite course of action but for the very same reason.

"So what do you propose we do?" I asked. "It seems like our only option is to stay here so that everyone is safe." I looked around the room, expecting someone to disagree with me, but the Deviants all seemed to be in varying states of shock or exhaustion.

"It's not our only option," Cleo's voice was strong and sure.

Quinnie was the one who answered. "What's more important

than our safety?"

"Freedom," Cleo said, turning to her. "And vengeance."

The room was silent and Cleo looked at each face before continuing to speak.

"I've read my file. I know what the Program did to my parents. You each have files in the osmium box, too. Secrets and pasts that they didn't think you deserved to know about. For some of us, they took us from families who wanted us. But the one truth that holds for all of us is that they stole our freedom and our futures."

She stood up and clenched her fists as her sides. "We never agreed to be become their experiments. They made that decision for us. They altered us, turned us into monsters, and when they discovered how dangerous we were and that they couldn't control us, they decided to hunt us instead." She turned slowly, looking everyone in the eye before speaking again. "I say we hunt them. They want to destroy us?" Tiny wisps of smoke curled from Cleo's skin as her hair floated on warm gusts of wind that seemed to swirl around her. "I say we destroy them."

Rune

~ 12 ~

Daddy Issues

"Are you sure this is the right place?" Persephone asked as I turned off the road and onto the long, dark, dirt driveway.

"This is the address I was given." In the distance I could see lights on in the farm house. Everything else was dark. There were no street lights or other buildings to pollute the air with light. Nothing but shadowy outlines of trees all around us and a crisp, clear, cold November night overhead.

"And you're sure we can trust her?" Euri was sitting in the passenger seat next to me, his knee bouncing nervously as his eyes scanned our surroundings, just as blind as the rest of us.

If Argus and Lux were here, they'd be able to tell us for sure how safe our surroundings were. But they, and their supernatural visual abilities, were probably still buried under tons of glass in the Inner Harbor. The sharp pang of loss at that reminder tugged uncomfortably against my stomach. No matter how dysfunctional we were as a group, I still felt the loss of those who didn't survive. I couldn't imagine a time when I'd ever be okay with what happened to them. I wanted to blame Delia for it all, but there was always that nagging reminder that if I hadn't intervened and saved Cleo, she'd probably be the dead one and everyone else would still be alive. But that wasn't an outcome I could have accepted either.

"Can we trust anyone? Everyone else we know wants us dead," I reminded him.

Persephone grabbed the back of my seat and leaned forward so that I could see her in my peripheral vision. "And who says we'll have any better luck here? They want us dead too—not to mention this is exactly the sort of place you take someone if you don't want anyone to find their body." She sounded bored. "We literally drove past acres and acres of cornfields to get here. I can hear banjos playing in the distance."

There was no easy way to shut Persephone up so I ignored her. I pulled up in front of the farm house, my breath tight in my chest, hoping that I wasn't dooming us to the same fate as our brothers and sisters. We got out of the car and before we walked up to the porch, I turned to give one last warning. "Remember what I said. No matter what happens, no one uses their deviation unless I say so. Our only chance is to be as unthreatening as possible." I turned my gaze to Persephone and pointed to her. "Not so much as a spark."

She rolled her eyes. "Get over yourself. You're not in charge, Rune."

"And yet you followed me here."

"Exactly. I followed." She crossed her arms. "And I can choose to leave any time I want."

"Don't ruin this—" My warning was cut off when the front door to the house opened inward and I turned to see a man silhouetted in the doorway just beyond the screen door.

"Show time," Persephone sang, pushing me forward.

For someone who made it clear on a regular basis that I wasn't in charge, she sure was eager to let me lead. I turned to flash her another warning glare and as we walked toward the porch, the front light flicked on.

"Stop right there," the man ordered, reaching for something to the side. When he pulled the object in front of him, I could see it was a rifle. I came to a halt at the bottom of the stairs. The porch light was more like a spotlight, and with it shining in my face, I couldn't see the man or anything beyond him.

"Hell of a welcoming committee," Persephone hissed. I could almost hear her smiling, relishing a fight.

Damn. This was not what I was hoping for. I thought they'd be expecting us, but I never actually considered it might be a trap...that we were brought here to be eliminated. Maybe I put too much faith in people. Or maybe hope made me blind.

"I'm Rune," I called out to the man.

"I know who you are. What I don't know is why you're here." He leaned against the edge of the doorway, but kept the gun where I could see it.

Didn't she tell him? When I contacted her about what happened at the Academy, she told me to come here, that we'd find refuge.

"The Program is hunting us. They want us dead."

The man huffed. "I know that. You still didn't answer my question. Why are you here?"

"Is it my turn to speak yet?" Persephone whispered, stepping up beside me.

I stretched my arm out, pushing her back behind me. "We had nowhere else to go," I told the man in the doorway.

He clicked the safety off the gun and I could feel Euri tensing beside me. Without a weapon, his deviation of perfect aim was useless. He was the only one in our group who was defenseless. Unless you counted the gravel under his feet.

"How did you find out about us?" the man asked. "Who told you?"

I took a deep breath. "Quinnie." The word barely left my mouth before I heard the sound of five quick gun shots. Confused, I noticed that the man hadn't lifted his gun to shoot, but a sudden sharp pain brought my hand to my neck. I grasped the object protruding from my skin and pulled. My vision started to blur as I looked at the dart in my hand.

The last thought I had before I slumped to the ground, unconscious was: Why five shots?

***

My arms and legs felt like they were weighted down and I struggled to move my fingers. I attempted to lift my arm and realized it was strapped down to something. My eyelids were heavy and although I tried to open them, I couldn't find the strength to make it happen.

"He's coming to." I didn't recognize the voice of the woman speaking, but she sounded older.

"You administered the counteragents, right?" It sounded like the man with the gun. For a moment, I was relieved to hear the word counteragents. That meant Persephone, Elysia, and Euri were still alive. There would be no need to give them counteragents if they were dead.

"Yeah. But there is no counteragent for him." That was Ozzy.

Well, at least I was in the right place. And luckily, still alive. Although for how long, I didn't know.

"I don't think he's here to hurt anyone. He saved my life," Cleo said.

Thank God she was here, too. She was the only person, aside from Quinnie, who I trusted. And if I was being completely honest with myself, I trusted her even more than Quinnie. But when I was looking for help, Quinnie was the only person I could turn to. Contacting her had been a desperate, last ditch effort to find allies.

"He might not be here to hurt anyone, but he brought them." Ozzy's voice was disgusted.

I couldn't really blame him. After what Delia and the Others had done at the Academy, he had every right to be disgusted with us. He had every right to hate us. I might have saved his girlfriend's life, but I didn't save all those Hounds that Delia executed. I should have done something to spare their lives, but I didn't. I let Delia follow through with her plan because...I don't know why I did. I wish I could say that I didn't know any better, but that wasn't true. Even then I knew it was wrong. I just didn't know how to choose differently. How to turn my back on all that I'd known my entire life.

The decision to stand by and let the massacre happen still ate away at me. What if we'd just refused to follow Delia's orders and turned ourselves in to the Academy? The Deviant Dozen wouldn't be on the run and neither would we. No one would have died. Except perhaps Delia. And that was a sacrifice I could have easily lived with. We would have been prisoners of the Program, but maybe that was a better choice than being hunted by it.

I wished I could turn back time and choose differently.

After a few more seconds, I was able to lift my chin and open my eyes. I blinked slowly, the blurred shapes finally coming into focus. A look around revealed that I was tied to a chair which was positioned in the middle of a barn. Horse stalls were to either side of me, the area was brightly lit from above, and the place smelled of clean hay, even though the stalls were all empty. The space looked brand new and modern, not at all what I would expect from a barn, except for all the hay of course. Close by were four more chairs with people tied to them—Persephone, Elysia, Euri...and Quinnie?

I turned my head sluggishly to scan the area and saw that the rest of the Deviants were gathered around, leaning against walls or poles. They looked relaxed, but I knew that was just for appearances. They didn't trust me, even if I was tied up. Ozzy stood closest, his gaze trained on me, his finger on the trigger of his gun. There was no counteragent for me. I was dangerous. We both knew it.

Quinnie was also awake and I was surprised to find that she wasn't screaming or yelling at the Dozen to let her go. Her arms were tied behind her back and her ankles were attached to the legs of the chair, but she was sitting proudly, with an ambivalent look on her face as if she was exactly where she wanted to be.

"Why did you tie her up?" I asked, nodding my head toward Quinnie.

"Because you told us she's the reason you're here." Ozzy kept his gaze trained on me.

"He's not going to hurt us, you idiot," Quinnie snapped. "That's not why I told him to come."

"No, you just thought you'd put us all at risk because you have a crush on him." Wesley pushed off the wall he'd been leaning against and crossed his arms as he glared at Quinnie.

She rolled her eyes. "So quick to throw blame. You're all trigger happy if you ask me." She shook her head as she looked at Ozzy. "I can't believe you shot me."

"You'd know all about being trigger happy," Arabella snapped. "Shooting first and asking questions later? That's pretty much your MO."

"Do you really think this is the time to argue?" Quinnie asked. "The Program is trying to kill us. They're hunting us—the Dozen *and* the Others. Inside, we were just saying how we don't have a chance if we split up, that we need to stay together to remain strong. Rune and the Others can be powerful allies to us."

"Just because we're all being hunted, that doesn't make us allies." Ozzy spoke to Quinnie, but didn't look away from me. "It doesn't change the fact that they're our enemies. They attacked the Academy. People we knew died, and he helped." Ozzy lifted the gun a little higher even though he didn't point it directly at me. His hand shook and I wondered how much control it took for him not to exact revenge on me for all the friends he lost.

"Rune didn't help with the attack," Quinnie reasoned. "He was our prisoner, remember? We never gave him a counteragent and he could have hurt any of us at any time. He never did."

My gaze cut over to Cleo and I cringed inwardly remembering how I'd attacked her in the training room. She didn't rush to disagree with Quinnie, but she wasn't exactly defending me either. I hoped that she was listening and would be the voice of reason in my defense, but she had her gaze fixed on Persephone, who was still unconscious. I wondered if Cleo was considering making Persephone's sleep a more permanent condition. After everything that

Persephone had done to her, it wouldn't be completely unexpected. But no matter how much Persephone might deserve it, I still wouldn't let anyone hurt her.

"That doesn't mean he's innocent," Wesley argued, bringing my attention back to the conversation. "And it certainly doesn't mean we can trust him, or any of them."

"Wesley's right." Cleo looked away from Persephone and turned her attention to me. "I want to trust you, Rune, but you brought them with you. You brought Persephone. Here. And you thought we'd be okay with that? That I'd be okay with that?"

"What was I supposed to do?" I asked her, my voice even. "Leave them behind?"

"Why not? She's evil."

"Would you have left Cassie behind? Or Arabella?" I raised my eyebrows in question, knowing the answer without her having to voice it.

Her laugh was bitter. "That's not even the same comparison. That thing is a monster," Cleo said, pointing to Persephone. "She's my enemy and I hate her."

I locked my gaze on Cleo's, willing her to remember our confrontation in the training room at the Academy when we'd lost our tempers and attacked one another. "We're all monsters, Cleo. Besides, Quinnie was once your enemy, too. Would you abandon her?" I asked.

Cleo spared a quick glance at Quinnie. "It's not the same. Quinnie's mean, she's not evil."

"Since when?" Arabella asked.

Quinnie glared at Arabella. "Shut up, loser."

"You're not helping your case, hag witch."

The room broke out into arguments as everyone fought to be heard. I could almost feel the storm of emotions and deviations swirling dangerously among us. A sharp whistle cut through the noise and everyone fell quiet, their attention drawn to the older woman who stood off to the side. She looked like a quiet little homemaker. A farmer's wife. How did she get a bunch of angry, frightened teens to quiet down with nothing more than a whistle?

"We're not going to turn our backs on them," the woman said. "First of all, they know about this place so we can't possibly send them away and risk them being captured by the Program. And we're not going to automatically keep them prisoner either." A few of the Deviants started to argue and she held up her hand until silence settled through the barn. "They're just as much victims as the rest of you, maybe even more so. They'll stay and they'll help us. Right?" Her hands were clasped in front of her and she looked directly at me, her expression that of a disapproving parent.

"Yes ma'am," I agreed. I didn't care what they needed us to do. If the Deviants were going against the Program, I'd stand with them. That was our best chance for survival.

"And do you think they'll agree?" the man with the rifle asked, nodding toward my still unconscious partners.

"Even if they don't, what choice do we have?"

The woman stepped forward, her expression softening. "You always have a choice, honey." She reached out and put her hand on my shoulder. "If you choose to help, you're choosing your chance at freedom. If you choose not to, well then that's your choice. But it comes with consequences. You searched us out and we can't let you endanger the lives of all the people here." She patted my shoulder in a comforting way, but her words were full of warning. She didn't have to threaten me, I knew what the consequences would be if we chose to go against the Deviants. If we risked their safety, we'd forfeit our own.

"I understand."

The woman looked down at me and smiled sadly. "Unfortunately, I'm sure you do. I'm sorry it has to be this way, that your life was forced on this path. It's not fair to you, or anyone else," she said, gesturing around the room. "But we're determined to set things right."

"That's all I want," I assured her.

Ozzy sighed. "Okay. Let's untie them."

"Took you long enough," Quinnie complained, rolling her eyes.

"Wait." Wesley walked to the middle of the room and stood facing Quinnie. "Before we untie her, I think she needs to come clean. She's been keeping a secret."

Although she tried to remain calm and unaffected, Quinnie's eyes narrowed and I could see the worry in them. "What are you talking about, moron?"

"I think it's only fair for everyone to know who your father is since he's the one who gave the order for us to be terminated. For all we know, you're leading him here just like you did the Others."

Quinnie's gaze flicked toward Cleo, accusatory and angry. "I thought I could trust you. So much for redemption, right?" she snapped.

Wesley laughed, but it wasn't an amused sound. "She didn't tell me." He turned to Cleo and gave her a disgusted look. "She's just as guilty as you, though. I overheard you two talking about it in the van while the rest of the Deviants were risking their lives to save Sterling."

"Wait," Sterling interrupted. "I missed something. Who is Quinnie's father?"

"Russell Baker," Wesley answered triumphantly.

There were gasps all around the room. I was surprised that this information was new to everyone. I just assumed they already knew who Quinnie's generous sponsor was. I figured that's why everyone was so scared of her at the Academy. Who wouldn't be afraid of the pride and joy of the leader of the Sophisticates? But by everyone's surprised reactions, it was suddenly clear that not only did no one know she was the daughter of Russell Baker, but that Quinnie didn't want anyone to know.

Delia had made no secret about the people who were the donors of the Deviant Dozen. She didn't know who my donors were, but she knew the rest. I could still remember the many times Delia tormented Persephone with the fact that her donors had tried to liberate Cleo from the Program so they could be a family again, and how they'd never given Persephone a second thought. Persephone loathed Cleo from the moment she knew about her. I knew that's why Persephone took it upon herself to torment Cleo at the Academy when she was supposed to be searching for the counteragents and top secret Deviant Dozen information that Delia wanted. Hatred was a powerful motivator. As was envy. Maybe that's why Delia's cruelty never fully took root in my heart. I didn't know who my parents were and I didn't have a twin in the Deviant Dozen to outshine me. I never felt the jealousy that Persephone had.

"Is this true?" Ozzy asked Quinnie, walking forward. "Russell Baker is your father?"

Quinnie stared back at him, her eyebrows raised in challenge.

She didn't answer him.

"And you've known this whole time? All these years and you never shared that secret." Ozzy turned around and glared at Cleo. "And you knew about this, too? Why didn't you tell me?"

Cleo flung her hands out to the side and shook her head. "It wasn't my secret to tell. She wanted to tell you herself."

"When are you going to learn that some secrets are too dangerous to keep? How am I supposed to ever trust you, Cleo? And you," he said, turning back to Quinnie. "Have you already given away our location to Baker?"

Quinnie's expression was nothing short of devastation. "You're kidding me, right Ozzy? Don't you trust me? We grew up together." She almost looked like she was going to cry. And that just seemed ludicrous.

He crossed his arms, backing away from her as if she was dangerous even though she was still tied up. "You never trusted me enough to tell me who your father was. Being the daughter of Russell Baker is a big fucking deal. Why should I trust you?"

Quinnie swallowed and seemed to regain some of her strength. "Well if our parents make us who we are, then maybe no one should trust you either, Ozzy. My father might have come up with the idea for the Deviant Dozen, but it was your sadistic father who actually created us." She yanked on her arms like she wanted to lash out at him, but the roped held tight.

Ozzy stalked forward getting right in her face. "What are you talking about?"

Her mouth stretched into a grimace. "Didn't you ever wonder why we were put in the same universities? Didn't you ever wonder why you were taken to the Academy so young?"

"I exhibited first," Ozzy countered.

"You exhibited first because he took away your counteragent early. He was impatient and couldn't wait to see his mutated DNA in all its horrific glory," she snapped.

Ozzy flinched. "Who?"

"Weren't you ever curious why Dr. Steel was so interested in you?" Quinnie yelled at him.

"Dr. Steel?" Ozzy stumbled back like she'd punched him in the face.

"Welcome to the world of daddy issues," Quinnie called out loudly. Her head was thrown back like she was announcing it to the world. When her words finally stopped echoing off the wooden walls of the nearby stalls, she lowered her gaze to fix it on Ozzy. "My daddy is the evil mastermind and yours is the mad scientist." Her voice was low and each word was laced with bitterness. "Isn't that right, Osbourne Steel?"

Ozzy threw a furious glance around the room, daring us to say something. When Cleo stepped forward to comfort him, he shrugged off her arm. His wild gaze traveled across each face again, noting all of the astonished looks his friends were giving him. The only people who didn't seem surprised were the farmer and his wife. I was surprised that Ozzy hadn't figured the truth out years ago. I'd always known. And it was becoming clear to me that I might know more about the Deviant Dozen than they knew about themselves.

Ozzy turned and stormed out of the barn. The stunned silence he left in his wake was oppressive.

"I knew Dr. Steel looked familiar when I saw him at Headquarters," Arabella finally said.

Suddenly, the Others and I weren't the worst problems on the farm.

CLEO

FORGE ME

I followed Ozzy out of the barn, but immediately lost him in the dark. I understood his need to be alone and process the fact that Dr. Steel was his father. I felt the same way after I opened up the folder about my parents. I only hoped that after he had time to deal with everything, I'd be the one he would search out first. Although, if his comments about not trusting me were any indication, that likely wouldn't happen.

How did I manage to so royally screw things up when all I was trying to do was the right thing?

And what was Wesley's problem anyway? If he was so concerned about Quinnie's secret, why didn't he confront us about it earlier? Why did he throw out doubt and accusations at the worst possible time? Letting Rune or the Others see we weren't a united front was dangerous. What Wesley needed was a good kick to the kneecaps, and I was just the girl for the job.

I stood out in the chilly dark for a few more moments, my arms wrapped around my chest, my irritation burning hot enough to keep me warm. I waited for Ozzy to return, but when it became clear he wanted to be lost for a while, I turned back into the barn. Persephone, Euri, and Elysia were all awake, but still seated in the chairs. The Deviants surrounded them, alert and ready. When I joined the group, I noticed Quinnie had been untied as well. She was standing on the other side of the room from me, but we both were getting our fair share of wary looks.

"...so, we'll be helping the Deviants." Rune's gaze travelled over the Others, deliberately pausing on each face. His comment was an order, not a request.

"We didn't come here to fight against the Program, we came here for help." Elysia glanced furtively around the circle. "I thought we were surrendering." She looked a lot different now than she had during our confrontation at The Rink. Back then she was confident, aggressive, and dangerous. Now she just looked frightened. For the most part, she looked just like Quinnie, but fear had turned familiar features into a completely different face. Odd how personality and expressions could do that. I wondered, now that everyone knew about Persephone, if they could see a difference between us as well.

"No, we came here for allies." Rune tilted his head toward Elysia as if daring her to argue. "They're going against the Program and we're helping."

Elysia's eyes darted around the room. "Are you all crazy? Do you know how badly we're outnumbered?" She shook her head and took a deep breath.

"We've always been outnumbered, Elysia. It never bothered you before." Persephone rolled her eyes and when she noticed me, a smirk found its way to her face.

"That's because the Program didn't know about us before." She leaned forward and dropped her head into her hands, mumbling. "We'll never survive."

Those words were all I needed to hear to know the true difference between Quinnie and her twin. Elysia was a coward—nasty and vicious when she had the upper hand, but spineless when she was no longer in control. As much as I hated to admit it, Quinnie was a fighter, one who embraced the monster within. She'd never surrender. She'd fight until the bitter end.

"What choice do we have?" Arabella stepped forward and crossed her arms, glaring down at Elysia. "It's either hunt or be hunted. I don't intend to sit around and wait for them to find me. I want to have the chance to live my life. On my terms for once."

Elysia looked up. "I don't see how we can possibly succeed."

"Easy." I stepped out of the darkness and into the circle of my friends. I could feel the eyes of everyone in the room on me, but I stared straight at Elysia. "We turn their army against them. And then we show them just how successful their human weapons are."

***

"You know, ever since you came back from your punishment in the cells, you've been kind of scary. And coming from me, that's saying something." Arabella sat on the couch with me in the War Room, otherwise known as the living room. Gina and Daniel brought Rune and the Others up to the main house to get them something to eat, and most of the Deviants were hanging out in the kitchen like security guards. Ozzy still hadn't come back and I was in no mood to be around Persephone, so I made a quick escape. Arabella followed. Knowing how much she wanted to spend time with her mom and dad, I was grateful for the sacrifice she made to keep me company.

"I know. I feel like they destroyed a part of me down in that cell. Like a piece of my humanity is gone and I'll never get it back. Especially with what we have to do now." I brought my knees up to my chest and wrapped my arms around my legs.

"If you don't want to fight, then why are you urging us to go to war against the Program?" Arabella picked up one of the doilies off the arm of the sofa and inspected it.

I shrugged, set my chin on my knees, and stared forward. "There will be a fight either way. We can't hide forever and they'll never stop looking. I just happen to think it's better if we take the fight to them. On our terms."

Arabella pressed her mouth into a tight line and raised her eyebrows in challenge. "I agree. I just don't want you to end up hating yourself."

"I don't—"

"I was there in the hotel room when you found out about the Others who died after the explosion." She took a deep breath. "I know how much you beat yourself up over what happened to them. And that was an accident. I just want you to understand what it will mean if we go up against the Program. People are going to get hurt. Maybe even die. Innocent bystanders could get caught in the crossfire." She looked away and picked at a string on the hem of her jeans.

We both sat in silence, lost in thought.

"I know," I finally admitted. "But what choice do we have?"

"Exactly." Arabella leaned forward to pull a candy dish off the coffee table and held it between us.

I reached in and took a handful of chocolate, tossing it in my mouth so I wouldn't have to talk. The room was filled with the crunch of the candies between our teeth and all of the oppressive thoughts neither of us wanted to voice.

Once our fingers started to scrape the bottom of the dish, Arabella asked, "Do you think we can trust them?" She nodded toward the kitchen.

I shrugged. "It's hard to tell who we can trust anymore. Do you trust me? Or is that why you're sitting out here? To keep an eye on me?"

She punched me in the arm. Hard.

"Ouch. What was that for?" I rubbed my arm trying to get the darts of pain to disappear. There would definitely be a bruise by morning. Damn Arabella and her ridiculous strength.

"We're way past our trust issues, babe. I won't ever doubt you again, so don't you dare listen to Wesley or Ozzy. Wesley is being an idiot and Ozzy is just over-protective."

My laugh was bitter. "I don't see how his anger at me keeping secrets is over-protective in any way."

"He thinks he's responsible for all of us so he's protective of everyone, but especially of you. He still doesn't think you can take care of yourself, that's why he wants to know everything, so he can determine if it's safe for you." She shook her head. "If only he could see that out of all of us, you're the one person we don't need to worry about. You're honest and trustworthy and brave."

The laugh that escaped me was full of disbelief. "I'm not honest. I didn't tell anyone when I found out that Rune could control his deviation. If I had, we could have avoided what happened at the Academy. We might not be running from the Program right now."

"Yes, but we also would still be at the Program's mercy." She leaned forward and put the dish back on the coffee table. "At least now we're free."

"But a lot of people had to die for that to happen." I rubbed my forearms as if I could rub away the blame I constantly felt. "And I didn't tell anyone about who Quinnie's father was."

"Just because you don't reveal someone else's secrets, that doesn't make you dishonest. You never lied and it would be ridiculous to pretend that none of us have secrets. We all do. Besides, I know why you kept Rune's and Quinnie's confidence. One was self-preservation, the other was kindness. Although to be honest, I'm confused as to why you'd be kind to Quinnie since she's never done anything to deserve it."

"True. But maybe that's why she needs it," I said, voicing my earlier thoughts.

Arabella laughed. "I don't know about that. My point is, you didn't lose any of your humanity in that cell. It only made you stronger and more determined. You used to be insecure, but you're not anymore. You know who you are and you accept it."

"But you said I was scary."

"Yeah. Scary because you're willing to take risks. You're unpredictable. And that makes me afraid for you because I don't think you're all that concerned about your own safety anymore."

I turned to look at Arabella to see that she was staring toward the kitchen. "You're one to talk about taking risks." I nudged her elbow with mine. "Where do you think I learned it?"

She sighed, forcing a smile to her lips. "I just think I found a reason not to take unnecessary risks anymore, though."

Arabella didn't have to explain, I knew exactly the two reasons she was so reluctant to take risks. At least with Sterling, she felt like he was an equal, like he could take care of himself. I think we were all a little worried about Gina and Daniel now. How our involvement with them could put them in danger. How the Others being on their ranch put them at additional risk.

"Do you think we can trust them?" Arabella asked again. "The Others, I mean."

I let out a long breath as I considered her question. Finally, I said, "I think the only thing we can trust at this point is that all of us have a common enemy. The Others are depending on us as much as we're depending on them. We can trust them until we take down the Program. After that, who knows?"

We sat in silence. I was lost in thoughts about how things had changed so much, and yet not really at all. We were technically free from the Program, but we didn't have true freedom. And trust, which had always been a rarity, was being tested in new ways. We had to trust untrustworthy people if we wanted to survive.

I was torn from my thoughts as the alarm blared through the house. Again.

"Shit," Arabella yelled from next to me as she jumped up off the couch and hurried across the room to the security monitor. "What is this? Grand Central Station?"

Daniel and Gina rushed from the kitchen, followed by...everyone. Except Ozzy, who still hadn't returned. We'd just gone through this routine a few hours ago when Rune and the Others unexpectedly showed up.

"Calm down," Daniel said, pushing his way toward the monitor. "I'm actually expecting someone this time." His eyes examined the vehicle that was making its way up the farm drive. Everything about Daniel and Gina's ranch surprised me. It looked like a sweet little farm house in the boondocks, but in reality, it had a military-grade security system that included heat-sensing cameras. I don't even think the Academy had security cameras that fancy. By the security footage on the monitor, I could see there were heat impressions of two people inside the car. Daniel grabbed his rifle as he made his way to the front door. While he waited, he turned to look at us. "Ozzy still isn't back?"

"There he is." Theo pointed to the screen where we could see the heat impression of someone shadowing the car.

Jesus. How far out on the property had Ozzy gone to get away from us? From me?

Daniel didn't seem concerned by the approaching car. He threw open the front door and strode out onto the porch. Turning off the lights in the room, we gathered near the windows, peering out into the darkness to see who Daniel was expecting. I'm sure I wasn't the only one surprised when the car stopped in front of the house and Geoffrey Lawless and Zelda Cain stepped out of the vehicle. What were my old History of Wormwood professor and the Academy librarian doing here? And why was Daniel expecting them?

"I see you made it safely." Daniel casually set the butt of his rifle on the ground, greeting our new visitors as if they were long-lost friends and not Program employees. Clearly, Daniel didn't consider Lawless and Zelda to be a threat. He said he had kept in touch with them and Professor Lawless had given us the osmium box, but they were still employees of the Program. And seeing them in our safe zone had me on edge.

"Did everyone make it out safely?" Lawless approached the porch, his hands tucked into the pockets of his khaki pants as if he were talking to a golf buddy and not the man who was harboring fugitives of the Program.

Daniel laughed. "I guess that depends. Exactly how many runaways did you send my way?"

"What do you mean?" Lawless was looking toward the house, but he couldn't see much with the porch light shining right in his face.

With a wave of his hand, Daniel motioned for us to come outside. Reluctantly we followed orders. I suppose if I had to choose which professors to face while on the run, Geoffrey Lawless and Zelda Cain would be at the top of that list. Right after Twyla Younglove.

When Lawless saw the Others with us, his eyebrows arched. "How did they find their way here?" He motioned toward Rune and his friends.

Daniel chuckled. "Long story. Come inside and we can swap news."

"Fair enough. Want me to pull the car around back?" Lawless asked.

"Better to be safe," Daniel replied. "It's not an Academy vehicle, is it?"

Lawless laughed. "You know me better than that, old friend." He got back into the car and drove it around back while Zelda Cain came up the steps. She hugged Daniel and Gina briefly before finding me and giving me an unexpected squeeze as well.

"I'm so glad to see you all safe. We've been so worried about you," she said to me. Her concern surprised me. She patted my arm and gave me a smile before she followed Gina into the house.

I watched as everyone made their way back through the front door. Knowing Persephone was among the group inside, I couldn't bear to go in and join everyone. I wasn't sure how we were going to be able to work together when all I wanted to do was destroy her. I wished she'd never come. I wished she'd been lost in the battle at the Inner Harbor.

My body shuddered as I acknowledged that dark thought...and the fact that I didn't feel guilty to have it.

Did I really feel that way?

Persephone caused my friends to mistrust me. She caused me to endure whippings for things I didn't do. She had been intimate with Ozzy.

Yes. I really did feel that way.

"Cleo." My name was accompanied by the sound of footsteps shuffling through leaves and gravel. I turned back toward the driveway as Ozzy slowly materialized out of the darkness. He stopped just within the circle of light from the porch, his gaze holding me in place. I wanted to run down the steps and into his arms, to reassure myself that everything was okay between us, but I couldn't bring myself to risk the rejection if he pushed me away again. I wished I could see the expression in his eyes so I wouldn't feel so confused.

"Do you think you'll you ever trust me again?" I finally asked.

He stared at me for a long moment. "The question is, will you ever trust me?"

I hated that he sounded so unsure. "I do trust you."

Ozzy shoved his hands into his pockets. "Then why is it so hard for you to tell me things?" He took a few steps forward, which I took as a good sign.

I took a deep breath and then released it, shrugging. "To be honest, we spend most of our time fighting for our lives. There are a lot of things I haven't had time to tell you."

Ozzy nodded his head as he looked at the ground and sighed. He finally looked up at me and gave me a sad smile. "I guess I got so used to knowing almost every little detail about you, I don't know how to handle waiting for you to tell me things now. I know it's not fair to expect you to tell me everything, but I want you to."

"I want to tell you everything." I descended the small flight of wooden stairs and stood on the quaint little pathway of stones that led to the driveway.

"More secrets?" he asked.

"More everything."

"More truths and lies?" he asked, looking off into the darkness as if he could see the events of the night he was referring to. His tone was almost playful, like it had been all those times when he'd snuck into my room at the Academy. I remembered the night we played two truths, one lie and how he tempted me with teasing, almost-kisses.

I shook my head. "No lies. Only truths. You have no idea how much you mean to me, Ozzy. I don't want to lie, and I don't want to keep anything from you," I admitted.

Ozzy's breath released in a relieved exhale and when he looked at me again, his gaze had softened. "I like knowing things so that I can keep you safe. I want to protect you. "

I took a tentative step forward. "But that's just it. You don't have to protect me. I don't want to be behind you waiting for you to fight my battles for me. I want to fight beside you. Just because I don't tell you every little thing that goes through my head, that doesn't mean I don't trust you or that you can't trust me. We've been through too much together to mistrust one another now. Please

Forge Me

don't doubt me, because I sure as hell don't doubt you."

"Are you sure?" He clenched his jaw. "You don't care about who my father is?"

I reached out and grabbed his arm. "That man is not your father," I insisted. "You share his DNA, but that's it. You are nothing like him."

"But I'm everything he thought I'd be." Ozzy looked away from me, but I could see the shame he felt. "I'm a killer. A damn good one. Just like he wanted. It was one thing when he controlled my actions, but knowing that he's my father, I feel like something on the inside has been tainted by him, too."

I reached up and grabbed his chin, turning him to face me. "You're more than he could have ever hoped you'd be, Ozzy. You're amazing. You're smart. Courageous. Generous. You're dependable. You cared about the Dozen when no one else seemed to. You cared about me when I couldn't even care about myself. There are a lot of things I'm not sure about, but you're something I have complete faith in. Don't let Dr. Steel define who you are. You're still the same person you were before you knew he was your donor. Don't let that information change anything for you, because it certainly doesn't change anything for me."

Ozzy lifted his eyes to lock his gaze with mine. I pressed my lips against his and he kissed me back gently. Even when he was confused and hurting, his kisses still tasted like sweet danger and addiction. When he pulled me into his embrace, I rested my head on his chest, grateful that he wasn't angry with me.

"Sorry I took off," he said. His voice was quiet, but the words vibrated through his chest.

"I understand. Sometimes you just need to be alone to think. I

125

felt the same way after I read my file."

He wrapped his arms more tightly around me. "We're going to make this right," Ozzy whispered into my hair. "I'm tired of running. I'm tired of having no control over my own life. I don't want to be who they made me to be."

I held on tightly until I could feel my heartbeat falling in tempo with his.

I agreed with him. Mostly. I was tired of being on the run and not having freedom, but right now, I wasn't scared to be who the Program made me to be. I used to hate my deviation and that it made me dangerous and unpredictable. After seeing how much heartbreak the Program had put us all through, I was glad that I had a way to fight back.

The Program was going to regret creating me. Mutating my genetics was unforgivable, but it was everything after my birth that made me truly dangerous. Every sin the Program committed against me, every time they beat me down, it only served to forge me into something more powerful. My pain made me stronger.

They wanted a weapon?

I was one.

OZZY

~ 14 ~

THE FIRE

The grass crunched beneath our sneakers, the delicate covering of frost splintering into tiny icy shards under our heavy footsteps. The sun cut across the ground in a harsh line, lighting up the frozen grass like glassy needles. Our breath curled around our heads in cloudy puffs as we followed the tractor Daniel was driving to the far end of his pasture. The hum of the motor broke through the quiet morning, startling birds out of nearby trees. The small trailer that Daniel pulled behind him was filled with boards and other fencing supplies.

He never actually asked us to help him, it just sort of happened. The first morning after Lawless and Zelda showed up at the ranch, he finished his breakfast, put on his jacket, and walked out the back door without a word. When I asked where he was going, Gina replied that he was doing his chores. So I got up and followed him, and so did most everyone else. When we asked if he needed any help, he gave us a list of things he wanted to get done and we split up the work.

I was surprised that after two weeks with the Others, everything had been rather peaceful. Our days were filled with mindless work and little reason for confrontation. The few horses Daniel had were being spoiled rotten. We tore down perfectly good fencing and replaced it with new boards, and we had enough firewood to last the ranch for several winters. More than once it crossed my mind that perhaps Daniel was making up these chores in order to keep the peace between us...idle minds being the devil's playground and all. But whatever his purpose, it was working.

I looked over my shoulder and watched as Persephone made her way from the house to the barn. She was followed by Wesley. Despite Rune's harassment, she refused to help out on the ranch, and Wesley refused to let her out of his sight. He'd taken it upon himself to be her personal shadow during the day. During the night, the duty of keeping an eye on the Others was split up between the rest of the Dozen in two person shifts. Last night was one of my shifts. We were in a routine of sorts, but it was impossible for anyone to sleep well with the Others in our midst. They weren't causing trouble, but that didn't mean they wouldn't.

Daniel stopped the tractor next to the fence and we started unloading the supplies, setting the new boards aside so we could put the old fencing in the trailer and repurpose it for fire wood. He lifted a bucket of nails and turned to hand it to me.

I reached out for the bucket and cleared my throat before speaking. "So, when are we going to talk about what we plan to do about the Program?"

His eyebrows arched in surprise and when he smiled, it was resigned. "That's up to you."

"Me?"

He let go of the bucket and the weight of the nails settling in my hands was heavier than I expected. Daniel leaned over the edge of the trailer and reached for a crate of tools, pulling it forward with a grunt of effort. "I told you that I wouldn't force any of you to do anything and I meant it. If you want to fight back, we'll help you. If you want to stay here, you know you're welcome." He turned to face me, the bucket cradled in his arms. "The Program has already taken too many of your choices away. This is one choice I wouldn't dare make for you."

"But I thought that's why Lawless and Zelda were here, to help us come up with a plan."

"They're here because they're running from the Program just as you are. If you choose to fight against the Program, they'll help just as Gina and I will. But none of us would force you to do anything. These are your lives, your futures, and your decisions. I've already done what I can to reclaim the life the Program stole from me." He glanced at Arabella who was on the other side of the trailer helping to unload it. "I would never assume to know what is right for you or any of the other Sophisticates. That's a decision you have to make for yourselves."

Marty came up to Daniel and took the crate from him. "Thanks, son," Daniel said, nodding to him in gratitude. When Marty walked away, Daniel took a few steps toward me and his large hand patted my shoulder twice before he squeezed it reassuringly. "No matter what you decide, I won't judge you. Take your time. Don't rush into anything, okay?" He patted my shoulder again and then headed for Arabella and Sterling. I could hear him directing where they could start dismantling the old fence and I stood there, bucket in hand, watching Daniel's easy confidence and the way that everyone trusted him so completely. And why shouldn't they? He was the first adult in our lives to show us how to live and not just tell us how to do it.

I only wished rebuilding our futures could be as simple as replacing a few old, worn boards.

***

I pulled Cleo close, tucking her under my arm, trying to ignore the way the cold air bit at my exposed skin. Alone time with Cleo was a rare commodity these days. With so many people around, any private spot didn't stay that way long, so we had to be creative. Taking a walk in the middle a frigid night wasn't one of my best ideas.

"Maybe we could go back to your room?" Cleo asked.

She didn't seem affected by the cold at all. The side of my body where she was touching me was warmer than the rest of me, but a shiver still seized my muscles. The weather never seemed to affect Cleo anymore, almost like her body was always on edge and ready to explode. Intimacy between us had become as risky as navigating a minefield. Even a kiss could send her over the edge if we let it go too far. But I didn't want to think about that or what it might mean for us. It didn't matter if we could never do more than kiss because I was hers, completely. I was hers before she even knew I existed.

I spun her around and opened my jacket, pulling her against my chest and wrapping my arms around her. She didn't need my warmth, but for once, I needed hers. "I don't have a room, remember?" I bent my head down and ran my lips along her hair. Without her perfume, she no longer smelled like a roasting creamsicle. These days it was more like toasted coconut. New shampoo, new scent. The only constant was the underlying scent of a just-struck match. "Unless you want an audience." I pulled back to look at her. "You into that, Flame Fatale?"

Cleo groaned and her head fell to my chest. "How could I forget? Everything about this place is pretty perfect. Except for the fact that we have roomies. I had to share with Eva last night after my guard duty shift. Did you know she talks in her sleep? And it's really creepy because she talks in different voices. At one point, I woke up terrified thinking Delia was in the room with me!"

"It could be worse," I reminded her. "I had to sleep in the bed Dexter usually sleeps in. There were holes in the mattress from where he drooled on it."

Cleo laughed and I loved the way her happiness vibrated through her chest to mine. "At least we're not on the run anymore. I guess we should be happy we have some place comfortable to sleep, right?"

"Right." There were only six bedrooms on the second floor of the barn. Arabella and Sterling were staying in the main house, the Others had been split up between two rooms, and the ten remaining Deviants rotated through the remaining four rooms depending on who was keeping watch and when. To make it easy, we had two rooms for girls and two for the guys. Privacy was definitely hard to come by.

"Well," Cleo said, pressing a soft kiss to my mouth, letting her lips linger as she spoke. "If we hurry, maybe we can find an empty one and lock the door behind us and claim it for our own."

Cleo's hands slid under my shirt, her fingers drawing circles on my chilled skin. For once, the heat of her hands was tolerable. Her mouth pressed against mine, her tongue slipping along the seam of my lips. She pulled back to look at me, her eyes fixed on mine, her mouth parted in anticipation. Her fingertips pressed into my back to pull me closer and when our lips met again, it was with a slick desperation to take as much as we could before our time was up. Before our bodies betrayed us—hers blazing uncontrollably and mine unable to withstand the heat.

My hands were in her hair, pulling her to me. Even through our clothes, I could feel that her body was feverish with the power of her deviation. Her lips and breath were hot against mine and yet I still wanted her so desperately that I continued to kiss her, every touch of her tongue against mine scalding and sweet.

Before the heat forced us apart, the porch light came on and it was like having a bucket of cold water poured over us. We broke the kiss and turned toward the light, shading our eyes with our hands. The frigid air that billowed around me cooled my flushed skin.

"There you two are." Gina was standing on the porch, holding the screen door open as she peered out into the darkness at us. "Daniel wants you to meet him in the back yard."

"What's wrong?" I asked, releasing my grip on Cleo so that she could turn and stand next to me to face Gina. I kept my arm around her waist, holding her against me.

A smile lit up Gina's face and she laughed. "Nothing's wrong, darling. That's exactly the point. Head on back." She nodded with her head for us to walk around the side of the house.

I raised my eyebrows in question, but then grabbed Cleo's hand. We found Daniel in the back yard standing among the Deviants and Others. Everyone was staring at a huge stone pit that was surrounded by various chairs.

"Oh good. Gina found you," Daniel said.

"What's going on?" I looked warily at everyone, almost expecting a problem. Things had been way too easy so far.

"Mr. Knight was just telling us he thought it'd be a good idea to have a bonfire," Cassie said.

I looked to Arabella, wondering if she was part of the idea. When she met my gaze she just shrugged her shoulders and raised her eyebrows.

"A bonfire? Are you serious?" Cleo asked.

"Apparently he is." Quinnie inspected her nails even though it was impossible to see them in the darkness. "He brought out hotdogs and marshmallows."

"Why do you want us to do this?" I searched Daniel's expression.

Daniel took his time looking around at all of us. "I want you to do this because you're young and you deserve a chance to act like normal teenagers."

"What's that supposed to mean?" Quinnie couldn't even manage to muster up her normal sass.

"It means, that you're free to do whatever you want. If you want to have a bonfire, go get some wood from behind the stable, make a fire, and roast some food. If you don't want to, don't. It's up to you." Daniel smiled at us in challenge before turning to walk back toward the house, meeting Gina who was standing on the back porch. He put his hand on her lower back and led her inside to the kitchen.

We stood around, staring toward the porch light, confused. Sixteen teenagers, with dangerous powers, and enough animosity between us to start another World War. And he just left us alone, suggested we start a fire, and told us to do whatever we wanted. No one had ever let us do what we wanted.

It was...strange. And refreshing.

"Come on." Cleo tightened her grip on my hand. "Let's go get some wood."

I noticed that Cleo glanced at Persephone as we walked by the chair she was sitting in. The skin on her hand flared hot for a moment, heating my chilled fingers, and then she looked away, regaining control. Persephone was turning something over in her hands, and she looked up as if she felt me staring at her. Her gaze was blank at first, but then she winked. I swallowed and looked away, feeling remnants of shame for what happened between us. How could I have ever made the mistake of thinking she was Cleo?

Behind the stable, Cleo and I each grabbed an armful of wood and brought it back to the fire pit. Marty stacked the smaller pieces into a teepee shape, arranging kindling beneath the pile. When it was ready, he stepped back and looked at it with his head tilted. "That should work. I'll get some matches from Daniel."

He was barely out of the way when a ball of fire streaked through the dark, smashing into the carefully arranged wood. The pieces tumbled over in a messy blaze of flames. I reached for my hip and pulled out the tranquilizer gun as Wesley lunged for Persephone, knocking her out of the chair. Out of the corner of my eye, I could see the motion of bodies stepping forward, the hum of electricity, the hiss of blades scraping against each other, and a flare of heat from Cleo. My heart pounded against my rib cage, memories of the carnage at the Inner Harbor racing through my mind.

Wesley was on top of Persephone who was face down in the dirt. He was wrenching her arms behind her back even though she wasn't struggling. She laughed, the sound of her voice wicked and pleased.

"I thought you gave her the counteragent?" Wesley was glaring at me, his gaze wild as he forced a knee into Persephone's shoulders to keep her pinned down.

I kept the gun pointed at her. "I did." I didn't like the accusation in his voice or the fact that he thought I'd willingly put anyone in danger. I'd been administering all of the counteragents regularly.

Persephone continued to laugh even when Wesley yanked her arms back more forcefully to try to get her to shut up. "The counteragent doesn't work on me anymore. It hasn't for the past two days."

"You're lying." The hate in Wesley's voice was surprising, as if he was somehow offended that she still had use of her deviation even with him watching her like a hawk.

"Let her up." Rune stalked toward Wesley. I let go of Cleo's hand and stepped forward as well.

"Don't you see? They can't be trusted, Ozzy." Wesley narrowed his eyes at me, never releasing his grip on Persephone. "We need to get rid of them."

"And how do you suggest we do that? If we send them away, the Program might find them and then the Program would find us."

"I don't mean send them away. I mean get *rid* of them." He glared down at Persephone, pressing his knee harder into her back causing her smile to turn into a grimace of pain.

"Do it," she whispered.

"Let her go." The words tasted bitter on my tongue, but I had no choice. If Wesley kept talking this way, there was only one way the night would end and I wasn't about to let that happen.

"What?" Rage contorted Wesley's features, the light from the fire twisting the anger on his face into ominous shapes.

"Let her go. I don't like her any more than you do. I don't know why the counteragent isn't working and I don't trust her. But you have to let her go. We need the Others as much as they need us. The only way she can earn our trust, the only way any of them are going to earn our trust, is if we give them a chance."

"You saw what she did."

"Yeah. She started a fire. And you weren't the center of it. If what she's saying is true, she could have done that to any one of us over the last few days," I pointed out.

Wesley opened his mouth to argue and I interrupted him.

"Look, we can't live like this forever. We can't keep watching the Others and our backs at the same time. Eventually, we're either going to go after the Program or they're going to find us here. Either way, we'll have to fight. For us to have a chance, we need every advantage we can get. We're going to have to learn how to trust one another even if we don't like each other."

"He's right," Arabella said. "I trust Quinnie even though I don't like her."

"Shut up, bitch." Quinnie waved her middle finger toward Arabella.

"You first, hag." Arabella stuck out her tongue.

"Enough." I glared at both of them and then turned to Wesley. "Let her up."

"Or what?" His grin was almost as malicious as the one Persephone usually wore, and for a moment, I couldn't see anything familiar about the Wesley in front of me.

"She might have built up a tolerance for her counteragent, but you haven't." I raised the tranquilizer gun until it was pointed at him.

"Are you really going to shoot me?" He released his grip on Persephone's arms, but kept one hand on the back of her neck forcing her face into the ground as he lifted his chest to get a better look at me. His eyes were narrowed in disbelief.

"Only if you make me."

"Ozzy?" Cleo's hand was on my arm. "Don't do this," she whispered. "You'll never forgive yourself."

My aim didn't waver. "It's his choice."

Wesley turned to look at his brother for support and I was grateful when Theo shook his head and said, "This isn't the battle you want to fight, Wes."

With a disgusted huff of breath, Wesley pushed up from the ground and took a few steps back, never looking away from Persephone. She stood up, brushed the dirt off her clothes, and then bent over to retrieve the black 8-ball she had been holding. I thought it was destroyed at the Inner Harbor.

She looked around the circle with a satisfied grin as she shook the ball in her hand. A few seconds later she turned the ball over and glanced at the purple screen. "I'm going to bed. Enjoy the marshmallows," she said, taking a few steps backwards. "You're welcome for the fire." She turned and headed for the dark shape of the barn, her pace unhurried. Before she was completely out of sight, Wesley released a frustrated breath and followed her.

"Wes—" Theo called after him.

"Don't worry, I'm not going to hurt your precious little terrorist. I'm just going to make sure she doesn't come back and kill you all while you stuff your faces." He turned his glare on me. "I hope you know what you're doing." No one spoke as he stalked away and the darkness swallowed him.

"Me too," I muttered.

RUNE

❧ 15 ❧

TAMING THE SHREW

"Did you know the counteragent wasn't working?" Ozzy was sitting in a chair across the bonfire from me. Cleo was settled in front of him, leaning against his legs.

I shook my head. "I found out the same time you did."

After Persephone and Wesley left, Eva passed out food and roasting sticks, and soon a strange sense of calm settled over everyone. I think we all were just tired of doubting one another and constantly being on high alert. The worst possible scenario—Persephone having use of her deviation—was now a reality. And if she was telling the truth, it had been that way for two days without incident.

"Would you have told us if you did know?"

I stared at him a moment. "I would have warned you, but I also would have protected her."

Ozzy nodded, his gaze leaving mine to settle on the fire between us. For a few moments, the only sounds were the snap of the flames while everyone ate. I still couldn't believe Ozzy didn't take Wesley's side and retaliate against Persephone. I could only assume he knew I would've defended her. Not because I wanted to, but because I felt obligated to. I wasn't going to let the Deviants gang up on her. She might deserve punishment, but maybe I did too. None of us were innocent. We all had sins and secrets. Even the Dozen.

I might be willing to protect Persephone, but I was still pissed that she didn't tell me her counteragent wasn't working. I was in the same boat as the Dozen, forced to trust someone who was impossible to trust. But then again, it was always that way with Persephone.

"What about you two?" Ozzy was looking between Elysia and Euri.

Elysia licked her lips. "The counteragent hasn't worked on me since yesterday."

Ozzy's eyes travelled over to Euri who held up his hands in front of him. "I have no idea. I haven't even tried to use it. The idea never even crossed my mind. I didn't know the girls were immune to it."

"You didn't tell him?" Ozzy's head was tilted to the side as he assessed Elysia.

She shook her head, looking down at her lap. "I was afraid of what would happen if anyone found out." Since she cut her hair short, she looked so different from Quinnie. And with her constant state of anxiety, it was now easy to tell them apart.

"The only thing I can think of is that it was designed to work on children. Perhaps the dose is too small and it's easy to build up a tolerance against it," Ozzy said thoughtfully.

Everyone was quiet as we waited for him to say more. After a few more minutes went by, Theo stood up from his chair and stretched his arms over his head before walking over to the table where the food was. When music started playing from the portable speaker Daniel had left, the tension disappeared, especially when Theo pulled Cassie up from her spot on the blanket and twirled her into several ridiculous dance moves. Before long, there was laughter and conversation. Exploding kindling was forgotten for now.

Quinnie leaned over and whispered in my ear. "Will you go get me a blanket?"

She wanted me to get her a blanket? Quinnie never asked anyone to do anything for her.

"Sure." I stood up and when a few people looked my way, I hooked my thumb over my shoulder toward the barn. "I'm gonna grab a couple blankets. Anyone else need anything?"

"Can you grab me a sweatshirt?" Sadie asked.

"Me too." Eva raised her hand to get my attention.

"Please bring back some music that isn't shitty." Arabella scrunched her face in disgust as she watched Theo and Cassie dance.

"Don't bother, Rune. We can't dance to angry girl music," Theo argued, throwing Arabella a challenging look.

"You can't dance at all," Arabella told him. She pushed up out of her chair, went to the speaker, and changed the music.

I walked toward the barn as Theo started arguing with her over song selections. I was glad for the easy banter because it gave me hope that things might work out between the Dozen and the Others. Eventually.

When I stepped out of the stairwell into the upstairs hallway, Wesley was sitting on the floor across from Persephone's door.

"Is she behaving?" I asked, nodding toward the room.

Wesley ignored me so I went into the room that Euri and I shared and grabbed a couple of blankets and extra sweatshirts. Gina didn't seem to care whether we were part of the Dozen or not. After we arrived, she got new clothing for the Others and treated us as if we were no different. It may have been a small gesture on her part, but it was the first time that I'd ever been treated as an equal instead of something less.

I came out of the room with my arms full and Wesley looked away from Persephone's door. "Don't think that just because Ozzy trusts you that we all do."

I held his gaze for a moment before answering. "I don't."

His eyes left my face and continued to burn a hole through the door in front of him. I wondered if he was using his deviation to its full extent. Was he just guarding the door, or was he looking through it?

"She's playing with fire," Wesley said, answering my unasked question. I didn't know if he meant that literally or figuratively. And I didn't care. If he wanted to waste his time spying on Persephone, that was his problem.

"In case you haven't noticed, we're all playing with fire," I told him. I jogged down the steps before he could answer and stepped out of the stairwell and into the dimly lit barn. The smell of hay was potent, but the horses were quiet in their stalls. The sudden grip of a hand on my elbow forced me to drop the blankets and I spun around, my hands poised and ready to strike.

"It's just me." Quinnie was standing in the shadows, her hand on her hip.

"I was bringing the blanket you asked for. Show a little patience." I grinned and pointed to the pile on the ground. The smile on my face was a foreign feeling. Something new that only Quinnie seemed to be able to conjure.

"I don't want the blanket." She reached out and fisted her hands in the front of my jacket. I didn't resist as she yanked me further into the shadows with her. Quinnie's body pressed against mine as her mouth skimmed along my chin. Her lips left a trail of hot kisses down my neck and then across my jaw before finding my mouth. My hands gripped her waist as I pushed her against the wall, kissing her slow and deep in the way I knew she craved. Quinnie seemed like the kind of girl who'd want it fast and hard—wham bam thank you ma'am. Everyone believed she was shallow. But that wasn't the Quinnie I knew. That wasn't the Quinnie who had gotten me to smile. Neither of us truly felt like we belonged, except for the times we were alone together.

"Did you miss me?" she mumbled against my lips.

When she pulled away to take a breath, I reached up and wrapped my hand around the front of her neck using my thumb to tilt her chin backwards. I kissed down her throat and she sighed with each stroke of my lips against her skin. "I missed this." I ran my other hand down the curve of her side, sliding it over her ass and squeezing.

"You're an ass," she whispered.

She didn't try to push me away. She let me take my time tasting along the sweet skin of her neck until I reached her collarbone and her head fell to the side in complete submission to my mouth. In this moment, we were the Quinnie and Rune that no one else ever saw. We were both vulnerable and needy. Exposed. And for once, feeling exposed didn't scare me.

She slipped her leg around my thigh, tucking her foot behind my knee to pull our hips close together. A soft sound of contentment echoed through her chest as I pressed my hips against hers in a slow rocking motion.

Her fingers slipped through the belt loops of my jeans, pulling me harder against her body. I slid my free hand around her back to hold her tightly to me. I kissed up her neck in a slow pace that had her body wriggling against mine. When my mouth touched hers, she let out a soft moan and opened her lips to the heat of my tongue.

"I knew you were a traitor."

We pulled away from each other, panting, and turned toward the bottom of the stairwell where Wesley was standing, glaring at Quinnie.

"Jealous?" Quinnie's voice was bored as she slid back into her emotional armor with ease. She acted as if Wesley's words harmlessly bounced off her, but the look in her eyes was stark naked vulnerability. Wesley's words cut her deeply, marking her. She acted like she didn't care what people thought because it was easier to hide her disappointment, but I knew how deep her emotional wounds were. I knew how little the others saw of the real Quinnie.

Wesley's top lip curled back over his teeth. "More like disgusted." He spun around and stomped his way back up the steps without explaining why he'd come down in the first place.

She stared at the space where Wesley had been standing and I lightly ran my fingers up and down the backs of her arms. "Maybe we should go back out to the bonfire."

Quinnie looked up at me and the hurt in her eyes made something flare hot inside me—made me want to protect her. "Why? So everyone else can sit there and judge me for the rest of the night? You're the only one who never has."

I hated the discouraged look in her expression, the look that proved just how desperate she was to be accepted. I pulled her against my chest and when she laid her head on my shoulder, I felt her sigh and I smiled to myself. I was the one person who could tame the bitch that Quinnie usually wielded. Under my hands and lips, the shrew was content and docile. Almost non-existent.

CLEO

❧ 16 ❧

THE VOICES

Three Months Later

Holding back the curtain, I stared down at the thick blanket of new grass covering the ranch—green as far as the eye could see. There was something comforting about spring and I loved how the world became soft and optimistic when under its touch. Almost hopeful. Spring made everything feel renewed.

I let go of the curtain and turned toward the two beds in the room, kicking the frames. "Get up or we're going to miss breakfast."

Quinnie turned over so her back was to me and she pulled the pillow over her head. "I'm not going," she mumbled from under the pillow.

At least that's what it sounded like she said. She came back to the room some time during the middle of the night. I had no idea where she'd been or what she'd been doing, but since I didn't like my whereabouts with Ozzy constantly monitored, I didn't nose around in her business either. I was still amazed that she chose to room with Cassie and me instead of Eva and Sadie, but ever since

Quinnie's secret was revealed, she seemed to want to distance herself from her old position as Queen Bee. Almost as if she knew she didn't need it anymore.

"Well I'm going. Gina and Arabella are making french toast this morning." I shrugged into my jacket.

Cassie groaned and threw back her covers. "Fine. I'm getting up. I refuse to miss grilled bread and powdered sugar. Even if Arabella has something to do with it."

We quickly dressed and then grabbed our toothbrushes and headed for the communal bathroom. Wesley was sitting in the hallway on his portable mattress across from Persephone's door. We'd been at the ranch for months now and although trust between the Others and Deviants slowly began to build, Wesley was steadfast in his distrust. He didn't accept any of the Others, but mostly his disapproval was focused on Persephone. And although I agreed that Persephone was still a liability, I couldn't waste the energy worrying about it every second like he did. She would either help us or betray us. There was nothing we could do about it until she made her decision.

In the meantime, I avoided her like the plague. I avoided Wesley, too, since he'd become his own sort of plague...on Persephone. If he kept going at this rate, following her around every minute of the day and night, he was either going to go crazy or completely wear himself out.

"Did she get into any mischief last night?" Cassie asked him as we passed. "Set any kittens on fire? Summon any demons? Dance naked in the moonlight?"

Wesley looked away from the door only long enough to glare at Cassie. It was hard to believe he was the same guy who used to follow her around like a lovesick puppy. There was nothing lovesick in his expression now. There was no sign of the sweet, shy guy I knew back at the Academy.

"I'm glad you think our safety is a joke. I wonder if you'll still think it's funny when she's standing over your body watching you take your last breath." He glared at us with that strange detached gaze of his until the bathroom door closed behind us.

"That boy is batshit crazy," Cassie muttered. "I can't believe how different he is from Theo. Hard to believe those two are related at all, let alone twins."

Cassie and Theo had been spending a lot of time together. A lot of alone time. I found it strange how some of us started pairing off, as if we could only be with someone else who could understand what it meant to be a Deviant.

"He's not completely wrong. He's just taking his fear to an unhealthy, obsessive level." I turned the water on at my sink.

Cassie leaned her hip against her own sink and looked at me. "Enough about Persephone's stalker. How about the original stalker? How are things going with you and Ozzy? Getting any better?"

I grinned. "He's not a stalker anymore. I like having him around now." I squirted toothpaste on my brush and sighed. "Things haven't gotten any better, though. We can barely kiss without him walking away with burns of some kind. Most of them are minor, but still. I don't want to hurt him every time I kiss him. Kind of ruins the romance, you know?"

"But that's the only time your deviation is out of control anymore, right?" Cassie ran her toothbrush under the water.

I nodded. "I don't understand it. I feel absolutely in control of my deviation in every aspect of my life. Except with Ozzy. Why is that? Anger used to be my trigger, but now lip-locking is? Why? How long until he decides I'm not worth the pain?" I roughly brushed my teeth, frustrated.

Cassie's eyebrows furrowed and she bit the inside of her lip as she stared at me. "I don't know. Once I learned how to use my powers by choice, I never had an issue with it happening accidentally. I wish I could help." She dropped her gaze to the floor for a few seconds before looking me in the eye again. "I don't think it's your deviation, though. I think it's you. There's a reason that this is happening. You used to be afraid of your deviation and didn't want to use it. Whenever you were pushed too far, you'd lose control and things would happen."

When I didn't answer, she turned to brush her teeth, watching me in the mirror.

I thought about what she said. She was voicing some of the same fears I already had. Deep down I felt the truth in what she said, I just couldn't imagine what my problem was. I spit into the sink and rinsed out my mouth. "I just can't think of a single reason why Ozzy would be my trigger right now. I'm not mad at him and I don't want to hurt him. So what's my problem? "

Cassie took a deep breath as she rinsed her brush. "Are you sure about that? Are you sure you're not even a tiny bit mad?"

I stood straighter, almost defensively, and furrowed my eyebrows in disbelief. "Why would I be mad at him?"

Cassie shrugged. "I have no idea." She used her finger to tap my forehead. "But I think there's something buried deep up here that's getting in the way."

I crossed my arms. "Or maybe my deviation is just faulty."

She crossed her arms too and tilted her head, smiling. "Or maybe I'm right. I usually am."

We both turned to the sink, brushing our teeth in silence, and I wondered again why I was the one that always seemed to have trouble with my deviation. No one else seemed to have any problems. Their powers came naturally and consistently, like breathing. My deviation was a royal pain in the ass. Just when I thought I had it mastered, it spiraled out of control again. And this time it was in the worst possible way. At least as far as my hormones were concerned.

When Cassie finished, she headed for the door. "You coming?"

"Yeah, just gotta go to the bathroom, I'll meet you down there."

After the door slammed shut, I placed my hands on either side of the sink, leaning forward to stare at my reflection, as if looking closely could somehow give me the answer to my messed up situation. What did my mind and deviation have against Ozzy? And if I figured out what it was, could I just reverse the issue? Or if I couldn't figure it out, could I just turn my deviation off? The thought occurred to me, again, that by taking the counteragent, my problem would be solved. But only temporarily. Persephone eventually built up a tolerance to the counteragent and it would be the same for me. Subduing my powers might fix my issues for a while, but it wouldn't solve anything in the long run. My deviation would still be there...waiting.

The sudden clatter of metal on the tiled floor echoed through the bathroom and I tensed. I thought Cassie and I had been alone in the bathroom. I never would have discussed my deviation problem if I'd known that anyone else was around.

I pushed off the sink and bent over to look under the doors of the bathroom stalls behind me. No feet. I walked around the wall at the end of the row of sinks and went to the other side of the bathroom where the showers were located. In the last shower stall, I could hear shuffling and quiet breathing.

I pulled back the curtain and then recoiled in shock, slamming into the wall behind me. Persephone was sitting on the floor of the shower with her back against the wall. Her arm was stretched out across her knee, bright red streaks criss-crossing down her forearm. Her head was tilted back and rested against the wall, her eyes glazed and dreamy. In the hand that rested on the floor by her leg, she held a razor blade that was glistening with her blood.

"What are you doing?" I was shocked. Disgusted. Afraid. Not afraid of her...afraid for her.

"It helps." She sighed dreamily, like she was high. The blood was dripping from the multiple cuts on her arm, sliding across her skin in bright streams, gathering on the floor in tiny puddles of red.

"It helps with what?"

"It keeps the voices away." She lifted the hand with the razor blade, but it was a weak gesture and she gave up.

"Are you trying to kill yourself?" And if she was, would I stop her? I felt bile rise in my throat at that thought. Was I really that inhuman that I'd let her do that? No matter how much I hated her, no matter how much evil she'd done, would I let her taker her own life?

She laughed and it sounded like it was in slow motion. "Don't act like you care. Besides, if I wanted to kill myself, I wouldn't try. I would just do it." She eased her head away from the wall to look me in the eye.

I turned to leave. "I'm getting Rune," I warned her.

She rolled her eyes. "I'm not doing anything he doesn't already know about."

"He knows you do this?"

"He knows it stops the voices."

I shook my head. Maybe Wesley was right. Maybe we were stupid to put so much trust in Persephone. She was clearly mentally ill. She needed help. Real help. Help we weren't qualified to give her.

"I know what your problem is." Persephone's voice was still content, as if she was in a drugged-out haze.

I edged back toward the door, afraid to leave her and yet too afraid to stay in the same room with her. "Doubtful."

"I know you better than anyone." Her voice became a little more lucid as her head lolled side to side before she looked at me again. "Your intimacy problem with Ozzy. I heard you telling your friend. I can help."

"You're the last person I want help from," I snapped.

"And yet, you want something you can't have, and I can tell you how to get it." Her smile was slow and lazy as it spread across her face.

I stopped my retreat and took a few steps forward to glare at Persephone. "I don't believe you."

"Your little problem with Ozzy didn't start until after you found out he'd been with me. Right?"

My lips flattened into a tight line. I wouldn't give her what she wanted. I wouldn't let her see my jealousy.

"You're insecure," she continued. "Deep down you worry that he'll compare us and you know you might never measure up. You're afraid."

The familiar heat flared through my body as anger clenched my chest tightly. "You don't know anything about me."

"Wrong." The word was harsh and loud as it echoed through the room. "I know everything about you. I am you. I hate you."

"You're nothing like me. And the feelings are mutual." The words felt so good. Like a breath of fresh air.

A bitter laugh tumbled out of her. "Oh I don't think you could possibly hate me as much as I hate you." She let the words echo through the bathroom for a few moments. "You see, I grew up knowing you were the one our parents wanted. You were the one they risked their lives for, even though you've always been the weaker one. I mastered my deviation before you were even in a training bra. They died for you," she said gesturing to me, "when they could have had me." She crossed her hands over her chest, the razor blade and her forearm leaving blood stains on her shirt. "You killed them."

I took a deep breath and swallowed past the lump in my throat. How did she know to say the things that I feared the most? It was as if she knew exactly the way to slice me to ribbons with just words. "The Program killed them, not me."

She looked away from me, gazing at a broken tile on the wall next to her head. "Whatever you have to tell yourself so you can sleep at night." She reached up and traced the tip of her bloody razor blade against the wall using her blood to make a mark that looked like a circle with an "8" in the middle.

I spun around and headed for the door, desperate to get away from her accusations and my insecurities.

"You shouldn't trust me," she called out. Her voice wasn't mean or hateful anymore, it was just sad.

With my fingers wrapped around the handle, I turned back to face her and when I laughed, it was without a trace of humor. "Don't worry. I don't trust you."

"But I'm right about your problem." She turned her eyes back to the blade in her hand.

I hurried out of the bathroom and down the hall.

"Is she almost done in there?" Wesley asked.

I didn't answer him. I made my way to the main house as quickly as possible and when I entered the kitchen, I headed straight for Rune. He looked up from his plate and when he saw the expression on my face, he paled. "What did she do?"

I held out my arm and drew lines across it with my fingertip. As silence fell around us, I could feel the gaze of every single person on us.

"Is she still...alive?" he whispered. I nodded. Rune sighed and it was a mixture of relief and dread.

"Does she do that a lot?" My voice trembled as I forced myself to look at him.

He cringed. "Define a lot." When I continued to just stare at him, he got up from his seat. "I'll go check on her. Thanks for letting me know."

I grabbed his arm before he could leave and turned him back to face me. "This is a stupid question, but should we be worried she's doing this?"

Rune shrugged. "She's been doing it for so long, I'd be more worried if she didn't do it. If the cutting ever stopped, I'd be worried she was finally giving in to the voices." He shrugged off my hand and pushed through the back door of the kitchen, leaving the room in total silence.

A little fear, a little disbelief, and a whole lot of "What the hell have we gotten ourselves into?" filled the oppressive quiet of the room.

OZZY

❧ 17 ❧

MORE THAN ONE QUEEN

The familiar hum of wheels on wood coaxed a smile to my face. I closed my eyes and the nostalgia was even more potent. This was the perfect distraction now that winter was gone. The crudely built track still smelled of freshly cut wood, and there was a fine sprinkling of sawdust across the surface making it slick. But that didn't stop the girls. As soon as the last nail was in, they strapped on the second-hand skates that Gina managed to track down. The patch of farm that hosted many of our winter bonfires had been transformed into a roller derby playground. There were no matching uniforms, we didn't have a brightly lit score board, and not a garish helmet panty was in sight. Hell, the girls weren't even wearing any helmets. But there were smiles on their faces and that made all the hard work of the last few weeks worth it.

"So," Daniel said, coming to stand next to me. "I've heard there's a lot of competition between these girls. Who's the queen of the track?"

I laughed. "I think you know my answer on that. Ask any of the guys and you'll probably get eight different theories. To be honest, I think we might find out there's more than one queen. They're all threats in their own ways."

Daniel stood in silence for a few moments. "I'd have to agree with you, son. And I have a feeling we're going to need every last one of them. Come with me."

***

I couldn't believe what I was seeing. The images were horrific. After months of secretly searching for us, the Program made a drastic move to flush us out of hiding, and now the stalemate was smashed to pieces. We knew that eventually the Program would find a way to come after us. I just couldn't believe they'd sacrifice so many innocent people to do it.

Death. Destruction. False accusations. All the things the Program was created to fight against were also things they were experts in creating. I don't know why their hypocrisy really surprised me since they always did what they thought was necessary to maintain control, even when those actions were monstrous. The difference was, now it was all out war.

I paced the room, too disgusted to watch the carnage on the television, yet unable to look away. The Inner Harbor at Baltimore was on fire. All of it. The USS Constellation, the old historic sloop-of-war that was moored at Pier 1, was now nothing more than floating wreckage. The hull of the ship, which had been blown apart, was split in half, creating two massive bonfires on the water. The broken masts jutted up through the fires like skeletons rising from the grave. Beyond the wreckage of the ship, what remained of the National Aquarium was now piles of smoldering rubble. Other nearby buildings were also engulfed in flames, and the survivors of the attack shuffled aimlessly around in the background, some visibly injured, others looked emotionally traumatized. Emergency personnel darted in and out of the chaos, overwhelmed by the staggering amount of destruction.

The camera swung back toward the journalist who was covering the story. "Program officials are securing the area and demand that residents and tourists avoid the Inner Harbor." He pressed his mouth into a grim expression as he finished his report. He looked like he was in a disaster movie with all the burning buildings, emergency vehicles, and fleeing victims behind him.

The image flashed away from the on-scene reporter to the news anchor in the television studio. "Thank you, Jim," said the anchor. "Be careful out there." He picked up his papers and tapped the bottom of the sheets against the desktop as he looked into the camera. "Now, let's speak with a Program representative to see what's being done about this tragedy."

The image split in half to show the Program's designated representative. My blood slid like ice under my skin when I saw the man now filling half the screen. He was none other than Dr. Steel, my donor.

Correction. My *father*.

"Dr. Steel," the anchor said, his tone serious. "Can you give us any information on who the Program believes is responsible for this attack? Is there any connection to the recent attacks that have occurred in Las Vegas and at Andrews Air Force Base? And does this have anything to do with the destruction at the National Aquarium that happened just several months ago?"

Dr. Steel nodded his head as he listened to the anchor's questions. "There is evidence that these attacks are all connected to a terrorist cell, named the Deviant Dozen, that we have discovered is based here on the east coast. We currently have Mandates searching for the fugitives in question."

The screen split again, and photos of me and the rest of the Dozen, plus Rune, were visible alongside the panel of Dr. Steel. With the stern expressions we wore in the photos, we looked every bit the criminal deviants the Program was painting us to be.

I clenched my fists at my sides. "Deviant Dozen?" I growled. "I can't believe they're actually naming us by the identity that *they* gave us," I muttered. "Bastards."

Daniel had crossed his arms and was glaring at the television. "Just goes to show how deep their arrogance runs that they'd dare use that term. They're throwing it in your faces because they don't believe they'll ever have to answer for what they've done."

I clenched my fists. Cleo was right. The Program had to answer for all the sins they had committed.

"Can you tell us anything more about the suspects?" The anchor asked Dr. Steel, bringing my attention back to the conversation. "There are thirteen, correct?"

Dr. Steel looked bored, as if speaking with the reporter was below him. "Yes. Thirteen who have been identified."

The anchor tilted his head and furrowed his eyebrows. "Anyone who looks at these images would agree that these all look like kids," he said. "I find it hard to believe they're responsible for the large scale attacks this country has suffered."

I frowned and spared a glance at Daniel. Everyone else was outside enjoying the unseasonably warm day and the brand new roller derby track, unaware of the lies being told about us. They had no idea the Program changed its strategy, that it was attacking its own people and blaming us for it.

Dr. Steel smiled in a way that made it clear just how foolish he thought the news anchor was. "Make no mistake about it, Bob. These fugitives may look like children, but each and every one of them is deadly and cunning." Dr. Steel looked directly into the camera. "We ask that civilians do not attempt to engage or confront the suspects. These terrorists are dangerous and very likely armed. The best course of action is to inform Program authorities with any available details."

"Good to know, Dr. Steel." The news anchor shuffled his papers without looking down at them. "One more question for our viewing audience. Is there a reward for providing information that leads to the capture of one or more of the fugitives?"

Dr. Steel's mouth flattened in a look of displeasure that I was all too familiar with. "Frankly, Bob, having these criminals off the streets and our civilians safe is reward enough." He paused for a moment and leaned forward on the desk he was sitting behind. He folded his hands in front of him. "However, yes. There is a reward. All that information can be found on the Program's website."

"Thank you, Dr. Steel," Bob said. With a final nod of his head, the image of my donor disappeared and was replaced with a video of the Inner Harbor as the news anchor recapped the breaking story.

I turned away from the television and stopped pacing. I put my hands on my hips and looked toward Daniel. "I don't understand why the Program is doing this." I gestured toward the television. "What does this achieve? They don't really think we're going to show our faces now, do they? If anything, this gives us more reason to hide."

Daniel rubbed his chin with the side of his thumb. "They're turning the public against you so you have *nowhere* to hide. People are going to want to see justice served for what they think you've done. There's nothing like a tragedy and a hunger for vengeance to bring people together." He leaned against the arm of the sofa and looked out the front window. "The promise of a reward will just fan the flames."

Now that I knew Dr. Steel's true identity, my hatred for the Program was more potent than before. My own father thought of me as nothing more than an object he could use and then throw away when he was finished with it. I could feel myself burning with rage, with the need to put things right.

"All the Program has done is made us more dangerous than we were before. When they come for us, we're not going to surrender. We'll fight, and people will end up getting hurt."

Daniel took a deep breath. "I don't think the Program really cares who gets hurt as long as they get what they want. They want to undo their mistake. They want the Dozen destroyed. "

Their mistake. A muscle in my jaw twitched and I wanted to put my fist through something. Preferably something that would shatter into a million pieces. "I'm not going to let that happen."

"Me either," Daniel said, holding my gaze.

Cleo entered the room and then halted, brushing loose hair back from her face with her hand. She was breathing hard and holding her skates in her hand. "There you are, I was wondering where you ran off to. We were just about to get started." She glanced from me to Daniel, noticing the tense mood between us. "Did I interrupt something?"

"No. There's just been a..." I cleared my throat. "A situation." I chanced a look back at the television and when Cleo followed my gaze, she gasped.

"Is that...is that the Inner Harbor?" She walked slowly toward the television, her face drawn into a look of dismay. "What happened?"

"The Program happened." I moved next to her as we watched the footage from the disaster. The reporter and cameraman had pulled back from the scene which now looked more like a war zone.

We watched as the camera zoomed in on a group of men who were throwing broken concrete and patio furniture through store windows before stepping inside and stealing merchandise.

"I don't understand," Cleo said, looking at me. "Who did this?"

I ran my hand over the top of my head and glared at the television. "According to the Program, we did."

Cleo's look of dread instantly morphed into indignation. "Us? Ridiculous. How are they going to prove that?"

"They don't need to. The people will believe whatever they're told," I admitted. The word of the Program, coupled with a reward, was reason enough for people to believe our guilt. To the Program, this was a chess game and we were their pawns.

***

Everyone gathered in the living room to watch the news updates. Reports of the rewards offered for us were being aired frequently, and the public was going mad with greed and a call for justice. All over the country, in all the major cities, people were protesting and demanding our capture. In some places, the protests had gotten out of control and riots were breaking out. We watched as law enforcement stood by, unable to do anything to control the violent masses of angry people.

"This is so sick." Arabella was seated on the floor in front of Sterling, her arms wrapped around her knees. We watched as shaky footage from a cell phone revealed a young family being dragged from their home, children screaming as a vigilante search party kicked open doors and turned furniture upside down, destroying the home in a matter of seconds.

What started out as a local tragedy in Baltimore, turned into a national witch hunt—the wicked feeding on the weak. And the Program was doing nothing to stop it. Not a single Hound or Mandate was to be found in the areas where the riots were occurring. When reporters questioned Program officials about it, they responded that every available Mandate was needed to search for the suspected terrorists and that local authorities could handle the general public. Unfortunately, it was becoming all too clear that the criminals were in control and the police were overwhelmed and outnumbered.

The truth was, the Program didn't want to stop the people from working themselves into a frenzy. They needed the public to turn itself inside out to find us, and that was exactly what was happening. Amateur video footage and helicopter surveillance showed rioters pulling innocent people from their homes and businesses in their search for us. The video recording we were watching showed the intruders grabbing high-end electronics and other valuables on their way out when it became clear that there was nothing to earn them a reward. They laughed when they realized they were being filmed, holding up the treasure they pillaged from their victims as if it was all a joke.

"Why did they think we were hiding in there?" Sadie asked. "It looks like they're just entering homes at random."

"They don't care if they find us." Cleo had her lip curled up in disgust. "This is just an excuse for them to steal. They know the Program isn't going to stop them. The Program hasn't done anything to stop any other rioters from destroying businesses or public buildings, why would they bother with protecting innocent families?" She huffed out a breath and shook her head, flicking her hand at the television. "I mean really, this is happening in Boston. None of the previous attacks occurred anywhere close to that city. There's no reason to believe we'd be there." She was sitting on the floor in front of me, leaning against my legs. I could feel the heat of her body increasing with her anger. It wasn't the wild uncontrollable heat that made an appearance when we were intimate. This heat was focused and measured, like a predator preparing to strike.

"Are we really going to sit by and let this happen?" Cassie asked.

No one answered her.

"The Program can't just let people terrorize one another, can they?" Eva asked. "How long are they going to let this go on?"

"It'll continue until they get what they want." Sterling rubbed Arabella's shoulders. "And clearly they want us pretty badly."

We sat in front of the television all day, unable to tear ourselves away from the devastation that was spreading across the country. Just when we thought the worst was over, another news story started, another family was torn from its home, another building was burning, another city was under attack from its own citizens.

"If they think we're going to show our faces after this, they're crazy." Quinnie chewed on the corner of her thumbnail, the only sign that she was nervous at all.

"If I were you, I'd be afraid to show my face too, hag." Arabella's insult was half-hearted and Quinnie didn't even bother to insult her back.

"Wait...what the hell?" Cassie shot up from her seat on the floor and crawled closer to the television for a better look.

"Oh my god. Why are they doing that?" Cleo had her hands over her mouth and her voice was choked as she and Cassie both stared in horror at the screen.

I recognized the guys that the Program Mandates were dragging away in handcuffs and chains. Justin, Brad, and Sam—Cassie and Cleo's childhood friends whom they lovingly referred to as the Homework Harpies—were being forced into a Mandate law enforcement van. They were hunched over with their arms secured behind their backs. Their faces were covered in blood and bruises.

Cleo grabbed the remote and pressed the volume button so we could hear what the reporter was saying.

"Program officials have confirmed that they've captured three suspects who they believe are involved with the thirteen terrorists responsible for the recent bombing in the Inner Harbor. The suspects will be taken to Headquarters where they will be questioned," the reporter said.

"Questioned?" Cleo growled as she pushed herself to her feet. "You mean tortured! It looks like they've already been beating on them!" She spun around, the ends of her hair floating eerily around her face and shoulders like angry vipers. I could almost see the waves of heat pulsing from her body. "We can't let them do this!" She looked around the room at each of us, her expression determined. "The Harpies haven't done anything wrong. They're being punished because of us. It's bad enough the Program is hurting random people and blaming us for it. Now they're going after the ones we care about. We can't just do nothing. We have to help them."

"Cleo," Marty said, speaking in a calm voice. "That's exactly what they want us to do. We can't go running off every time the Program imprisons someone we know. We'd be walking right into a trap."

Cleo spun around to face Marty, her eyes flashing angrily. "That's easy for you to say now, but what happens when they take someone you care about?" She scanned every face in the room, searching for support. "They know every detail of our pasts. They know who to hurt to get to us. It's only a matter of time before they drive a knife into each and every one of our backs. I'm not going to just sit around and let the Program do what they want and hurt innocent people—especially people I love. They want me?" She threw her arms wide and tiny flames danced across her palms. I don't even think she was aware of it. "They can have me."

"Cleo—" Marty started.

She spun around to face him again, her expression resolute. "I'm going. Even if I have to go alone, I'm going." She lifted her chin, daring him to argue with her.

I stared at Cleo, but I could still hear the sounds of rioting coming from the television. The Program was making moves to draw us out, but we didn't need to play by their rules. They might think they had checkmate, but I knew they were underestimating us.

The queen protected the king, but the Dozen had more than one queen to play.

I stood up and crossed the room, putting my hand on Cleo's shoulder. "You won't be alone," I said. "We'll get them out."

"I know we will." Her eyes flashed dangerously and flames curled around the ends of her fingers as she dropped her arms to her sides.

This game was about to get vicious.

Rune

~ 18 ~

LOVERBOY

"So you're just leaving me here? You trust me to be on my own with your precious Cleo?" Persephone lounged on my bed as I packed my meager belongings which consisted of the small collection of outfits that Gina purchased for me since we arrived. I also had the communication equipment and weapon that Ozzy had given me. Persephone eyed the pistol and ammunition as I packed them in my bag, but she didn't say anything. I didn't worry about her trying to take it. We both knew she was more dangerous on her own than a gun could ever be. My deviation, for that matter, was also more dangerous than the gun, but it was nice to have it as back up anyway. We had no idea what kind of trouble we'd be up against once we left the farm.

I looked up at her, refusing to rise to her bait at the mention of Cleo. Persephone wanted a fight and I wasn't going to give it to her. "Does it matter if I trust you? We don't have a choice. I have to go and you have to stay."

She grinned and shook her head. "That's where you're wrong, loverboy."

Loverboy? What was she talking about?

"We do have a choice," she continued. "You're just choosing to go along with the Dozen's plan. Don't act like you *have* to do this. You *want* to."

I stuffed a shirt into the bag without bothering to fold it. "So? What if I do?"

Being on the farm was nice. But that's all it was. Nice. I felt like we were all in a holding pattern and there was no satisfaction in a holding pattern. No matter how nice life at the farm was, it was still a prison of sorts. We had choices, but they were limited. And that made our freedom feel like a joke. I needed action. I wanted change. I craved true independence.

Persephone sat up. "This isn't your fight, Rune. What do you care if a bunch of idiots riot and steal from each other? What does it matter if some of the Dozen have friends in prison? That has nothing to do with us. You're putting yourself, and the rest of us, in danger by agreeing to split up. Euri is going with Ozzy, you're going off with your side piece, and Elysia and I have to stay here with my lovely bitch of a sister. Chances are one or both of us will be dead within the first day."

Side piece? I didn't realize that Persephone noticed Quinnie and I had been sneaking time together. I should have known better than to underestimate her. She was paying attention even when you didn't think she was—*especially* when you didn't think she was.

"You and Elysia will be fine. You're safer here than anywhere else."

"I'm not talking about safety, dipshit. I'm talking about the fact that Cleo hates me almost as much as I hate her. I haven't forgotten about the Inner Harbor and trust me, she hasn't forgotten that I've been with her boyfriend." Her laughter held absolutely no guilt for her actions.

My jaw twitched at Persephone's admission. She was as heartless as she was ruthless. She had no remorse for any of the things she'd done, at the Academy or anywhere else. In her depraved mind, Persephone believed that Cleo deserved awful things to happen to her. Punishing others gave her almost as much pleasure and relief as when she punished herself by cutting.

I wondered if the rest of the Dozen saw me the way that I saw Persephone. I might not be clever and witty like Sterling and Theo, or confident and trustworthy like Ozzy, but did they think I was as depraved as Persephone?

I shook my head to clear my thoughts. Who cared what the Dozen thought of me? I was here to survive, not make friends.

"Cleo might not like you, but she doesn't want you dead," I told Persephone. "She's the one who warned me about those," I said, nodding to the barely healed slashes on Persephone's arm that she was currently running her nails over. "If you don't fight her, she won't fight you."

Persephone blinked slowly and a wicked grin slid across her lips. "What if I want a fight?"

I released my breath in annoyance and shrugged. "In that case, good luck. She kicked your ass once, there's no reason she can't do it again."

Persephone's eyes narrowed and she tucked her tongue in between her teeth and lower lip. "That's what you want, isn't it? To get rid of me." Her tone of voice made me feel like I just kicked a three-legged puppy. I refused to feel sorry for her.

"If that were the case, I wouldn't have dragged you away from the Inner Harbor. I would have left you there for the rest of the Dozen to tear you to pieces." I balled up a pair of jeans and shoved them in the bag before pulling the zipper shut.

She arched her eyebrows. "Did you consider leaving me?"

I leveled my gaze at Persephone, but didn't answer.

Her wicked grin returned. "You did, didn't you?"

"I came back for you. That's all that matters." I hefted the backpack and slung it over my shoulder.

"Maybe. Maybe not. But now you're stuck with me." She laughed and pulled at a string hanging from the hem of her jeans, wrapping it around her finger. "And I think you regret it." She leaned back against the headboard of my bed and pulled her new 8-ball from her pocket. She stared at it while she shook it. When she flipped it up to view the answer in the window, her smile turned hard and cold. "Maybe some questions shouldn't be asked," she mumbled.

Exactly my thoughts. I didn't want to know what was going through Persephone's mind. I headed for the door. "I'd tell you to be good, but I don't think you really care what I say."

Persephone clutched her heart and pouted. "That hurts, Rune." Then she laughed. "Or I guess it would if I actually had a heart."

I shook my head and reached for the doorknob.

"By the way—" Persephone nodded toward the door. "I don't like him."

"Ozzy? It doesn't matter if we like him. I trust him."

She shook her head. "No, you idiot. Wesley. That kid is slimy. I don't trust him."

I chuckled. "I have a feeling he'd say the same thing about you."

Persephone shook the ball, watching the little window inside. "The difference is, everyone knows I can't be trusted. That kid is a disease."

"Well, he's going with Ozzy's group to recruit Vanguards. I think I'm safe."

Persephone chewed on the inside of her cheek as she shook the 8-ball and looked at the window again. "Don't say I didn't warn you."

CLEO

∼ 19 ∼

FALLING INTO PLACE

"I feel like a slacker." I laid my cheek against Ozzy's chest and I felt the coolness of his body through his shirt. At my touch, his skin instantly warmed where I pressed up against him. Being outside with him when it was cold worked out so much better for us. The burn of my dysfunctional deviation took longer to affect him when it had to battle through the chilly weather. For that reason alone, I loved winter and early spring. When summer came, I probably wouldn't be able to get within three feet of him.

Ozzy and I had hiked halfway across the property to be alone. Now that our plan was in motion, it wouldn't be long before we had to part ways. We wanted to be together for as long as possible before we had to say goodbye. I couldn't stop worrying about the fact that if things didn't go the way we planned, this goodbye might be permanent.

I shouldn't even entertain that fear. The idea of it was too awful.

I hated the plan that the Dozen agreed on, but I was outvoted.

We discussed the situation for hours, and debated the pros and cons of our options for even longer. When the decision was finally made, I was stunned. We were doing the one thing we all agreed we should never do.

We were going to split up.

Ozzy and Daniel argued that it was the best course of action we had. No one was content to sit back and stay at the ranch forever, but it would be a suicide mission to take Headquarters head on, even with all of us working together. The Program would be expecting an attack on Headquarters—that's why they televised the arrest of the Harpies. They were trying to lure us there. Chances were, however, that they weren't expecting us to hit them from all sides. We were outnumbered no matter what we attempted to do, but we had the element of surprise on our side. If we could distract the Program long enough, we just might have a chance of getting the upper hand. Or so Ozzy and Daniel insisted.

"Slacker? Where do you get that from?" Ozzy lifted my chin and ran his finger along my jaw before leaning in to press his cold mouth against my burning one. My hands gripped his shoulders and my lips teased against his, fiery kisses licking along his skin. The air between us flared hot for a second before I pulled away.

I took a deep breath. "A slacker because I'm going to be here while people I care about are out risking their lives. I want to be with you, helping."

He tucked a chunk of hair behind my ear. "You will be helping."

My fingers traced along his collarbone. "Are you sure you're not leaving me behind because of some misguided need to protect me?" Ozzy might say he needed me at the Ranch to hack into the Program's computer system and watch over Persephone, but I remembered all too vividly the times he tried to protect me, to keep me from using my deviation to fight. Like I was somehow breakable. "I want to be there with you and everyone else. I want to help. I'm stronger than you think."

He grinned and slipped his hands around my back to hold me close. "I never said you were weak, Cleo. I know how strong you are." His laughter was resigned. "But you're also our best hacker. We need you here doing what only you can do. We each have our part to play if this plan is going to work. Unfortunately, that means you and I have different paths to follow."

I slid my finger over his shoulder to trace up to his neck. "So you keep telling me. I just wish this wasn't the only thing I could do to help."

"I never said it was the only thing you could do. It's just what we need you to do." He ran his hands up and down my back, but I stared down at my lap, unable to take comfort in his words.

"I don't want to have to say goodbye," I admitted.

"It won't be forever."

I lifted my gaze to him. "How do you know? Things never go exactly the way we want them to. I don't know if I could bear the thought of something happening to anyone. Especially you." I took a deep breath and was quiet for a moment. "And with what's going on between us and my deviation, I feel like I'm driving you away." Persephone's words in the bathroom had been echoing through my mind, chipping away at my confidence. And with the stress of Ozzy's imminent departure, I couldn't ignore them any longer. They just bubbled up and out of my mouth.

"What?" Ozzy pulled away and tried to catch my gaze, but I refused to meet his eyes. "Driving me away? How could you possibly think that?"

I shrugged and threw my hands up into the air. "Because we can't even be intimate. What kind of girlfriend am I if you can't even kiss me without getting your lips burnt off? Every kiss is like torture for you."

He laughed and reached up to run his thumb across my lip. "Trust me, there is nothing torturous about your kissing." He leaned in and touched his lips to the corner of my mouth before I turned my head to break contact.

"I'm worried that what Persephone said was true," I admitted in a whisper. I bit the inside of my lip as I felt Ozzy's body go rigid next to me.

His embrace around me loosened. "Persephone? You were talking to Persephone about us?"

I felt my eyes widen as I realized what I said. "Oh god. It's not what it sounds like..."

Ozzy reached up to run his hand through his hair and sighed heavily when his fingers met nothing but the fuzz of a buzz cut. He shaved off his dark brown curls earlier in the day and bleached the rest of his hair blond as a disguise. He looked so different. Harsher.

"If you wanted to know what happened between us, you should have just asked me. I would've told you. I wanted to tell you, remember?"

"Of course I remember." A sick feeling settled deep in my gut. When he tried to confess everything to me months ago, I asked him not to. I was the one who couldn't handle the truth. I didn't want to hear him recount the story. I thought it would be easier to ignore if I didn't have to hear every disgusting detail of what happened when Persephone snuck into his room pretending to be me. I wanted to forget that it ever happened.

"Why did you go to Persephone?" Ozzy's voice was defensive, guarded. "How could you trust her over me?" His jaw twitched as he stared past me.

My hands reached up to the sides of his face, my fingers flaring with heat as I forced him to look at me. "No. It wasn't like that. Persephone overheard me confessing my problems to Cassie." I held his gaze, begging him to understand. "I had to talk to someone and I didn't know Persephone was there. She heard what I said, and she just..." I swallowed and then cleared my throat. "She suggested that maybe my deviation is out of control because I'm insecure about what happened between you and her. She said my problem is that I'm worried that you'll compare us." My voice lowered and the words felt like they were scraping their way up my throat as I forced myself to continue. "And ever since she said that, I've wondered...I've worried that maybe she's right."

I stared straight into Ozzy eyes, but he didn't say a thing.

"Is she right? Is this my way of protecting myself? Does my deviation stop me before I can go too far and find out the truth—that I might be less than her?"

Ozzy reached up and slipped his hands around mine, pulling them from his face before lacing our fingers together. He squeezed gently and took a deep breath. Before he could say anything, the rest of my fears poured out of my mouth in a rambling rant. "And now you're leaving and I might never know. Something could happen to you."

I started to speak again and Ozzy leaned forward, his mouth silencing mine. My lips were unyielding at first, almost scared, but he reached up to cup the side of my face and hold me to him. Finally my resistance faded and I melted into the kiss with a quiet sigh of surrender.

When Ozzy finally pulled away, I ducked my head and rested my forehead against his shoulder.

"Persephone might look like you," Ozzy finally said, "but she could never be you. She could never compare to you." He reached up and ran his hand down my hair, gripping the strands between his fingers and pulling my face closer to his until we could see nothing but each other. "You can't imagine how much I regret that night. I want you to understand that when I was with Persephone, I thought I was with you. In my mind, I was with you. She means nothing to me, and the only part of me she had was a physical part."

"But that's just it." My body felt boneless. "I can't even be physical with you. She owns a part of you that I might never experience. I mean, I know you didn't have sex..." I looked away, focusing on the dark outlines of the trees, and my voice shook with each word. "But I can pretty much guess what happened." I rubbed the heel of my palm against my forehead, desperate to get the images out of my thoughts. "And I hate that I'm feeling so jealous and insecure about this. I don't want to be weak."

Ozzy's hands moved down to my arms and his thumbs smoothed over my shoulders in soothing circles. "Listen to me. Persephone is only a shadow of what you are, Cleo. She owns a memory, that's it. She doesn't own any other piece of me." He lifted my chin up so we were looking at each other again. "She can't because you own everything—my thoughts, my needs, my wants, my future. I know things have been different for us lately because of your deviation, but it doesn't mean you're less than her. To me, you never could be. You've always been more to me, even before you knew I existed."

My heart kicked into high gear, beating erratically in my chest. His words searched out all the broken pieces of my confidence and gathered them up carefully. The intensity of his gaze was so strong I felt it sliding the pieces back together, his admission making me into something even stronger than I was before.

Ozzy pulled me in for a kiss. My skin was scorching hot, but he held on, almost as if he was desperate to prove that what happened with Persephone was insignificant. That he would endure anything just to be with me. He continued to kiss me, but I could feel myself holding back. His willingness to sacrifice himself to, and for, me was frightening. Over the last few months, we learned just how far we could go before my deviation became too much for him to withstand. Right now, he was pushing the boundaries. With my emotions in turmoil, I was on the edge of a flare up and we both knew it. The only difference was, he was willing to risk it to show me how much I mattered to him, and I didn't want to hurt him.

"Come on, Flame Fatale," he mumbled against my lips. "I just poured my heart out to you. Time to wipe that memory of Persephone clean away for both of us. I already know she means nothing to me. Now you have to believe it. Prove to both of us that you're the only one for me." His hands reached to the back of my head and he tangled his fingers into my hair, holding me close. He pressed a quick kiss against my lips. "You're the one I want." Another kiss, this one chaste. "You're the one I think about." A smoldering kiss. "The one I dream about."

Against my will, my lips opened slightly when he kissed me again.

"You're the only one I love." His words trickled over my lips, into my body, and made a bee line for my heart, filling in all the dented and cracked parts.

My eyes flew open in surprise and I met his gaze. "You...love me?"

He grinned. "Don't act like you didn't know."

"But...you can't. You don't know me well enough yet. You don't know..." *Please tell me to shut up. I want to believe you.*

He eased his hands up to cradle my jaw and slid his thumbs over my lips to keep me from talking. He smiled when my questions became jumbled behind the press of his fingers and I finally went quiet.

"Cleo. I know everything about you." When my mouth started to move in response, he chuckled. "Okay, maybe not everything. You have secrets, I get it." He gave me a cocky smile and his green eyes lit up with amusement. "But I l know the important stuff. And I love you. Before you even came to the Academy, you ruled my thoughts. Now, you completely own me."

The wild beat of my heart refused to calm down. I took a deep breath. "You're serious?" I mumbled.

His voice dropped low and his thumbs spread out along my lips to rest on my cheeks. He stared at my mouth like he might devour me. "I can't wait to show you how serious I am."

I've heard the saying that a tongue has no bones, but that it's strong enough to break a heart. With Ozzy's words echoing in my mind, I realized the tongue is also strong enough to heal a heart with just a few words. Three to be exact. He loved me.

Before Ozzy could say another word, I climbed into his lap, my lips and hands ravenous and careless. I touched every part of him. I couldn't have stopped if I wanted to. I was pulling off his jacket as

I kissed him and between each touch of my lips, I apologized. "Sorry"..."Don't want to hurt you"..."Need to kiss you"..."Have to touch you..."

I could feel urgency, heat, and hunger in every part of my body and along every inch of my skin.

"Cleo," Ozzy managed to say between kisses.

I was a wildfire, ravaging everything I touched. Unstoppable.

"Cleo..."

I was starved, a being made of nothing but cravings. And I wanted Ozzy.

"Cleo," he said again, almost as if he was in pain.

My name was a slap to my face bringing me to my senses. I lifted my hands to stop touching him. What was wrong with me? Three little words and I lost all restraint.

"I'm sorry. I didn't mean to lose control. I just wasn't expecting you to say that," I rambled. I bit the end of my tongue and then smiled ruefully. "I...I liked hearing that. A lot. And I wanted to show you how much I liked it. I just...I just don't know how to do it without hurting you." I held my hands up like I was under arrest.

Ozzy wrapped his arms around my back and pulled me close again. "Then get back to showing me. I'm not in any pain. Trust me. No burns. See?"

My eyebrows furrowed as I inspected his lips. "None? But I felt so hot."

His cocky grin was rooted firmly on his mouth. "Yes, you are. But your deviation was under control this time."

"It was?" I tilted my head in question, still unsure. "But you said my name."

He grinned. "Just letting you know how much I was enjoying

it."

"So do you want me to go back to kissing you again?" I touched his face with my fingertips experimentally, sliding them back into his hair when he didn't flinch.

He leaned in, nipping at my lower lip with his teeth. "I want your lips on mine. Again. Now," he growled. When he leaned in to my touch, my breath came out in a ragged sigh and I dove in for another round of touching every inch of him I could.

My lips crashed into his and we didn't speak or let our mouths part for more than the need to take a breath. After months of stolen moments and risky kisses, being able to touch Ozzy without fear was exhilarating. My hands were fisted in his shirt and when I started to pull it off, Ozzy rolled to the side until we were lying next to each other on his discarded jacket. I still had a tight grip on the fabric stretched across his chest, but I merely held on as he propped himself up and stared down at me like we'd both just won the lottery. My other hand trailed up the bare skin of his arm. "I can finally touch you," I said.

"Then don't stop." He ran his finger along the neckline of my cotton shirt, pulling it down just enough that he could lean over and kiss my shoulder. That light touch of his lips sent sparks of excitement spiraling through my body.

I made a small sound in the back of my throat and my eyelids fluttered closed. "Why?" I whined.

"Why what?" He continued to kiss along my skin, up my neck, over my jaw, to the corner of my mouth.

"Why can I finally be with you just when you're getting ready to leave? It's not fair." I turned my head to kiss him full on the lips. My hands roamed under his shirt and my heart raced with every seeking touch of my fingers and mouth. I'd missed this. God, how I'd missed this.

He didn't answer me, he just continued to kiss me as if it might be our last chance. My heart fell out of rhythm when I realized maybe it was.

I don't know how much time passed before I heard a throat clearing. We were breathing heavy when Ozzy broke our lip lock to see who had interrupted us.

Sterling was staring back toward the house, running his hand over his head, mussing up what was left of his hair after his transformation for the mission. He was pointedly avoiding the sight of us.

"Your timing sucks," Ozzy growled.

"Sorry." Sterling risked a look at Ozzy. "We're ready to head out. You wanted to leave at midnight, right?"

Ozzy lifted his wrist to look at his watch. "Already?"

"Yeah. I'll just…" Sterling jerked his thumb over his shoulder toward the house. "I'll just wait for you back at the house."

Rubbing his forehead, Ozzy nodded. "I'll be up in a bit. Just give me a moment."

"Friggin' awkward," Sterling muttered as he turned to walk away. "Nobody told me you two were out here swapping spit and getting ready to make the beast with two backs…" He hurried off, still talking to himself.

Sterling wasn't even out of sight before the uncontrollable laughter started. *The beast with two backs?* Such a Sterling thing to say.

Ozzy stood up and offered me his hand. "I can't believe he just insulted us with Shakespeare."

I let him pull me up and then melted into his embrace, wishing I could freeze time so that midnight never came. "I can't believe we can finally touch each other and you're leaving."

"All the more reason to get this done as quickly as possible." He gave me a quick kiss and then grabbed my hand, turning to lead me to the house.

We walked in silence for a few moments. I was stunned. Persephone was right—my insecurity had been causing my deviation to derail. And what was even more unbelievable was that three little words from Ozzy was all it took to set things right again. I was amazed by how much power words had.

I peeked to the side to stare at Ozzy's profile, which was now unfamiliar without his curls.

He grinned as if he could feel my gaze, and I wondered if he expected me to tell him I loved him, too. There was a part of me that knew, without a doubt, that the way he made me feel could only be called love. But there was another part of me that worried that I hadn't known him long enough to know for sure. How could I say those powerful words to him when I couldn't even admit them to myself? All I knew was that I didn't want him to leave, and it made me sick to think about the fact that he would be in danger.

"Ugh," I finally said. "I don't have to thank her do I?" I asked, avoiding the subject I was really obsessing over.

"Who?" Ozzy's voice was oddly content, despite the fact that every step brought us closer to goodbye.

"Persephone. For pointing out what I was too blind to see," I admitted.

Ozzy grunted. "It was the least she could do."

I turned my hand slightly so I could twine my fingers between

Ozzy's. I squeezed, staring off into the darkness. "So. You really love me?"

Out of the corner of my eye I saw him turn his head and I could almost feel his cocky smile as he stared at me. "You really can't tell?" He lifted our hands so he could run his lips over the backs of my fingers. My entire body lit up, tingling from the tips of my fingers all the way to my toes. One touch, one look, a few words and I was lost in him. I belonged to him.

Maybe it wasn't just his words that were powerful.

"When did you know for sure?" I pulled my bottom lip between my teeth, holding back the nerves that were snapping through my entire body.

He shrugged. "I don't know." His thumb traced a light circle against the inside of my palm. "I think it was a slow fall. I don't know the exact moment I went over the edge, but I'm not sure it matters. All I know is that every moment I spend with you I fall even deeper."

My smile grew wider, but I didn't say anything. We walked in silence, and for a selfish moment, I wished we could just turn and walk the other way. Away from all our responsibilities.

"It's strange," I said, finally breaking the silence. "Just when I thought things were falling apart, it was really all the pieces falling into place." When he turned to look at me, I knew my gaze revealed everything. I didn't tell him I loved him, but he could see it in my eyes.

OZZY

EXPOSED

We beat the sunrise to the Penn State campus. The night was still a cold purple and the bare limbs of the trees stretched out against the sky, coaxing daybreak to appear. The night was just as impatient for the sun as we were.

Leaving the ranch was harder than I expected, mostly because Cleo was staying behind. But driving down the long driveway and onto the main highway was also a bit like taking our first steps after a deep sleep. I'd been away from the Program for so long that being on a mission now, risking my life, was an alien feeling. In the past when I went on missions for the Program, I was anonymous. A face-less killer. There was no longer such a thing as anonymity. Now our pictures were on every television and social media source in the country. No matter how I attempted to disguise myself, I still felt exposed. A target. Was it karma that the hunter had become the hunted? The only difference was that my prey never knew they were being hunted until it was too late to do anything about it. I, on the other hand, could feel the target on my back as if it were a living thing.

I lifted the night vision goggles to my eyes and carefully surveyed the area around us. The campus was still asleep, the Sophisticates unaware that the Program's most wanted was within reach. The question was, when given the choice, would our fellow Sophisticates choose freedom, or would they try to apprehend us? I wanted to believe they hated their existence in the Program as much as I did.

The sound of a shoe scraping along the pebbled concrete forced me to drop the goggles and look to my right. Sadie gave me an apologetic shrug of her shoulders. She hadn't stopped fidgeting since we agreed that we'd go to Penn State—her old university. Confronting Devon, the boyfriend she hadn't seen since she was taken away to the Academy, had her all but busting out of her skin. We needed help recruiting Vanguards to our cause, and Devon was our first source. If we were going to chip away at the power the Program had over Sophisticates, we needed to start with our old friends, people we could trust. Penn State was close enough to the Knights' farm that the trip took just a few hours. It was as good a place to start as any.

I rubbed my forehead as I glanced at my watch. As much as I tried to stay sharp and focused, my thoughts kept replaying the last moments at the ranch—when I told Cleo I loved her and her deviation finally obeyed her. Admitting my feelings to her hadn't been part of my plan. But once she voiced her doubts, I couldn't leave knowing she believed that any of what Persephone said was true. So I told Cleo I loved her, and she didn't tell me she loved me back.

To be honest, I didn't want her to.

I gripped the goggles tightly in my fist. No, that's not exactly true. I wanted her to, but I knew she wasn't ready to believe it herself. I respected the fact that she hadn't just echoed my words. It would have made the words mean less. I knew she loved me and that's all that mattered. One day she'd figure it out and when she could finally admit it, I'd know it was her heart speaking and not some sense of duty.

Now all we had to do was get free of the Program so we could focus on the lives we wanted to live and not the ones that the Program were only too eager to snatch away.

Sadie reached up to pull her braids into a ponytail, a motion I'd seen her do a thousand times. A look of loss flashed across her face when her hands met empty air. Like me, her hair had been drastically cut and colored in an effort to disguise her appearance.

"Are you sure he'll help us?" I asked Sadie to distract her.

She scratched the back of her neck, as if that's what she meant to do all along, and rolled her eyes. "I wouldn't have suggested him if I had any doubts." She would have hated if she knew I could hear the anxiety in the words she was trying so hard to instill confidence in.

Pulling her bottom lip between her teeth, she took a deep breath. "I can't believe I'm finally back here," Sadie muttered. Her eyes darted up to mine and she added. "I didn't realize how much I wanted to see him again. I'm nervous."

I put my hand on her shoulder. "I won't let anything happen to you. You have the two best marksman ever created protecting your back."

"I'm not afraid of being attacked." She sighed in exasperation and played with the zipper on her jacket for a few moments. "Devon was the only guy I ever kissed and I didn't get a chance to say good-bye. I'm excited to see him, I just don't know how he feels about me."

I went still. "I thought you were sure he'd help us." I gripped her shoulder and turned her to face me. "Sadie, if you have any doubts about Devon, you need to tell me now."

Her eyes flew wide in surprise and she shook her head. "No, no! He'll help us. Of course he'll help us. Even if he doesn't care about me like that anymore, we'll always be friends. He'll help."

"And you think he has pull with the other Sophisticates here?"

"Yeah." She nodded frantically. "He was always charismatic, the charmer. They have him on track for politics. He's a leader. And now he's one of the older Sophisticates here. He's the right person to reach out to. I wouldn't have risked our lives if I didn't trust him."

I studied her for a moment and then looked up at the horizon where the sunrise was bleeding into the sky. "Cleo's search of his files says he lives in that building there." I pointed to the dormitory where windows began to fill with light. "According to his schedule, he should exit sometime within the next thirty minutes to make it to his class on time. You'll talk to him first and we'll just stay in the shadows so he doesn't get spooked."

Sadie chewed on the edge of her lower lip and took a deep breath through her nose. She never took her eyes off the building and I swore I could hear the pounding of her heart in the quiet of the shadows.

I glanced over my shoulder to find Euri leaning against the wall, checking his weapons. I never thought that I'd ever be able to turn my back on him, especially when he had a weapon in his hand. But his chance at freedom was wrapped up in the success of this mission just as much as mine was. We trusted one another only because we shared a common enemy. We were on the same side until the Program was out of the picture. After that...who knew? Maybe we'd have to turn our weapons on one another again.

Marty and Wes were at the other end of the building, guarding our backs. We waited in silence, the darkness slowly disappearing as the sun rose higher in the sky. I was surprised at how empty the campus was. I hadn't seen a single Hound patrol the entire time since we arrived. Did the Program have them out searching for us?

"That's him!" Sadie whispered excitedly, pointing toward a figure that was making his way toward us. Cleo's assumption was right. Devon was right on time, right where she thought he'd be.

Sadie ran her hands down her thighs and took a deep breath, preparing to step out of her hiding spot. I inched back into the shadows where we were waiting and pressed my body up against the wall behind me. Euri stood from his crouch and flattened himself against the opposite wall. I drew my weapon and motioned with my hand for Sadie to intercept Devon when he got close. She nodded, a look of determination settling on her face. I turned to give Wesley the signal to use his deviation to scout our escape route in case we needed to make a quick getaway, but he wasn't paying attention.

"Wes!" I hissed into the microphone of my headset. He jerked his head over his shoulder to meet my eyes. "Focus," I demanded in a whisper. I gave him the signal to keep watch and then turned back around in time to see Sadie give her outfit one last nervous tug before she stepped out of the shadows. Weak, early morning light filtered through the trees and onto the sidewalk, but our target didn't immediately notice her.

"Devon," she said. All the nerves from before were gone. That one word was full of hope and longing.

Devon turned, his body flinching in surprise. Noticing Sadie, he tilted his head in confusion and narrowed his eyes, inspecting her as he stepped closer. When he was within arms distance, he reached out for braids that weren't there, his hand hovering over her shoulder. "Sadie? Is that you?"

Her smile was brilliant. "Yeah, it's me. Look, I came here to ask you..."

Devon's posture stiffened slightly and he looked around anxiously. "Your face has been all over the news, Sadie. They say you're a terrorist."

I flipped the safety off my gun and raised it a little higher, flashing Euri a glance to see he'd done the same. My other hand reached down to my hip to grip my other weapon.

Sadie was shaking her head. "No! You know me, Devon. You know that's a lie. I'd never do anything like that. I came here to talk to you. To help you." Sadie moved forward, reaching for Devon.

He stepped back, putting his hands up in a defensive position. Devon was glancing around like he was either going to yell for help or make a run for it. This was not going well. Sadie needed to talk fast. Her ex was quickly becoming a liability and I really didn't want to have to shoot him.

"Devon!" Sadie wielded his name like she was snapping a whip. Her hands went to her hips, her confidence slamming back into place at Devon's slight rejection. At the sound of his name, Devon halted, his eyes flying wide open in surprise. "Don't you dare walk away from me. Don't treat me like I was nothing to you. Don't act like I'm the bad guy. I was the one who patched you up when they dragged you back after your escape attempt. Remember?" She tilted her head in challenge.

Devon ran? That meant he'd probably suffered the same fate as Sterling and Cassie—beatings to force him back into submission. So, that's why Sadie was sure he'd help us. She knew he wanted out and that he had a vendetta against the Program. That's also why he probably looked so skittish. He knew the punishment for breaking the Program's rules. The question was, why would Devon have run in the first place? Vanguard positions in the Program were coveted. Especially if what Sadie said was true and that Devon was slated for a political position of some kind. He had little reason to run.

"No matter what the news says, I'm not the enemy. You know me, Devon." Sadie took a step closer and this time he didn't back away.

Devon nodded as he looked down at the sidewalk, silent for a few seconds. When he looked up, I could see determination in his gaze as he met Sadie's eyes. "What do you need me to do?"

Sadie smiled and reached for his hand. It wasn't the arrogant smile that she wore back at the Academy so often. Her face and mouth were set in a look of contentment I'd never seen on her before. I was reminded just how much we were forced to change the moment each of us were taken to the Academy and became a member of the Dozen. Change was the only way to survive. We wore the face of the weapons they expected us to be, even if our hearts remained as vulnerable as before.

"Come on," Sadie said, pulling Devon toward our alley. "We'll explain everything. We're going to set Sophisticates free. All of them. And you're going to help us."

RUNE

FREEDOM TUNNEL

I'd never been to Headquarters. If all went as planned, that was about to change.

Dexter parked our SUV in the abandoned garage and we all got out, donning winter jackets and hats. Spring was well on its way, but the lingering bite of winter gave us a reason to disguise ourselves in bulky clothing. The morning was still cold enough that my breath was visible in anxious bursts of white clouds as I looked around. I wasn't the only one whose eyes were scanning every dark corner of the building we were currently in. Lawless swore we could trust the people we were meeting, but I didn't hand out my trust easily. My fists were shoved in my pockets, one hand wrapped tightly around the handle of my handgun, the other tingling with the power of my deviation.

"What do you think?" Quinnie asked me. "Want to take a guess how long it'll be before one of us needs to use our deviation?" She flexed her fingers. "I'm feeling the itch to let loose a little. It's been a while." Tiny sparks flickered at her fingertips and she shivered.

"Cold?" I asked, rubbing her back.

"Excited. I might get to see dear old dad face-to-face." She curled her fingers tightly into her palms until the sparks were swallowed by her fists. "You didn't answer my question." Quinnie tilted her chin up to look at me. "How long until all hell breaks loose?"

Before I could answer, Arabella sidled up beside us, glaring at Quinnie while tucking her gun into the holster hidden under her jacket.

Quinnie groaned. "Go away. Save your insults for the Mandates. That is if we actually manage to make it inside Headquarters." Quinnie rolled her eyes and turned from Arabella to check her own weapon. Quinnie exuded indifference about our mission, but that couldn't be farther from the truth. She was desperate to see Russell Baker face-to-face. This might only be an undercover mission to free the Homework Harpies and swing as many Mandates to our side as we could, but she fought with Ozzy to be sent to Headquarters. If the opportunity arose for her to take out her father, she wanted to be the one to do it. She argued it was her right more than anyone else.

"No insults. Just a promise." Arabella rubbed at the sleeve of her jacket as if knocking off dust. "If you do anything reckless on this mission that endangers the safety of the rest of us, I will make you suffer."

Quinnie rolled her eyes. "I accidentally walked in on you and Sterling a few days ago. Both of you were naked. I've suffered plenty already."

"I hope you learned something useful." She smirked as she pulled on gloves. "I'm serious, though. Don't screw this up," she threatened again.

"It hurts that you still don't trust me," Quinnie joked.

Arabella blinked slowly, but didn't look away. "I'll trust you when you earn it."

Quinnie pursed her lips. "I want to see Baker and Steel dead just as much as you do. Probably more than you do."

"Just as long as you don't get the rest of us killed in the process." Arabella snapped.

"I'm on the same side you are, nag." Quinnie's arms were crossed and she was wearing her patented look of boredom.

Arabella leaned in to hold Quinnie's gaze a moment longer. "Prove it," she said before turning on her heel and walking away to join Sterling and Dexter who were pulling out the rest of our equipment.

"I haven't fried you yet," Quinnie muttered as she stared after Arabella. She looked up at me. "That should be proof enough, right?"

I chuckled and shook my head. "She has a point. You do tend to fly off the handle. I've heard the stories. You're kind of a trouble-maker."

"Don't act like it doesn't turn you on." She gave me a flirty expression as she looked me up and down. "You like it when I'm feisty." When I grinned and didn't deny her accusation, she grabbed my arm and led me toward the others. "Come on, let's go make some trouble."

***

After securing our weapons and earpieces, we exited the old building into the harsh sunshine. Usually morning had that soft feeling to it, but this early New York light was blinding as it cleaved through the frigid air and threw long, severe shadows behind us. Almost as if it was warning us that we shouldn't be here.

Without a word, Sterling led us toward the overpass where we were supposed to meet our contact. The sound of vehicles speeding by on the nearby interstate was in stark contrast to the quiet stillness of the forgotten, overgrown area we were walking through. Abandoned streets, empty buildings, scraggly brush forcing its way through cracks and rubble—even the civilians knew better than to tread too closely to the Program's borders.

Our boots scuffed loudly on the cracked concrete as we neared the small group waiting for us under the overpass. From what I could tell, there were only half a dozen people and they were dressed in dark, winter jackets like us.

"You're on time," the woman in front commented as we got close. Her graying hair was pulled tightly back into a low bun which accentuated the sharp angles of her face. Despite the ratty appearance of her clothes, her eyes were bright blue and alert as her gaze darted over us, lingering on Sterling the longest. She reminded me of a hawk with the way her head twitched as she surveyed us, her watchful gaze absorbing every little detail. Even though I knew our deviations were a hundred times more powerful than the woman and her entourage, there was something about the way she looked at us that made me feel like prey. Like she knew more about us than we knew about ourselves.

As the leader of our expedition, Sterling stepped forward to answer the woman. "Thanks for meeting us. Lawless said you could help us get into Headquarters undetected."

The woman nodded once in agreement.

Sterling cleared his throat at the woman's strange silence. "This is Arabella, Dexter, Quinnie, and Rune," Sterling said, pointing to each of us in turn.

"Rune." Her eyes narrowed as she looked at me. "So you're number thirteen." I didn't bother to deny it. She was making an observation, not a question that needed my confirmation. "I knew your parents," she said simply.

Her comment was so unexpected, I felt momentarily unbalanced. Delia never told me who my parents were. And I never cared to ask. I couldn't figure out why this woman felt the need to tell me that information. Before I could come up with a reasonable response, she turned her attention to Sterling. "And you're my contact?" she asked.

"I'm Sterling."

Genuine curiosity flashed through the woman's eyes, but she blinked and a moment later it was gone. "Sterling." She repeated his name like it was a word she'd heard but couldn't remember the meaning of. "Sterling Flintlock?"

Sterling's forehead creased in confusion. "Yeah. Uh...that's what my file said. That name will take a little getting used to, though. How did you know?"

The woman smiled, her expression softening even though her teeth showed bright white and sharp out of her tanned, weathered face. "I met you once before. Seventeen years ago."

Sterling stared at her in silence, his mouth hanging open like he didn't know what he should say. Arabella stepped forward, her head tilted as she examined the woman. "He told you our names, what's yours?"

The woman looked away from Sterling, fixing Arabella with an amused, predatory look. "I'm Josie. Josie Flintlock."

***

Josie Flintlock. Sterling's mother.

It didn't seem possible.

Josie didn't rush to hug Sterling, which to be honest, I think he was grateful for. She was nothing like Gina Knight, a sweet farmer's wife with a big heart. Josie looked like a homeless rebel who might feed on any one of us if she got hungry enough. She was intelligent and capable, that much was evident by the way the rest of her group stood quietly behind her. But it was still debatable whether we could trust her or not. I wouldn't be surprised if she handed us over to the Program for a loaf of bread and the security code to launch a nuclear weapon. She looked both that desperate and that calculating.

Sterling reacted to Josie's confession better than could be expected. He didn't say anything and neither did she. They just stood staring at one another in silent assessment even though the truth was hanging over them like a treacherous black cloud.

"Alright then," Josie finally said, shaking her head as if to clear it. "Let's get you into Headquarters." She spun on her heel, gesturing for us to follow her. She had none of Sterling's temperament or sense of humor. I wondered if that was a result of her current situation, or because she never was that way to begin with.

Sterling quickened his pace to come up alongside her. "How do you plan on getting us inside? Lawless said he would put us in touch with the leader of the tunnel dwellers, but I still don't see how we can use your tunnel to get into the city undetected. They'll see us coming from a mile away."

"You thought you were going to use the Lincoln Tunnel?" Josie huffed a laugh, waving her hand as if the thought was ridiculous.

"The Lincoln Tunnel is useless for getting into the city unless the Program wants you to come. The people who live there have nothing to do with us and have no idea we even exist. It works out for us. The Program knows about the dwellers of the Lincoln Tunnel so their camp works as sort of a decoy." She raised her eyebrows in challenge and then looked forward again, motioning for us to follow her. "The Program hasn't even bothered to search elsewhere for other camps. They have no idea we exist or how much we've infested their precious city. Their greatest weakness is underestimating those of us who aren't Sophisticates. Just because we weren't altered to be smarter and stronger, that doesn't mean we can't still outsmart them." She grinned over her shoulder at the rest of us and I couldn't decide if her comment was meant to encourage or threaten us.

Soon, we were picking our way through rubble and weeds so overgrown it was almost as if the edges of the city were rotting away. In the distance I could see the entrance to the Lincoln tunnel, but we weren't headed that way.

"Here," she said, pushing aside some weeds and vines to reveal an opening. Under my feet, I could see the outline of metal rails disappearing into the leafy-covered darkness beyond. We stepped through the foliage into a cold gloom that reeked of dampness and age. Josie and her companions pulled out flashlights and when the lights snapped on, I realized we were in a man-made cavern. All along the walls, colorful graffiti clung to the cracked concrete. Broken crates and trash littered the surrounding area. The place felt like a dirty, broken tomb that had been ransacked and then used as a garbage dump.

"Homey," Quinnie said under her breath to me.

Josie cast an annoyed look at us. "This was part of the old railroad tunnel a long time ago," she said, swinging her beam of light over the walls. "This passage runs alongside the Lincoln Tunnel all the way under the Hudson River. It went unused for decades until the homeless started using it in the early 1980s for shelter. That's where all the graffiti came from," she said, shining her light on the intricate artwork. "The city ignored the fact that the homeless overtook the tunnel because it kept the destitute off the streets which meant they were no longer the government's problem. Come, follow me." Josie lifted her flashlight and started down the tunnel and we fell into step behind her.

"Over the years," she continued, "the tunnel became its own small underground city, filled with unwanted people who developed their own community and laws. Back then it was called the Freedom Tunnel, but after *Wormwood*, everyone who lived here died along with the rest of the city and this place was pretty much lost and forgotten...until we found it." As we got farther away from the entrance, the graffiti on the walls remained, but the trash diminished until the ground around us looked almost clean.

"I looked at all the maps when I was held in Headquarters," Sterling said, "I don't remember seeing this tunnel marked on them." His eyebrows were furrowed as he examined our surroundings.

"You wouldn't." Josie turned to look at Sterling, her inspection lingering on his profile. "Like I said, it was easier for the city to just let the homeless have the tunnel. They made half-assed efforts to block it off, but they didn't truly want to keep people out. If it wasn't on their maps, if they just pretended it didn't exist, they didn't have to put out money or effort to maintain it."

"And this thing goes all the way under the Hudson River?" I asked. "Right into the city?"

Josie's grin was ruthless. "My dear Rune, this thing doesn't just go into the city, it is the gateway for traveling underground. The Program sealed off the subway tunnels when they seized New York, but they never even knew this was here. You can get almost anywhere in Manhattan undetected by using the Freedom Tunnel."

Our footsteps echoed against the stone as the ground made a gradual descent. In the distance I could see a soft glow.

"If you have access to everything inside the Headquarters compound, why haven't you attacked the Mandates before? Tried to kill Baker or Steel?" Arabella asked.

"Yeah. You're not exactly very dangerous rebels," Quinnie added.

The men and women who'd been silently following behind Josie shifted nervously, their shoulders slumping slightly as they looked to their leader to answer.

"I never said we were rebels." Josie slid her hand over the top of her head as if smoothing back stray hair even though it was all still perfectly slicked back in her bun. "We don't have the numbers or expertise to take on professional soldiers. We can nick food and supplies, but a battle with the Mandates would be suicide for us. We're nothing but pests to the Program. Cockroaches."

"Then why do you stick around here? Living underground can't be much of an existence," Dexter said. I'd almost forgotten he was with us. He'd been as silent as Josie's guards.

"We represent hope. As long as we're here, there is someone keeping an eye on the Program and the hope of rebellion is alive." Josie's voice raised slightly, passion and emotion pulling her words

out. "As long as we're here, it means someone remembers all of the children who were stolen from their families." Josie's gaze flicked over to Sterling, but when he turned to meet her eyes, she looked away, capturing Quinnie and me in her hawk-like gaze. "As long as we're here, you have a way to get in and save your friends." She paused and took a deep breath. "As long as we're here, that means the Program isn't as untouchable as they think they are."

We continued walking and as we came around a bend in the tunnel, we saw lights hung along the wall, buzzing with electricity.

"Well," Quinnie said. "At least you're not living in total poverty. You have electricity."

"Poverty? Give us some credit." Josie laughed. "We weren't chosen to be parents of Sophisticates for nothing." Up ahead, a wall of brick and stone had been erected across the tunnel with a metal door set in the middle. When we reached the door, Josie rapped her knuckles on it in a series of complicated knocks. The door opened inward and I had to shield my eyes against the brightness that radiated from the other side.

"Welcome to Liberty," Josie said, holding the door wide. "We've been waiting for you."

***

Liberty, I quickly discovered, was the name of the underground city that was located in the Freedom Tunnel. Despite the fact that they were living in an abandoned subterranean passage, the people of Liberty were not living in poverty. Not even close. Large tents and structures were erected along the edges of the wide tunnel in a kaleidoscope of colors and textures. As we passed, people came out of the doorways of their small homes to inspect us.

Along the center of the tunnel were organized common areas

where other residents were gathered to cook and eat. Television screens were placed at intervals in the common area and I noticed security cameras flashing their red lights along the edges of the ceiling. There was electricity and running water and so many people I was speechless. Even buried underground, Liberty was bright and vibrant, just like its name. It was like a gypsy commune with tents of every color crowding the sides of the tunnel and blending in with the old graffiti. Lights were strung from the roof and were so bright, they chased away the dank, coolness I expected to find.

"Come," Josie said, pulling our attention away from the unexpected surroundings. "Have something to eat."

She led us over to the tables and benches, calling for food to be brought over. After seeing Arabella with Gina and Daniel Knight, I expected Josie to have a reunion of sorts with Sterling now that we were safely inside her dominion. I was wrong. She brought over a tablet and hooked it up to a nearby television. As we ate, she explained the layout of the tunnel system, where the exits were located, and how many guards we could find at various locations. She was all business.

"What is your first objective?" Josie asked Sterling as she folded her hands on the table in front of her. There was no warmth from her and no curiosity from Sterling. I couldn't figure it out. Even I would be curious if I was seated in front of the woman who gave birth to me.

"We want to talk to a few Mandates, see if we can sway them to our side."

Josie's eyebrows arched. "And how are you going to do that? Just march into their barracks and ask if anyone wants to betray the Program?"

Sterling regarded her coolly and I leaned forward to answer. "We have a list of Mandates and Hounds who we think might be sympathetic to our situation. Cleo hacked into the computer system and found out their schedules and when and where we might have the best chance of confronting each of them without an audience."

"I see. And what of the three boys taken into custody who were accused of conspiring with you? Lawless told me that you planned to get them out." She looked at each of us in turn. "You do realize that if you botch up a rescue attempt, you put not only those boys in danger, but my people as well."

Sterling was a blur of motion as he shot to his feet. "Don't worry," Sterling snapped. "We won't endanger *your* people." He spun around and stomped off as we all stared after him in surprise. He'd gone from indifferent to enraged in less than ten seconds.

"Where are you going?" Arabella called after him.

"Bathroom," he said without turning around.

Arabella raised her eyebrows and looked at Josie who only shook her head and pointed in the opposite direction. "It's over there."

With an annoyed huff, Arabella abandoned her breakfast and went after Sterling.

Josie was silent and tried to pretend that she wasn't watching Sterling, but she wasn't as sly as she thought she was.

"So, you're Sterling's mom," Quinnie said, taking a bite of her eggs.

"I was his donor." Josie's back was ramrod straight and she wouldn't look at us.

"But you're not living in one of the fancy Program houses." I pointed out. "Did they take him from you like they did to Arabella and her parents?"

Josie shook her head. "You don't know what it was like back then, after *Wormwood* and all the terrorist attacks that followed. I was doing my part for my country."

"You didn't fight to keep him?" Dexter asked.

Josie lifted her eyes to meet each of ours in turn. "I volunteered to be part of the experiment. Back then, I thought it was my duty."

"Duty?" Quinnie sneered. "That's bullshit. You let the Program experiment with your child. You're a shitty mother."

Josie's icy expression fractured with hints of pain, but she quickly regained control of her expression and forced it into calm again. "I never said I wasn't."

"What happened?" Dexter asked. "If you volunteered, why are you down here? What happened to your payout?"

"I never took the payout. I was chosen to help protect our country and I did what I thought was right at the time."

"You just handed him over?" The feeling in my chest was foreign. I knew many of the Sophisticates were given willingly to the Program, but even with having the demented childhood I did, actually talking to someone who sacrificed their child to the madness made me feel sick.

"I was young. And stupid." Josie's fingers were twisted together on the top of the table, but her expression was wiped entirely clear of any emotion. There was no regret, no sadness, no anger. Just nothing. "I wish I could say I didn't know what I was doing. I knew. I just didn't understand. I thought I was doing the right thing." She looked down at her hands. "I realized later that by giving away my child, I'd destroyed a part of myself."

"So, that's why you live down here and work against the Program? To atone for what you did?" Quinnie sat back in her chair, judgment rolling off her in hateful waves.

Josie met her eyes. "There is nothing I can do that will ever make things right for me or Sterling. Just finally seeing him again is more than I deserve." Her chin wobbled and her eyes became shiny, but she blinked hurriedly before any tears fell. She cleared her throat and then took a deep breath. "That's all I'm going to say about Sterling. Anything else you'd like to know?"

We were all quiet for a few moments and Josie reached for the tablet, bringing up the maps of the tunnel again.

"You said you know my parents." I kind of hated myself for bringing it up. I never cared before about them. Never wondered who they were. Why now?

Josie stared at me, her eyes sparking with an emotion I didn't understand. "Knew. I knew your parents."

"They're dead?" No emotion. I didn't care. Did I?

She licked her bottom lip. "Your mother loved your father. She never suspected that her fertility treatments were anything more than just that. When she found out what he'd done, that he experimented on her baby and turned him into a deadly weapon, she was distraught. He gave her a child she'd never get to hold, never get to raise, so she decided to take matters into her own hands. A knife," Josie said, sliding her hand across her stomach. "Right across here."

"Jesus!" Dexter exclaimed. "That's messed up."

I waited to feel something. Disgust. Loss. Anything. But the place in my soul where I should have had love for a mother had been hollow for so long that I felt no different. I didn't know my mother. I'd been created in a test tube and grown in the body of a woman I'd never met. The only mother figure I knew was Delia.

And honestly, there was nothing Josie could say to top anything Delia had done.

Should I hate my biological mother? She was just as much a victim as me. The Program, the man she loved and trusted, had taken her choices away and turned her into a tool. She might have wanted to destroy the thought of me, but I understood. I admired her for fighting back against the Program even though her methods were horrifying.

"She killed herself and the baby?" Quinnie looked like she might throw up. "With a knife?"

Once again I could see the cracks in Josie's expression. No matter how hard she tried to be cold and detached, this particular memory had affected her, maybe even more so than the fact that she gave up her own child. She nodded. "She said she wouldn't bring a monster into this world."

"A baby isn't a monster," Quinnie snapped.

"I never said it was. I'm just giving Rune the facts." Her shoulders slumped a bit, as if the weight of all the truths she knew were too much for her to bear anymore.

"What about my father?" I asked.

Josie's gaze fell to the table and she picked up a fork, digging the tines into the soft wood of the table. "After what I told you, are you sure you even want to know?"

"It can't be any worse than my mother."

"Don't be so sure," Josie warned.

"Just tell him." Quinnie's face was pale, as if she was worried for me.

Josie looked around to see if anyone was paying attention. There were curious looks thrown our way, but most people were staying far away from us and going about what appeared to be their normal routines. "Your father is still alive and has a very important position in the Program. I'm actually surprised he didn't have you brought in when he found out that you existed."

"What do you mean?"

"He let you stay at the Academy when Younglove discovered who you were." Josie was digging the fork so hard into the wood that she left gouges.

"Why would he want to see me? As far as Younglove knew, I had no deviation." I thought back to the time I spent at the Academy, and how even though I was a prisoner, it was better than the time I'd spent with Delia. "What would he have done with me anyway?"

"Ask Ozzy."

"And how would he know?" Ozzy. Why did everyone always treat Ozzy like he was the Emperor of Deviations? He was a decent guy and all, but he didn't know everything.

"Because," Josie said, leaning forward. "Dr. Steel is Ozzy's father too."

"Holy. Shit."

At the sound of the curse, I turned to find Arabella standing behind me with her hand over her mouth and her eyes wide. A look at Quinnie revealed she was just as surprised.

"Holy. Shit," Arabella repeated. "You and Ozzy are brothers?"

Cleo

～ 22 ～

RECLAMATION

Hacking into the Program's secure system was a lot easier with Lawless beside me, helping me sidestep all of the digital booby traps. But still. Looking up the locations of Sophisticates and finding their schedules was boring as hell. Ozzy and Arabella were out there risking their lives. The only risk I had was the possibility of getting a paper cut when I wrote down information in my notebook. Pathetic.

Theo was seated beside me, reprogramming video surveillance as we needed it. I hacked in and he made the cameras look the other way. The ones on the Penn State campus? They had no idea Ozzy and the rest of the group had been anywhere nearby. As a team, we were flawless at making the Deviants and the Others invisible. I just didn't want to do it. Which was weird because when Delia informed me I was going to the Academy all those months ago, I argued for the chance to stay and become a Vanguard. It only took facing my worst fears to realize I would have been miserable sitting behind a desk all day with nothing but a computer and coding for company. I was worried about my friends. I wanted to be there to help.

"I don't see why you need me here at all," I said to Lawless as I leaned back in my chair. "You know what to avoid."

"Yes, but I don't have the skills to actually hack into the system. I might know where the pitfalls are, but my skills are limited to remembering facts about *Wormwood* history, not outsmarting electronics." He watched as my fingers flew over the keys, digging through the code to find what I needed. It was like a treasure hunt and I was always amazed how the pathways seemed to be so obvious to me, but not to others.

I narrowed my eyes as I scanned the screen. "What did you say we were looking for again?"

"The Reclamation files. They are the ones that will have the lists of all the Sophisticates who have tried to run away only to be tracked down and punished." Lawless leaned forward and scrubbed his hand along his chin as he stared at the screen. He was trying to help me look for any clues, but I could tell from the glazed look in his eyes that to him, my screen looked like a flood of meaningless letters and numbers. "After talking to Sadie's friend, Devon, Ozzy thought that we'd have the most success getting Sophisticates on our side if we knew they had tried to escape before."

"Makes sense." I typed a few keys and the screen lit up a prompt for a password. I'd seen this one before and it only took a few more taps before we were in through the next security level.

Cassie walked into the room and dropped a kiss to Theo's cheek before turning to face me. "Just talked to Ozzy."

I spun around in my chair, abandoning the maze of coding, a

smile spreading across my face as I held out my hand.

"What?" she asked.

"Don't mess around. Where's the phone?" I looked down to her hands to realize they were both empty.

Her eyebrows pulled together. "He already hung up. They just finished talking to Devon again and now they're heading to Marty's old university. They didn't want to be on campus any longer than they had to so they got back on the road to find a place to stay. He wanted me to have you look up these names, though." She reached into her back pocket and pulled out a folded piece of paper.

I tried to ignore the twist in my gut that I'd missed a chance to talk to him. I knew he was on a mission and couldn't very well put everyone in danger by forcing them to wait around as he talked to me, but...I missed him.

"Right," I said, unfolding the paper and giving it a cursory glance before placing it to the side. I'd look at it as soon as I was done with the search Lawless had me doing.

"What are you looking up now?" Cassie asked, looking over my shoulder.

"Reclamation files," Lawless answered for me. "Information about runaway Sophisticates. They are the ones we want to approach first. We think they'll be more sympathetic to our goal and more passionate about recruiting."

Crossing her arms, Cassie's laugh was forced. "Reclamation? That's what they called it? I wouldn't say I was reclaimed. That's way too tame a word for what they did to me. They treated me like a dangerous animal."

"You are dangerous," I reminded her, trying to lighten the mood.

Theo wrapped his arms around Cassie's middle and pulled her down onto his lap, and I shook my head in confusion. Theo—the guy who wouldn't even let me hug him in gratitude—was snuggling with my best friend. Cassie was known for being prickly and petulant. Neither of them were what I would consider cuddling material, making the scene beside me both sweet and disturbing.

Despite Theo's attempts to comfort her, Cassie was still scowling and I didn't blame her. I remembered all too well the punishments the Program bestowed on those who broke rules. I'd never forget how they whipped me in the bowels of the Academy like a war criminal for something I hadn't even done. Cassie and I had shared a room for months now. We'd both seen the evidence of the Program's punishments on each other's bodies. Even Quinnie, the daughter of the Program's mastermind, wasn't immune. The whip marks faded, but would never completely disappear. The Program's methods left scars on all of us. Some that could be seen, but others that ran far deeper under the skin. All of them were permanent.

"The only person that will lay a hand on you from now on is me," Theo said, burying his face in Cassie's neck.

Ew. Gross. I felt a blush rise up my own neck and turned away from them.

"I'll make sure no one ever does that to you again," Theo promised.

Out of the corner of my eye, I saw Lawless cast Cassie a sympathetic look. "We're going to make sure they never do that to anyone again."

Yes we would. The flash of indignation that raced underneath my skin made my resolve grow. We'd find all the Sophisticates who'd been reclaimed and get them on our side and then we'd convince them to persuade others to join us. We'd turn the Program's methods against them.

"Oh, another thing," Cassie said, leaning her head on Theo's shoulder while burrowing into his embrace, "Ozzy wants us to brainstorm ways to break the tracking tattoo."

I looked up from the keyboard and frowned. "We already know how to break the tracking tattoo. Electrical shocks."

"I know." She twirled a piece of Theo's hair around her finger. "But if we're going to create a mass uprising, we're not going to be able to take out the tattoos sporadically one at a time. The Program will notice when Sophisticates start to blip off their radar. We'll lose the element of surprise. Besides, Devon spoke to some other Sophisticates and although they were interested in what he had to say, they weren't very eager about shocking themselves to get the tattoo to stop working. Besides, can you imagine the logistics of trying to locate thousands of tasers?" Cassie reached up to rub her forehead as if the idea was too much for her to even contemplate.

"What am I supposed to do?" My strength might be languages and computers, but that didn't mean I had any skills in strategy. I wasn't even sure how the tattoos worked to begin with or why a shock would cause them to stop working in the first place.

Cassie shrugged. "Brainstorm. We've got the time. Maybe I should go get Persephone and Elysia. See if they have any ideas."

I glared at her. "Persephone would probably suggest we dig the tattoo out with a spoon or something else equally bloody," I snapped.

"You don't have a very high opinion of me, do you sis?"

I looked over my shoulder to see Persephone leaning against the door to the war room. Her hands were shoved into the pockets of her jacket.

"Actually," she said, "the spoon wouldn't be my first choice. Although I can't deny it might be more satisfying." Her eyes reflected the malice between us.

I spun around in my chair to face her. "You don't have your guard dog following your every move now, why don't you go back outside and play?"

"That's right," she said. "There's no one here to babysit me. Does that worry you?" Persephone's lips pulled into a sneer and her eyes were narrowed like she wished she could break me in half with just a look.

"The only thing I'm worried about is putting an end to the Program. But first we have to put an end to the tracking tattoos." I faced the computer screen again, tired of the constant verbal battles between us.

"Then I suggest you shut your fat mouth and listen to me." Persephone pushed off the wall and crossed the room to stand in front of the computer. "The tracking tattoo is powered by a blood battery and runs off the bio-electricity of its host. Sophisticates have a slightly higher level of bio-electricity than the average person. This fuels the tracking part of the tattoo which is inserted into every Sophisticate."

"How do you know this? And even if you're telling the truth, why would we believe anything you say anyway?" I countered.

Persephone stepped closer until we were only a few inches apart. "I was right about the problems with your deviation. Wasn't I?" She lifted her eyebrow and when I didn't deny her claim, she grinned. "I knew it." She stepped back and looked at Cassie, Theo, and Lawless in turn. "You forget that Delia had access to almost all of the top secret Program information that her sister did. Everything Delia knew, we knew."

I bit back a growl that rose in my throat. She always knew the right words to cut the deepest. "I still don't understand what bioelectricity has to do with disabling tracking tattoos."

Persephone rolled her eyes, unimpressed. "You already know that when you overload the tattoo with electricity, it stops working. But since you don't want to mess with tasering every single Sophisticate, I'm suggesting that you overload the tattoo with the bio-electricity of the hosts instead."

It was almost scary how normal and intelligent Persephone was when she wasn't trying to destroy or threaten anyone. Theoretically, I knew she had designer DNA just like the rest of us, but I'd always seen her as just a cold-blooded killer. The fact that she was smart too made her infinitely more terrifying.

"I'm a hacker, not a scientist. How exactly do we overload the tattoos without tasers?" I was getting really fed up with her smug expression. Annoyance smoldered in my gut, spreading the heat of my anger through my body.

"Actually," Lawless said, turning toward me with a triumphant grin, "If you can hack into the tracking tattoo program, we can force the blood batteries of the tattoos to draw on the body's bio-electricity. We can trick them into thinking they need more power. A sudden, intense draw of power might be enough to disable the tattoos."

"But what would happen to the host?" Cassie asked. "If you make a large draw on the bio-electricity, would it hurt the person?"

Lawless shrugged. "We'd have to test it. I'm assuming it would be such a short amount of time that maybe the worst that would happen is the person might pass out for a few seconds. The body is pretty resilient. It'll kickstart itself back into gear quickly enough."

I bit my bottom lip. If what Persephone and Lawless were saying was true, this could be the solution we needed. We could free the entire Sophisticate population in one fell swoop. And if there were Sophisticates who didn't want to be on our side? Well, we could use the same technique to knock them unconscious. Theoretically.

I grinned at the idea. The tattoos—the one thing the Program thought they could use to keep us under their thumb forever—just might be the ticket to our freedom. There was just one problem.

"We need to find someone we can test this on," I said.

OZZY

PLAN B

Road trips always sound like a great idea, but in reality, they lose their luster pretty quickly. We'd been on the road for only three hours and Chicago was still more than five hours away. The one person I wanted to be on a road trip with was in the opposite direction, sitting in front of a computer, probably wondering why I didn't talk to her when I called. I couldn't. After leaving Penn State, I was already tempted to turn the car back toward the ranch. Hearing her voice again would have been too hard to resist.

At least Wesley was happy. The University of Chicago was our next stop and that was where he and Theo were trained. I was there years ago and I could understand why he missed it so much—the campus was a beautiful collection of old gothic buildings which were covered in ivy, giving the place an ancient, majestic appearance. Despite its beauty, however, the campus was set smack dab in the middle of the city. Chicago had been hit hard by *Wormwood* and although the university was now thriving with Sophisticates, the surrounding city was still desolate and abandoned. Apocalyptic even. Much like Washington, DC and Manhattan, only the Program hadn't taken over the rest of Chicago yet. Sneaking in was going to be trickier than Penn State since it would take planning and finesse to make it undetected through a deserted area. At the very least, we'd need the cover of darkness. That meant finding some place safe to rest tonight and all day tomorrow.

I figured Akron was a big enough town that we could easily blend in for a short time. There hadn't been any news reports about riots occurring there and it was on our way to Chicago. After exiting the main highway, I found a nondescript motel and pulled around the back where our SUV was mostly hidden from view. The Program didn't know what we were driving since we were using one of the Knights' vehicles, but I liked to play things safe. We needed to stay to the shadows whenever possible.

"Want me to go in with you?" Marty offered as I gathered the cash I needed to book us a room.

I shook my head. "One person is more forgettable." Zipping my winter jacket up, I put on the black thick-rimmed glasses Gina got for me, hoping my newly-dyed blonde hair and unshaved face would look nothing like the pictures the Program had been circulating around. I caught a glance of my reflection in the rearview mirror and hardly recognized myself. Looking at the stranger staring back at me, I thought about how much I had changed because of the Others and Delia. And for the first time, I was grateful. They gave us a chance to change our future. We were running for our lives, but we had choices.

And this time, I wasn't choosing the Program.

***

"Where are you going?" Sadie asked. She was sprawled out next to Marty on one of the beds in our motel room as they watched television and ate dinner. Euri was in the armchair cleaning his gun, and Wesley was on the other bed, eyeing me warily.

I held up the phone. "I need to check in with home base."

Sadie grinned. "You mean you need to whisper sweet nothings to Cleo. We're not stupid, Ozzy."

"I need to find out where the best place will be to intercept our targets, and it's too loud in here for me to concentrate," I argued. I opened the door and stepped out onto the dark walkway.

"Sure," Sadie called out to me. "Keep telling yourself that, Romeo."

I ignored her and headed for the solitude of the SUV. She wasn't wrong, but I hadn't been lying either. I needed to get some planning out of the way tonight, but I also needed to hear Cleo's voice. Alone. I made my way through the deserted parking lot, thankful for the lack of street lights.

When I shut the car door behind me, I was enveloped by the heavy darkness as I dialed the number for the ranch phone.

"Hello?" Cleo was breathless when she answered and I instinctively thought back to our last night together. Memories of hungry kissing and whispered confessions lodged deep in my chest. Cleo was one of the most dangerous women I'd ever met in my life, and even though I knew fragile was a word I could never honestly use to describe her, that night she seemed breakable. And I liked thinking I was the one who held her together.

"Kilgore Falls," I said.

The silence stretched out for several seconds.

"Crap!" Cleo swore. There was rustling on the other end of the line and I could hear the sounds of papers shuffling and things falling onto the floor. "I don't remember that code word. What the hell is going on?" She was growing anxious as the sounds of a frantic search intensified. "Ozzy? Ozzy are you okay?"

I chuckled, wishing I could see her face. "Calm down Flame Fatale or you'll end up setting the whole house on fire. I'm fine. It's not a code word."

She huffed out a breath. "I don't understand. What does Kilgore Falls mean?" When she spoke, there was still worry in her words. I could almost hear her shaking her head in confusion.

I pulled the lever on the seat and leaned it backwards, staring up at the dark roof above me, pretending I was sitting right next to her instead of hundreds of miles away. "Kilgore Falls used to be part of Rocks State Park before the Program took it over. You can only get to it by following a trail through the woods and that trail hasn't been used regularly in about 30 years. Everything is completely overgrown now, but it's worth the hike because at the end, there is a free falling waterfall in the middle of a rocky gorge."

She cleared her throat. "Okay?"

"It's beautiful and secluded. It feels like freedom there."

I imagined that her forehead was creased in adorable confusion as she tried to decode my words, searching for hidden meanings. "Sounds nice," she finally said.

I ran my hand over the top of my cropped hair, wishing I was burying my fingers in her hair, holding her so that I could kiss her. "That's the first place I'm going to take you when this is all over." The SUV was quiet, my words swallowed by the intense darkness I was sitting in and I swear I could hear the seconds ticking by as I waited for Cleo to respond.

She sniffled. "I needed to hear that. So much."

Relief consumed me as I let out the breath I hadn't realized I was holding. I laughed quietly. "You needed to hear me say Kilgore Falls?"

"No." Her voice cracked. "I needed to hear you say that we have a future to look forward to. That we're going to make it through this. And at the end of it all, it'll be me and you. Together."

A weight was lodged in my chest and I felt the full impact of the distance between us when she said "together." There were so many obstacles we had to get through before that could happen, but I was determined to make it true. "There's no other way I'd possibly let this end," I swore to her, my voice dropping low with sincerity. "I won't stop until we're free of the Program. I'm not going to let them win."

"I know you won't." Cleo's answer didn't even hold a hint of doubt and I loved the confidence that she had in me.

We sat in silence for a bit, just listening to each other breathe, neither of us bringing up any of the obstacles that still stood in our way. Just for a little while, I wanted to pretend that this was a normal conversation between a boy and a girl who were in love.

"Where's the first place you'll take me?" I finally asked. I needed to hear that I was her future, too.

She hummed, her voice low and husky as she seemed to contemplate an answer. Finally, she said, "My bed."

My blood shot through my veins with a sudden and intense need. I could barely arrange my thoughts. The only thing my mind could focus on was Cleo in her bed. With me.

"Your bed?" The words were strained, pulled out of me because I didn't want to give them up. I wanted to keep them to myself, something to revisit long after the phone call ended.

"I'm finally able to touch you again," Cleo said. "When this is all done, that's all I want to do. For a very long time."

***

Sadie was leaning up against the wall, twirling a piece of ivy between her fingers, contemplating what I just told her about my conversation with Cleo the night before—the non-romantic parts of course.

"So do you think Devon will be willing to test out Persephone's theory?" I asked. "We'd be there with him, prepared to extract him from the university as soon as it was over. We'd get him out."

Sadie narrowed her eyes in thought but before she could answer, Wesley came up beside me. I hadn't even heard him come back from his bathroom break.

"What theory?" he demanded.

I didn't like his tone and considered ignoring him. But he was part of the mission and had every right to know the risk we'd be taking. I turned to face him, crossing my arms over my chest. "I asked Cleo to research ways that we could break the tracking tattoo en masse since using tasers isn't feasible. Since the tattoos function off of a Sophisticate's bio-electricity, Persephone suggested that we could use that in the same way as a taser. In theory, anyway. We need to test it on someone to see if it's even possible. I want to see if Devon is willing. Of course there's a risk since we don't know if it will work or cause any sort of injury."

The disgusted sound that came out of Wesley was a cross between laughter and disbelief. "Please tell me you're not actually banking the success of this mission on something that Persephone suggested." He said Persephone's name the same way he might talk about dog shit. Like he didn't even want to think about it.

I shrugged. "I'm willing to test the idea out."

"And get us all caught," Wesley growled.

"You think Persephone is willing to risk her own freedom just so she can cause trouble for you?" Euri asked without looking up from his gun. "She might be a nasty bitch most of the time, but she's not stupid. We all know that the more Deviants this mission loses, the greater our chance of being captured and killed. She might hate you, but she values her own life. You don't have to like her, but you can trust her. In this at least."

"See?" I nodded toward Euri. "Sometimes you have to take a risk to succeed. We're not going to get any Sophisticates on our side if we can't promise that they won't be easy pickings for the Program because of the tracking device."

Wesley huffed out a breath and narrowed his eyes at me. "We should be handing Persephone over to them, not listening to her."

Euri pushed himself off the ground and the steps he took toward Wesley were heavy with menace. "Careful. If you become a danger to this mission or anyone else, you'll have to be decommissioned."

"Is that a threat?" Wesley spat, puffing out his chest as he advanced on Euri.

Euri merely shrugged. "Just a fact. I'm not letting my safety be jeopardized by your prejudice."

Wesley clamped his mouth shut, glaring between me and Euri. I stepped between them to defuse the situation. "This isn't a decision we're making lightly, Wes. Our ultimate goal is freedom for us and every other Sophisticate out there. I want to dismantle the Program and I'll do whatever I have to do to make that happen."

"Even endanger our lives?" Wesley snapped.

"Our lives are already in danger. They have been since the moment we were born."

***

"Where's Wes?" I asked, searching the dark space between the buildings where we were hiding.

"Bathroom." Euri didn't look up at me when he answered, which I was grateful for. Even though he had colored and styled his hair into a different disguise than mine, it was still like looking into a mirror when I spoke to him. Having my reflection talk back to me was creepy as hell.

"He has the bladder of a damn two-year old," I snapped. "Didn't he take a piss as soon as we got here? He's going to get us caught."

Euri just shrugged and clicked the barrel of his gun back into place. "Don't ask me. I'm just here to shoot shit."

A moment later, Wesley marched back into view, tucking something into the back pocket of his dark jeans.

"If that's your weapon you're putting away, don't bother," I told him. "We'll be on the move any minute now."

"Oh, yeah. No," he said, pulling his hand away and patting the front of his jacket. "Got my weapon right here." The smile he gave me was forced and I clenched my jaw. Ever since our earlier conversation, he'd been blatantly distracted. If he wasn't careful, he'd end up on the wrong side of a bullet. I couldn't worry about his safety and everything else at the same time.

"Is Marty all right?" I asked. "Is he still where we left him?"

Wesley tensed. "Yeah. Guarding the escape route like you told him. Why wouldn't he be?"

"No reason. I figured you must have passed him on your way

to the bathroom." I adjusted the dark hat I was wearing over my shaved head.

"I did. He's fine. Don't worry."

"Ready to do this?" I nodded my head toward the sidewalk just beyond our hiding spot where we hoped to intercept Jackson, a friend Wesley had while at the university. Jackson actually evaded the Program for three whole days before they managed to reclaim him. I didn't want to think about what kind of scars that escape earned him.

Wesley shrugged. "Yeah. Of course."

I frowned at his nonchalance, but then turned my focus back to the sidewalk where Jackson was supposed to appear. I pulled my tranquilizer gun out of my holster and clicked off the safety.

"Drop your weapons!" The unexpected voice cut through the shadows and I spun around, instinct taking control as I ignored the demand. I fired and the tranquilizer dart made contact with an unfamiliar Sophisticate who was standing just a few yards away. Wesley stood behind him, his arms held by two other Sophisticates. I couldn't understand why he didn't warn us. Why wasn't he struggling? Didn't he understand that the Program wanted to kill us? It didn't make any sense.

The guy I hit collapsed, unconscious, to the ground. Euri dropped into a crouch at the same time, firing at the guards holding Wesley. They let out surprised screams of pain and released their hold, falling as they clutched their thighs where they'd been hit. Euri wasn't using tranquilizers, but he also hadn't started killing. Yet.

"Pull out," I shouted. "We've been compromised." I turned toward Sadie who was standing behind me.

There was a resounding crack and Sadie's eyes went wide as blood welled out of a hole in her throat. She dropped to the ground, her body jerking as she fought for breath.

"Sadie!" I bent over to help her but my attention was pulled away as Sophisticates rounded the corner behind her. Without a thought, both guns were raised in my hands as my survival training kicked in. I didn't even take time to shout a warning before I pulled the triggers. All I knew was that I was staring down the barrels of too many guns and if I looked at the faces behind them, I'd hesitate. I couldn't afford to hesitate. Every time I saw a weapon raised, my deviation pulled my aim straight and true, stopping the threat before it started.

"We're surrounded," Euri shouted from behind me. I could hear the echoes of his shots and I had to trust that he had my back. I couldn't risk turning around to see the other end of the alley, there were too many nameless Sophisticates still swarming toward me.

I was on autopilot, the sound of my gunfire followed by bodies tumbling to the ground, either unconscious or bleeding. My attention was focused on the threat coming toward us in waves of unfamiliar Sophisticates, but I could hear Sadie's struggle on the ground in front of me as if she was on full volume. She grabbed at my ankle and fear was choked in my throat because I couldn't help her. I couldn't pause for one second or I'd be lying on the ground next to her.

It was amazing how easily my deviation responded, as if shooting someone with flawless precision took no effort. Rage tugged at my skin. Disgust tore through my chest. The bodies collapsing to the ground were just teenagers...kids who were younger than me. Even though my shots weren't kill shots, those who had been hit by bullets instead of tranquilizers abandoned their weapons and were calling out for help. They weren't even attempting to fight back. They probably didn't even know how to take the damn safety off their guns.

And then there was Sadie whose frantic tugs on my leg were starting to weaken.

We'd been so careful. How did the Program know we were even here?

When I took down the last Sophisticate, I finally risked a glance down. Sadie's blank stare was fixated on me, her fingers splayed wide and lifeless across my shoe. She wasn't breathing.

I dropped to my knee, looking back out into the still-dark morning as I placed my fingers at Sadie's neck.

No pulse. She wasn't breathing. This wasn't supposed to happen. Not possible.

My gut twisted as my fingers slid around the blood on her neck, desperately looking for a pulse. It had to be there.

Only it wasn't. It wasn't!

How did the Program know?

Behind me, Euri was still shooting. I quickly reloaded my gun. How many times had I already done that without a thought in the last few minutes?

"Stop!" Wesley yelled. "Ozzy! The Program will give us another chance if we surrender. If you keep shooting, you're going to kill someone."

"Sadie is dead!" I yelled back. "They killed her!" Another Sophisticate came around the corner and I lifted the gun with the live ammo, sending a single bullet right through his heart.

Now we were even. The Program took Sadie, and I took one of

theirs.

"They just want the Others!" Wesley yelled. "They promised me that if we turned ourselves in, we'd get another chance."

They promised me.

Wesley betrayed us?

They promised me.

Wesley betrayed us. He chose the Program over us. My body went rigid with horror. After everything the Program had done, how could he trust them? How could he sacrifice all of us for the Program's lies?

"Should I shoot him?" Euri asked, his voice identical to the one inside my head.

I took a deep breath. "Switch," I told him. "I'll take Wes, you protect my back." We spun around, Euri's body shadowing mine perfectly as if we'd done it a hundred times.

I didn't risk looking behind me to see if any other Sophisticates were coming. My anger was trained on Wesley. The alley behind him was empty except for Euri's victims. I didn't even want to look too closely to see if they were injured or dead. I didn't want to know how much damage I'd done with my decision to bring Wesley with us.

"Is Marty alive?"

Wesley swallowed. "They promised they were just going to detain him."

I could hear shouts echoing from the direction where we left Marty and I felt my heart stutter.

"Has our getaway vehicle been compromised?" My hand was starting to shake, anger and fear mixed with the need to take revenge on something. Someone. Wesley.

The clench of Wesley's jaw confirmed he told them about our getaway car. He probably told them everything.

Shit. He told them EVERYTHING.

Rune warned me and I didn't believe him because the warning came from Persephone. I still couldn't believe it.

Hatred pressed my eyes into narrow slits. "You told the Program about the ranch?"

Wesley swallowed.

"I can't believe how fucking stupid you are!" I never knew fury could be so possessive, so all-consuming. I had to force myself not to pull the trigger. Theo would never forgive me if I did. I advanced on Wesley and he backed down the alley, matching me step for step.

"I'm stupid? I'm not the one who invited the Others to stay with us. That was you!" he accused me. "Persephone is pure evil. You brought this on us!"

My jaw twitched and my arm lifted until the gun was pointed at Wesley's chest. And then I remembered he was wearing a bullet proof vest so I lifted the gun until it was level with his forehead. "Persephone didn't betray us. You did."

"I'm trying to save us!" Wesley looked over his shoulder as if hoping for backup, which only incensed me more. I was his backup. I'd been his backup for years now. And this was how he repaid me. This was how he treated his friends...sacrificing us to get his revenge on Persephone. *Christ!* His brother was back at the ranch. Didn't that mean anything to him?

Don't squeeze the trigger. Don't.

"Sorry, man. Sadie's gone." Euri's voice sounded as choked up as I felt.

"I know," I managed to say.

"We should get the hell out of here while we still can," Euri warned.

"SUV's been compromised." I reached up and gripped the back of my neck, trying to decide whether I should leave Wesley or take him with us. He betrayed us, but leaving him behind would be a betrayal to Theo. If I left Wesley, he wouldn't survive. No matter what the Program promised him, they wouldn't let him live after this. "And we'll have to find Marty."

At that moment, a Sophisticate came hurtling around the corner behind Wesley, the barrel of a gun glinting in the pre-dawn light. Just as I lifted my weapon away from Wesley to fire, a dark streak came hissing through the air and struck the Sophisticate in the chest. The boy fell to the ground, a long blade embedded in his chest. I glanced up to see Marty leaning over the roof of the building.

I breathed a sigh of relief. Marty hadn't been captured. We still had a chance.

In the distance I could see a mass of people heading our way and I fired off a few warning shots toward the end of the alley to send them scattering back for cover. I unhooked the smoke grenade from my belt, pulled the pin, and Wesley ducked when I tossed it over his head. Within seconds, the space between the buildings filled with thick smoke. The Sophisticates on the other side began shouting, but none were brave enough to blindly run through the smoke and risk my aim. I yanked another smoke grenade from my belt and chucked it down the other side of the alley beyond Euri. We were now hidden between two walls of smoke, hopefully buying us enough time to escape.

Marty tossed a roll-up ladder over the edge of the building and the metal rungs snapped against the bricks as the ladder unfurled.

"Go," I told Euri. Gun shots rang out, pinging off the top of the building, scattering shards of brick when the Sophisticates on the other side of the smoke saw Marty above. Marty sent a flurry of blades raining down on the Sophisticates below to cover Euri's climb.

When Euri was over the edge, he pointed his gun at Wesley and I finally holstered my weapons and hurried up the side of the building.

A few seconds later, I leaned over the edge. "Come on," I told Wesley. "We don't have much time."

He shook his head. "They have our SUV. We don't have a chance of getting out of here."

"That's why we're following Plan B."

He looked over his shoulder where the smoke screen was starting to fade. "There is no Plan B."

"There's always a Plan B. You just didn't know about it."

Wesley didn't even have the guts to ask why. I almost wanted to tell him why there was a part of the plan he knew nothing about. But Sadie was dead, and it was all his fault. He didn't deserve to know.

"Let's go," I repeated. "Theo is expecting you to come back. We can't wait any longer." I heard the roar of helicopter blades behind me and felt the relief uncoil inside. I didn't know if it was luck or destiny that Jackson's route to class passed by the campus helipad, but I was grateful either way.

Wesley shook his head and slowly walked backwards. "I can't."

"Don't." I told him, gritting my teeth. "They'll kill you."

Wesley pressed his mouth in a tight line and then spun around and jogged down the alley, disappearing into the thick smoke. I watched the spot for a few more seconds to see if he changed his mind before I unhooked the ladder and threw it over the edge of the wall. The metal rungs and chain clattered to the ground. As I turned toward the helicopter, Marty stood up to follow me and then roared in pain, clutching his chest before falling to the ground. I ducked down behind the wall as bullets rained over my head, taking chunks out of the concrete.

I crawled over to Marty and pulled his hand away to see that a bullet had pierced his body armor. He was pulling in shallow, hurried breaths as he gritted his teeth in pain. I knew I shouldn't move him, but I had to. If I didn't, he'd die for sure. I slung his arm over my shoulders and dragged him over to the open door of the helicopter, apologizing through gritted teeth when he screamed out in pain. I propped him in the backseat and then climbed in next to him, shutting the door behind me.

"We have to go," I yelled to Euri. "Marty's been hit and Wesley took off."

"He's not coming." Euri stated Wesley's betrayal simply.

I shook my head once, sharply. I clenched my fist, fighting the urge to jump out of the seat and go after Wesley. That would be a suicide mission. And even if I caught up to him, I wasn't sure if I wanted to save him or kill him.

Euri grabbed a box off the seat next to him and handed it to me. "Toss this out the window."

"Black box?" I asked, opening the door so I could drop the metal box onto the concrete.

"Wouldn't be much of a Plan B if they just followed us would it?"

Marty groaned and I slammed the door shut again. "Time to go," I said, reaching over to fasten a lap belt over Marty's legs. "You really know how to fly this thing?" I asked, snapping the buckle shut.

Euri raised his eyebrows, twisting the grip between the front seats before pulling the handle up. "What? You don't?" His grin was more of a grimace and then he faced forward. The helicopter rose into the air and Marty's upper body jostled against the window. The helicopter rose over the building and with a few subtle movements of Euri's hands, we took off toward the sunrise. Below, I could see Sophisticates scrambling around in confusion. A few lifted weapons, but we were already moving too fast and they were unprepared. I searched for Wesley, but he was nowhere to be seen as we left Chicago and flew over Lake Michigan, the sun turning the water into a sheet of gold.

The leader in me, the part that had protected the Dozen for so long, hoped Wesley was okay. That he'd been able to make a clean getaway. The friend in me, the part that could still feel Sadie's blood on my fingers, was sick, wondering who else we would lose because of Wesley. But it was the last part of me that I was most afraid of, the soldier inside. Wesley had stupidly put all of us in danger—the Dozen, the Others, the Knights, and worst of all, Cleo. A soldier didn't care what happened to traitors.

Marty writhed in pain on the seat next to me and panic chased away my thoughts of Wesley. I needed to find out where he'd been injured. I pulled his flak jacket off and found that the front of his body was entirely soaked in blood. I lifted his shirt up and guessed from the location of the bullet wounds and his labored breathing that he'd gotten hit in the lung a few times. The flak jacket was no match for whatever the Sophisticates had been armed with. Forcing myself to be calm, I tried to remember all of the first aid measures that were drilled into my head over the years.

Stop the leak. Let him breathe. That was the first thing I needed to do. I rummaged around in the cock pit and my pockets for a credit card or some other piece of plastic. Something to create a seal over the holes in his chest. If I could keep him breathing, we could get him to medical help. The wounds were bad, but a good doctor could save Marty. I'd hold a whole hospital hostage if I had to make that happen.

Marty coughed, his breathing ragged. "I'm going to die," he managed to say.

I shook my head and when I couldn't find any suitable plastic, I grabbed his shirt and pressed it against the wound. "We'll get you help. Just stay strong. Keep breathing."

He shook his head. "If you take me to a hospital, you'll be caught. You can't sacrifice yourself for me. The others need you."

"Let me worry about that."

Marty grabbed my hand, trying to pull the fabric away from his chest. "It's too late for me." He struggled to take a breath. "Make my life worth something. Don't let my death hurt anyone else." His voice was quiet and weak. "Don't let the Program take any more of us," he begged. Marty's breathing stuttered, like it was caught on something.

"Find a hospital," I ordered Euri. He didn't even argue, he just tilted the helicopter away from our current course.

I grabbed my phone and opened a browser, searching for the nearest hospital. A sharp intake of breath by Marty and a subtle jerk of his body caught my attention. I looked over to see that his eyes were wide open, his arm draped over his chest, his mouth hanging open.

"Marty?" I tried to lift his arm, but it was stuck to his body. One of the thin black blades that he was able to throw from his skin was still attached to his arm and embedded deep into his chest. Right through his heart.

"Marty!" I yelled. My fingers fumbled against Marty's neck, confirming what I already knew. "He's gone," I choked out. He sacrificed himself so we wouldn't take him to a hospital.

Euri looked over his shoulder at me and if I'd had any doubts before about him, they evaporated when I recognized the apology in his gaze.

I slid my hand over Marty's eyes, closing them. "Continue on with Plan B," I told him. "We need to get out of the sky before they find us and shoot us out of it." The order was carved out of me like granite from the side of a mountain. Sadie and Marty. One left behind, one sacrificing himself, both dying under my watch.

It was all Wesley's fault. Wesley the traitor.

I considered that last part of me. The cold-hearted soldier. I hoped wherever Wesley was, he was suffering.

RUNE

⟋ 24 ⟍

NEW RECRUITS

Life was easier before I knew the truth. I never cared about my donors or felt any sort of loss over who they might have been. I never really cared about anyone else or felt the need for a family— to mean something to someone. Going to the Academy changed everything. A few months ago, I felt a vague sense of duty toward Euri, Persephone, Elysia, and the rest of the Others. But I knew if it came down to it, I'd choose myself over everyone else. I was that selfish.

And then there came the day when I didn't choose myself. I didn't help Delia attack the Hounds in the cells. I lied and told her I'd been given a counteragent. I didn't let Pirro kill Cleo at the Inner Harbor. I saved her life. I didn't just walk away from Euri, Persephone, and Elysia. I brought them with me to the ranch, even though I knew having Persephone with us might get me killed.

Life was easier before I knew what it was like to care. Quinnie, Cleo, Euri, Persephone, and Elysia. They all snagged a piece of my loyalty that I couldn't take back.

And now I had a brother. A big brother. Damn it.

I could feel things changing. I was changing. And what was even scarier...I wanted the change.

If I took a good look at myself, I had to admit that maybe I'd started changing when I met Quinnie. What started out as a few kisses in the shadows of the Academy transformed into a deeper understanding. We were two-of-a-kind. Deep down I knew that when the time came for the Others and Deviants to go their separate ways, that Quinnie and I would choose the same path. I couldn't explain how I knew that except to say that no matter how hard we both tried to act like this thing between us was nothing, I found more reasons to believe that it was something. We pretended that we could walk away, that our relationship was about convenience, but I saw the truth time and time again. We could try to pull away as much as we wanted, but we rebounded back to each other against our will.

I wouldn't call it love. I didn't even know what love was; I had never experienced it. But the draw to Quinnie was more than just physical. Maybe if Wesley hadn't skulked around like some sort of conspiracy hunter intent on thwarting everyone's romantic lives, I might have figured out what that draw was before the mission to Headquarters started.

And now I was in the Freedom Tunnel with Program rebels, wondering about Quinnie and trying to reconcile the fact that Ozzy, and by default, Euri were truly my brothers. I never needed a family. A family would only be a burden. No, I definitely didn't need it.

But maybe I wanted it.

"You're freaked out, aren't you?" Quinnie sat down next to me, setting her lunch on the table and looking over at the food that I hadn't bothered to start eating yet.

"I'm still trying to decide how I feel." I stabbed at the pasta with my fork, realizing I was really hungry after our adventure earlier in the morning. We approached a few Mandates that Cleo hand-picked from her Reclamation list. So far, so good. They were not only willing to listen, they were eager to join us. Ozzy suggested that the Mandates would be an easier sell against the Program than the Vanguards, and he was right. The Mandates were treated as if they were expendable and they were tired of it. Too many of them had lost friends to anti-terrorist missions.

"It doesn't change anything," Quinnie said. "Ozzy is your brother, but that doesn't mean you have to automatically give him your loyalty. You don't have to make yourself any promises right now."

"I know that—"

"That being said," Quinnie interrupted, pointing her fork at me, "you couldn't choose anyone better to give your loyalty to." When I gave her an incredulous look, she rolled her eyes. "I'm serious. I may act like a shallow bitch, I may even *be* a shallow bitch, but I know our chance of success is good with Ozzy."

"How do you know that?"

She shrugged and took a bite of lunch without looking at me. After chewing and swallowing she said, "Because he's known me my whole life and no matter how horrible I am, he's never abandoned me."

I was about to explain to her that their lifelong relationship had a lot to do with his commitment to her, but Sterling and Arabella sat down opposite us. Dexter wasn't far behind and he set down a large canvas bag as he took a seat across from us.

Arabella crossed her arms on the table. Her face, although dry, was splotchy as if she'd been crying. Sterling looked absolutely heartbroken. "I've got bad news," she said in a low voice. "Ozzy's mission in Chicago went badly."

Quinnie's fork clattered to the table. "What? Is he okay?"

"He's fine." She shot me a look and I realized I could let loose the breath I was holding. I told myself I was only worried because of how important his mission was to the rest of our goals. Not because of any recent news. Definitely not.

"It was Wesley," Dexter said. His voice cracked and he reached up to pinch the bridge of his nose with his finger and thumb. "He betrayed them."

Quinnie snorted. "Your information must be wrong. Wesley? He would never."

Arabella bit the inside of her lip and struggled to hold back her tears. "We just spoke to Cleo. Ozzy contacted her after he and Euri safely made it out of Chicago. Wesley told the Program everything. He betrayed their mission."

"What about Sadie and Marty?" I looked between Sterling, Arabella, and Dexter.

Arabella shook her head and looked down at the table as Dexter cleared his throat. "Sadie and Marty didn't make it," he finally said. "Killed in crossfire by Sophisticates who were tipped off by Wesley."

I ground my teeth together, causing my jaw to pop. "And Wesley?"

Sterling and Dexter shared a look. "Even after what he did, Ozzy gave him the chance to come with them." Sterling uncrossed his arms and leaned forward on the table, his body slumping in defeat. "Wesley chose the Program."

The silence that fell over us was almost deafening. Finally I asked, "Do we know how much Wesley told the Program?"

Dexter rubbed his forearm. "We assume that everything was compromised. Ozzy's mission and ours. Ozzy thinks Wes even told them about the ranch."

The ranch? How could that be true? Theo was back at the ranch. Why would Wesley betray his brother?

"How did Ozzy and Euri manage to get away?" Quinnie asked, her words broken. I'd never seen her so vulnerable before. I had the urge to reach out to comfort her, but I knew her well enough to know it wouldn't be welcome.

Arabella finally looked up from the table, her eyes welling with tears as they met Quinnie's. "Ozzy knew that if Jackson turned them in, they'd have a hard time getting out of the university undetected since Chicago is still pretty desolate. He had a backup escape plan. Luckily, one he didn't share with Wesley. Maybe he knew something wasn't quite right with him." She looked back down at the table. "I just...I just can't believe Marty and Sadie are gone. Forever."

Even though Euri and Ozzy had made it out alive, I couldn't help feeling some of the blame for Sadie's and Marty's deaths. I followed Delia's orders to get taken to the Academy, never questioning why I didn't just turn against her. Everything since then was a result of my silence. I never warned anyone at the Academy about my connection to Delia or what her plan was. I could have saved so many lives. Seventeen years is a long time to live under certain assumptions. Funny how life-long beliefs and loyalties can come crashing to the ground in such a short amount of time. The Academy changed me. I learned that everything I'd been taught, everything I believed, had been forced on me by Delia. The Academy gave me the chance to be different, and in the end, I embraced that opportunity.

But even so, so many Hounds died in that attack. So many Others were dead. The Deviants were on the run for their lives and now Marty and Sadie were gone, too.

"I'm sorry, Arabella. I didn't realize you were so close to them," I said.

Her eyes flashed to mine, anger igniting in her gaze. "I don't have to be close to someone to mourn them. They didn't deserve to be slaughtered like that. None of us deserve that! I'm tired of being treated as if we're nothing but garbage that the Program can toss aside when they're done with it. Our lives mean nothing to them. They have to pay for what they've done to us."

We sat in silence for a few minutes, everyone avoiding eye contact.

"So what do we do now?" I asked. "If Wesley told them everything, it won't be long before the Program comes looking for us."

Sterling shook his head. "Wesley didn't know about the Freedom Tunnel. We didn't even know about it when we came up here, remember? He just knows we were sent to rescue the Homework Harpies and get intel on Baker and Steel. We can assume he told them that much, but we still need to continue on with the original plan. It might be harder for us to get close to Baker and Steel now, but we've made contact with the Mandates and some of the Hounds. We can still carry out our mission."

"How can you be sure those Mandates won't just turn us in or set a trap for us?" I countered.

Sterling gave a bitter laugh. "I can't be sure of anything. I was sure Wesley was trustworthy and look how that turned out." He laced his fingers together in front of him and tilted his head as he held my gaze. "But I can tell you this, the Mandates are motivated to change things. They want freedom as badly as we do."

"How do you know?"

"Remember that theory Cleo proposed about disabling the tracking tattoo through a computer virus?" Sterling gathered strength as he continued talking.

I nodded.

"There's a squadron," he explained, "an entire squadron, who is willing to let her test that theory on them."

I found it hard to believe that Mandates would be so trusting. "They're willing to take a risk like that? Did you tell them you don't know if they'd even survive?"

Dexter leaned forward and said in a low voice, "They're not only willing to risk it, they're eager. These are Mandates. The Program sends them into battle as if they're nothing more than pieces on a chess board. They're not treated like humans, they're treated like tools. To them, the possibility of freedom is worth any risk that comes with it."

"Okay," I said. I still wasn't convinced, but for the sake of argument, I asked, "Cleo tests the theory and then what? We sneak them out through the Freedom Tunnel? We can't risk Josie's people like that. There are children here."

"We're not going to sneak them out. Not right away. Why not have more invisible soldiers on our side inside the city walls?" Sterling rubbed the bottom of his chin with his hand and took a deep breath before speaking. "Even without Wesley's betrayal, the Program knew we would come to rescue the Homework Harpies. That's why they televised their capture in the first place. They were luring us here. The good news is, we just learned that the Program is planning to move the Harpies to a different location. This can work to our advantage."

"I don't see how that helps us," Quinnie said. "It took us two days to find out where the Harpies were being kept in the first place. By the time we figure out where they've been moved, it will be near impossible to get them out since the Program now knows we're here. Wesley destroyed any element of surprise we might have had." She picked up her napkin and folded it, her hands leaving charred fingerprints where her hands sparked against the thin paper.

"That's the good part, though. The squad who offered to have their tattoos disabled is the same one that will be responsible for the Harpies' transfer."

I narrowed my eyes. "If Baker and Steel trust them enough to put them in charge of the transfer, what makes you think we can trust them?"

"Because," Sterling said. "They're the ones who helped me escape Headquarters and get into hiding before. The Hound who took the fall for my escape was punished and she's being held with the Harpies. Her squad wants us to help get her to freedom, too."

Quinnie huffed out a laugh. "This sounds...complicated. There are so many ways this could go wrong. First of all, we don't know if Cleo's virus will even work. She might end up killing our so-called allies. Not to mention that once an entire squad blips off the radar, the Program will know exactly where to start looking for us. They'll know we'll be where the Harpies are."

"That's why we have these." Dexter took a small bag out of the duffel by his feet and set it on the table between us.

"What are those?" I leaned forward to look at the bag to find it was full of tiny metal squares that were no bigger than a pencil point.

"The new squadron." Sterling grinned for the first time. "Josie's team nicked these trackers a while ago and we've already forwarded the IDs to Cleo to have her recode them to replace our test squadron. She'll activate these when the time is right—at the same time our test squadron goes missing."

"That's actually...clever." Quinnie pursed her lips together. "But where are you planning to put them? They won't work if they're not hooked into the bio-electricity of a body. Right?"

There was a clank on the table between me and Quinnie and I looked over to see a cage full of large, New York City sewer rats. Josie was standing behind me, her hand resting on top of the cage. "Meet Squadron 54, newest recruits of the Program."

CLEO

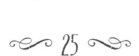

GOING DOWN IN FLAMES

"We don't have much time, Cleo. Grab what you can." Gina was oddly calm considering she was being forced to leave her home. The Knights gave us sanctuary, and in return, Wesley stole their safety. Gina and Daniel should be raging over the unfairness of it, but instead they stayed composed as they directed us on what things we absolutely needed to take with us. I had a feeling the worry that was carved into Gina's expression wasn't for herself. It was for Arabella.

Theo was the person I was most worried about, though. Homes and belongings could be replaced. Brothers? Not so much. He hadn't said a word since Ozzy's phone call. He followed Gina's orders and carried boxes out to the waiting vehicles, but he moved as if he were numb. Empty. Absent. The loud boisterous guy I knew was gone and in his place was a shell of the boy who once believed in me enough to risk his own safety to save me from punishment in the Academy's torture cells.

I carried the last box of computer equipment to the car and slid it into the trunk. Gina pulled the back door of the house closed behind her and quickly crossed the yard before climbing into the front seat. We needed to be on the road soon. The Program would no doubt come looking for us and we had to be long gone by the time they showed up. We were already cutting it too close by attempting to salvage anything from the house at all.

"Go ahead," Daniel said, ushering us toward the vehicles. "Hop in so we can be on our way." His gaze swept over the property in a silent farewell. I expected to see pain and regret, but it was almost as if he expected this day to eventually come. He was resigned.

Lawless and Zelda were already in the front seat of one of the vehicles and Cassie, Theo, and Elysia climbed in the back seat. That left me, Eva, and Persephone to ride with the Knights. I looked around, expecting to find Persephone lounging in one of the Adirondack chairs alongside the roller derby track. I walked over to Elysia's window and peeked inside.

"Have you see Persephone? We have to go." Annoyance flared along my already tense nerves.

Elysia shoved a folded piece of paper through the open window. "As soon as you got Ozzy's message, she left. She told me to give you this when we were ready to leave."

What the hell? I snatched the paper and unfolded it as Daniel came beside me to read over my shoulder.

C- You need a diversion. That's what I'm good at. Don't let it go to waste. Oh, and I'm not doing this for you. I'm doing it for Rune. -P

I flipped the paper over only to find that it was blank on the other side. "What does this mean?" I asked Elysia.

She shrugged. "She's creating a distraction so we can get to safety."

"That doesn't sound like something Persephone would do. What—" There was a loud booming sound and I swore I felt the ground shake beneath my feet. Off in the distance, birds took flight out of the trees as the sunrise seemed to tremble.

"She knows you're the best hope for the mission's success. Without you, everyone would be going into battle blind." Elysia turned to face straight ahead. "We should go. Persephone is great at creating chaos, but I don't know how long she'll last on her own. Like she said, don't let her sacrifice go to waste."

My stomach clenched and I refused to believe it was guilt.

"You just let her go alone?" The accusation slipped out before I could consider what it meant that I felt the need to say it.

Elysia refused to look at me. "I never gave you the impression I was a hero, why are you surprised?"

I wasn't. Elysia was confident and violent when she'd been with Delia because she had power. But once she was faced with her own weaknesses, she'd become a coward.

"Come on," Daniel said, grabbing my arm and pulling me away before I could think of a retort.

I let my eyes stay on Elysia, wondering how she could let Persephone go off alone. She never met my gaze. I got in the backseat of Daniel's car with Eva and he shoved the key into the ignition, quickly changing the radio station to a local channel when the engine roared to life.

"...interruption. We don't have any details, but authorities are asking that you stay in your homes and that you avoid the Chesa-peake City area," the deejay said. "All traffic should detour to other bridges along the canal until further notice."

Daniel put the car in drive, following Lawless' vehicle as he sped down the pothole-riddled dirt driveway. I held onto the door handle as I bounced back and forth, a million worries jostling around in my head. I wondered if Euri and Ozzy were still safe. I was heartbroken for what happened to Marty and Sadie. I worried about Sterling and Arabella and how Wesley's betrayal would affect their mission and safety. Lastly, a minuscule part of me was con-cerned for Persephone and I didn't know why. She'd done horrible things to me and those I cared about. But in the back of my mind, I remembered Quinnie trusting me with her secrets and admitting that she didn't want to be anything like her father. If Quinnie could change, why not Persephone? Maybe everyone was capable of re-demption if given the chance. Maybe even the girl who tried to de-stroy me.

Seriously? Was I actually worried about Persephone?

I rubbed my forehead as if I could wipe away my fears and I tried to focus on the radio broadcast.

"We're getting reports that several nearby buildings are on fire," the deejay continued, "and that the scene of downtown Chesa-peake City resembles that of the Inner Harbor just a few months ago. I repeat, stay away from the area until authorities have it se-cured."

Daniel turned on the main road, heading the opposite direction of Lawless.

"Aren't we going to the same place?" I asked him, turning in my seat to watch the other vehicle disappear down the road.

"Eventually." He glanced up into the rearview mirror to meet my eyes. "I figured we might swing by and pick up your sister before the Program does." Daniel's jaw was clenched tightly.

Sister.

I leaned forward in my seat until I could touch his shoulder. "That's not necessary. It's too dangerous for you and Gina. Arabella would never forgive me if I let anything happen to you. This was never part of any plan. Persephone made her choice."

Gina reached over and placed her hand over mine. "And we'd never forgive ourselves if we let anything happen to any of you when we had it within our power to help. Chesapeake City isn't that far away. Hopefully we can get there before the Program does. We'll convince Persephone to come with us."

I sat back in my seat, fingers drumming across the dark leather while I leaned to the side to peer out of the window.

The entrance to the bridge over the canal was blocked, traffic backed up down the road as people got out of their cars and milled around. I saw the dark smoke spiraling into the sky before I saw the source of it. From the heavy black cloud hanging above in the early morning light, it looked like Persephone had set the entire town on fire. Despite the warnings on the radio, Daniel drove along the side of the road and down into the center of town, passing vehicles that were crowding the road on their way out. Turning onto the small street that ran alongside the canal, I finally got a view of Persephone's diversion. Across the water and underneath the bridge that spanned the canal, there was a huge wall of fire. Persephone was standing at the end of a long pier, her arms held straight out to the side where balls of blue flame hovered above her palms.

Daniel pulled off into the grass and I got out of the car, hurrying to the edge of the water where others were gathered to watch. People stood around with coffees in their hands, rubbing their eyes as if Persephone's pyrotechnics were merely an interesting way to help them start their day. They had no idea she was death incarnate, that she literally held their futures in the palms of her hands. She was across the water, but that meant nothing if she decided to target this side of the canal.

Behind her, two buildings with signs that said "Schaefers" were ablaze. Between them, flames licked up the skeleton of a large gazebo making it look like an enormous torch. All along the pier, boats were on fire, bobbing on the water and sending black tendrils of smoke into the sky. The smell of burning fiberglass hung heavy in the air. All the fire was reflected in the water below and Persephone stood in the middle, the spark in the middle of a firestorm. She looked up at the bridge and although she was too far away for me to see her expression, I knew her smile was wicked when she flicked her arm upward. A ball of fire screamed into the underside of the bridge and the explosion that followed felt as if it had rocked the earth off course. Even though I was far enough away from the danger, I instinctively ducked as jagged pieces of metal swung from the bridge, falling into the canal below and throwing the water into a roiling mass of pitching and hissing fire.

Worried gasps and screams echoed around us as people backed away, but kept watching. Like an accident on the side of the road, they just couldn't turn away no matter how horrendous.

"She's bringing down the bridge," I muttered. I stepped forward, unsure whether I planned to stop her or help her.

Daniel grabbed my arm. "We'll have no way to get to her if she takes it down." He looked around and his gaze fixed on a small marina down the road. "Unless I steal a boat."

It was my turn to grab his arm. "She'd probably just throw fire at you too."

The sound of a helicopter cresting over the trees on the other side of the water caught my attention just as an army of vehicles surrounded the burning buildings behind Persephone. I stood helpless, the water between us like an endless chasm. I'd never be able to get across to help her in time. As if aware I was nearby, Persephone's head turned toward where Daniel and I stood. She was too far away to know for sure if she was looking at us, but I could feel her gaze and somehow I knew she could see us. Looking away, she flung both arms upward again and when her fire slammed into the bridge, the force of her power twisted the metal, crushing it as if her fireballs were a giant fist.

The crowd around us screamed, falling over each other, trying to get away as the middle of the arched bridge swayed and then crumbled in slow motion into the water below. Daniel threw his arm over my head, curling me into his body as we stumbled to the ground, the bridge's collapse causing tremors that knocked our feet out from under us. I immediately pushed myself up to look back across the canal. I was just in time to see Persephone standing alone on the pier, watching me as the water swelled up in a tidal wave and swallowed her whole.

OZZY

❧ 26 ❧

BLAME GAME

A thick blanket of fog rolled in over the water as Euri flew over Lake Michigan. The heavy mist swallowed everything in its path and soon the city faded away behind us. The farther we got away from Chicago, the more numb I felt. Hidden in the curtain of the low hanging clouds, Euri turned us north before circling back around to the west in hopes of confusing anyone who might have been trying to follow us. The Program would follow eventually, but at least the poor visibility would slow them down, especially without the black box to track us.

As we crossed back over land and continued west, the fog slowly faded away until we were back into clear air. The miles disappeared beneath us in a blur of greens and browns as the silhouettes of closely spaced buildings gave way to fields, forests, and rivers. I lost track of time. I imagined Sadie's last moments over and over again, wondering what I could have done to make things end differently. I couldn't even look at the seat next to me. I couldn't stop blaming myself.

I chose Wesley to come with us. I was in charge of the mission. The fact that he even had the opportunity to betray us fell on me. Rune's warning about Wesley acting oddly back at the ranch had been enough to convince me that I needed to have back up escape plans, but honestly, I never thought I'd have to use any of them because of Wesley. I figured Persephone would find some way to ruin our plan, or maybe the Vanguards wouldn't be willing to listen. But Wesley?

My eyes were drawn to Marty. He looked like he was asleep and I could almost convince myself that the whole thing never happened.

Forty minutes later, Euri flew low over a tree line, finally landing the helicopter in an open area that was close to the edge of a forest. He turned off the engine and the blades continued to spin as he opened the door and hopped out. My gaze was fixed on Marty.

"I'm sorry. We don't have time to bury him." Euri leaned on the edge of the seat and gave me a determined look. "The fog helped, but it still won't be long."

I nodded and then opened my door, jumping out onto the long grass. "Let's go," I said without looking back. If I looked back, the guilt would be too much. Not only did I fail to keep Marty safe, I couldn't even give him a proper burial. I was almost ashamed that I had to put my own safety first. But if I didn't, I had no hope of helping the rest of the Deviants. They were still depending on us to make it back safely.

Euri turned and jogged along the edge of the trees, heading east, and I followed behind him. We didn't try to hide our tracks and we made sure to leave our scent stamped all over the place.

After a mile or so, we headed deeper into the woods and left our jackets before doubling back toward where we started. I couldn't bear to look at the helicopter or the body inside as we passed. I kept my eyes trained on Euri as he made his way down toward the river, careful to step on rocks so as not to bend a single blade of grass.

Somewhere in the distance I could smell a campfire and I remembered Euri said that he was setting us down in Starved Rock State Park because it was close to our destination and it would be easier for us to move undetected. Hidden in the state park, the Program wouldn't be able to search for us from the air and we could disappear into the woods like phantoms.

Together, we jumped into the edge of the river, splashing our way into deeper water. Frigid fingers of liquid circled my calves and dipped into the tops of my boots. I fought the urge to head back to shore and leaned over to run my hands through the water. I was still covered with Sadie and Marty's blood and I quickly rubbed my fingers together, desperate to get them clean. Blood was caked under my fingernails. Every line in my skin was stained with red. I scrubbed my hands until the water all around me was tinged in pink.

Euri grabbed my elbow, pulling me up and forward. "Later. We don't have time."

I looked down at my hands, covered in drips of pink and red and I just wanted to be clean. But he was right. Every second counted. Besides, I couldn't imagine I'd ever get my hands clean enough again. I wiped my palms on my pants and then hurried to follow Euri through the icy current. My breath cleaved in and out of me as we trudged on. I was grateful for the cold and how it made it harder to think about anything else. Or anyone else.

We followed the river for a while and when Euri saw some fisherman in the distance, he motioned toward the woods on our left and climbed back onto dry land so they wouldn't see us. Without second guessing his direction, he picked his way through the woods until we were on a hiking trail. It was still early in the morning, but I knew we weren't alone in these woods. We needed to not be seen. Whenever our sensitive hearing picked up the sounds of fellow hikers, we strayed off the path to make ourselves invisible. We passed impressive canyons of rock with waterfalls spilling over their edges and I added another place to my list of things I hoped to one day show Cleo.

I would show her. I wasn't going to let Wesley's betrayal be the end of our future.

"In the dead of winter, the falls freeze over," Euri said, finally breaking the silence. "Beautiful walls of ice." He gestured to the waterfall.

We were crossing through a rocky canyon that was shaped like a huge stone bowl. Water cascaded over the top in a glassy sheet before dropping into a clear basin at the bottom. It might not be cold enough for the water to freeze right now, but winter still had a grip on this place and the canyon felt like an ice box. I wanted to ask Euri why he was familiar with this area and how long it had been since he'd last been here. But I couldn't bring myself to say anything. I hadn't said anything since I'd abandoned Marty. I didn't want to think about Euri's past with Delia. There were too many terrible thoughts already crowding their way into my head.

Overhead, the familiar thudding of helicopter blades echoed far above the tree tops and Euri looked at me and grinned when we heard them heading in the direction we'd come from.

"By the time they find our real trail, we'll be halfway to New York." He beckoned with his hand and we climbed out of the gorge and back under the canopy of trees.

Our hike was long and tedious, my wet socks rubbing blisters on every inch of my feet. The discomfort was something I could focus on. The pain actually felt good. After passing through the canyon with the waterfall, we didn't speak anymore. There was nothing to say. It was useless to worry about the rest of the Deviants and Others until we could talk to them and get facts, to find out just how much damage Wesley had done. Our only goal at the moment was to get back on the road and join our friends. Until that happened, there was no use talking about new plans.

"Almost there." Euri's words were the first ones that had been spoken in a long time. The sun was high in the sky so I knew we'd been hiking for a few hours.

He turned off the main trail and we crashed through untamed underbrush for another twenty minutes. Eventually, the woods started to thin and through the trees I could see a house. It was run down and looked almost abandoned, the lawn and gardens overgrown and neglected. We crossed the yard and walked up the steps of the porch that wrapped around from the back of the house to the front. Cobwebs hung from the corners of the roof and there was a thick carpet of damp leaves scattered over the wooden boards. Despite the dilapidated appearance of the house, there was a digital keypad on the back door. Euri punched in a series of numbers before turning the handle and pushing the door open.

"Wow. It still works." He walked inside, his gun drawn as he kept his back against the wall. I followed, closing the door behind me once we were both inside. The place looked nothing like I expected. Half the first floor was a kitchen, hosting a long table with a dozen chairs around it. The only other room on the first floor was in the front part of the house. Blinds were closed across the windows and from what I could see, the room looked like a classroom. A video screen filled one wall and desks were spread out across the floor facing the screen. Euri ran his hand along the back of one of the chairs, disturbing the thick layer of dust.

"Doesn't look like anyone has been here since we left." He rubbed his hands together, cleaning off the dirt.

"What is this place?"

"We had houses like this near a few of the cities where universities were located. I haven't been in this one in about three years, but when we lived here, we spent a lot of time training out in Starved Rock. I know those trails like the back of my hand." He leaned against the edge of one of the desks, glancing around the room with meaningful looks, as if cataloguing all the old memories it held.

"You lived here? You and the Others?" I didn't know much about the lives of the Others before the last few months. I didn't talk about my past and I didn't ask about theirs.

"We trained here." Euri cut his gaze away from the desk and looked at me. "Training is all we knew. Looking back, I wouldn't call anything we did living. But back then, we didn't know any different. Come on," he said, pushing away from the desk and leading me to a set of stairs that led down into what I assumed was a basement. "I'm sure we can find a change of clothes somewhere."

"If the Program investigated Delia, does that mean they know about this place?"

He shrugged. "This house wasn't in her name. None of the places were. Janus Malleville owned The Rink, and this place was owned by someone else. She was careful to keep her associations hidden. Maybe if they looked hard enough they'd find it, but I think if they knew about it, they would have already raided it."

At the bottom of the stairs, there was another door where Euri typed in a code. Once we were through the door, he flipped on a light to reveal a large gym filled with weights, targets, training mats, and an entire wall of cabinets. That's where Euri headed.

"How did she keep you hidden for so long?" I asked.

"She had a lot of money. You know how the Program paid off parents who sacrificed their children to be Sophisticates?"

"Of course, everyone knows that."

"Well, Delia and Twyla were both given to the Program for experimentation and their parents got double the payout." As we crossed the room, Euri reached out to touch things—well-worn targets, practice dummies, climbing ropes—and I wondered if this room gave him good memories or bad ones. "When the experiments went wrong," he continued, "Delia and Twyla were returned to their family with even more money because of the side effects they experienced. They weren't disabled, just...affected."

He stopped to pick up an old boxing glove that was laying on the ground. Like the rest of the house, it was covered in dust.

"That's why Professor Younglove's skin was so dry and brittle," I said. I knew her condition was from Program experiments. I'd heard rumors, I just didn't know the entire truth.

Euri nodded. "She was one of the experiments prior to the Deviant Dozen. I guess you could say she was Cleo's predecessor. Twyla was meant to be a weapon of fire." He tossed the glove to the corner of the room and headed for the cabinets.

"And Delia?"

"Cassie is everything they hoped Delia would be. That's why she was so obsessed with getting Cassie after Sphynx died." He took a deep breath and swallowed. He was quiet for a moment.

No one had talked about Sphynx or any of the Others who'd been lost at the Inner Harbor. Euri, Rune, Elysia, and Persephone had been with us for months at the ranch, but their lives with Delia were still a huge mystery. One I wasn't sure I wanted to unearth.

"Anyway," Euri finally said, "Twyla chose to work for the Program and Delia stayed with her parents until they died and she inherited their money. Blood money she used to call it."

"Died?"

Euri rubbed the back of his neck. "She never kept it a secret that she killed them. At least from us. She made it look like an accident, but she drilled it into our heads that those who experimented on us and then just tried to throw us away should pay. She wanted revenge on everyone who had done her wrong, so she started with her parents."

"And you were her method to get revenge on everyone else she hated."

Euri fumbled with the keypad on the outside of the cabinet. "I agreed with her back then." He shrugged. "But I see things differently now. You have to understand that we only ever had Delia's side of the story. Her rage. Her bitterness. Her theories. We were prisoners under her, we just didn't know it. Over the last few months I've realized that it's no excuse for what we willingly did for her, but it's the truth." He finally got the lock undone and threw open the cabinet doors. The shelves were filled with weapons, clothes, and other gear.

"Take whatever you want," Euri said, motioning to the shelves. "I want to be on the road in ten minutes."

"Sounds good to me." I reached for some clothes and the biggest damn gun I could find.

***

"You've got to be kidding me." I stared at the tiny truck that Euri was currently stuffing gear into. It was an equal amount of blue paint and rust, and had to be nearly four times as old as I was. "There's no way this thing is going to run. And even if it did, it'll never get us to New York. We'll end up pushing it there. I think this piece of crap has been sitting in this garage since the house was originally built."

"Glad to see you're feeling a little better now that you have some clean clothes on," Euri replied, folding himself into the driver's seat. "Get in. I'm driving first."

I was surprised when I opened the passenger door and it didn't immediately fall off the hinges. I was even more surprised when Euri managed to get the truck started. The engine sputtered for a few seconds before rolling into a consistent growl. Euri looked over at me. "Buckle up. We've got a long drive ahead of us."

Fourteen hours. Fourteen hours until New York. I pulled out my phone, but it was dead, the charger for it still sitting in the SUV that we'd left back in Chicago. I hadn't talked to anyone since right after we left Chicago. A quick warning to Cleo and the bad news about Sadie and Marty were all I had time for. I had to hope that Cleo and everyone else on the ranch had gotten away safely. I couldn't bear to think otherwise.

I switched the radio on as Euri backed out of the garage. The house was set back down a long driveway and the road he turned onto was pretty deserted, too. We weren't too far from the state park. Chances were we'd be driving along a lot of desolate roads. Leaning my head back against the seats to rest, I realized I couldn't remember the last time I'd slept. I think it was back in Akron. And even what little sleep I did get hadn't been good.

We travelled for a few minutes, the rough dirt roads finally giving way to smooth pavement.

I'd see Cleo again soon. I had to. Fourteen hours. If we were lucky. If she'd been lucky. I had to believe that they'd gotten away before the Program showed up.

"Shit," Euri muttered, swerving so abruptly I hit my head on the window. My eyes flew open as I reached to my hip for my gun. Euri pulled into a gas station and came to a stop next to one of the pumps.

"We need gas already? The tank was half full wasn't it?" I leaned over to look at the fuel level. Yup. Still half full. "I thought you wanted to get out of town as quickly as possible?"

"I do," Euri growled, pulling his ball cap further over his head and sliding on a pair of sunglasses. "I couldn't very well pull a U-turn in front of that check point."

I followed where his finger pointed to see the flashing lights of police cars blocking the road ahead.

"A wild guess tells me that's not a sobriety check point." I looked at the other figures standing with the officers who were checking the vehicles going by and noticed the guns slung across their chests. "Hounds," I pointed out. "The ones with the guns. Probably sent from Headquarters. They don't give just any Mandates weapons like that. Those are trackers."

"Shit." Euri slammed the palm of his hand against the steering wheel. "We're going to have to take the long way out of the city." He looked over his shoulder as if he could see the path we'd need to take and then faced forward again. He rubbed his chin with his finger as he stared at the wall of law enforcement vehicles and armed Hounds. We watched as the next car on its way out of town was stopped and thoroughly inspected.

I reached for the handle and opened my door. "I'll run in and get some food and pay for gas. When I get back, we'll just head west. They're expecting us to go east. They can't block every single road out of the state."

With a nod, Euri turned toward me. "I know some good back roads we can take." He got out to pump gas while I went in to pay for it.

I kept my head down as I quickly made my way through the store, yanking things off the shelves. I dumped the armful of food on the counter along with a six-pack of water. I stared at the bag of caramel corn mixed with cheese corn. Half the snack aisle had been filled with different types of popcorn and I grabbed a bag at random. Now that it was on the counter, I considered exchanging it.

"This stuff is so good," the cashier said, grabbing the bag and ringing it up. She snapped her gum and winked at me, her hoop earrings swinging wildly as she reached for each item and put them in the plastic bag. When I didn't answer, she stared at me with raised eyebrows and I looked down, pulling my hat lower before reaching in my pocket for money.

Shit. Last thing I needed was a chatty cashier remembering my face. "Really?" I asked. "I've never tried it." I handed her a wad of cash, avoiding her gaze. "Can you put twenty on pump three?"

"Sure thing, sugar." She reached out to touch my arm and snapped her gum again. "And that popcorn? Oh honey, it tastes so good you'll think you died and kissed an angel itself."

"Right, thanks." I grabbed the bags of groceries and gave her a nod of my head without looking at her straight on.

I pushed out the door and hadn't gone ten feet before I felt something hard shoved in my back.

"Long time no see, huh, cheesedick? I thought you sounded familiar in there. Can't believe they sent me on this wild goose chase and you were stupid enough to fall in my lap."

My back stiffened as my entire body went on high alert.

Jerry. Fucking Jerry. Of all the Mandates sent to search for us, I had to accidentally cross paths with the one who would recognize me no matter how good my disguise was. Come to think of it, if the Program had any sense at all, they would have sent every single Hound I ever worked with to come look for me. Civilians might be fooled by a haircut and dye, but not the men and women that I spent years working alongside. I cast a quick glance at the roadblock, wondering how many of the Hounds were ones who had been sent on missions with me. The only saving grace in this situation was that it was Jerry, and not someone more capable, who found me.

I put my hands out to the side in surrender, the plastic bag dangling from my fingers. "How did you find me?" I forced worry into my voice, knowing that Jerry loved the power he currently held over me and that it would make him careless.

"You're not as slick as you think you are. We found your helicopter."

No shit, Sherlock. It's not like we could hide it under a pile of leaves. Instead I said, "I'll make you a deal. You let me go, pretend you never saw me, and I'll make it worth your while."

He chuckled. "This is already worth my while." He pressed the gun into my spine. "Do you have any idea the kind of reward that's out for you? Dead or alive. It makes no difference."

It was my turn to laugh. "You don't think the Program is going to pay you a reward do you? That reward is meant for civilians, not Sophisticates."

The gun wasn't pressing so hard against my back anymore. "Of course they will." His words held no conviction because he knew I was right. Finding me was his job. There would be no reward, probably not even a pat on the back.

"Look, Jerry. The only thing they'll give you for my capture is even more responsibility. They'll see you as a success and send you out on more dangerous missions. Is that what you want? You can say goodbye to that cushy gate duty job. You'll be waist-deep in enemy territory by next week. But if you agree to let me go, I can pay you."

His laugh was bitter. "Pay me? How? Where did you get money? You've been running from the Program for months."

I nodded my head toward an expensive luxury car in the parking lot of the restaurant next door. It was sleek and black and just the lie I needed. "Same place I got the car. I stole it."

Jerry hesitated for a few seconds, but then he pushed me toward the car, just like I knew he would. Greed was so easy to control. He grabbed onto my jacket as we walked forward, keeping the gun pressed into me. I dropped my arms to my sides as I walked and Jerry didn't seem to notice when my hand slid into my jacket.

The sound of a stuttering engine sidling up next to us was followed by, "Hey, can you give me some directions?"

Jerry had barely turned before my knife found his heart. Perfect aim and the force of years of hatred with a twist of grief. Within seconds, Euri was out of the truck, supporting Jerry on the other side as we dragged him behind the gas station. We let go of him and he collapsed against the wall next to the dumpster, shock still on his face. His hands weakly grasped at the hilt of the blade still protruding from his chest. He didn't have much longer. Maybe seconds.

I looked at Euri. "Take care of the security footage. I'll take care of him."

Euri nodded and then pulled on the door leading into the back of the building, his eyebrows lifting in surprise when it opened easily. He slipped inside and I turned to face my childhood bully. Jerry's mouth hung open and his eyes stared blankly toward the car that was his undoing. After so many years of putting up with his shit, I'd imagined his death more times than I could count. Only now that he was dead, I didn't feel any sense of justice. All I could think about was that we didn't have long before his tracking device started to fade off the grid and the Program sent someone looking for him. And that was assuming they weren't already looking for him. How long had he been gone from his post already?

I moved him to the other side of the dumpster and leaned him against the corner. I didn't even consider taking the knife with me. I left it embedded in his chest, a message to the Program. They took some of ours? I'd take ten times as many of theirs if they kept sending them. I was covering Jerry with broken down cardboard boxes when Euri emerged from the back door again. He handed me a pack of baby wipes and hand sanitizer.

"Destroyed the footage. It's like we were never even here.

You've got two minutes to clean up," he said.

I lifted my hands to see they were sticky with blood. Sadie, Marty, Jerry...my hands might never be clean again.

RUNE

～ 27 ～

BAD BEHAVIOR

Rats bite. Although, I guess I would too if someone tried to put one of those trackers in me. Josie asked me to get the first rat out of the cage and the damn thing decided to gnaw on my hand. It took all of my willpower not to air blast it across the room. Considering the rats were caught down here in the tunnels and had probably survived through the *Wormwood* poisoning, I'd be lucky if the bite didn't turn me into some sort of radioactive mutant. I was already deadly enough. I didn't need spiderwebs shooting out of my ass or anything...or any other mutant diseases.

I ran my finger over the thick dressing that Josie put on my bite mark, and watched as Sterling slid a pair of thick gloves on to extract the rat. One of Josie's doctors tranquilized the rodent so it couldn't squirm during surgery, or bite anyone else. Since the procedure was almost microscopic, there was a video screen set up so we could see what was being done. We watched as the doctor implanted the tracker in the incision. The device was so tiny that she had to do the procedure with the use of a camera. When the tracker came in contact with the blood, minuscule silver fibers snaked out of the metal, embedding into the surrounding tissue. They were so tiny, they were almost invisible. The device itself wiggled, burrowing deeper until it could no longer be seen. After a few seconds, a tiny light on the computer screen blinked to life to show that the tracker was now functional.

"The tracker is fully embedded," the doctor said. She used a tool to blot a bit of clear gel on the edges of the rat's skin before pulling them together and closing the wound.

Arabella rubbed her tattoo as she watched. "I feel like there's an alien inside me now." She shuddered. "I'm totally creeped out."

Josie turned her attention away from the doctor and to Arabella. "Your tracker is no longer embedded like that. We could cut it out without any problem. Once it was overloaded with the electrical shock, all those little tendrils would have shriveled up."

"What about the tattoo?" Arabella asked. "I thought the tattoo was part of the tracking."

The doctor finished her work and motioned for the next rat. "The tattoo was mainly used as a brand. It's located over the incision spot, but it serves no actual tracking purposes. It's called a tracking tattoo, but technically, the tracker is below the tattoo."

"Then, why the tattoo?" Sterling asked, lifting his arm to look at the mark on his wrist.

"Like I said, it's a brand," the doctor explained. "A way for Sophisticates to be easily identifiable. All of a Sophisticate's personal identification is coded into the tattoo like a bar code. That way if the Program scans it, they know exactly who you are." The doctor faced Arabella. "For instance, a Sophisticate could wear a disguise, but one simple scan will tell the program your name, blood type, and every single thing you've ever done in the Program. Or against it."

Arabella's smile was wicked as she ran her fingers over her mark. "I can't wait to see what my scan says when this is all over. I plan for it to be a very long list of bad behavior."

***

After we saw the procedure performed on the first rat, I was done. I didn't particularly want to watch those tracking devices burrow their way into anything else. Quinnie and I left the medical tent and made our way past one of the common areas. Ozzy's call had arrived hours ago, but we still hadn't heard from him or anyone else at the ranch yet. The rats would be ready to go soon and we could only hope that Cleo would make it here in time to hack into the system. The whole plan to get the Harpies out would be pointless without Cleo to break the tracking tattoos. Everything depended on the assumption that she was safely on her way to the Freedom Tunnels.

"Oh no." Quinnie grabbed my elbow and pulled me toward the television. The residents of Liberty were gathered around the screen, watching news footage of another city that was on fire.

"I thought the riots were starting to die down," I said, taking a step closer.

"Those aren't riots." Quinnie pointed to the screen. "Don't you remember that bridge?"

"What bridge?"

"Exactly. Someone blew up the bridge that used to be over that water."

After a closer look, I could see what she was talking about. A few supports were left standing on the edges of the canal, but the entire middle of the bridge was gone. Underneath where it should have been, twisted metal stuck up from the water like a half-sunken ship. In the background, buildings were on fire and broken pieces of boats were scattered in the water. Even destroyed, the place did look slightly familiar.

"It was dark when we crossed over that bridge on the way to the ranch," Quinnie said. "But I remember it. It's only about ten minutes away from where the Knights lived."

One of the tunnel dwellers in front of us turned to face us. He was an older man who I'd seen doing various repairs around Liberty. "One of your own did that." He nodded his head toward the television. "Happened a few hours ago."

"It wasn't one of us." Quinnie was frowning. "We have no reason to blow up a bridge."

His eyebrows lifted in disbelief. "Don't believe me? Let me show you the video." He motioned for us to follow him over to a laptop that was sitting on a nearby table. "The Program isn't allowing the original footage to be shown on television, but some amateur videos popped up online. I saved them to our backup drive." He sat down in front of the computer and with a few clicks, he pulled up a video file. It was shaky and looked like it had been taken with a phone. We leaned closer to get a better look. The person taking the video had been standing on the side of the canal. On the opposite side, a girl stood on the pier, fire dancing over her hands. Military vehicles and helicopters swarmed around her, but she stood tall, a tiny figure amidst a sea of fire. We watched as she threw a fireball at the bridge and it came crashing down into the canal. The resulting wave washed her from the wooden planks and devoured her in a matter of seconds. Terrified screams blared from the laptop speakers and the footage became increasingly shakier as the videographer attempted to run away while still filming at the same time.

When the video cut out, Quinnie and I stood in silence, staring at the blank screen.

"Do you..." Quinnie cleared her throat. "Was that Persephone or Cleo?"

"Persephone." My answer was quick and sure. "Cleo would have attacked the threat. Persephone had another purpose." My chest was hollow as visions of Persephone being swept under the water replayed through my thoughts.

Quinnie shook her head, reaching for the computer to watch the video again. "What could she have possibly been doing?" she muttered.

I knew exactly what Persephone was doing. "This," I said, gesturing to the screen, "this was her way of giving us a fighting chance."

Quinnie crossed her arms. "I don't understand."

"Wesley betrayed us. Who knows how much of a head start the Program had on the ranch before Ozzy gave Cleo the warning? Persephone created a diversion to give them a chance to get away. She knows most of our plans revolved around Cleo and her ability to hack into the system. She did this to keep Cleo safe. If there is one thing Persephone knows how to do, it's create chaos."

"But that doesn't sound like Persephone. She hates Cleo. Why would she risk herself like that? Why would she care? Why wouldn't she just run and hide?"

"Because there's one thing she hates more than Cleo." I turned away from the video replay. I didn't want to see Persephone taken by the water again.

"And what's that?"

"The Program."

Quinnie's attention was fixated on the screen. "Do you think she survived?" she asked quietly.

"I don't see how she could have." The screams echoed on the video. "She sacrificed herself."

Quinnie was torn between horrified and impressed. "I didn't know she had it in her."

I wasn't sure how to feel. Persephone had been embracing her own destruction her whole life—all the cutting on her arms and deadly risks she routinely took. She welcomed death. Maybe she was making the sacrifice for us, or maybe for herself, but either way, I wasn't sure I could have done the same thing if I was in her position. I don't think I could have given my life to save those who hated me. Did that make Persephone fearless? Stupid? Selfless? Was she more honorable than the rest of us? Or was she just crazy?

Whatever it made her, I finally had the answer to the question I'd asked myself all those months ago. I knew that one day, all the cutting and gashes wouldn't be enough and that Persephone might eventually do something more permanent to hurt herself. At the time, I wasn't sure if that would be a blessing, or a tragedy. I knew now. Persephone had been damaged, maybe even beyond repair, but I'd seen a glimmer of hope in her. Standing on the pier, calling the Program to her like a siren drawing sailors to their deaths, I'd seen that spark that told me Persephone had a soul worth saving.

Only now it was too late.

***

"Come on," Quinnie said, grabbing my hand. "We might as well go get some rest while we still can."

I'd started to drift off as we watched the news reports with the residents of Liberty. Josie and the rest of our team were still with the doctor observing the tracker procedures on the future Squadron 54. Quinnie pulled me to my feet and tugged me toward the tent we'd been sharing with Arabella, Sterling, and Dexter since our arrival.

It wasn't really fair to refer to the Liberty homes as tents since they didn't at all resemble the flimsy structures that people used at campgrounds. The Liberty homes were framed out of wood and covered with heavy fabric. They reminded me of gypsy tents with pitched roofs, vivid colors, and plenty of privacy. Quinnie pulled me inside and released the fabric from the hook that held it open to create a doorway. Light from outside the tent filtered through the blue panels of fabric, bathing the space in cool light. The floor was covered in a patchwork of throw rugs to battle the chill of the concrete, and five cots were crammed inside.

Quinnie let go of my hand and backed up toward her cot as she removed her hoodie, never taking her eyes off mine. She hooked her finger at me and I obeyed, closing the distance between us until I was in front of her. For once, I didn't mind having someone tell me what to do. She lifted her chin to look at me and I wrapped my arms around her, pulling her up against my body. She kissed my chin and I closed my eyes, relishing the softness of her lips, a softness that was meant only for me. I liked that Quinnie never showed that side of herself to anyone else, that she felt safe enough to toss away her emotional armor when we were alone.

"I thought we were going to rest," I joked, tilting my face down so that our mouths could meet. She kissed me gently, each touch of her lips like an apology—soft, hesitant, wanting more.

She pulled away and grinned before spinning me around and pushing me back on the cot until I was lying down. She crawled over top of me and my hands slid to the outside of her thighs, anchoring her to me. Quinnie dropped her mouth to my jaw, pressing kisses there between her words. "I lied. There's no time to rest. If we die later on, I don't want to think I wasted my last moments with you by sleeping them away."

"And what if we survive? Then what?"

Quinnie flattened her body against mine and I swallowed a groan as she leaned over to whisper in my ear. "Then we celebrate. No clothes necessary." Her fingers found the bottom of my shirt, pulling it up until I was forced to remove my hands from her and lift my arms so that she could take it off.

I reached up and hooked my finger in the collar of her shirt, pulling her back down until her mouth was just an inch away from mine. "It looks like you're celebrating a little early." I yanked on the fabric and erased the distance between our lips, her sweet slow kisses replaced by eager, desperate ones. Quinnie's hands were in my hair, her mouth was hot on mine, and every inch of her was pressed up against me—moving. Wanting. I reached for her waist, my hands finding the delicate skin just above the waistband of her jeans. My fingers tingled when I touched her, like her body was a live wire ready to shatter into jagged bolts of lightning. There was so much power simmering and sparking under the smooth expanse of her skin.

Soon her shirt was gone and my pants were unbuttoned and there was so much exposed, every touch charged with urgency.

"Why me?" a voice whined from the other side of the tent.

Quinnie and I broke apart to glare into the light of the open curtain where Sterling now stood.

"Why me?" he shouted again, covering his eyes. "First Cleo and Ozzy, now you two. And I thought watching rats get operated on was nauseating."

"Maybe you should have knocked first." Quinnie was sitting up and glaring at Sterling, her arms crossed over her chest which was only covered by a skimpy bra to begin with.

Sterling huffed, keeping his eyes covered. "Explain to me how I'm supposed to knock on a curtain."

"The curtain was closed. That means we wanted privacy." Quinnie made no move to put her clothes back on.

"I thought you were sleeping," Sterling muttered. "How was I supposed to know you were doing the horizontal mambo in here?"

"We hadn't gotten that far, thanks to you." Quinnie looked entirely comfortable sitting on top of me, half-dressed. "Well? Are you waiting to be invited to join in, or is there a reason you're lingering in the doorway like a perv?"

Sterling finally had the courage to look our way. "Join in? In my nightmares maybe." He jerked his thumb over his shoulder. "We got intel that everyone from the ranch just entered the tunnels. They should be here soon."

"Everyone?" I asked.

Sterling's gaze cut back to me. "Everyone but Persephone." He paused and shoved his hands into his pockets. "I saw the footage. What she did..."

"Yeah."

"Anyway," he shrugged. "Thought you'd want to know." He

turned and left through the doorway, allowing the curtain to fall back in place.

Quinnie sighed and put her hands on my chest, leaning forward to place one, last lingering kiss on my mouth. "Hope that can hold you for a while, loverboy. Looks like it's time to be a hero."

CLEO

RAT SQUAD

The strap of the laptop bag bit into my shoulder, but I hardly noticed it. The tunnel seemed to stretch out endlessly before us and the echoes of our steps beat a relentless rhythm in my head, along with the visions of Persephone being pulled under the filthy water of the canal. I was so tired. I was ready for this to be over. For everyone I cared about to be safe. For the Program to leave us alone. No one had heard from Ozzy since right after the incident in Chicago.

Incident. How could I even call it that? It was a betrayal. A massacre. My hand went to my chest and I clutched the fabric over my heart as if that could somehow protect me. It did no good. My fear for Ozzy was a bloodthirsty animal hell-bent on rampaging through my chest and I no longer had any defense against it. My heart couldn't hold all the emotions that were constantly tearing through me. Worry for Ozzy, grief for Sadie and Marty, fury at Wesley, and an unfamiliar emotion for Persephone. I couldn't even think about what she'd done.

I took a deep breath and hitched the strap of my bag higher, telling myself that no news was good news. If the Program had caught Ozzy, they'd be boasting about it on every media source available. Right?

I reached up to rub my forehead. I just...I just needed to hear his voice. To know he was okay. I needed to see my friends with my own eyes—Sterling, Arabella, Quinnie, Rune, and Dexter. I had to know that we were going to get through this. Together. A small smile snuck across my lips at that thought. When did I start thinking of Quinnie as my friend? I couldn't remember the exact moment, but I liked knowing we were allies now. It was so much easier than being enemies.

"Cleo!"

I looked up to see a blur of color rushing down the tunnel toward us. I realized it was Arabella just before she crashed into me, pulling me into a rib-crushing hug. "I missed you, girl," she said. "The hag witch is so much worse when you're not around. You're like hag antidote or something."

"Hag antidote?"

"Quinnie."

I smiled. Leave it to Arabella to help me remember to laugh. She released me and I got a good view of her red, white, and blue streaked hair.

"What's this all about?" I asked, reaching up to rub some of her hair between my fingers. It didn't matter how many times I saw her change her appearance with just a thought. I'd always be amazed...and jealous of her deviation. Seriously. Perfect hair and looks with no effort? Unnatural strength? The ability to grow back body parts? Stretchy limbs to reach things on high shelves? Arabella hit the jackpot when it came to deviations. She got useful variety, and I got death and destruction. Not fair.

"This?" Arabella grinned. "I guess putzing around in the Freedom Tunnel and hanging out in Liberty sort of inspired me. I did it once and the kids in the camp thought it was cool, so I kept it."

"I like it." I took a deep breath as Arabella grabbed my hand and led me down the tunnel from where she just came. Her presence was a balm, her bright personality smudging away the dark feelings I'd had moments ago. "Any word from Ozzy?" I asked.

Arabella squeezed my hand and shook her head. "Not yet. But I have faith in him. He and Euri will figure out a way to get back to us. I have to believe it."

I nodded, wanting to believe it, too.

"In the meantime, we have work to do. Squadron 54 is up and running, just waiting to be activated. And when I say running, I mean running. Sterling created a little maze for them to fool around in to entertain some of the kids at camp. The stupid things have been running wild for hours now." She shook her head. "Dexter started organizing some races, putting up odds and wagers. It's like Las Vegas in there. Only with rats."

I cleared my throat. "Sounds like you guys are making the best of it."

Arabella cast a worried glance my way and squeezed my hand. "We're all scared, Cleo. Sometimes it's easier to prepare for the hard stuff when you're making the best of the present. You know we're all devastated about Marty and Sadie. We're worried about Ozzy and Euri." She looked over her shoulder where Theo walked with Cassie before whispering, "We have no idea how to feel about Wesley. It's like we hate him, but still want him to be safe."

"I know," I mumbled back.

She blew out a breath. "And Persephone. God. We're shocked. What she did was so unexpected."

"And it saved us."

Arabella paused, giving my hand another squeeze. "Who would have guessed she had it in her?"

I didn't know how to answer that. I was still having a hard time believing it was real. "How is Rune?"

"Quiet. As always. I know he's upset about it, but kind of relieved, too." She turned to look at me. "I think he and Quinnie are serious about each other."

"Rune and Quinnie?"

She nodded.

Interesting.

"Here we are," Arabella said as we approached a large metal door set in a brick wall. "Wait until you see Liberty. It'll knock your socks off."

***

I looked at the maps spread out on the table in front of us and set my laptop to the side.

"From the information the real Squadron 54 gave me, they will be coming along Madison Avenue with the prisoners," Sterling said, pointing out the path on the map. "That's where we can make our move. Once they reach the intersection here, you overload their tracking devices and activate the Rat Squad."

Rat Squad. Yes. We were actually calling them that. "Why has the Program waited so long to move the prisoners? Why not do it right away when Wesley went to them?" I asked. The situation didn't make sense to me. It felt like a trap. "How can you be sure we can trust these Mandates?"

Sterling narrowed his eyes at me. "How did you know you could trust Quinnie when you first found out who her father was and decided to keep it a secret?" He held his hand up toward Quinnie to stop her argument. "I have a point," he said to her before turning back to me. "Look, I know in my gut that these Mandates are on our side. We can trust them."

I took a deep breath and held it for a second before releasing it in a rush. "If you're sure."

"I am." He pinned me with a confident stare before pointing back down at the map again. "Okay. So, the Harpies were originally placed in cells here at Headquarters." Sterling indicated the old Empire State building where we knew Baker and Steel had offices. "They expected us to come crashing in through the front gate, desperate to get to the Harpies as soon as we found out they'd been taken into custody." He swept his finger along the main gate from the Lincoln Tunnel. "They underestimated us and didn't anticipate the possibility that we'd have a plan. See that's the Program's fatal flaw. They gave us genetically advanced intelligence, but never thought we'd actually use it on our own."

"Exactly." *Preach on, Sterling. Preach on.*

"Anyway, as I was saying, they thought we'd come in through the front gate so they had plenty of Hounds and Mandates prepared to take us down before we could even make it to the Harpies. The incident in Chicago and Persephone's stunt threw them for a loop. They weren't expecting guerrilla warfare. It never occurred to them that we might try to sneak in or that it was even a possibility. If it wasn't for Chicago, they'd still have no idea what we were planning."

Sterling didn't call out Wesley's treachery even though it was the elephant in the room, the one thing no one wanted to mention in front of Theo. Since Ozzy's phone call, Theo had been strangely silent. He hadn't spoken a single word. I didn't know if it was because he was in shock, or pissed, or hurt. Maybe it was all three.

"So now that the Program knows we plan to sneak in," I said carefully, "Where are they planning to move the Harpies?"

Rune jabbed his finger on the map in a spot that was closer to where he was sitting. "They're creating a holding cell here in Grand Central Station. It's not that far from the Empire State Building, but it'll be harder for us to get them out of there. The Program plans to lure us in there, and then destroy the building with us inside. That's why we need to initiate the rescue attempt when the transfer is en route."

Destroying a building with us inside just to take us out? Talk about overkill.

"And how did you find all of this out?" Cassie asked. "It seems pretty convenient that someone would tell you exactly how Baker and Steel plan to eliminate us." She picked at her nails with the tips of the blades that had slid out of her knuckles. It was still hard for me to accept that my best friend—the one with top notch fashion sense—could also be a ruthless killer if she needed to be. With the blades fully extended from her knuckles, she looked like Wolverine's little sister. I wouldn't dare tell her that, though.

"We have to be smart about who we trust and what we believe, but we're not going to win without taking risks. The point is, if someone offered you a chance to get away from the Program, would you take it?" Sterling asked.

Cassie lifted her eyes and the blades slid back into her skin, her hands delicate and harmless looking again. "Of course."

Sterling spread his hands wide. "The Mandates feel the same way. Let's take a chance on them."

"Let's take a vote," I said. "Those in favor of using the Rat Squad plan to test the mass tattoo disabling in order to rescue the Harpies, raise your hand."

All hands went up, even Cassie's. Despite her concerns, she was just as eager to get the Harpies to safety as I was.

"Perfect." I pulled the laptop back in front of me and started typing away on the keys.

"Let's go," Rune said, standing up from the table. "We managed to get a hold of some uniforms. We should get everything organized. You two have everything you need from us?" Rune asked me and Theo.

I nodded. "Good to go. I'll let you know if we have any questions."

Cassie leaned over to kiss Theo on the top of the head before leaving. Within minutes, the table was empty except for me and Theo. He was in charge of disabling and looping video where necessary. I was picking my way through all of the delicate webs of Program security. With Lawless' guidance, I'd gotten pretty good at it over the last few months. Both Theo and I were staying behind to monitor the situation. Elysia would be staying behind too. She'd been gun shy ever since the battle at the Inner Harbor, but since Persephone left, her cowardice was immeasurable. She downright refused to be a part of any rescue attempt or mission against the Program.

"What are you doing?" Theo asked, breaking his silence.

My eyes darted to his, surprised he finally decided to speak.

"Breaking into the tracking tattoo program so I can set everything up."

"Exactly how will it work?"

I paused my typing to turn and give him my full attention. "I insert a virus into the tracking program that will force the devices to draw excess energy from their hosts. That should cause the trackers to short out. The virus should be able to take out all of the trackers in the entire Sophisticate program at once. That's the long term plan, anyway. For now, I'm just going to individually overload the seven that are in the squadron, plus those of the prisoners, as a test. If it works, our rescue mission is a success. If we successfully get these people off the grid without hurting them, then we know we can do everyone."

Theo folded his arms over his chest and leaned back in his chair. "Have you seen any new security in place since Wes..." He cleared his throat. "Since he sold us out to the Program?"

I shook my head. "I've been in and out of the Program's databases a thousand times over the last few months." I waved my hand in front of the laptop. "Everything is exactly the same. Either he didn't understand how I was going to break the tattoos or he didn't tell the Program about it." My fingers hovered over the keys while I stared at the screen. "It's not like Wes paid any attention to what the rest of us were doing at the ranch. It's likely he didn't even know I was rooting around in the Program's databases."

Theo looked down at his hands as he cracked his knuckles one by one. "Probably not. He was so concerned with Persephone, he didn't really pay attention to much else."

"Why do you think he was like that?" I asked. "None of us trusted her, but he took it to extremes." As I was talking, my eyes and fingers moved again, picking out the well worn path I'd made through the Program's security.

Out of the corner of my eye, I saw Theo shrug. "I'm not really sure. He didn't confide in me much once we got to the ranch. He'd been all out of sorts since you and Cassie. And me."

I jerked my hands away from the keyboard and spun in my chair to look at him. "Since me and Cassie and you what?"

He glanced up at me, a look of disbelief on his face. "You know he had a huge crush on you, right? You chose Ozzy. Then he set his sights on Cassie, but she chose me." Theo took a deep breath before releasing it in a rush. "Wes has always been insecure and I think he felt misled with the attention that you and Cassie initially gave him. When neither of you were interested in him, he took it hard. Especially when Cassie chose his twin brother over him." Theo gave me a sad smile. "He was the nice one. I was the jackass."

I frowned, feeling defensive. "I never gave Wes the impression we were dating. We went to that dance as friends. I even said so. Anything he inferred beyond friendship is on him, not me."

Theo raised his hands against my rant. "I know. Trust me, I know. I never said it was your fault. I'm just...I'm just as confused as you about why he did what he did. The only thing I can think of is that he was hurt or humiliated. And he took up Persephone as his own personal mission. Then when he found out we were trusting her ideas, he lost it. He felt overlooked. Again."

Explained that way, I could sort of understand Wesley's state of mind. But that didn't make what he did acceptable. "I feel bad for him, but I'm not ready to forgive him," I admitted. "I might not ever forgive him. Sadie and Marty died because of what he did. So did Persephone."

Theo's gaze fell to the table, heavy with the shame of his brother's actions. "Trust me. I'm not ready to forgive him either. He's my brother and I love him, but I'm so fucking pissed at him I can hardly see straight." He ran his hand back through his hair, clutching the ends in his fist before taking a deep breath. He shook his head as if clearing his mind, and looked up at me. "So. Do you feel pretty confident about the plan? Do you think overloading the tattoos will work?"

I nodded, grateful to change the subject. "Lawless and I have been over this dozens of times. The tracking device is a lot more fragile than you think. It won't take much of an energy surge to do the job. Using the tasers was excessive. This new plan will do the same thing, but with fewer side effects."

Theo tilted his head toward the screen. "Once you break in, do you need to stay here and monitor the breach, or can the hack be kept open even if you're not here?"

I thought about it. "They haven't realized I've been getting in. Nothing has changed about their security in the last few weeks. If everything is exactly the same today, I see no reason why I need to be here to oversee it once it's open. I mean, I think I could totally take control of their entire system if I wanted to. Why?"

Theo rubbed his jaw and glared at the computer, lost in thought. "You're our biggest weapon." He turned his eyes to me. "They're going to need you watching their backs during the rescue. You're going to be much more useful than Eva in the field if anything goes wrong."

"But someone has to be here to actually put everything in motion."

He shrugged. "I'm going to be here watching over the video. If you open the digital gateway and explain to me what to do, I can take care of things."

My mouth hung open as I stared at him.

Theo's lips pressed together. "I know my brother just betrayed us all and got our friends killed." He took a deep breath in through his nose. "But you can trust me. I might look like Wes, but I'm nothing like him."

I flinched in shock. "No! That's not what I was thinking at all." I reached across the space between us and put my hand on Theo's arm, squeezing gently. "Theo, I remember what you did for me back at the Academy, how you believed in me when no one else did. I know that you took risks to get proof that Persephone was responsible for all those horrible things that I was blamed for. I *know* I can trust you." I put my palm to my forehead and shook my head. "I'm just surprised that I didn't think of this first. Of course I'm not needed here. Why waste all this firepower just to sit around holding a digital door open and pressing a few buttons?" I released his arm and held my hand out as flames licked across my palm.

Theo sighed in relief and when he looked at me, I could see pain in his eyes. "You trust me with all of these lives?"

"Theo..."

He leaned forward and grabbed my arm. "I can't undo what Wes did, but I can do everything in my power to give us a chance to come out on top. I want to."

I was quiet for a few moments as a plan formed—exonerating the Deviant Dozen, freeing the Sophisticates, and destroying Baker and Steel. "This could be our one chance to set everything right."

Theo's gaze was resolute. "Let's do it."

I smiled, rubbed my palms together, and turned back toward

the computer. "Well then. We don't have much time for me to show you the ropes. Let's get Operation Rat Squad in motion. It's time to take the Program by their digital balls."

OZZY

❧ 29 ❧

DETOURS & DEVIATIONS

The miles disappeared behind us, and the only thing that seemed to change was the position of the sun. Even though I knew we were getting closer to our destination, the entire trip had been like one of those bad dreams where you're running toward a door and no matter how fast you run, the door gets farther and farther away. Because of Jerry and the checkpoint, it had taken us hours to get out of Illinois. Thankfully, Euri knew his way around so we managed to evade the checkpoints and helicopter surveillance. I felt like I'd seen every inch of the damn state and I had no desire to ever go back. Except to the canyon, because I wanted to show that to Cleo. If we got out of this alive.

Scratch that. *When* we got out of this alive.

"What do you think about that bridge collapse in Chesapeake City?" Euri asked. He reached to the side and pulled the handle that sat his seat upright again.

The media didn't come out and say it was a terrorist attack, or that it was connected with the Deviants in any way, but from the few details we gleaned over the radio, we knew that either Persephone or Cleo had been involved. Chesapeake City was just too close to the Knights' ranch for one of them not to be involved in some way.

"I wish I could say it wasn't Cleo's style, but she did accidentally destroy the National Aquarium last time she and Persephone got in a fire fight. It's entirely possible either of them, or both of them, were involved." The only comfort I felt was that the Program hadn't made any announcements about capturing anyone. I had to hope that meant everyone on the ranch was safe or still on the run.

Euri grabbed the open bag of chips from behind my seat and shoved a few in his mouth. "Had to be Persephone," he mumbled as he chewed.

"Why do you say that?"

"She'd been idle too long. She needed to get that out of her system."

"Do you think everyone at the ranch got out of there before the Program showed up?"

Euri shrugged. "Dunno. We have no idea how much warning Wes gave the Program. I hope so though."

"Me too."

Not being able to get in touch with everyone had both of us on edge. When I spoke to Cleo right after the disaster in Chicago, she said they'd be heading up to New York to join the others and I promised that we'd meet them there. What should have taken us fourteen hours had taken so much longer. The Program had surveillance set up all along Route 80; the interstate we planned to take to New York. Instead, we had to take the long way around, looping down south along the Pennsylvania/Maryland line. We knew the Program would be looking for Illinois license plates, so getting a new vehicle was a necessity as soon as we crossed over into Indiana. In fact, every time we crossed a state line, we went shopping for a new vehicle. We had to be picky about what we stole. We couldn't take anything that would stick out or be traceable and we tried to find cars that wouldn't be missed for a while.

All of that took time. Time we didn't have.

We took turns sleeping, but the truth was, I was spent.

My foot pressed heavily on the gas and the headlights and tail-lights of the cars around us turned into streaks of red and white. I felt myself zoning out to the monotony of the view when bright flashes of blue and red filled the car. I looked into the rearview mirror. A police car.

"Shit!"

"Just go," Euri urged. "We can lose him."

I shook my head. "He'd just call in our license plate and then we'd have helicopters and every cop in the surrounding area chasing us down. Don't worry. I've got this." We were coming up to an underpass and I pulled to the side of the road, right under the bridge.

It was late and dark out so not many people were on the road. I knew if we waited for the cop to come to us, he'd already have called in our license plate and location. I opened the car door and pushed up out of my seat. Within seconds, the cop was out of his car, hiding behind his open door and yelling for me to "freeze." His gun was pointed at me, but I didn't hesitate. I lifted my hand and pulled the trigger.

He slumped to the ground.

***

Euri peered into the rearview mirror and into the backseat where the unfortunate officer was still unconscious from the tranquilizer dart. His arms were handcuffed behind him. We'd already dumped his car behind a building at the last exit. Now we had to find somewhere to dump him. Preferably someplace someone would find him after we were long gone.

"If you'd shot him with the other gun, we wouldn't even have to worry about this. We could have just left him with the car." Euri tapped his fingers on his knee. He was alert and aware as he gazed out of the window.

I clenched my jaw. "I'm not killing anyone unless it's necessary."

"I'm just saying. You wanted to get to Headquarters quickly. This," he jerked his thumb over his shoulder at the cop, "is the opposite of quick."

"I'm not going to let the Program turn us into the monsters they're accusing us of being. That guy was just making a routine traffic stop. I'm not going to take his life for that. He's probably got a wife and kids back home."

"Or, maybe he's a crooked cop who takes bribes and smacks his old lady around," Euri offered.

"No way. I read his badge. His name is Milo."

Euri barked out in laughter. "Milo. What's that got to do with anything?"

I turned off the highway and followed signs to a nearby elementary school. "Milo is too nice. He probably volunteers at soup kitchens on the weekends or works with one of those groups that builds free homes for low income people. Milo. Milo's a good guy. Milo doesn't deserve a bullet to the head."

Euri chuckled. "If you say so."

I pulled up next to the playground. "Come on. Help me get Milo to the swings. By the time the kiddies find him, we'll be at Headquarters and his old lady will have pancakes ready for him."

We dragged the officer to the swing set and I used another set of handcuffs to cuff him to one of the poles. He started to stir and we hurried away before he could wake up and get a look at our faces.

"Should we get a new ride while we're here? He knows what our car looks like. Probably the plate, too," Euri asked.

"No. Let's just go." I slid into the driver's seat. "We're just north of Philly. We'll be in New York before he has a chance to report us." I started the car and then pulled out of the parking lot.

"What do you think everyone is doing?" Euri asked as I took the next exit ramp back onto the interstate.

"Hopefully, brainstorming. We still need to find someone to test Persephone's theory to see if we can remotely break the tracking tattoo." I squeezed my hand into a fist and tapped it against the closed window while I thought. "Once we get to Headquarters, we can come up with new plans." We were almost there. Everything would be fine. "I just wish we could talk to them so we knew that everyone got there safely."

"Good news," Euri said, holding out his hand. "I grabbed the cop's phone when I was driving his car to the drop off. It's fully charged."

"What?" I made a grab for the phone to toss it out the window, but Euri held it out of my reach. "We can't use his phone. It's traceable."

"True. But it's the same model as your phone and he had these in his car." Euri held up his arm where cords dangled from his fist.

I raised my eyebrows. "And?" The truck we were driving was so old it didn't have the proper receptacles for a charger.

Euri smiled. "And I can use these to boost a charge on your phone. Want to talk to your girl or not?"

I turned my attention to the road. "You know I do."

He hooked it up and when my phone finally had enough charge for the screen to light up, I held out my hand. Euri dialed the number and handed my phone back to me. After three rings, someone picked up.

"Cleo?" I asked before they could even say "hello."

"Ozzy?" A male voice answered. "Jesus. Where have you been? Things have been crazy. We—" It was Theo.

"Where's Cleo? I need to talk to her," I interrupted.

Theo cleared his throat. "Um. She's not here."

"Is she okay? Where is she?"

"Right now?" Theo paused. "In the tunnels. Near Headquarters."

Shit. Cleo was near Headquarters? Without me?

An hour and a half had seemed so close just seconds ago.

A car pulled up alongside us and when it slowed down to keep pace, I glanced over. In that split second, I recognized the guy sitting in the passenger seat. Marco. One of the Hounds who'd been on the mission to assassinate Rasool ur Ra'ahmah back in the fall. He turned to look at me, smiling as if he'd known it was me all along. When he raised his hand, I didn't even wait to see what he was holding. I slammed on the brakes and veered to the side.

Euri grabbed the handle above his door. "Do you know that guy?"

"Yeah," I grumbled, spinning the car around and crashing over the median before heading down the highway in the opposite direction. "His name is Marco. We went on several missions together. He definitely recognized me."

"Where are you going?" Euri's voice was calm.

"There was an exit a mile back. We need to get that new car you've been wanting or else we'll never make it to Headquarters." I looked in the rearview mirror to see if Marco had turned around, too. He hadn't.

An unfamiliar ringtone sounded and I looked down to see Marco's name lighting up the screen.

Euri raised his eyebrows.

"Answer it," I growled. "Might as well find out what he wants, how he got that number, and how the hell his fucking name is on my screen."

Euri hit the answer button and then put it on speaker. "Ozzy isn't available to talk right now. Can I take a message?"

Marco laughed. "Crazy. You sound just like him."

"He wants to know how you got this number." Euri pointed out the exit and I took it.

"Wesley gave it up. The Program has been waiting for it to show up on cell records. You're lucky I'm the one closest to you the first time you use it," Marco said.

I clenched the steering wheel in a grip so hard I was surprised it didn't break in half.

"Why's that lucky?" Euri asked.

"Because," Marco answered in a slick voice. "I'm on Ozzy's side. And if he's heading to Headquarters like I hope he is, he's going to need an army at his back. I can provide that."

"An army for what?" I asked. Marco and I had always been friends. But I wasn't sure I could trust our past enough to trust him. The Program would much rather I surrender to them than fight. His offer was likely a trap.

Marco sighed. "Come on, Oz. How many missions did we do together? I know you, and I know you aren't responsible for what the Program says you did. And if that's true, then I know that they're the ones terrorizing their own people. I'm not the only one who feels that way. We've been waiting months for you to come out of hiding and fight back. We're ready to fight with you. So are you going to turn that piece of shit around and lead us into Headquarters or what?"

"How do I know I can trust you?" I asked, even though deep down I knew I could. We'd saved each other's backs more times than I could count. And that kind of loyalty was stronger than any direct order given by the Program.

"Oz," Marco said. "I was following you for a mile. I may not have perfect aim, but I was following you long enough that I could have easily put a bullet or two in you."

I laughed. "You're not that good," I countered.

"I'm good enough. Now are you coming or what? Word is Baker and Steel are both hunkered down at Headquarters. It'd be a shame to let that go to waste."

"On my way," I said, grabbing the phone from Euri and tossing it out the window. I hated to give up the only link to Cleo I had left, but I couldn't risk giving the Program the ability to track me. I turned to Euri. "Looks like I'll have to get you a new car later. This one will have to get us to Headquarters."

"Or," Euri said. "You can just give me that motorcycle of yours once this is all over and we can call it even. It's still at the Academy, right?"

I turned to glare at him. "You're not getting my bike."

"We'll see."

Rune

❧ 30 ❧

Mistaken Identity

According to Josie and her people, once the Harpies were taken into custody, all the Mandates in the Manhattan compound started roaming the streets dressed in battle garb. The Program was expecting us. Helmets and flak jackets were standard gear, although I couldn't imagine what sort of protection either would provide against someone like Cleo, Quinnie, or me. The good thing was that the current dress code of Mandates made it easier for us to get around undetected. With battle garb on, we looked just like any other Mandate.

I followed Arabella, Sterling, Cassie, Quinnie, Dexter, and Eva up the stairs of the subway station. The Program might have a tight grip on the bridges and most of the tunnels entering the city, but they had no control over the thousands of tunnels, both known and forgotten, that snaked below the city. They never needed to before because they thought they had complete control of Manhattan. The Program had no idea Liberty was hiding right under their noses.

Josie and her people knew all of the tunnels and had spent years mapping them out. Everything from the sewers to the old subway lines was fair game for getting around the city undetected, and they were experts.

When we stepped out onto the street, cold wind whipped around my body. The sky was dark, but the moon was bright, illuminating everything in an eerie glow. The sign at the corner of the sidewalk was battered, but still legible—Madison Avenue and 42nd Street. We were right where we were supposed to be. We quickly crossed the street, confident in the knowledge that Theo was turning the Program's eyes the other way. There were video cameras everywhere, but with Theo at the helm, we might as well have been invisible. Our safety was at the touch of his fingertips.

Once we entered the building across the street from the subway, I relaxed a little. The doors were unlocked, just like we were told they would be, and we found ourselves in the lobby of some long-forgotten office building. I wondered what it had been like forty years ago, before *Wormwood*, when it would have been full of people going about their everyday lives. The building was empty and somber now. Nearly all the buildings in Manhattan were like that. Some were used for training exercises for the Mandates, but mostly they stood tall and empty.

Everyone took off their helmets, so I did too, my eyesight slowly adjusting to our new surroundings. There were surprised gasps and muttering and I spun around to see what the problem was.

I came face to face with Cleo and my helmet slipped from my hands to clatter on the floor.

What the hell? Cleo wasn't supposed to be with us. Eva was. But

Eva was nowhere to be seen. I tried to remember if I saw her before we left Liberty and realized I hadn't. We were all in helmets and battle gear.

"Cleo! What the hell are you doing here?" Dexter was immediately in her face, furious.

"I'm here as backup." She forced a smile and snapped her fingers, a tiny flame bursting between her fingertips before it curled toward the ceiling in a wisp of smoke.

"What the hell are you thinking?" he growled. "You're supposed to be back at the compound to knock out the tracking devices. The Mandates transporting the Harpies are depending on us to get them off the grid. You've just royally screwed this entire mission," Dexter shouted. "There's no way we can pull this off now." He gestured wildly toward the window. "We didn't even bring a taser. Even if we follow through with the plan and intercept the transfer, the Program will just hunt everyone down again because of the damn tracking devices." He pointed a finger in Cleo's chest. "Which you're supposed to be disabling. Isn't that the whole point of this mission? Testing out the theory?" Dexter took a breath as if to continue and Cleo put her hand up.

"Don't worry. Everything is going to plan. I breached the security system before I left," she said as if it was as easy as turning off a light. "I went over all the steps carefully with both Theo and Lawless. They can do it just as easily as me. Well," she said, shrugging, "maybe not *just* as easily, but we can trust Theo. He's been hacking into the Program's video surveillance system as long as I've been hacking into their other files. He can follow a few simple instructions. Everything will be fine. They don't need me there to push a few buttons."

Dexter's jaw twitched. "And Eva?"

"She's with Theo and Lawless. If something unforeseen comes up, she can always place a call to help out. She's been studying those recordings of Baker and Steel that Josie's people had. Her deviation will do more good back there than here. Just like I'm more valuable here watching your backs in person than from behind a computer screen."

Dexter shook his head and gave Cleo a dirty look. "Fine. Whatever." He tucked his helmet under his arm and walked toward the window for a better view of the intersection. "But this wasn't the plan we agreed on. If this fails, it'll be all your fault."

Cleo gritted her teeth and narrowed her eyes at him.

Arabella snorted. "So does that mean if this plan succeeds, you'll be ready to kiss her ass in gratitude?"

"Shut up, Arabella," Dexter snapped. "Maybe you don't care that we lost Marty and Sadie because someone deviated from the plan, but—"

He didn't get to finish the rest of his sentence because Arabella's arm had stretched across the room quick as lightning and her hand was around Dexter's throat, pinning him to a column. He struggled against her grip, clawing at her hand.

"I. Do. Care. Asshole." She bit out each word like she wanted to tear his throat out with her teeth.

Sterling just shook his head at Dexter. "Dude. You know better than to stay stupid shit like that. Especially to Arabella." Coming up in front of Arabella, he tilted her chin so she'd look at him. "You know he didn't mean it. He's just being a pissmonkey because he misses his friend. We all miss Marty and Sadie. Let's give him a break, yeah?"

Arabella took a stuttering breath and released Dexter before spinning around and stomping off to a dark corner to be alone. She would never cry in front of the rest of us. I was choked up too, reminded of the warning that Persephone had given me about Wesley before I left the ranch and how she paid the ultimate price for his betrayal. It was still hard to imagine she was gone and that she sacrificed herself for someone else. We'd already lost so much so I could understand Dexter's distress. We stood to lose even more if Cleo's gamble didn't work out.

Sterling stared after Arabella for a moment, but wisely chose not to follow her. He came up alongside me where I was leaning up against a wall and we watched as Cleo headed for Arabella. "What do you think? You okay with this?" He nodded his head toward Cleo.

I shrugged. "We don't have much choice. The decision has already been made for us. Too late to send her back. And we'll know pretty soon whether Theo can pull this off, right?"

Sterling reached up and rubbed his jaw in thought. "If he can, then she's right. She'll do more good here. Her deviation is the best defense we've got if things go south."

I nodded. "Let's hope it doesn't come to that."

My earpiece buzzed with static and I watched as nearly everyone in the room reached up to touch their ears at the same time. Theo's voice came through clearly. "The transfer vehicle just left Headquarters. All occupants are accounted for. Seven Mandates, three Harpies, and Elena, the Mandate who helped Sterling escape. Vehicle ETA to your location is about two minutes."

My stomach flipped with a surge of adrenaline and I pushed away from the wall, picking up my helmet on the way, as we mobilized near the front doors of the building. Theo would keep the Program's eyes off us, but we had to assume there would be someone monitoring the transfer from a computer terminal somewhere. The video wasn't a concern, but the timing for disabling the tracking devices and activating the Rat Squad had to be perfect so that nothing would seem amiss. We had to be quick and move before the Program realized anything was wrong.

I felt like I'd barely taken a breath before the black, non-descript van carrying the Mandates and prisoners stopped at the intersection. I turned to look at Sterling, who was studying the scene with narrowed eyes. The door to the front cab of the van opened and the Mandate who had been driving got out, casting a curious glance toward our building.

Theo's voice came back over the headset. "And...done."

The Mandate standing out on the street flinched and then reached for his arm and rubbed it where the tattoo should be.

"Mandates are offline," Theo's voice echoed through the earpiece. "Rat squad is online. It's amazing. I saw their tracking dots blink out in the middle of the intersection on the map and then reappear near the subway station."

I glanced to the small cage we'd left near the exit to the subway station. The new Squadron 54 was inside, hopefully not gnawing on one another.

"Perfect," Sterling said. "We're moving in now." He motioned forward with his hand and everyone put their helmets back on. We filed out of the building and into the street, guns raised, eyes wary as we scanned our surroundings. It was dark out, but with the night vision of the helmet visor, I could see that the only people nearby were the ones in the vehicle. We hurried across the street fanning out protectively around the van as the Mandates got out of the back, leading four figures who were bound and hooded.

Sterling stepped forward and lifted the visor on his helmet to speak with the driver of the van. I went to fetch the Rat Squad.

"So, everything good?" the Mandate asked Sterling as I returned.

"Yup," Sterling said. "You're invisible now."

I held up the cage. "Meet the new Squad 54 and prisoners."

The Mandate smiled and rubbed his wrist again. "I could tell exactly when it happened. It was like a surge of adrenaline and then I felt a stinging sensation at the tattoo, like someone scooted across the carpet in socks and then shocked me on the wrist. Dull, but noticeable."

I glanced over at Cleo and saw that she couldn't contain her smile. It worked. Leave it to Persephone to figure out how to solve our problem. Suddenly, the small smile that fought its way onto my mouth felt awkward. Persephone finally did something to redeem herself, but it was too late for her.

Sterling looked at his watch. "Time to get out of here. It won't be long before someone realizes the prisoners haven't made it to the new location yet. Let's head out."

The Mandates who were guarding the prisoners made quick work of removing their hoods and bindings. Arabella pulled off her helmet and rushed forward to give quick hugs to the Harpies, smiling. "Come on," she said, grabbing their hands. "Time to go."

"Move out." Sterling motioned with his hand for us to follow him, and the rest of the rescued Mandates and prisoners did just that as he made his way to the subway tunnel.

Cleo, on the other hand, never took her helmet off or approached the Harpies. She merely stared at their backs as they left before turning to me and holding out her hand. "I'll take Rat Squad."

I frowned at her. "Why?"

"Because if we leave them here, Mandates will be sent to investigate and they'll eventually find the subway tunnel and figure out what happened. We have to make sure they're looking in the wrong spot and that they don't figure out how to get to Liberty."

"Wouldn't it make more sense for Sterling to do it? He can make a quick getaway," Quinnie pointed out.

Cleo held Quinnie's gaze. "I plan to leave a message with the trackers. One Sterling can't deliver."

I held my hand out slowly and Cleo grabbed the cage and then jogged over to the van, tossing the box of squealing rats on the floor behind the driver's seat. We stood, dumbfounded, staring at her. This wasn't part of the plan either. She turned around to look at us, waving toward the tunnel. "Go!"

"I don't think so," Cassie said, rounding the van to the passenger side. "I'm coming with you."

"I don't need your help—"

Cassie held up her hand. "Don't even start with me, Cleo."

Cleo snapped her mouth shut and faced forward, holding back a smile.

"We're coming too," Quinnie said, grabbing my hand and pulling me toward the van. "Who knows what kind of trouble you'll get yourself into?"

Cleo rolled her eyes. "This is getting ridiculous. You guys don't need to risk yourselves like this. I can handle it."

"Fine," Quinnie retorted, pulling the sliding door shut. "Handle it on your own. I'm just coming along because I'm curious and feel like being entertained."

With a sigh, Cleo took off her helmet and tossed it to the side. She put the van in drive and did a U-turn heading back down Madison Avenue in the opposite direction toward the Empire State building. If anyone in the Program was tracking the Rat Squad, they were probably confused as to why the prisoners were heading back toward Headquarters.

Cleo reached up to touch the side of her headset. "Theo? You still there?"

"Still here, boss." Theo's voice echoed through the earpiece.

"Cleo!" Arabella's voice crackled over Theo's. "Where are you? I thought you were right behind us. We're in the tunnels and you're nowhere to be found."

"I have something to take care of. Just get the Harpies to safety. Quinnie, Cassie, and Rune are with me. They're fine." She turned to look at us. "For now, anyway."

"This isn't part of the plan," Dexter complained. "What are you doing?"

Cleo took a left turn and then another left onto Park Avenue.

"Theo," she said, ignoring Dexter. "Broadcast the SSA we made. Then unleash the virus once it runs." After we'd gone several blocks, Cleo stopped the van and in the distance I could see Grand Central Station, the three large arched windows and elaborate statues overhead heralding the entrance.

"SSA?" Quinnie asked. "What's that?"

Cleo reached into her jacket to pull out a tablet. She swiped her finger across the screen to bring up a video. She handed it to Quinnie. "This explains it. Now get out."

Cassie crossed her arms. "I will not get out."

"GET OUT!" Cleo yelled, spinning to face her friend. Her hair lifted as a heated blast of air swirled around her. "We don't have much time! You'll ruin everything."

Cassie flinched and then opened the door to escape. We all stumbled out onto the sidewalk as Cleo continued to urge us to go. Once we were out, she reached over and yanked the passenger door shut before facing forward. She narrowed her eyes and then the wheels of the van squealed against the pavement, the back end fishtailing as the tires fought for purchase. The van hurtled up the two-way road, which was raised like a ramp over the streets crossing beneath. There were short walls on either side, and Cleo picked up speed as she drove up the ramp like a stunt car driver.

"She's not slowing down." Cassie's hand flew to her mouth. "Why isn't she slowing down?"

Suddenly, the driver's side door opened and Cleo tumbled out onto the road, just before the van made impact. The vehicle crashed through the short wall surrounding the building and launched itself up over the step, narrowly missing a statue before smashing through the middle archway. Glass shattered with the impact and not a second later, Cleo leaned up on her elbow and thrust her hand forward. Flames rocketed away from her, engulfing the building with a wall of fire. There was a deafening roar and then stone and glass succumbed to her power, blasting away from us and crumbling inward.

Cleo pushed herself into a standing position and quickly limped down the ramp toward us as the building imploded in on itself behind her. Cassie rushed to meet her, yelling at her for being so stupid.

Quinnie elbowed me in the side and held the tablet up for me to see. "Look at this."

Cleo was on the screen, Theo at her side. "Hello fellow Sophisticates. Whether you're a Mandate, Vanguard, or Hound, this message is for you because we're all the same. We're all prisoners of the Program. I know my face looks familiar. The Program would like you to believe that I'm the enemy. That I'm the one who can destroy everything this country knows and loves. That's not true." She leaned forward on her elbows and smiled. "With your help, I'm one of the people who is going to free you."

***

"I don't think everyone got your message," I said to Cleo. Using the tunnels, we'd made our way to the Empire State Building unseen. Now we were watching Headquarters from afar, and the place was swarming with Mandates in battle gear. "Or if they did get it, they didn't believe it."

"No matter." Cleo was covered in bloody scrapes, and her uniform was in tatters because of her jump out of the van, but she seemed even more determined than before. "It's almost time," she said, looking at the watch on her wrist. "I want to see what happens when Theo sets the virus loose."

After we left the remains of Grand Central Station, we watched Cleo's SSA, or Sophisticates Service Announcement, as she called it. Even with the possibility of facing off against the Program, she hadn't lost her sense of humor. The video was broadcast to every device available to Sophisticates: laptops, televisions, phones. The audio was even transmitted over speaker systems in buildings and compounds to reach as many Sophisticates as possible. In the recording, Cleo briefly explained what the Program had done to the Dozen and how they were framing us for crimes we hadn't committed. She promised to free the Sophisticates from the Program's grip and her first promise was to break the tracking device, which was supposed to happen in just a few short minutes.

The Mandates we were watching were alert, yet nervous, as they prowled the area around the entrance to Headquarters. Some looked at their watches, the only sign that they were aware of the broadcast Cleo sent out.

"Tell me again why you had to risk your life murdering the Rat Squad and destroying yet another beautiful building," Quinnie asked, coming up alongside Cleo. "Don't get me wrong. It was cool and all, but I just don't understand."

Cleo sighed. "First of all, if anyone was tracking Squad 54 and the prisoners, I wanted to lead them away from the scene of the crime to give Arabella and Sterling a chance to get them to safety. Secondly, they were planning to bring that building down on us when we tried to rescue the Harpies. It was filled with booby traps. It had to come down. And lastly," Cleo said, a cruel smile claiming her mouth, "Persephone isn't the only one who can cause chaos. It was a threat and a diversion. When they send Mandates to investigate the situation, there will be fewer for us to deal with when we go after Baker and Steel."

"I hate to interrupt," Theo said over our headsets, "but the virus is going live in thirty seconds."

"The virus," Quinnie repeated with a laugh. "You should have come up with a catchy name for it. *The virus* sounds so boring."

"Insurrection." Cassie twirled her blades through the air in boredom. "That sounds like a disease."

"I like it," Theo agreed. "Insurrection in 10 . . 9...8...7..." his voice buzzed in our ears. "3...2...1."

It was as if someone threw cold water over the guards below.

As one, their posture stiffened and then they reached for their wrists, pulling up sleeves and rubbing the spots where their tattoos were located. They looked around at one another. If they had seen Cleo's SSA, doubt, disbelief, and hope were only a few of the questions on their minds.

"Done," Theo said. "Every single blip is gone from the screens. Sophisticates are digitally invisible to the Program now."

"That's it," Cleo said, pushing back from the window. "Let's hope it's enough to throw a few of them to our side. We have to strike now while we still have the element of surprise. Theo has control over the Program's entire system, but I don't know how long it will last. We jumped the biggest hurdle and broke the trackers, but now we have to cut off the head of the snake. Steel and Baker are in there," she said, pointing to Headquarters, "and this is our best chance at getting to them."

"Music to my ears," Quinnie muttered. "I don't care who takes out Steel, but Baker is mine."

Cassie cleared her throat. "But he's your father. Are you sure you can do it?"

Blue sparks danced along Quinnie's fingertips. "That's exactly why I can do it."

Cleo turned away from her view of Headquarters and looked at each of us in turn. "I'm not asking you guys to go with me. I can do this alone."

Cassie laughed. "Yeah, that's what you said that time we climbed the tree outside Ms. Wellington's classroom. Remember that? She had to call the fire department to get you down."

Cleo glared at her. "I was six. And you dared me to do it."

Cassie put up her hands. "Just saying. If I hadn't been there to go run and tell Ms. Wellington that you got yourself stuck up there like some hair-brained cat, your ass would still be stuck in that tree."

Cleo shook her head. "Fine. Do whatever you want. You will anyway."

Cassie grinned. "Good. I'm glad we understand each other. Quinnie? Rune? You guys coming?"

"I'm in," Quinnie said. "Do we have a plan or are we just going in, deviations blazing?" She batted her hands around like guns, tiny bolts of electricity shooting from her fingertips before sizzling into nothingness.

"There's a plan," Cleo confirmed. "It's half-assed, but still a plan."

"As long as in the end Baker dies, I don't really care how half-assed it is." Quinnie eyed Cleo. "Tell us what we need to know."

CLEO

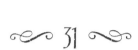

DEVIANTS TO THE END

I was created to be a weapon for the Program, one who could eliminate any enemy that tried to harm our country. That was what they claimed.

Funny how my enemy turned out to be the people who created me. I was dangerous, that much was true, but I refused to let the Program use me. I was a living thing with choices, and power, and a taste for revenge. I'd heard the saying that revenge is a dish best served cold, but I wasn't satisfied to wait long enough for it to get cold. Marty and Sadie deserved more. Besides, I wanted Baker and Steel to see me coming. When they were destroyed, I wanted them to know that I helped make it possible. I wanted to look them right in the eye when death finally stole their last breath. I wanted them to know I was doing it because of Marty, Sadie, my parents, and all the failed experiments leading up to the Deviant Dozen. Baker and Steel didn't deserve quick deaths, but as long as death finally took them, I didn't care much how it happened.

We were in the lowest level of Headquarters, far below street level. Another one of Liberty's mapped tunnels dumped us into a storage room. The tunnel was smaller than most of the others we used, and it was rough and unkempt which made me think that it was possibly a tunnel someone dug out on their own rather than one the city purposely created. It seemed only fitting that revenge should come in through an ugly, dark, unknown path.

"Baker and Steel are in their office on the 86th floor, but there are no cameras in there," Theo said through the earpiece. "I can secure the elevators to take you up there, but I can't guarantee what you're going to be facing once you get in. I don't know how many Mandates they might have in there, and by now, I'm sure they're expecting you. Or at least they're expecting something. We've had control over their network for hours now and they've been working hard to wrench it back from us."

"Then we need to hurry," I said. "Before they figure out how to break through the obstacles I put up. How do we get to the elevators?"

After assuring us the coast was clear outside the room we were in, we followed Theo's directions until we were in front of a set of shiny doors. Even down in the basement, the elevator was decked out in gold and trimmed in the art deco silhouette of the building.

I turned to face my friends. "You can still turn back. It's not too late."

"Oh, but it is, pussy cat," Cassie said. She reached out and a blade slid from the knuckle of her index finger and she pressed it against the button that would call the elevator to us. "I'm in this until the end." She dragged the edge of her blade across the elevator door leaving a deep gouge in the shape of an 'X' in the metal.

"I already sent the elevator to you, babe," Theo told Cassie through the headset. "No need to scratch up those pretty blades just yet."

Cassie looked up at the camera in the corner behind us that was faced toward the elevator. She smiled and blew a kiss to it. "Don't worry. I'll save some for you, baby."

"Ugh." Quinnie screwed up her face in disgust and looked at Cassie. "Please tell me that's not some sort of dirty sex talk. One, that's just stupid. And two, I don't want to think about you two that way. I can't afford to double over in dry heaves right now."

Cassie grinned and held up her hand, the blades flicking out of her knuckles as she fanned them in front of her face. "These are really useful when clothes get in the way."

Quinnie put up her own hand, electricity crackling along her skin in irritation. "Not listening."

I didn't try to stop them from arguing because I knew them both well enough to know it didn't mean anything. It was just something to do while we ignored our nerves. Like Theo said, we had no idea what would be waiting for us on the other side of those doors when we finally reached the 86th floor. A cheery ding echoed through the vacant hallway and then the doors opened.

"Your chariot awaits," Theo said.

We got in and then the doors slid shut. The elevator started moving up and my stomach dropped with the speed of our ascent.

"Shit," Theo said. "Cleo, I'm blind."

Reflexively, I reached up to my ear, sure I heard him wrong. "What?"

"You have to get out of there. I'm shut out. Completely shut out." Theo, who was always calm and collected, now sounded panicked.

"The video feed went down and I'm totally blind. I can't see you. I can't see anything. Something is wrong. I have a blank screen."

We pushed the buttons on the wall, trying to get the car to stop on another floor, or just stop altogether, but nothing worked. The elevator continued to rocket toward the 86th floor and an unknown situation. Static filled my ears and through it, I could barely hear Theo calling our names. And then it went dead.

"Theo?" I called. When he didn't answer, Cassie called his name into her own headset. She didn't get a response either.

The car came to a sudden stop and there was a moment of quiet while the doors stayed shut.

"Looks like it's just us," I said quietly. The doors started to open, and Rune stepped in front of us, blasting the doors outward with a gust of air before they fully opened. The metal panels were ripped out of the doorway and flew forward, knocking over the Mandates who were standing guard just outside. Quinnie pushed Rune behind her and moved her hands in front of her body, the protective electrical shield springing to life just before shots were fired. Bullets ricocheted off the shield, pinging against the floor and embedding in furniture and glass. Mandates ducked for cover to avoid being hit.

"Hold your fire!" a voice demanded.

I looked toward the person who gave the order to see that there were two men standing in the middle of the room. They were dressed impeccably in dark suits and although I'd never seen either of them before, I knew that they must be Baker and Steel. There were Hounds and Mandates standing to either side of the men, some with weapons pointed at us, others staring in shock at Quinnie's shield. I vaguely noticed a figure with a hood over its head, tied to a chair near the desks.

I raised my hand toward the men in the middle of the room and my palm warmed as my deviation surged to life under my skin. A Hound took a step toward me, blocking my aim. My hand snapped forward, tongues of flame crashing at the man's feet, forcing him backwards. I looked back toward Baker and Steel as fire gathered around my fingers.

"Before you finish that thought, young lady, you need to listen well." The man with white hair and matching goatee was looking straight at me. "You harm us, Liberty will be destroyed."

Liberty? His words were like a fist around my throat. *How did he know about Liberty?* It was all I could do to hold back my deviation.

As if to answer my unspoken question, the man with white hair grinned. "We know all about Liberty thanks to a little bird." He beckoned with his hand and the Mandates parted to allow someone through.

Eylsia. Her first few steps through the Mandates were unsure, but she gained determination as she neared Baker and Steel.

Rune stepped forward, but didn't go beyond Quinnie's protective shield. "What have you done, Elysia?"

"What I had to do." She refused to look him in the eye. "The Deviants' plan would have gotten us all killed."

"And you thought this would help?" Rune clenched his fists, sneering at her.

She lifted her chin, her blue eyes turning glacial as she eyed him. "I knew it would help *me.*"

The white-haired man laughed. "Hear that, Steel?" He turned to face the other man. "See that was our mistake. We tried to make weapons out of the good genes." He gestured toward us where we were still hidden behind Quinnie's shield. "We should have been working with the damaged ones. They have no conscience." He put his hand on Elysia's shoulder and she stood a little taller, confidence flowing through her for the first time in months.

Dr. Steel stood unfazed, his hands folded in front of him as he gazed at us. He took his time inspecting each of us before he settled on Rune. "Want to rethink your allegiance, son?"

"I'm not your son," Rune growled.

Dr. Steel tilted his head in interest. "Hm. I thought someone would have told you by now that you're mine. That you have my DNA to thank for your existence."

Air pulsed around us, warping Quinnie's shield and Rune clenched and unclenched his fists as if trying to keep everything under control. "They told me who you were, I just chose to deny your claim on me."

Steel's mouth pressed flat in annoyance and he flicked his hand toward a Hound off to the side. "Turn on the video footage so our guests understand the importance of the request I'm about to make."

The Hound nodded once in agreement before moving to the desks near the windows and hitting a button. A large video screen off to the side flickered to life and I recognized the inside of Liberty. The residents were gathered into the middle of the tent city, sur-rounded by Mandates in battle gear. With pride, I noticed that no one was cowering in fear. Every resident, from young to old, stood proud and courageous. Josie was in front, defiant in every nuance of her posture. Arabella and Sterling were missing. They must have still been making their way back from rescuing the Harpies.

"You might have gotten control of our system for a while, but we still found our way into your compound," Dr. Steel said. "Put down your shield, or we'll start picking those people off one at a time. We'll start with the children. That should move this along more quickly."

Quinnie laughed bitterly. "If I put down my shield, you'll just kill us one at a time and then kill every single person in Liberty when you're done." She was answering Steel, but her eyes were fixed on Baker. "No deal."

"Elysia," Steel said, "go fetch Wesley. And then have one of the Hounds take you back to Liberty. We may need to have you make an example of some of the residents if your sister refuses to cooperate."

So, Wesley was still alive.

"That coward is not my sister," Quinnie snapped. Her shield flared brightly in anger and Elysia cast her a smug look before leaving the room.

"You share the same DNA," Baker interjected. "Technically, you're sisters."

Quinnie scoffed. "Technically I share DNA with you, too, but the only word that comes to mind when I think of you is..."

I elbowed Quinnie in the arm. "Don't make things worse than they already are," I whispered.

"News flash, chica. Things can't get worse," she hissed back.

"We just need to give Theo a little more time," I reminded her.

The door Elysia left through opened and Wesley came in, carrying a metal briefcase. I heard a sound of angry disgust and I wasn't sure if it was coming from Quinnie or Cassie. They both looked like they wanted to rip Wesley into tiny pieces. He set the briefcase on the desk and opened it, pulling out a gun and fitting a dart into it. His expression was calm and controlled, but I noticed his hands shaking.

Without even thinking about it, I raised my hand again, thoughts of revenge flaring along my fingertips.

"Don't," Baker warned. "If you open fire on him or any of us, our Mandates will do the same to Liberty. And if that's not enough of a deterrent for you, maybe we should start taking a trophy for every moment you delay in putting down the shield." He walked over to the desk and ripped the hood off the figure who was tied to the chair.

I gasped when I realized it was Professor Younglove. She was even more emaciated looking than before. Her skin clung to the bones underneath and when she lifted her chin and squinted through the bright lights to look at us, I could see how full of pain and exhaustion her eyes were. Baker pulled a knife out of the belt of one of the Mandates close to him and then slid it against the nylon rope that was wrapped around Younglove's body. She didn't even struggle when he pulled her arm free and slammed her wrist against the table, holding her arm hostage.

"I'll start with her hand since she was so careless as to let you get away in the first place."

Static crackled in my ear and I had to school my features to ignore it. "I'm back," Theo said. His voice was quiet. "Mandates took over Liberty, that's why I cut out. But I managed to get away. I'm patched back into the video feed. Do what you have to do."

I reached up to straighten my jacket and noticed Cassie doing the same.

"Drop the shield." The knife in Baker's hand was resting across the backs of Younglove's fingers.

"This is only a counteragent," Wesley said, holding up the gun. "They don't want to kill you. They just want to take you into custody."

Counteragent? Custody? I couldn't be hearing him correctly.

"Of course they want to kill us, you idiot," Cassie shouted. "That's why we've been in hiding for months. That's why they already killed Marty and Sadie."

Wesley flinched. "That was an accident." Regret was clear on his features as he put aside the gun and loaded another one. "The Program needs you alive. They need to prove to the people that they caught the terrorists responsible for all of the recent attacks."

"The Program was responsible for the recent attacks!" Quinnie glared at Baker and Steel in turn. Her shield flared erratically with her fury, the edges of it snapping wildly with stray bolts of electricity. Mandates stepped back out of reach.

"We are not terrorists." I turned my glare on Baker. "The Program orchestrated the attack on Baltimore and framed us for it. We had nothing to do with that and you know it. You terrorized your own people."

Baker didn't deny it. "We do what we have to do to keep the country safe," he said. "Baltimore was a small sacrifice and a means to an end. The Deviant Dozen is the real threat against this country. If we had to burn a small piece of the city to flush the Deviants out of hiding, so be it."

I stepped forward. "We're not a threat. Not to the people anyway." My voice was calm, but I was a riot of emotions inside. I just had to hold it together a little longer. "You allowed the people to riot and terrorize one another all over the country while they went on a wild goose chase for us. The Program was created to protect the American people and the only thing you've done is protect yourselves. You're hunting us because you don't want the people to know that you created weapons that you could no longer control."

Baker grinned. "Such a big mouth for such a little girl. We'll have our control. And you know how I know this?"

I sucked in a breath as Baker pressed the edge of his blade down across Younglove's fingers. She clenched her jaw shut and looked away, trying not to make a sound as blood welled along the edge of the blade.

His eyes held mine. "Because we're willing to do whatever it takes to have control. People have sacrificed their children into the Sophisticates Program to give us power over our enemies. We've sacrificed our *own* children." He glanced at Quinnie, a feral grin stretching across his mouth. "And I will seize control no matter what I have to do." He slammed the knife down with all his weight and the blade sliced clean through Younglove's fingers. Her scream echoed through the room as her body arched out of the chair. Baker pointed the knife at the screen, blood splattering across the floor in a glossy arc. "Choose one of the children," he ordered. "The smallest one you can find."

"Cleo," Wesley begged. "Drop the shield. It's only a counteragent." His eyes flicked to the screen where a Mandate was pushing through the crowd. "Don't let anyone else die."

"Quinnie," I murmured, putting my hand on her arm. "Please. We have the confession. We can't let them have a child, too."

Without argument, she dropped her hands and the shield vanished. I braced myself when I heard the distinctive pop of a gun and then reached up to pull out the dart that was embedded in my arm. The Mandates lifted their guns and trained them on us once again as they moved to surround us.

The counteragent. Wesley shot us with the counteragent. He told them to give it to us so we couldn't use our deviations. They didn't want us dead yet. They wanted to use us. Maybe public executions? Who knew...I shook my head. It didn't matter. We got what we needed from Baker and Steel. Even if we didn't end up surviving, I knew we'd be taking them down with us. I only wished Younglove hadn't been caught in the crossfire. She was now clutching her wrist against her body, blood running down her arm. I didn't expect her to be here. That wasn't part of my plan.

"A child!" Baker yelled at the video screen. "As a reminder to these fools that they need to listen to my instructions the first time."

The Mandate emerged from the crowd, dragging a young boy along with him. Panic seized my lungs and I couldn't breathe as the soldier pulled a gun from his holster. The people of Liberty started to scream, rushing forward to get to the boy. Before they could breach the wall of guards holding them back, a loud sound exploded through the video feed and people ducked instinctively. The Mandate holding the boy jerked once before crumpling to the ground and out of view. The boy ran back into the crowd to safety.

The people of Liberty and the Mandates went still, looking blankly at something off screen.

"What is going on?" Steel walked toward the video monitor as if that would help him see better.

A group of Hounds walked into view and physically separated the Mandates from the residents of Liberty. Instead of bullying Josie's people, however, the Hounds aimed their weapons at the

Mandates, disarming them before forcing them to lie face down on the ground.

"Explain yourself, officer," Steel demanded. "Who are you?"

The Hound in the middle of the screen who was directing the ambush turned to face us. He reached up and pulled his helmet off, tossing it to the side. I swear my heart tried to fight its way out of my chest at the sight on the screen.

It was Ozzy.

I hadn't dared to think of him at all since we left Liberty earlier today. I wasn't sure if I'd ever see him again and now that he was so close, yet so far out of reach, I thought I might crumble with the overwhelming relief I felt at knowing he was safe.

"Lesson number one about Sophisticates," Ozzy said, holding up his gun. "Friendships are more powerful than dictatorships." He laughed, looking around as Hounds yanked off their helmets and tossed them away. I didn't recognize any of them. "Funny how those same people who trusted me with their lives on all those missions, still trust me. I win, Steel."

Dr. Steel's face turned bright red. "You win nothing, Osbourne. You can have that worthless city for now because I will eventually take it back. I still have your friends." He threw his hand out toward us and grinned. "We'll see how quickly you play my game once you see the life draining out of them. They're completely at my mercy now."

"Actually," Quinnie said. "You're at our mercy and it seems we're fresh out of that." Her hands spun wildly and the shield sprung to life in front of us again.

Cassie, Rune, and I spun around to face the Mandates who had come up behind us after the counteragent was administered. One of them raised his gun and Cassie was a blur of fury and shiny metal as she knocked it out of his hand and slashed across his forearm before turning toward the Mandate next to him. Rune waved his hand to the side, bursts of air brushing soldiers off their feet and away from us as if they weighed nothing. I flung handfuls of fire out, creating pillars of heat that sent the rest of the Mandates cringing away and looking for safety. I spun around to face the middle of the room again.

"What?" Baker backed away from Younglove, the knife dropping out of his hand and clattering to the floor. "You can't...you can't. The counteragent..."

"We spent the last few months building up a tolerance," Cassie explained. Her fingers were curled in toward her palms and her blades stuck out from her fists, dripping blood from the tips and reflecting the bright blur of Quinnie's electromagnetic shield along the edges. "We could have taken you out at any time. We just needed something from you first." She tapped the pin at the top of her jacket, a similar video camera we were all wearing.

"What?" Baker asked again as he moved toward Dr. Steel.

"Your video confession to clear our name," Rune explained. "I'm sure once we go through this place from top to bottom we'll find all the proof we need to corroborate it. So, now we have no further use for you." He raised his arms, a deadly promise wrapped in such innocent looking hands.

"You can't do this..." Baker darted a glance toward Steel, but Steel stood transfixed by Quinnie's shield as if he could see their empire crumbling beneath them.

"Oh do go on, father. I would love to hear you beg," Quinnie sneered.

"Please..." Baker muttered.

Quinnie made a disgusted sound. "Shut up! Don't you understand sarcasm? Rune, can you...take out the trash?" She nodded toward Baker and Steel.

He raised his eyebrows. "I thought you wanted to do the honors?"

She narrowed her eyes. "I just want them out of my sight. Immediately. I'm ready to go home."

"My pleasure." Rune raised his arms and with a simple motion of his hands, there was a thundering crack that caused the Mandates to drop their weapons and cover their ears. The power released by Rune's hands was invisible, but vicious. It was as if two unseen fists shoved Baker and Steel backward. Their bodies flew through the room, slamming against the windows, shattering the glass, and tossing everything out—86 floors above street level. Quinnie and Rune were expressionless as their fathers, our creators, flew over the edge and plummeted out of sight.

Cassie rushed over toward Younglove, speaking in her headset as she went. "Theo, we need medical help for Professor Younglove. She's been injured."

Rune and Quinnie walked toward the broken windows and peered out into the open sky. I looked at the Mandates scattered around the room, their eyes wide and disbelieving. I let flames gather in my palms and crawl up my arms, singeing my jacket sleeves.

"We're dismantling the Program. You held your weapons against us, but I'm giving you a second chance. A chance to choose redemption."

Weapons dropped to the ground, the last grip of the Program

falling away.

OZZY

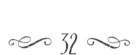

KILGORE FALLS

Cleo's arms were wrapped tightly around my waist, her body tucked close against mine. My motorcycle rumbled beneath us as we prowled the deserted roads. A few hours ago, these roads were the property of the Program. Technically, they still were, but that was a matter of paperwork. The Program was going to change. Everything would change.

There was still a lot to be discussed and decided, and I knew that at some point, we would have to be part of that. But not today. Today I was fulfilling my promise. I told Cleo that when our mission was over, the first place I was going to take her was Kilgore Falls. And maybe things weren't quite over yet. Maybe there was still a lot to do. But today, I was giving her a taste of freedom. I didn't care that we had to drive three hours to make that happen. As soon as we confirmed that Theo had the video confession that Cleo worked so hard for, we left.

No hugs goodbye, no tearful promises, no excuses. We'd waited too long and had endured too much, and I felt no guilt over being greedy. I was ready to ignore responsibilities for once and keep a promise to the girl I loved. I was going to enjoy my freedom immediately.

Of course, a taste of freedom wouldn't be complete without my bike, so we had to make a pit stop for that. We also needed a change of clothes since both of us were covered in memories we'd rather forget. So we swung by the Academy. We entered through the front door, which had never been repaired. I found it strange how in all those months after Delia's attack, it stood vacant and as unchanged as the last time we set foot in it, much like all the land that the Academy owned around the campus to preserve their privacy.

I pulled my bike into the overgrown parking lot and turned it off. Cleo didn't immediately pull away. She kept her face pressed against my back and her arms tight around my chest.

"I'm almost afraid to let go," she admitted. "I'm afraid I'll wake up and find out you're still gone. Or worse. I'm dead."

Chuckling, I said, "I wouldn't let that happen to you." I reached up to wrap my hands around hers before gently prying them apart. She swung her leg over the seat and dismounted, but I didn't let go of her hand.

I got off the bike and pulled her into my arms. Cleo's face automatically tilted up and our lips met in a heated kiss, much like they had hundreds of times in the last few hours. Much like they would for the rest of our lives. Now that I could kiss her any time I wanted, I didn't really have plans to do much else.

Shifting Cleo's hand in mine, I laced our fingers together before leading her down the path. No one but me had been down here in years and the forest was slowly, but surely, reclaiming the path as its own. Cleo didn't seem to mind when prickly vines snagged at her clothes or we had to duck under low hanging branches or climb over fallen trees. She held onto my hand like I was her lifeline.

When the sound of the falls could finally be heard off in the distance, she squeezed my hand in excitement. The path eventually dropped us at the edge of a river and Cleo giggled as I helped her navigate the slippery rocks in order to cross to the other side. A giggle. From the deadliest girl I knew. It only seemed fitting that her personality was the exact opposite of her abilities—a soft heart to temper the deadly fire.

Cleo gasped when she got a look at the falls. "It's more beautiful than I expected." Her eyes were bright and carefree as she took everything in—the soaring walls of rock, the glassy sheet of water cascading over the edge, the sparkling pool of water at the bottom of the falls, and the lush green canopy of trees overhead that nearly dripped with the fullness of spring.

"Come on," I said, guiding her up onto the enormous boulder that jutted in the middle of the water. Once on top, I unrolled the blanket I'd grabbed back at the Academy and I spread it over the rocky surface. I sat down and pulled Cleo between my legs so that her back rested against my chest and I could wrap my arms around her.

We didn't speak. We didn't have to. All we needed was to be together, to enjoy our freedom, both from the Program and with each other. We sat, watching the falls for so long I was sure Cleo had fallen asleep.

She reached up to wrap her hand around my arm, her fingers trailing along my skin thoughtfully. "You know, when you and Euri snuck into the city?"

"Yeah?" I leaned down to kiss along her neck and she moved her head to give me better access.

"I'm surprised you didn't come for me first." Her fingers slid over my arm to my knee, tracing a path along my shins.

"Surprised or offended?" My first instinct was to go straight for Cleo, but after finding Theo, I not only knew I wouldn't make it to her in time, I knew I couldn't go even if I wanted to.

"Surprised." She sighed. "But I'm glad you didn't. We never imagined that Elysia would give us up. We thought Liberty was safe. I'm glad you kept it that way."

I kissed her neck again and she shivered. "It was the hardest thing I ever had to do, to not come to you," I told her. "But deep down I knew that as much as I wanted to protect you and keep you safe, you're perfectly capable of doing it on your own. When Marco heard the call come in to capture Liberty, I knew where you'd want me to go."

She smiled and I pulled her closer to me, capturing the corner of her smile with a kiss.

"Can I tell you something?" she murmured.

"Of course."

"I like that you trust me. But I also kind of like that you want to keep me safe." She turned her head fully to look at me.

I caught her lips with mine and she let me kiss her, deep and slow. "Then you won't complain the next time I try?"

She shrugged. "As long as we're together, I don't think I'm going to complain about anything."

I ran my hand up into her hair and held her to me as I kissed her again, lifting and turning her so that she was sitting in my lap. Her arms snaked around my shoulders and my pulse pounded in my chest as I realized there was no out-of-control deviation, no meddling friends, no Program to step in and stop us.

Cleo must have realized it at the same time as me because her hands went to my chest and she pressed just hard enough to break our kiss. "We have to slow down," she murmured.

"We do?" I craned my head forward to steal another kiss, but she evaded me, somehow wriggling out of my embrace and standing up.

"Yes." She grinned, peeling off her jacket and tossing it to the rock. "Because if you keep kissing me, I'll never get a chance to jump off this boulder and you promised me it would be a rush."

I stood up, peeling off my own jacket as Cleo stripped off her shirt, never taking her eyes off mine.

"Remember that night we played two truths, one lie?" she asked.

"Yeah." *How could I forget?* Trying to drive her insane with anticipation had nearly driven me insane. Best night of my life.

Her smile was so wicked, it could have charmed me to do just about anything. "Here's my two truths and one lie," she said. "I want to go skinny dipping with you..." She held up her index finger. "I'm going commando right now..." She winked and finger number two flipped up. "I love you." Finger number three joined the first two.

I ...what? Two truths, one lie. I stared at her, confused. Two truths one lie.

"I can see you're having trouble remembering the rules, so I'll refresh your memory," she said quietly. She unbuttoned her jeans and then hooked her thumbs in the belt loops, yanking her pants down. She stood in front of me in nothing but her bra and underwear. "You see, I'm not really going commando, but I really do want to go skinny dipping."

I was so dumbfounded, I completely missed her removing the rest of her clothes. She looked over her shoulder and gave me a sassy smile before leaping off the rock, butt naked, and squealing all the way down until she splashed into the frigid water.

And I stood there like an idiot with only one thought ringing in my head.

Cleo loved me.

RUNE

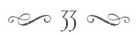 33

LEGACY

A Year Later

A Year Later

The thing about a legacy is that people assume it's some sort of consequence. Something handed down to you, the aftermath of those before you.

Our legacy wasn't given to us freely. We stole it. Earned it. Demanded it. It was rightfully ours.

What exactly was our legacy? The deaths of Baker and Steel. And hopefully a better future for Sophisticates.

We knew it would take time for things to settle down, but we refused to allow things to get out of hand. We were barely adults, some of us not even considered adults by most standards, but we were seizing our future and we made sure that point was clear. To everyone.

The sad state of affairs was that the Program had been controlling so much of the business and military future of our country, the government had been little more than a figurehead monarchy for the last 30 years. Through the power of the Program, Baker and Steel regulated everything, so handing control back to the government was likely to be a slow, painful process. The good news was that Lawless, Younglove, the Knights, and Josie were all willing to step in and help make the transition successful. The idea that the future of our entire country rested on a few teachers, jilted parents, and orphaned teens was almost too hard to believe.

But then again, who would believe the Deviant Dozen and Others could possibly exist?

Faced with the video confession Cleo pulled from Baker and Steel, along with the mountain of evidence we unearthed in Headquarters, the government had no choice but to go along with our suggestions. Cleo had all but freed the Sophisticates and if the government wanted them to return to their positions, both in business and in the military, it would be a return that was made by choice. No Sophisticate would ever be forced to do anything against their will again. The country was at our mercy, but we were determined not to take advantage of that.

It had been a year since Baker and Steel were eliminated, and things were finally starting to settle down. Vanguards, Mandates, Hounds, and even the Deviants were finding their places in the world, and making choices they never dreamed they'd have the opportunity to make.

Arabella and Sterling returned with the Knights to their ranch. Arabella didn't have much skill with horses, so it was no surprise to any of us when she opened up a skating rink in town and hosted roller derby events once a month. Quinnie told me that Arabella was booked up solid every other day of the week giving skating lessons to young girls and a few brave boys. She was also making almost as much money off her wig fashion line as she was giving lessons. Apparently, her students were as addicted to colorful hairstyles as Arabella was.

Sterling opened up a gym right next door to Arabella's which offered Free Running and Parkour. All I knew is that whenever I showed up to visit, kids were running up walls, jumping off things, and flipping all over the damn place.

Cleo and Ozzy? We didn't see them much. When they were on the east coast, we all tried to get together and hang out, but it didn't happen often. They were constantly on the move, traveling and discovering new places. They wanted nothing to do with the Program, although it had been renamed Legacy. Legacy, unlike the Program, held no control over Sophisticates or the government. It was merely an advisor to political leaders and an advocate for Sophisticates everywhere.

Why was it called Legacy? Because after the dust settled, Quinnie and I were the ones answering the questions that were asked, demanding the rights that were necessary, and guiding those who needed direction. Against all odds, we had somehow inherited the empire our fathers built, and we found ourselves in charge of dismantling every ugly piece of it and turning it into something useful. I didn't mind. Theo and Cassie were around to help, as well as Euri, Dexter, and the Homework Harpies. To me, it was worth it to uncover the friendships that I eventually recognized as a family.

Eva, like Ozzy and Cleo, wanted to get as far away from Legacy as possible. She was off pursuing an acting career in California, but she made an effort to come back frequently to visit. I think she needed that family tie as much as the rest of us. Not all of us had been as lucky as Arabella to go through the Sophisticates Program and come out on the other side with parents who were waiting for us. Even Sterling, who'd found Josie, chose to treat the Knights as parental figures. Most of us did.

On the good days, I took comfort in the fact that Sophisticates were finding their place in the world and that they were being accepted by civilians. On bad days, I remembered the lives that had been lost because of Delia, the ones that I could have prevented if I'd been stronger at the time. It was the bad days that kept me working toward the good ones. I would probably spend the rest of my life atoning for the mistakes I made under Delia.

But at least I was better off than some others. Elysia and Wesley didn't survive the attack on Headquarters. I'll never understand why Wesley told Baker and Steel that the counteragents would work on us. He knew they wouldn't. After we discovered that Persephone, Elysia, and Euri had built up a tolerance against the counteragents back at the ranch, the rest of the Deviants decided to do the same. The fact that Wesley would suggest that Baker and Steel use counteragents on us when he knew they wouldn't work made me think that he felt guilty for what had happened to Marty and Sadie. That he was trying to give us an advantage by creating that ruse.

We'll never know the answer to that, though. After the battle at Headquarters was over and we searched the building, we found the bodies of Wesley and Elysia in a stairwell. Both of them had gaping holes in their chests as if they'd been shot with a missile at close range. Or as if someone had punched a hole through them. There were no bullets or other weapons, only faint charred marks around the skin and clothing, the hole cauterized in a creepy, unexplained way.

Quinnie thought they both tried to run and were caught by someone with a score to settle, but we had no idea who. All we knew was that ex-Program officials would occasionally show up dead after trying to run from justice, one or two a month, and they always had the same gaping wound. It was a mystery. If I didn't know better, I might suspect Cleo, but she'd been with us the entire time in Headquarters. She never had a chance to search out Wesley on her own. Besides, brutal assassination wasn't Cleo's style.

"Hey you, what are you thinking?" Quinnie came up behind me and leaned over the back of my chair, wrapping her arms around me and kissing the top of my head. She was careful not to act this way in front of others. She had a reputation to uphold, after all.

"I'm thinking it's time to get out of here and go home." I spun my chair around, grabbing her waist and pulling her into my lap. "Or I could just keep you here and have my way with you." Sometimes I couldn't believe the way my life had turned out. I had friends. I had purpose. I had a home. I had Quinnie. And even though Arabella routinely insisted that the last part was a curse, I knew differently. Quinnie needed to be saved just as much as I had. And Cleo was the first person to give each of us that chance.

Quinnie reached up and ran her fingers through my hair. "Messing around at the office is no fun. Why don't you take me home to have your way with me?"

"Why me? Always me?" a voice hollered from the other side of the room as a door slammed shut. "*Go up and get them, Sterling. They're probably still working, Sterling*," he whined in an imitation female voice.

I spun the chair around and broke out into a smile when I saw Sterling standing just inside my office. He looked unhappy and disgusted. "Hey there, Sterling. What's up?"

"I don't want to know!" he shouted, putting his hand up and turning away. "I have no interest in knowing if Quinnie has you pitching a tent over there. I'm outta here. Cassie and Theo sent me up here to get you guys." He opened the door. "Assholes," he muttered, before leaving.

The door banged shut behind Sterling and I pulled Quinnie against my chest. "I guess I'll have to take a rain check since our friends are waiting."

"Hmmmm," she agreed. "Friends." She pulled back to look at me. "That sounds weird, doesn't it?"

I shrugged. "I kind of like it. I say we keep them."

She stood up and held her hand out to me. "They are kind of entertaining, aren't they?" She looked around the office. "Did I leave my skates in here?"

I picked them up from under my desk and handed them to her. "Yup. Go kick butt, babe."

CLEO

～ 34 ～

DAMSELS OF DISTRESS

Coming back to Headquarters was still hard for me. They didn't call it Headquarters anymore. It was known as New York again, but it would always be Headquarters to me. It would always be the place where my nightmares resided. Legacy did a good job fixing it up though. They'd turned it into a refugee city, giving first dibs to Mandates, Vanguards, and Hounds, as well as the people of Liberty. The wall was torn down, buildings fixed up, and monsters hunted down and exterminated.

And when I say monsters, I mean both the genetically mutated creatures in the tunnels, and those hiding in human form. Sometimes I think the ones who were human were worse than the experiments that were found in some of the old tunnels. I almost felt bad when the monstrous experiments were destroyed because the only difference between them and me was that I'd learned to turn off my deadly abilities. It's not as if they could just stop being animals. And I wondered: if there were genetically mutated animals, and genetically mutated people, what other horrific secrets had the Program been hiding? I hoped I never found out.

"This feels like old times," Arabella said, tossing a helmet panty at me.

I couldn't hold back my grin. "This will be fun. Although now instead of being a Damsel of Distress, we're playing against them." I looked over at Quinnie and Eva. "It's going to be weird playing with you two instead of against you."

"Just so you know, I'm playing jammer," Quinnie said, swiping the helmet panty that Arabella had thrown at me.

"I don't think so." I reached for it and when she held it away and stuck her tongue out at me, I tossed a little fire at her. Just a little.

She threw up a lazy shield of electricity and rolled her eyes at me. "All that vacation is making you slow."

"Good thing *I'm* still on top of my game," Cassie quipped, yanking the jammer panty from Quinnie and snapping it over her helmet. "You two can be my blockers. I'm jamming this time."

Quinnie and I started to argue and Cassie's blades slid out like a fist of switch blades. "It'd be a shame to lose half your uniform during the match, huh ladies? I can be so clumsy when I don't get my way," she purred, scraping her blade across my uniform strap.

I pulled back. "Fine, psycho. You be jammer." I patted the strap of my outfit. "Just keep those babies sheathed."

"I can't make any promises," Cassie purred, wiggling her fingers until the blades disappeared.

In the distance I could hear the echo of announcements being made. It was almost time to go out. This was going to be the first derby match in New York at the newly refurbished track. Since the

Damsels had all moved to New York, they followed Arabella's lead and opened their own rink. They invited us to an exhibition match, Damsels against Deviants.

"We better line up," I said. "I think our names are about to be called."

"Oh!" Arabella said, grabbing my shoulder. "I almost forgot. I had cards made up especially for this night."

"Cards?" Eva asked.

"Player's cards so that we can toss them out to our fans afterwards," Arabella explained.

"We have fans?" I smiled, remembering my first match at the Academy when I'd played with the Damsels, how we'd beaten Quinnie's team, and how I'd saved one of my player's cards to give to Ozzy.

"Don't be ridiculous. Of course we have fans." Arabella opened up her locker and pulled out a cardboard box.

"Boyfriends don't count," Eva countered.

"We should call them boyfans," Cassie giggled.

"Anyone who calls out my name is a fan." Quinnie inspected her fingernails. "And trust me. Rune calls out my name plenty."

"Ew," we all groaned in unison.

"Here." Arabella shoved a stack of cards into each of our hands. "I had the girl who does the cards for my students do some for us. I told her what I wanted and she whipped them up last minute. I think they turned out pretty good."

I looked down at mine and had to admit it was cool. It was an illustration of me as a superhero, Flame Fatale, my skates and hair nothing but ribbons of fire. I tucked one in my bodice to give Ozzy later. He'd totally get a kick out of it.

"You've got to be kidding me," Quinnie screeched. She threw her cards onto the bench. I looked down to see what the problem was. The title across the top of her card said 'Electribitch' and the image was of a girl who looked like she was getting electrocuted...and was super pissed about it.

"You don't like it? Next time get your own done." Arabella was only half-hearted in her comeback, and even though Quinnie pretended to be angry, I saw her pick a card up off the bench before we left the locker room and stuff it into her bodice.

"Let's go girls. Our boyfans await." I pushed the door open from the locker room and even through the darkness, my eyes immediately found Ozzy. He smiled and my heart was full. I had love, I had friends, I had a future, and I had choices.

Freedom was a beautiful thing.

Epilogue

She pulled the eight-ball out of her pocket as she watched them and tossed it back and forth between her hands. The water inside caused the ball to spin with a wobble, but her hands were steady. Always steady.

For Deviants, they were hiding their nature pretty well. Sweet smiles, easy laughter, love in their eyes. If she didn't know better, she'd never guess they were as wicked as she was.

Then again, maybe they weren't. Maybe she was the only broken one now. Maybe they figured out how to turn it off. Maybe it was supposed to be this way.

"Should I let them know I'm here?" she asked herself. She wanted to. The urge to let her presence be known was an itch she wanted to scratch. Not the same sort of digging and scratching she used to do. No, that urge was gone. She didn't know when it had disappeared, but she knew that with it went the haze that seemed to always cloud her brain. She saw things more clearly now. She saw her own wretchedness and she wasn't afraid. She was what she was made to be. A killer.

"Should I let them know I'm here?" she asked herself again. She shook the ball and then turned it around so she could see the screen. The object inside floated to the top with her answer.

Outlook not so good.

"You're right," she told the ball. "It's better this way."

She sat in her seat in the dark, watching as they circled the track, warming up for the match. The hatred that had been so potent between some of them was long gone, replaced with the same acid jokes, but newfound respect. She wondered if maybe someday that could be her, if they could ever look at her with anything other than mistrust and disgust.

A shake and a peek.

Cannot predict now.

Yes. Of course. Not now. There was still so much to be done. So many Program scum hiding away, dodging their punishments. She still had to hunt them all down. She was the only one who could. The one who should. Evil was good at finding evil. And eliminating it.

"Maybe I'll just leave this here," she thought. "A sign." She shook the ball and flipped the screen up.

Without a doubt.

She smiled and set the ball on the short wall. She gave it one last lingering look before pushing it over the edge. She melted back in the shadows and disappeared as the ball bounced over the edge, rolling down the staircase until it came to rest at his feet, the one with the dark hair and green eyes. He picked it up, and then stood up quickly, searching every inch of the arena.

She was long gone.

ACKNOWLEDGEMENTS

I can't explain the immense feeling of accomplishment that comes at reaching the end of a trilogy. I hope *Redemption* surprises you, exceeds your expectations, satisfies you, and makes you love all the characters and their flaws as much as I do. Thank you for going on this journey with me and for all the support. I couldn't have done this without each and every one of you.

Johnny Manzari...you will always be the first person on the list because you're the most important. You're my foundation, my inspiration, and my happiness. I'm so lucky that you believe in me and support my dream. I love you.

To Johnny, Alex and Chloe, my adorably brilliant kids, thank you for sharing my love of books and for thinking that a trip to the book store on a Friday night is the most fun ever. I love that you make your own books just like mommy and I hope one day you're able to follow your dreams and do the things you love every day of your lives.

Many thanks to my beta readers: Rich Sanidad, Laura Ward (author of *Not Yet*, *Past Heaven*, and *The Pledge*), Dani Fisher (author of *A Bit Witchy*), Laurie Marin, and Amber Hodgson for taking the time to read the first draft of *Redemption* and for giving me valuable feedback on everything from the manuscript to the synopsis. Laura, you have been my biggest gift since I started writing. I'm so glad we get to take this journey together!

From the bottom of my heart I want to thank Rich Sanidad and Shelly Burch who took the time out of their busy lives to thoroughly edit my manuscript. Your brilliant red pens and insanely good advice made my book so much better.

There are so many special bloggers out there to thank. Book bloggers really are such an important part of a book's success and I appreciate the hell out of all of you. I'd like to specifically thank: Ethan Gregory from *One Guys Guide to Good Reads*, Maria from *Book Junky Girls*, Stephenee Carsten and Gladys Atwell from *Nerd Girl Official*, Sarah from *Girl Plus Book*, Jenna from *Star Angel Reviews*, Lindsay Self from *Broke Book Girls*, Merissa from *Archaeolibrarian*, Maja from *Maja's Books*, and Lauren from *Northern Plunder.* Thank you also to blogger Kim Baker from *KimberlyFayeReads* for your continued support and friendship.

A special thanks to Candace Robinson, Alice Hamer, Bekky Levesque, Kristen DeMarino, and Rosemary Britton. Your interaction with me on social media is so appreciated.

I can't have a proper acknowledgment section without thanking the two people who created the weird little monster that I am today. Mom and Dad, thank you for being the kind of parents that let me believe I could do anything (no matter how weird or crazy that thing was) and for always being there (no matter how far you had to travel to support me). You let me know it was okay to be different and I'm forever thankful for the beautiful, unconditional love you've always given me.

My deepest gratitude goes to all my friends and family who have been there to give me virtual high fives or words of inspiration in person and on social media. Thank you for buying my books, reading them, reviewing them, and suggesting them to others.

Lastly, a special thank you to those of you who have been with me from the beginning and have eagerly awaited each book. I write for you.

Thank you for reading Redemption. If you enjoyed this story, please consider leaving a review. Reviews are incredibly important to indie authors.

REDEMPTION PLAY LIST

Kill of the Night by Gin Wigmore

Guilty All the Same (feat. Rakim) by Linkin Park

Every Breath You Take by Chase Holfelder

Do or Die by Thirty Seconds to Mars

Dead! by My Chemical Romance

Supermassive Black Hole by Muse

Come Along by Vicci Martinez & Cee Lo Green

Famous Last Words by My Chemical Romance

Tainted Love by Marilyn Manson

I Bet My Life by Imagine Dragons

Teenagers by My Chemical Romance

I Am by AWOLNATION

Could Have Been Me by The Struts

Figure It Out by Royal Blood

I'm Not Okay (I Promise) by My Chemical Romance

Best Day of My Life by Chase Holfelder

Out of the Black by Royal Blood

Sugar, We're Goin Down by Fall Out Boy

Heaven Knows by The Pretty Reckless

I'm Only Joking by KONGOS

Welcome to the Black Parade by My Chemical Romance

#1 Crush by Garbage

Animal by Chase Holfelder

I Lived by OneRepublic

Battle Cry by Imagine Dragons

ABOUT THE AUTHOR

The first thing Christine does when she's getting ready to read a book is to crack the spine in at least five places. She wholeheartedly believes there is no place as comfy as the pages of a well-worn book. She's addicted to buying books, reading books, and writing books. She even turned her dining room into a library—reading is more important than eating. She also has a weakness for adventure and inappropriate humor. Christine is from Forest Hill, Maryland where she lives with her husband, three kids, and her library of ugly spine books.

CONNECT WITH CHRISTINE MANZARI:
Website: www.christinemanzari.com
Facebook: www.facebook.com/ChristineManzari
Twitter: www.twitter.com/Xenatine
Instagram: http://instagram.com/xenatine
Pinterest: www.pinterest.com/xenatine
Goodreads: www.goodreads.com/Christine_Manzari

BOOKS BY CHRISTINE MANZARI:
Deviation (The Sophisticates Book 1)
Conviction (The Sophisticates Book 2)
Redemption (The Sophisticates Book 3)
Hooked (Hearts of Stone Book 1)
Hitched (Hearts of Stone Book 2)
The Pledge (College Bound Series Book 1)
The Color of Us (College Bound Series Book 2)

69380420R00196

Made in the USA
Columbia, SC
12 April 2017